THE DOOMSDAY EQUATION

Also by Matt Richtel

FICTION

The Cloud

The Floodgate: A Short Story

Devil's Plaything

Hooked

NONFICTION

A Deadly Wandering

THE
DOOMSDAY EQUATION

MATT RICHTEL

WILLIAM MORROW
An Imprint of HarperCollins*Publishers*

THE DOOMSDAY EQUATION. Copyright © 2015 by Matt Richtel. All rights reserved. Printed in the United States of America. No part of this book may be used or reproduced in any manner whatsoever without written permission except in the case of brief quotations embodied in critical articles and reviews. For information address HarperCollins Publishers, 195 Broadway, New York, NY 10007.

HarperCollins books may be purchased for educational, business, or sales promotional use. For information please e-mail the Special Markets Department at SPsales@harpercollins.com.

FIRST EDITION

Designed by Diahann Sturge

Library of Congress Cataloging-in-Publication Data has been applied for.

ISBN 978-0-06-220118-8

15 16 17 18 19   ov/rrd   10 9 8 7 6 5 4 3 2 1

For Meredith
All my love

THE DOOMSDAY EQUATION

PROLOGUE

S ALAM, YOUR MAJESTY."
The woman taps on the quadruple-paned glass, thick enough to swallow her whisper and the greeting of her index finger.

The beast behind the glass does not stir. It is rolled on its side, heavy eyes closed, heavy paws stretched out, lazy with confidence, even in sleep.

A hat pulled tightly over the woman's short black hair does little to protect her from the predawn chill. Nor detract from her radiance. From the pocket of a black wool knee-length coat, she pulls a hard-earned skeleton key.

Without taking her eyes from the animal, she takes three steps to her left. She stops in front of the tall bars of the cage door. She inhales the scent of damp fur and old meat. She inserts the key. The lion twitches.

She thinks: San Francisco is supposed to be so humane. A zoo is a zoo. She turns the key. The lion lifts its head. It draws open an eyelid. Blinks.

The woman slightly bows her head. "Guardians of the City.

At your service." Her accent carries generations of migration, ports of call, millennia of weariness and duty.

The lion flops over, facing the woman now, but still in repose. The woman smiles. She understands this to be the most docile time of the lion's day. She pushes open the door.

The lion springs. The door slams against its liberator.

"Salam," she expels the word with a laugh.

Feels razor claws reaching her through the bars.

Salam, she thinks. At last. Peace.

CHAPTER 1

To do.

Jeremy rolls the pencil in his fingers. Lets the tip fall on a jagged scrap of paper. He looks at the words. To do. He hears Emily's voice. How about cleaning up your desk?

Next to the paper scrap an iPad rests on two books, *Superstring Theory: Volume I,* and *The Complete Idiot's Guide to Dating*. In their shadow, on a rectangular black mat covering the blond wood desk, sit two cell phones. A sweetness floats in the air, owing to something starting to turn in a Chinese food takeout container over the small fridge.

Jeremy squeezes the pencil, feels its rubbery vulnerability. It could snap. He flips it to the floor, where it lands beside a crumpled *Inc.* magazine with a headshot Jeremy had nearly deigned to smile for.

How's that for clean, Em?

With his right thumb, he rubs circles on the tender spot just inside his left shoulder, suppresses a wince. He closes his eyes. When he opens them again, a long moment later, he finds his gaze aimed at the computer's on/off switch. It's right beneath the second from the left of four computer monitors, the one with the map.

To do.

Options: Jog; spend the last sixty-five dollars on clothes or a haircut; pick up a thirty-something subverting hunger for children into some exotic erotic position? In the morning, maybe he'd put too fine a point on her transparency to find out if truth inspires yelling or tears.

Nobody, Emily tells him, is less qualified to predict and prevent armed conflict, war. "It's like M&Ms crusading against childhood obesity," she said.

She had pointed this out in their last conversation—not the last *last* conversation but the one before that. They were parked in front of Walgreens and she also pointed out that, in the prior few days alone, Jeremy had proved himself smarter than (and infuriated): a former congressman turned big-name Silicon Valley investor; his former business partner; the guy behind the counter at Walgreens.

"One percent hydrocortisone is not the same as 0.05 percent hydrocortisone. He works at a pharmacy, Em. It's like a zookeeper not knowing the difference between a snake and a bird."

"Maybe. But you needn't have said so. A guy at Walgreens looking at me and smiling is not the same as the guy being a jackass."

"It's bad parents."

"What?"

"Stupid, lazy parents cause childhood obesity, not M&Ms. It's one of many flaws with the simile."

Silence creeps heavy through the front seat, then Emily says: "I'm a world-class mom."

"I wasn't—"

Jeremy shakes his head and looks at the monitors. The one on the far left has all the data, scrolling, 327 precious inputs constantly updating; next to it, the map with the countries pulsing mostly green with a few yellows and oranges, Libya and Syria; then the magic, the genius, the monitor that shows what it all means, what all the data adds up to; and then the fourth monitor, the one with online Scrabble. It's the one he's paid attention to lately.

He scans back across the screens and sees beneath them the off button for the whole contraption, and quickly averts his eyes.

They fall on a picture of a boy wearing overalls and a grin. Transparent tape holds the four-by-six, unframed, against the base of the second monitor, a faint thumbprint smudge beside the bookcase next to the boy. Words pop into Jeremy's head, skirt across his mind's eye. "My bad, bud," but he swallows the whisper that would carry contrition. He looks at his iPhone, Emily and Kent a call away.

A crunching noise pulls him from his thoughts, sounds he hears before realizing the door has opened with a visitor.

"You move well for a big guy." He turns to find Nik. "But your snacks precede you."

Nik stands in uniform, his lumpy corpus—six foot two and 260 pounds—loosely covered in a T-shirt and sweatpants. A thick brushed metal cross hangs around his neck. Over his shoulder hangs a pregnant leather gym bag, a sweatshirt poking through the zipper.

"Go look for a job," Jeremy says.

Nik raises a greasy eyebrow. Nik, short for PeaceNik, christened Perry Dutton, nicknamed by Jeremy not long after he wandered into the Oxford lab and joined the team. Now he's the last loyalist, the final Templar, a deckhand waiting with the captain for the last part of the stern to sink. Jeremy imagines Nik goes to the little boxing gym where he spends his off-hours, suits up, then lets people hit him and never falls down.

Emily, while she likes Nik—who doesn't?—says he's a man so devoid of Earthly ambition that Jeremy can't possibly conflict with him. Still has a clamshell flip phone. And Evan once joked that if Jeremy was Richard Nixon, Nik was like that muted, bizarre version of his wife, Pat, in the famed Checkers Speech, named for the Nixon dog. Nik's got a mutt, a big, plodding white girl called Rosa, slobbery jowls, droopy eyes, currently lumbering behind him, loyal to Nik as Nik is to Jeremy.

"You've got unopened mail," Nik says.

Jeremy half nods. "Jesus can't save you from disodium guanylate."

Nik pops a Cool Ranch Dorito into his mouth, turns and plods away, Rosa in tow.

Jeremy notices that slid beneath the door is the unopened mail. Bills or something from Evan's lawyers.

Jeremy rubs the spot inside his shoulder. He stands and pushes away from the desk.

OUTSIDE THE OFFICE, on the waterfront, Jeremy ignores after-work commuter foot traffic and the rules and steps over the railing.

He sits on a concrete slab beside an iron boat tie. Waves lap the slab, splashing the bottom of Jeremy's feet.

Genius was supposed to pay off better than this.

His paper, "Conditions of Conflict," published in the *Journal of Dispute Settlement,* was seminal in its combination of two disciplines: computer science and history. Over eight years of doctoral study at Oxford, Jeremy used original algorithms to break down the conditions of the world before, during and immediately after conflicts from World War I to Vietnam to the Rum Rebellion in 1808, the Pastry War with France and Mexico and on and on.

To crunch the numbers, Jeremy persuaded the CS department to lend him hours of time with the supercomputer. Later, Jeremy managed to streamline the algorithms so that he no longer needed the supercomputer and could instead run them on regular-strength desktop computers jerry-rigged to perform multiple streams of concurrent parallel processing.

At first, a prestigious journal called *Peace* had rejected Jeremy's paper (not on merit so much as on charges he sought to intimidate a peer reviewer), so Jeremy approached the *Journal of Dispute Settlement,* a decidedly not prestigious journal and a competitor of *Peace.* It had the desired effect—at least in the academic community. How, people wondered, had *Peace* failed to land research that, within days, would generate a mountain of media and, within weeks, millions in prospective investment dollars? He was invited to travel the world to lecture, talk about conflict, how to avoid it.

There were media mentions, and plenty of cheap turns of phrase. *Popular Mechanics* asked hyperbolically if Jeremy Stillwater had invented the Digital Messiah.

The editor of *Peace* sent a congratulatory email to Jeremy, who responded by proposing a resignation letter that the editor send to his bosses.

The editor got the last laugh.

Something catches Jeremy's eye. A boat, *The San Francisco Experience,* brimming with tourists.

Jeremy looks down at the water. It doesn't look that cold.

The investors insisted he take on Evan. That's just Silicon Valley. The creative types get paired with the money types, the marketers who spin gold into a lot of gold. But at a price of input, especially on the marketing.

Jeremy grudgingly admitted some of Evan's ideas were good. Evan came up with the map with the hot spots lit up, changing with the changing conditions of the world, changing by the minute. On a typical day, Libya, yellow and mellowing; Iraq the same, but tinged with orange; Iran and Syria, a light, almost pulsing orange; central Africa deeper orange still, inflaming but not in flames; the cool blue of Norway suggesting terminal calm; and, always, the 38th parallel fluctuating between a deeper orange and red. Next to each hot or warm spot, a gauge, like the gas gauge in a car, suggesting the direction in which conflict is headed. Lots of arrows headed near north, meaning: conflict ongoing or looming.

The map had people at hello. The second that customers or investors saw the map, they were ready to listen.

Then Jeremy could talk about the data, a flurry of hundreds of inputs pouring in from around the globe. Specifically, 327 inputs. Oil and food prices, temperatures and tides, population density, migrations from rural areas to cities and back, birthrates, election cycles, high-level executive movements, stock market indices, news reports and a "rhetoric" measure, which reports the language used in speeches by major political and business leaders and in headlines from newspapers and blogs around the world.

More eyes lighting up. Can it really work?

"The data, that's monkey junk," Jeremy would say. With the

Internet, anyone can collect data. "It doesn't mean anything without this."

And then he would talk about the algorithm. It took all that data, all the inputs, and collated the incoming data, mashing and weighing it, giving it relative value. A change in leadership in a relatively stable country is valued at X, while a change in an unstable country equals X-plus-some-quotient. Prices for commodities or oil get a baseline given weight that is subject to changes in value depending on time of year and other variables, like precipitation; it is astounding, Jeremy thought, how much the weather dictates the likelihood that certain conditions will lead to conflict, because, when it comes down to it, invaders and attackers prefer clear skies. See: D-Day.

Sometimes, he'd get applause.

Part of him knew he was a show pony, a hub for the spokes of idealistic thinkers about the nascent field of data-driven peace and conflict studies, someone awesome to invite to and point out at parties.

Now Evan is trying to sue Jeremy's pants off to get access to the guts of the algorithm. He was never interested in conflict stuff. Jeremy knew it. Evan, PowerPoint Peckerhead, as Jeremy calls him (not *completely* without affection), and the investors wanted to apply the technology to predicting what would unfold in the world of business.

They wanted to sell it as a consulting tool to help Verizon understand how telecommunication was likely to change or to McDonald's to presage the next trends in food production or consumption. They wanted real, predictable revenue streams.

And who could blame them? It didn't take a supercomputer and a genius man-child to realize that investors make money by helping companies and other investors make money, not by predicting the outbreak, length and nature of a conflict in some island in the Sea of Cortez, or where-the-fuck-ever, as one of the big Valley investors had put it.

Besides, there was another problem, a kind of basic one. Jeremy's fancy invention didn't appear to be actually working for its stated purpose: predicting conflict.

He looks down at the water. He stands and raises himself over the iron barrier, and looks into the murky distance.

He glances back at the water. Not that cold. Not for a computer.

CHAPTER 2

BACK IN THE office, Jeremy sits. He checks the two phones, the iPhone and the other one. Same old story. Nothing, as it has been for more than two weeks, excepting unrequited badgers from the law firm of Pierce & Sullivan, and a call from a debt collector with a wrong number looking for Song Yung Li. With that one, Jeremy played along for three minutes until, just for fun, he duped the caller into revealing the debtor's Social Security number and then let her have it with both barrels.

After the paper came out in the *Journal of Dispute Settlement,* Jeremy worked briefly on a contract for the Pentagon and the Department of Defense, took in a mountain of their data about the conditions in Afghanistan and Iraq and made two decidedly horrific projections.

While working for the DoD, he predicted an insurgency in the Al Anbar province that never happened. And, separately, he had a 98 percent certainty that guerrilla movements in a particular mountain range near the Afghan-Russian border would subside within three months. They went on for two years, the unsettling and unconvincing back-and-forth with the military.

The initial paper had provided ironclad proof of the validity of the method. But then when it came time, when the opportunity came to do it for someone other than academics, it flopped. It didn't add up. None of it added up.

Jeremy looks around the room. Academic papers and newspapers and trade journals and a *Wired* and a *Maxim* on the rack of servers to his left, power cords jumbled on the floor and, everywhere, that smell. Emily, you can take a bite out of my ass if you think it's because I fear order that I don't want to clean up. It takes more than a bachelor's degree and single-motherhood experience to play armchair analyst.

The office was supposed to be Jeremy's think pad away from the main office down in Silicon Valley—walking distance from the ballpark and the swanky condo Jeremy bought at the peak of the market. A perk afforded a genius that has turned lease waiting to expire.

He rubs the inside of his shoulder, then his pectoral.

The fourth monitor shows the Scrabble board where he spends his hours playing people he's never met at the highest levels of the virtual Scrabble world.

He almost never wins. Because he never finishes a game. He's usually ahead but then he makes some suggestions to his opponents about the word they probably should have played, and they disappear. Many just won't play him anymore, even though, at Emily's counsel, which he took in this case, he prefaces his suggestions to opponents by asking if it's okay if he offers up an idea.

Jeremy catches his reflection in the Scrabble monitor. Something in the dull image reminds him that his monthly haircut is forthcoming. That's forty-five dollars that is not currently falling off the trees, but is also nonnegotiable. When it comes to his hair and other personal grooming, Jeremy subscribes only to the strictest ergonomics. He still doesn't understand that, even without a great haircut, he'd get the girls. He's muscular with long, toned runner's legs, and a sturdy, full face that hints more at the handsome qualities of a rugby player than an actor, having long since shed the slump-shouldered geeky kid who formed a chunk of his self-image.

He closes his eyes.

It's something between a catnap, daydream and slide presentation. His mom is there, bony and wispy and still totally in control of her emotions. There's Kent, just the opposite, childlike, a child, smiling and asking Jeremy to come over to build a fort. There's Peckerhead waving a pen, and there's Emily. Her eyes are red but dry.

Then Harry. Not alone, with Andrea. Both of them, together, laughing. Laughing and laughing. He strains to hear what they're saying but he can't. He can just feel their laughter rippling through him.

The three chirps startle Jeremy.

He clears his throat and opens his eyes. He blinks.

The computer beeps again. Three beeps. Those three distinctive beeps.

He looks at the monitors, starting with the one that is second to his right. Data, scrolling. Then the next one with the map.

His first impulse is less curiosity than disappointment. "Monkey junk."

Red. Bright red. The red he's never actually seen, not this bright. And never heard these chirps, not these three. Not since he programmed the computer to make such a sound.

Three beeps that mean something very dire is about to happen. Three beeps with all this red means it's nothing short of apocalyptic, the apocalypse.

Jeremy twirls around in his desk chair. He looks at the server, and up in the corners of the walls. He sees the door is closed.

He looks at his phone, checks the clock. He's been asleep, or daydreaming, for just a few minutes, less than an hour. It's a bit after eight.

"I'll humor you."

Jeremy scoots in, cocks his head like a bird. Looks at the map. Then begins tapping on the keyboard. On the monitor to the far right, the Scrabble board disappears.

In its place appears the web site of the *New York Times*. The lead headline is about a press conference in which the president is asked about the latest job figures. Below that, in the middle of the page, there's a picture of a man wearing a robe and sitting in a wheelchair, a feature about a judge in Brooklyn who is trying out for the Paralympics. There's something masquerading as breaking news that looks to be a roundup of technology company earnings.

Nothing to explain what's happening on the map. Nothing to explain why his computer is predicting there is going to be a massive global conflict, engulfing the world in death and destruction—and that the calamity is imminent.

Jeremy clicks and the *New York Times* disappears.

He clears his throat. Taps his fingers absently on the edge of the keyboard. After a full minute, he moves his cursor onto the first monitor, the one most to his left, the one with all the scrawling data points, and, with a few keystrokes, causes the flurry of data to appear also on the fourth monitor, where the *New York Times* had just been.

He moves his cursor onto the fourth monitor and starts moving up and down through the data with his cursor. The data is moving too, updating with every second, the inputs changing in real time: gas prices, stock market indices, weather. It comes in so fast from around the world that even Jeremy—for as much time as he's spent with these programs—can't quite grasp and make sense of it. He scrolls up, looking at the various measures, looking at time stamps.

Is there some needle in this haystack? Something that changed or stands out, or explains the map?

Nothing stands out. Of course not. No way for the human brain to make sense of this flurry of data. That's what the algorithm is for. And it speaks through the map. That's where the predictions show up in the nice accessible way, just as Evan envisioned.

Now it's mostly pulsing red—North America, for sure, Latin America, Europe. Even the Southern Hemisphere shows hardly a spot neither red or orange, and a few bits of yellow.

He puts his cursor onto the map. He clicks on a gauge, a cross between an odometer and a clock. He clicks on it. He reads the prediction. He clenches his teeth.

He pushes back from the desk. He stands and looks up at the corners of the room. He peers alongside the metal shelf holding the servers. No cameras. No overt signs someone is setting him up for the YouTube humiliation of the century when, finally on the verge of giving up on his creation and tossing it into the sea, he freaks and screams, "I told you so!" because the app is reporting that the world is going to end.

No signs someone has tapped into or tampered with the computer. Who could do that? Few, if any. They don't have the password to get inside the machine. No one does. Who might want to? Start a fucking list of the let's-turn-Jeremy-into-a-marionette. Evan the Peckerhead, Professor Harry Ives, the disgruntled investors.

How long was he gone outside at the water? Did someone get in?

Jeremy pulls out two middle fingers and shares them with the room.

He eyes the envelopes on the floor under the door. He kicks them over and confirms they are both, as he suspected, from the lawyers at Pierce & Sullivan, representing Evan, who is suing for access to the conflict algorithm so he can predict the future of mobile communications or fast food. Jeremy grinds the envelopes with his shoe.

He picks up his iPad, scrambles around the mess on the desk for the white cord. He plugs the iPad into his desktop and clicks a few keys.

While he's waiting for it, he walks out to Nik's cubicle. He pauses before the violation, then shuffles through Nik's papers. Sees late-payment notifications, legal correspondence, bureaucracy.

He bends over and reaches for Nik's computer mouse. Fiddles with it. The screen comes to life. He sees a black backdrop and a few windows open at the bottom. Jeremy clicks them. One is an email folder, left open, with mostly spam. Another is World of Warcraft, Nik's guilty pleasure, an innocuous enough time sink, his connection to a community of shut-ins and night owls.

Emily says Nik and Jeremy are like photo negatives of one another: Nik, a quiet and deferential loner who, on the Internet, commands armies and plays war; Jeremy, aggressive and confrontational, who uses the Internet to make peace.

Taped to Nik's desk, Jeremy finds a list of phone numbers and emails—contact info for all the big players, like Andrea, Harry and Evan. Even Emily. Nik is Jeremy's shadow, secretary, baggage handler, designated driver, still holding out hope.

Jeremy walks back into his office.

The iPad has finished doing its thing. He stuffs it into a briefcase, snags his phones, shuts out the light and closes the door.

Chapter 3

FORTY MINUTES LATER, Jeremy stands at the counter of a South of Market café. In a Tumi bag slung over his shoulder is his iPad, which he's synched with the computer at his desk. He thinks of its prediction, massive global conflict, three days and counting. More precisely: 71 hours, 15 minutes. Projected impact: 14 million killed, from not just the first hypothetical attack but, the computer estimates, the subsequent attack and counterattack.

It's simple math, really, game theory. The computer, upon predicting conflict, then plays out the likeliest scenarios for what will follow based on the state of affairs in the world.

Jeremy looks around the hipster café, a work-away-from-the-home-office joint during the day, but, now, nine fifteen on a Wednesday, a place for first dates and people seeking them. A tapestry of the African savanna hangs on the opposite wall, hovering above closely placed tables. There's a fireplace next to the counter, sputtering with a low flame and Wilco on the speakers.

The right amount of white noise to allow him to think; the right concentration of eye candy, chicks.

"What can I get you?" It's a guy behind the counter with a soul patch and a flannel shirt, which are all the rage.

"Peanut Butter Mocha." Sugar, protein, caffeine.

Soul Patch blinks: I've no idea what you're talking about.

"It's a mocha but you toss in a scoop of peanut butter. I've ordered it here before."

"Not from me," the guy says smiling. "We gotta stick to the menu."

Jeremy smiles back.

"It's complicated. You mix a scoop of peanut butter into the mocha."

Guy clears his throat. "I wouldn't know how to charge you."

"Oh, right. I understand. Generally, the way you charge is by keying in the numbers in the cash register and then taking my money. But maybe this is one of those dummy registers with pictures, like at McDonald's."

Guy serves Jeremy a mocha. With a scoop of peanut butter on the side.

He sits, unpockets his phones. In a fit of pique a week earlier, he'd purged his speed dial of those he felt had betrayed him. Emily, of course, though that number he knows by heart. Evan. Harold Ives, aka Harry War, the eccentric Berkeley war historian, Jeremy's rare equal in being a pain in the ass, whose research and, more importantly, support, proved instrumental to Jeremy's conflict algorithm. But, really, hadn't Harry asked for it by turning on Jeremy first?

He'd purged too the number for Andrea Belluck-Juarez, the tattooed and pierced junior officer at the Pentagon. His conduit to that whole messed-up situation.

Evan, Harry War, Andrea. The three he'd most likely have called—even as recently as six months ago—in the event his computer made the three sharp beeps and the map glowed red. He can always find their phone numbers in his email. He flips the phone onto the table.

He's not going to give them the satisfaction. Not even these three, once his last line of defenders. He doesn't need to hear the recriminations, the cackles. *So, your magic computer thinks the terrorists are coming? Can it predict what they'll be wearing? Can it guess which card they'll be thinking about? The four of hearts?* Harry had jokingly dismissed Jeremy's device as "iPocalypse."

Or, if the world is in fact going to end in seventy hours and change, then what's the point of exposing himself?

He looks around the room. To his left, two younger women, late twenties, conspiring after they appear to have gone for a late-night exercise session. One of the pair wears a ponytail with dark frizzy hair extruding around the edges. She's got light freckles and an easy smile and Jeremy ranks her as the best-looking chick he's seen in weeks. Not far behind in the looks category is the woman sitting to his right. Jeremy figures her at thirty-two years old, with a D-cup. She's got light brown hair, a spiral notebook that must serve as a diary, and she's lost in *The World According to Garp*. Relatively smart chick.

"Not okay to call them chicks." Evan had admonished Jeremy after a business meeting with investors and their science advisors, including two female Stanford Ph.D.s. "How about using 'hoes'?"

"Women call themselves chicks all the time. You talk like a brochure and I'll talk like a human."

Jeremy eyes his iPad lying flat on the blond wood table. Next to it is *The Complete Idiot's Guide to Dating*. He's purposely half obscured the cover as if to make it look like something he's trying to hide.

On the tablet, he opens the map. At the bottom, there's a feature called the "countdown clock." It reads: 70:36:05. Hours, minutes, seconds. Until attack. Or some huckster popping out of a cake and pointing at Jeremy and laughing.

At the top of the map, Jeremy clicks on a menu. Under the "view" line, he clicks "recent history." As the screen splits in two, he briefly relives the eons he put into not just selecting each category in each tool line but learning the basic program in the minutest detail so that the user interface would be precisely how he envisioned. He left nothing to chance, automation or outsourcing. He didn't spend much time thinking about other passionate creators, like Steve Jobs, but, when he did, he tended to think they were lazy for hiring other people to do the engineering.

On the iPad, the left window displays the current map, projecting massive conflict on the left; the window on the right is devoid of color. On a drop-down menu above the clean map, Jeremy chooses "45 minutes." The conflict map as it stood forty-five minutes earlier appears, filled with oranges and yellows and dull reds, but absent the rampant glowing red representing the imminent onset of massive global conflict. Jeremy looks at the digital clock in the corner of his monitor. It is 9:26, Wednesday night, late March, Jeremy tries to remember the date but can't. Forty-five minutes earlier, he thinks, his computer claims, something in the world changed. Exactly when? What?

"When" is the easy part.

Jeremy taps on "advance." The map begins to change, at first, ever so slightly. The colors are mutating slightly around the edges, their boundaries moving almost infinitesimally.

Jeremy must admit to himself that this feature, though it is another brainchild of Evan's, more sizzle, is pretty fucking cool. It's like watching a storm map on the Weather Channel. Not storms, conflicts. High-pressure societies and low-pressure societies, colliding power bases, the prospect of war. A key difference is that weather maps tend to have constant motion, the clouds and weather systems swirling and moving. On the war map, the changes are very subtle, unless you bring the clock back a decade and spin it forward at high speeds to see various regions go from blue to yellow to orange to red and back again.

And then: wham. Everything turns red.

This time, watching it unfold, Jeremy is not feeling disappointed, or privately skeptical, but, for an instant, startled. This is an image for his dreams or nightmares. The world pulsing crimson; the United States and China and Russia and Europe, pinkish hues swallowing the smaller and poorer places, Africa, tiny island nations. He swallows hard, then coughs, peanut butter lodged in his throat.

Jeremy paws the device. He rewinds the map again. Now he watches it evolve in slow motion. He's leaning forward, face inches from the screen. He sees what he's looking for: the first sign of red. The first indication something in the world has changed or, rather, is poised to change, four days hence.

He looks at the time stamp above the map. It reads: 8:06 P.M. He puts the cursor over the clock. An infobox pops up next to it with details. The moment he's frozen in time on his conflict machine, the moment the clock started ticking, was 8:06:42 on Wednesday, March 29.

He eyes the first onset of red. He puts his cursor over it, even though he knows what he's looking at. An infobox pops up: 37 degrees north, 122 west. "San Francisco."

When they refined this infobox, Jeremy had argued with Evan that there was no need to put the name of the city. All they needed was longitude and latitude. Actually naming the place was condescending to a smart audience, and a waste of manpower to double-check.

San Francisco. Right here, he thinks, a little more than three days.

He looks up and around the café. He catches the eye of a tall woman sitting by the door, looking in his direction, a model's figure, symmetrical features obscured by a baseball cap. She lowers her gaze.

A complete joke. Or maybe three days.

Jeremy grits his teeth and closes his eyes and discovers in his mind's eye an image of his frail mother in hospice, six months earlier. Last time he'd seen Eleanor alive. He can't recall much of it, just the plate of lumpy, syrupy, buttery mashed potatoes on the table next to a yellow rotary phone. She mutters something. Existential? Jeremy leans in close and realizes he's wondering if she's telling him that she loves him, maybe, finally. Once. She repeats herself: "Make peace." That's what she said. No, no nurturing words here. She's counseling him, giving him an edict, one that she could well stand to hear herself. She was his original sparring partner. And then the huge fight in the parking lot with Emily, the intensifying pain near his neck, the lump, everything spiraling.

Three days. It's March 29.

Three days.

"Oh shit," Jeremy mumbles.

He opens his yes. Three days is April 1.

April Fools' Day.

"You want war?" Jeremy suddenly mutters to no one.

He shakes his head, looks up, lands his gaze at the woman sitting to his right, with the D-cup, reading *The World According to Garp*. She peeks with light blue eyes at him over the top the book. Maybe wondering why he's talking to himself. Maybe just making contact.

He swallows. She's attractive, bordering on more than that. He lowers his iPad. Ready to stop being the patsy.

CHAPTER 4

"GARP IS WET," Jeremy says.

The woman's hand slides slightly down the book's spine, giving Jeremy a tingle.

Jeremy extends a napkin. "Sorry for interrupting. But you've got coffee on your cover. Or hot chocolate. Or whatever is your poison."

She looks at the book. Sure enough, she'd spilled some coffee on the nurse's hat on the cover. It's damp but almost imperceptibly so. She takes the napkin from Jeremy. Either she's not bright enough to see his obvious move or she fully recognizes it and is playing along anyway.

"A guy with an iPad taking so much interest in protecting the honor of a print book. You've got a sense of tradition."

"May I interrupt you further with one small bit of trivia?"

"Sure." A little wary.

"The tranny saves the day."

"The what?"

"The transvestite." He's looking at the book.

"Am I to understand that you're giving away the end of *The World According to Garp*?" Mock exasperation.

"I don't know. I didn't actually finish it. I saw the movie. Most of it. Fell asleep."

Slight smile, cautious, intrigued, she's dealing with a smart one, in a good way, feeling her brain tickled.

"So you didn't finish the book or the movie but you know how it ends. Can you see the future? What are the odds I'm going to be discovered?"

He laughs. Genuine. Good line and she's got no idea of Jeremy's complicated relationship with the future. He feels suddenly serious and makes a decent attempt to cover up the wash of feelings, return to compartmentalizing, channel his irritation into something much more strategic, which he can do with the best of them. He pushes away an intruding thought about September 1939, how willing the Poles must have felt to ignore obvious signs of imminent German attack. Obviously, he thinks, his computer is being punked, not warning him of apocalypse. Right? When, Jeremy thinks and then instantly dismisses the thought, did he start doubting himself and his computer?

"I'm reasonably good with the past. With some degree of certainty, I can tell you what happened yesterday." He delivers it well enough that she sees only witty repartee.

Twenty minutes later, they're still at it. He's managed to slip in just enough about himself—the entrepreneur thing and the "grad school in England thing" but not yet the Rhodes scholar thing—but also to leave room for her and her exploits such as they are. She went to law school to do good, like everyone else who went to law school, and wound up doing corporate law and then, unlike many others, scrapped the whole thing. She teaches social studies at a private high school on the theory she'll have a long life to try different things. The master plan involves saving enough to hike the Andes in the next three years.

The café lights flicker once. "Last call."

As she glances about at the beehive of activity, he opens the iPad, notices the screen saver. It's a picture of a boy sticking out his tongue. Kent, Emily's son. Jeremy grits his teeth, closes the red cover over the top of the gadget. He puts his hand on his sternum, just inside the left shoulder, paws around, trying to feel a lump or something to explain the dull ache and occasional sharp pain. He refuses to believe the pain and the overall malaise he's been feeling are related to stress but doesn't like any of the other explanations, like his immune system in conflict against something serious. Like the cancers that took his father at about his current age and, later, his mother.

He's struck with an idea. A way to figure out how to check what's going on with this computer. Then looks up to see the woman's packing her bag and looking at him. He shuts the cover.

"Want to get a drink?"

Ten minutes later, darker atmosphere in a danker place and margaritas. Jeremy's trendy sneakers lightly stick to the gummy floor as his knees bounce under the table with his inexhaustible energy. The talk is witty and mundane; movies and pop culture, then a discussion Jeremy finds more than mildly interesting about historic waves of civil rights movements, not a political statement she's making but, indirectly, one about global social systems and how they flex and bend and ebb and flow. Big-picture stuff, and he feels himself light up. She's getting prettier, only a hair shy of beautiful. Who is using who?

"School tomorrow." She stands to use the bathroom. He watches her confident walk in the well-fitting jeans, tingling, appreciating the good looks of a worthy foe.

He pulls out his phones. He already knows from the absence of buzzing the last two hours that he hasn't had a call or text. But he checks anyway. He considers checking his iPad in the backpack near his feet but he risks blowing the way he's positioned himself as laid-back enough and in-the-moment.

He glances up and finds himself catching the eye of a thin woman at the far end of the bar, near the door, her back turned to Jeremy but inexplicably with her head swiveled in his direction. Baseball cap pulled down tight over hair hanging to the middle of her back. She drops Jeremy's gaze but not before she's made an impression; Jeremy's sure that he's seen the woman before. Where? Wasn't it in the café earlier? Jeremy feels a surge of adrenaline, a conflict cocktail. Who is this joker: some legal server, an agent of Evan, or Harry War, coming to watch Jeremy implode?

"You okay?"

Jeremy sees his new friend has returned. He looks back at the bar to see the thin woman nowhere in sight.

"Where are you headed?" he asks.

"You sure you're okay?"

He nods. Her tone irks him.

"Want to walk me home? It's not far." She picks up her backpack. In the bathroom, she's brushed the hair off her face. In spite of himself, Jeremy feels like Charlie Bucket from *Willy Wonka* looking at her full, moist lips.

At the doorway of a two-story flat on a residential block plagued by the dull hum of a nearby highway overpass, they kiss. There's a reprieve in the chill, a stillness in the night air.

She takes his hand to guide him up the stairs. "Nice move, by the way."

"What's that?"

"*The Complete Idiot's Guide to Dating*. Well planted. Obviously, you're not a complete idiot."

He feels a sizzle, the crackling inside his head. Before he can even think about it, he strikes: "Nice neon sign."

"What?"

"*Garp*."

She turns on the stair. It's not just his words but the tone of voice, something icy, cruel.

"What about *Garp*?"

"The ultimate demand for attention. Works for the dumb guys and the smart guys. A pseudo-intellectual clarion call for attention. A quasi-literary welcome mat."

She shakes her head, trying to bring this creature into focus.

"Instead of a bookmark, you could use a condom."

The sounds of the slap gets absorbed by a honk from the highway overpass. The sting doesn't hurt Jeremy. It feels like victory.

"BALLPARK."

The driver nods. His puffy loaf of curly black hair reaches nearly the roof of the cab.

Jeremy realizes his jaw hurts. Not from the slap, but from clenching. He takes a deep breath. He thinks about how he could be in coitus right now with a lovely stranger. He could've held his tongue and gotten his victory in the bedroom, then the couch and then the shower. He wonders whether he sabotaged it because he's got more important stuff to think about. Or maybe he picked the fight with her because she is easier prey than whatever else, or whoever else, is haunting Jeremy? He unzips his backpack, which rests on his knees. He pulls out the iPad. He swipes away the screen-saver image of Kent to get to the algorithm.

It's still there, unchanged. Taunting Jeremy. But he knows how he might start fighting back. It's a simple task, really. He needs to get someplace settled and run a test. He needs to check the List.

The List is a set of 327 statistical inputs that, Jeremy believes, together describe the state of the world. Oil prices and population density and weather systems and all the rest. No human being can possibly track and understand the collective movement of these systems, and properly weight them. No intuition—well, maybe that belonging to Warren Buffett or some other savant wasting his talents on Wall Street—can even sense, let alone pinpoint, the direction of the world. Not like Jeremy's data set, at least when properly valued.

Jeremy's simple questions: Has someone messed with the inputs? Has someone altered the List? Easy way to find out. Jeremy can just ask. He can run a check to make sure that the variables the computer is using as the basis for its apocalyptic prediction do, in fact, match up with the actual variables in the world.

"Just out front?"

They're three blocks from the ballpark, passing the petering nightlife in this gentrified concentric circle around AT&T Park, home to the San Francisco Giants. The high-rise condos emerge onto the gray skyline. These are home to the future leaders of Silicon Valley and the engineers who will make them rich.

Jeremy picked the ballpark as his destination because it's

roughly equidistant from his apartment and his office and he wasn't sure where he'd want to wind up.

"Thirtieth and Balboa."

"I thought you wanted the ballpark."

"And I've changed my mind."

"So now you want to go to the Richmond."

"That's what I said."

Cabbie shrugs. It's another easy fare. He's no stranger to people wasting time in his cab doing computing. In fact, he's managed to squeeze out a few extra bucks now and then while circling the block while the fare, oblivious, plays a video game on the phone.

He turns a sharp right, changing direction. He clicks on the windshield wiper for a single swipe at the foggy condensation.

Jeremy feels acutely for the first time the light numbing from the tequila. He doesn't like the feeling, not tonight. He has an on-again, off-again relationship with booze. He's in an off-again stage, one of those times it serves only social functions. Other times, he craves the taste and the feeling, but not to the point he's ever in danger of overuse.

He looks at a young couple on the street, together but the man walking a quarter step ahead of the woman. Human nature, Jeremy thinks, the need of one creature to dominate another, even by a quarter step.

He closes his eyes. Puts his hand on the iPad. He pictures a conference table, surrounded by brass. At the head of the table, a real big shot, a lieutenant colonel, taking all the air out of the room. Flanking him, majors in uniform with the oak leaves and medals, one in khakis, white shirt, red tie. Projected onto a screen, there's a videoconference feed. It's an image from Berkeley of Dr. Harry Ives, the Cal scholar who introduced Jeremy to these monkeys. The aging man looks impassive, ensconced in a white beard, old eyes hard to read. It's at least eighteen months earlier, in a lifeless room at the Pentagon, Jeremy's technology on trial.

"Bullshit," Jeremy says.

A major purses his lips, not appreciating the language.

"Mr. Stillwater, they've taken a new village in the last twenty-four hours, their largest yet."

"And I'm bin Laden's pet monkey."

Jeremy cannot believe that the rebels continue to push through the mountains. His computer, armed with a ton of rich and updated data, was all but 100 percent conclusive: this mini-insurgency should've died weeks ago.

"Jeremy." It's Andrea.

He looks at her, raven-black hair in a ponytail, a silk shirt covering the Day of the Dead tattoo on her left forearm, her whole package buttoned-down and ironed. Then turns to the head of the table, to the Army intelligence guy who must be important because he has the confidence not to have a crew cut, never carries any papers or BlackBerry or anything, and because he rarely speaks.

"You messed with my data."

"I assure you . . ." Andrea starts.

He cuts her off with a wave. He's not even sure how they would've messed with his computer. Maybe on his last visit to Washington; he got drunk with Andrea at a karaoke bar and left his computer in his room. No way; he dismisses the thought. He was the one who ran the tests, scoured the data, knows he's right. He's sure they're lying.

"Where's my iPad?"

"You surrendered your device for security reasons at the

front, just like everyone else. And you'll get it back when you leave. This is a high-security facility and we're all equally privileged and burdened by the trappings." It's one of the oak-leafed majors.

Jeremy shakes his head. "Prove it. Prove I'm wrong," he suddenly demands of the man at the head of the table. Everyone tenses at the direct challenge to someone who clearly doesn't hear such talk except from one-star generals, and higher.

It's another of the majors who responds. "Mr. Stillwater, I understand you're frustrated. You're obviously very bright. Your technology holds promise but we're fighting a war and we can't afford to be your beta test."

Could it be more condescending?

"You want the casualty reports?"

Jeremy's eyes widen a tad. It's a rare utterance from the man at the head of the table. His voice is near a whisper, with a very slight northeastern drawl, the stuff of the Ivy League. Jeremy had failed to find any public information on this lead dog, no official bio, no smattering of personal details; but that might not mean much since he looks to be in his late forties, at least one full generation before people started sharing everything about their lives on the web.

"They can be doctored," says Jeremy.

The lead dog looks at everyone and no one. "Somebody get Mr. Stillwater the casualty reports, ours and theirs; show him the pictures from Patwa, the empty cache, the insurgents' recruiting figures, everything, all the classified stuff."

"Oh, and make it rhyme, like Dr. Seuss."

"Jeremy."

The lead dog puts up his hand to Andrea, looks at Jeremy.

"You know Mitchell Stevenson?"

Jeremy feels immediately defensive. He's being sucked into a rhetorical trap, being asked to answer questions he doesn't know the answer to, leading down who knows what path.

"Is he the guy who came up with the idea to pretend the insurgency is still raging? Or did he write *Green Eggs and Ham*?"

"Maybe you read a feature story about him in the *Times* a while back. He's one of the best mop-up guys we ever had."

There's a pause. Jeremy isn't sure what this means. Everyone can sense the cocksure geek's lack of comprehension but no one wants to interrupt or correct the lead dog.

"Had," the man continues. "A sniper blew off Colonel Stevenson's face. A sniper from a band of still-raging insurgents owning us in the mountains around Patwa."

After a pause, Jeremy says: "I'm not sure what that proves." He's lost a touch of his hostility. "I told you the insurgency was fading. I didn't tell you no one else would die."

"Fair point, Mr. Stillwater. We took a calculated risk to send in one of our best men to assess whether you and your computer had been accurate. And he walked into a hornet's nest. That doesn't speak particularly well to our own intelligence but then again we've never professed to have an Oracle of Delphi." He pauses. "You're right, though, that our paperwork proves nothing. It can be doctored, though I doubt the military has the technology to make it rhyme."

He half smiles. He's practiced, unlike Jeremy, in the art of defusing conflict. The others in the room aren't sure whether to laugh. He continues: "The only way I can prove it to you would be to send you and your computer to the region and let you do a field test. And that's a good way for you to wind up like Mitch, seriously and truly dead."

The man stands. He's tall in the way of people who command power, with slightly slumped shoulders, and he has an emerging belly in the way of people who spend their days looking at monitors. Two of his lieutenants stand too but they stay when the man walks out.

Just before he hits the door of the big conference room, he turns back to Jeremy.

"Take the money."

"What?"

"Take Silicon Valley's money. Use your magic eight ball to do business intelligence, predict the future in some sector where no one gets hurt. I bet it'll do wonders projecting the future of mobile apps."

He reaches the door.

"Send me. I dare you."

The man pauses, turns back.

Jeremy continues: "Send me to see for myself."

Now the lieutenant colonel smiles, in full. "I was hoping you'd fall for that." He looks at Andrea. "Work out some time that Mr. Stillwater can go to the region. Let him take his computer and run the tests real-time. Maybe he could get it to work. We sure could use the technology, if it could be refined into something not decidedly at odds with reality."

He shuts the door.

JEREMY FEELS THE cab slow. At the time, Jeremy wasn't sure who had won the exchange, but he subsequently learned. The lieutenant colonel was teaching Jeremy a lesson in patient disengagement. There were a few follow-up calls, Andrea never able to get the timing together on a trip, the budget not there; at one point it seemed like he was poised to be able to study a battle in southern Iraq, preparations made, then the thing evaporated, one thing after the next, and then it all just faded away, like the rest of Jeremy's opportunities. The crafty lieutenant colonel, the Pentagon, had slipped away from Jeremy, without even giving him the satisfaction of a fight.

And, thereafter, Jeremy started running all the diagnostics. Programming the algorithm to test itself, run war games, simulate conflict to see if it can rightly predict the outcome. Jeremy, even if he doesn't quite admit it, started to question his computer, started challenging it, demanding that it prove itself right. And it seems always to be so. It can see and predict things that elude all possible human foresight. Can't it?

"Here?"

He nods. The outer Richmond, predictably, is foggier than downtown, fog cum drizzle. He hands the cabbie a ten-dollar bill, which represents the fare and a fifty-cent tip, but Jeremy might need the last $20 in his wallet.

He glances at the countdown clock, 67:17:17, then puts the iPad into his backpack. He steps into the wet, the computer strapped to his back, like a papoose, or an albatross.

Chapter 5

FIVE HUNDRED MILES away, also damp, a dim light, projecting the shape and yellowish hue of a dying moon, illuminates a slick floor. Then it flickers, and dies.

The thin man smacks the cool cylinder against his palm. The flashlight returns to its half-life. "Friggin' thing."

He takes two more steps, then slides his heavy boots on the metal, imagining himself skating, breaking the monotony of the chore. He raises the angle of the light, looking at the edges of the boxes and huge containers, the mountains of white rice, cell phone screens, car batteries, undershirts, kids' pajamas, who knows what myriad of stuff piled high to the distant ceiling of this cavernous belly.

He looks up into blackness that, he imagines, could stretch to infinity. He thinks: I should have asked her to marry me. I should have, I should have. Now she thinks I'm on the fence. He pictures her sitting in a café in Hong Kong doing those tortuous emotional somersaults she can do, capable of deciding on an impulse to call off the whole relationship.

And he can't call. His cell phone hasn't worked in two days, the signal apparently unable to find a satellite in the vastness of sea. Or maybe it's the weather. Even in the hull, surrounded by mountains of boxes, he can hear the crashing and lashing of waves.

He looks back down, scoots along the narrow path, flash-light lit, thinking of her, looking at nothing. He sees the pants. Not pants, he realizes, legs with pants. A pair of legs jutting into the path, extruding from between huge containers. Give me a break, he thinks.

"Bryan."

The legs remain motionless. He sighs.

Louder: "Yo, Bryan."

Of the handful of shipmates on the skeleton crew, it's the sarcastic and confrontational Filipino called Bryan who is most likely to have drunk himself into a stupor. The thin man uses his right foot to nudge a leg.

The body rouses.

"They're gonna be pissed if they catch you down there."

The thin man wants to keep it as neutral as possible, not be seen as a cop or do anything to make an enemy if they've got to spend another half week together at sea.

The legs bend, then the body starts to rise in the dark be-tween the cold metal containers. In an unintentionally synchro-nized fashion, the thin man raises the flashlight, illuminating the tall figure wearing a long black peacoat and sporting a beard in full blossom.

"I fell asleep," the bearded man says. He sounds surprised.

It's not Bryan, the thin man realizes, not anyone he rec-ognizes. Jesus, a friggin' stowaway. Even as he thinks it, he's transfixed by the beard. As much as it is full and wild, it looks deliberate, like something that would've been fashionable in some distant biblical era.

As neutrally as possible, the thin man says: "Come on with me. We have hot showers upstairs." He wants to get this guy to the captain without a fuss, keep things simple.

The bearded man looks behind him, into the near-black crevice between the containers. He makes out the outlines of the backpack, the tattered brand-name knockoff bearing an otherworldly treasure, given him in a wordless exchange in an alley in Morocco. He was surprised that so much divine power and truth could be so light.

He turns back to find the flashlight upturned at his face. The bearded man closes his eyes, listens for other voices or footsteps. Hears none. He looks at the rail standing before him, a pasty, Earthy shell of flesh and bones. But a human being, a spark of life.

The bearded man mutters something.

"I can't understand you. Bring your things. You can take them with you upstairs."

The bearded man takes a slow breath, processing the inevitability of the logic, the undeniable rationale. After years of modest duty, he has been summoned, like his brethren, for divine purpose. It can only be that there is a gravest threat. As a Guardian of the City, he cannot doubt. His is a life of faith. He must act with purpose. Without reservation.

There is a flash of movement and the thin man feels himself turned, lifted. He feels intense pressure on his neck. He thinks: I should have asked her to marry me.

The flashlight drops to the floor.

"I said: 'God forgive me.'"

Chapter 6

As Jeremy stands in the Richmond fog, he knows that what he's telling himself he's doing and what he's doing are two different things. He's telling himself that he's come to the Last Cup, the rarest of all-night cafés in San Francisco, a city in which the eateries tend to close by ten, infuriating East Coast visitors and giving them a justifiable feeling of superiority. Here, Jeremy tells himself, he'll run some diagnostics on the conflict algorithm.

It is true that Jeremy has spent more than one night lingering over a bottomless coffee at the Last Cup, working through a manic muse or dozing in a beanbag chair by the piano. It is also true that he has generally done so after a fight with Emily, who happens to live one block away from the Last Cup.

He's standing in front of her flat, not admitting to himself that the real reason he's here—not the café—is to connect somehow with Emily, even just to peek into her window. Jeremy's reality is spinning off its hinges and Emily's always the touchstone. She used to tell him he was the same to her. She'd concede that his antagonism, his snipes and counterpunches, while antisocial, often spoke deep truths others would not speak. And she, unlike others, didn't get threatened by them.

Her puke-green flat, so painted by an intransigent land-lord, one of innumerable stubborn men who seem to surround her, stands between flats packed with large Chinese families. Jeremy points out to Emily that he has never had a single verbal altercation with the Chins and the Chus and Emily points out that that's because the families speak no English.

Jeremy shivers from the chill but the feeling quickly passes. He tends to be impervious to changes in weather; Emily says Jeremy feels words and ideas, not physical conditions. She's told him he'd endure physical torture without blinking just so long as it wasn't accompanied by someone questioning his intellect or tousling his newly cut hair.

Her Jetta is not in the driveway.

Tomorrow must be garbage day, Jeremy realizes; that explains the line down the street of black trash bins, blue for recycling, green for composting. The city recently hired a group of right-minded young people at minimum wage to go block by block to see if people have properly distributed their waste. Once, Emily got a knock on the door from an earnest SF State student explaining that she'd done a "very good job" segregating her recycling. "But, if you're up for it, it'd be great if you could be just a tad more vigilant with the newspaper. Mother appreciates it, y'know."

"Mother?"

"Nature."

"May I?" Jeremy bellowed from the other room.

Emily smiled, closing the door. "Too easy. This one's beneath you. Let's see if we can work off your venom in bed."

Jeremy takes a step toward the trash bins. If he looks inside, will he find evidence telling him whether Emily's Jetta is miss-

ing because she's on a date or a sleepover? Maybe she's on a date
with someone less like Jeremy and more like Emily, fluid and
easygoing, artistic, Jewish, not that Emily ever considered religion a deal breaker in a mate. Emily finds prayer calming. She
likes knowing "something bigger is out there," an amorphous
philosophy that drives Jeremy nuts. On Emily's ankle is a Star
of David tattoo, which Jeremy points out makes it impossible
for her to be buried in a Jewish cemetery, and therefore, Jeremy
razzes her, means she's not consistent with her beliefs, like most
of the freaking world. Inside the house, a dim light. Jeremy figures it's the cheap standing lamp next to the couch. He pictures
a babysitter on the couch, reading a trashy romance. Jeremy's
stomach sinks. Someone who is not him or Emily put Kent to
bed, read him *Madeline* or *Jamberry*.

When it comes to Kent, and virtually only when it comes
to Kent, Jeremy's emotions are precisely what they appear to
be—to him and anyone else paying attention. There is a one-
to-one relationship between what Kent makes him feel and
what he expresses. It's linear. It adds up. When the two boys
are hanging out, Emily says, Jeremy experiences no disconnect.
She loves and loathes that Jeremy feels more comfortable with
her son than he does with her.

She also cannot fully understand the phenomenon. Kent
challenges Jeremy as much as or more than anyone else. "Why,
why, why?" Kent asks Jeremy. Kent cries, he's mercurial, he
comes and goes, he becomes furious when Jeremy (or anyone
else) can't find his stuff, he rolls on the floor with giggles, then
throws a tantrum when blood sugar fades. He's nine and he
exhibits all the behaviors of the most annoying of Jeremy's investors. And Jeremy absolutely fucking loves him.

Loved him. Or whatever is the correct verb tense for a situ-

ation where you've lost contact with someone, perhaps indefi-
nitely, because you've lost contact with his mother, for at least
the last three weeks. To top it off, a few nights before his breakup
with Emily, he and Kent actually had a disagreement—and
now Jeremy feels estranged from the boy, too.

Jeremy takes the first step of the slick stairs at Emily's flat.
He feels a buzz in his pocket. He pulls out his phone. He ex-
amines it for incoming stimuli—a text, a call, an instant message. But there's nothing. He pulls out his other phone, from
his other pocket, even though he didn't feel a buzz coming
from it. Nothing. He rechecks both phones. They are devoid of
incoming stimulation.

Maybe I imagined it, Jeremy thinks, without finding that
possibility at all remarkable. He recalls some research paper
that documented the growing phenomenon of "phantom buzzing," whereby someone feels the tug of a device even though it's
not actually beckoning. Researchers theorized that the phantom buzz might actually be serving as a reminder to the person
of something he or she had wanted to do. The phone as proxy
for the subconscious. The human brain and the computer becoming intertwined, even when the person is offline.

A sharp gust of wind blows down the street, stinging Jeremy's face. He shivers. He looks at the phone's clock. It's just
before midnight.

He puts his head down and walks to the café, heading into
the wind. Instinctively, he realizes, he's got his fingers gently
pushing a fleshy spot on his left pectoral, where the nagging,
pulsing pain seems to start. He rubs the spot. Then moves his
fingers a few inches to the right and wraps them protectively
around the key fob hanging from a chain around his neck. The
key to getting into the guts of the program.

It's what Evan's suing over; even though Jeremy came up with it, it was so clearly his idea, Evan contends he owns or shares the intellectual property rights to many of the underlying ideas. The user interfaces, the countdown clock, the sizzle that has so many business applications. He's put together a well-heeled startup, SEER, to spot business trends. Evan claims the technology doesn't work to predict war but it's good enough to "intelligently guide" corporations about the future of their industries. His tagline: Not predicting the future, shaping it.

Over the last year of their partnership, Jeremy and Evan were increasingly at odds. Evan seemed intent on showing Jeremy the potential business applications and Jeremy was intent on telling Evan where he could shove it.

And so, now, in short, their relationship has devolved into a patent dispute. Jeremy thinks this is the most vile, uncivil form of conflict in the entire world, so cruelly administrative. And really, in the end, just a negotiation, not a search for truth. But it's also utterly du jour in Silicon Valley, with companies wielding armies of lawyers to vie over who came up with what idea first. And then smiling and signing royalty contracts, one company agreeing to pay the other such-and-such licensing rights because, well, the stupid fucking court can't really disentangle.

At its heart, Jeremy tells himself, his opposition to such compromises is the kind of thing that drives his inability to let the little things go. One day, you let the barista at a café act like an idiot, the next you're giving away your ideas, your soul.

Emily tells Jeremy that it's just an excuse to act like a jerk and that Jeremy isn't allowing anyone else to even contribute to finding productive uses for the technology.

And then Emily adds insult to injury: she says that Jeremy is jealous. Jealous! In particular, she says Jeremy can't stand that

Evan had become tight with Harry, who for so long was Jeremy's advocate and mentor. Evan and Harry seemed not just to become fast friends but to consult professionally. Maybe Evan, tired of Jeremy's antics, was consulting Harry instead. Emily says Jeremy can't stand to see anyone get along, especially people in his inner circle.

In any case, if Evan wants to shut down Jeremy's efforts and get access to the technology he claims to have helped develop, then Evan's going to have to come and get it.

Jeremy's working on a theory: Evan's doing just that. He's somehow messing with his algorithm, trying to drive a wedge between a man and his machine, to get Jeremy to give up. Take the payoff, licensing fees, royalties, and then go work on something else. Fat chance.

Jeremy wipes the drizzle from his arms and walks into the café. He orders a decaf and nods his nod to the Jabba the Hutt, who works the overnight shift behind the counter. Jeremy plops into a blue beanbag chair in the back. The place is about half full but there's no buzz or hum to it, the sound and energy sapped by the inclement weather, fog and drizzle as insulation. On the ratty orange couch, a guy with a beard quietly plucks a guitar and taps its face in rhythm to some song he's polite enough to almost keep to himself. Toward the front, some college-student types bury themselves in earphones and texts. No talent, Jeremy remarks in his neurological recesses, referring to the fact that there's not a single worthy chick.

He plugs the iPad into an outlet, signs on to the wi-fi, calls up, sees the machine come to life, paws the conflict map to bring it to life, then hears the machine beep. Three beeps, *those* three beeps, the same ones from the morning.

The war machine has an update for him.

CHAPTER 7

B EFORE HE CAN check the device, Jeremy feels something nag at him and looks up. He discovers he's being stared at by the bearded guitar player, who quickly lowers his head. Jeremy recoils into his beanbag, tilting the iPad so no one else in the place could possibly see it.

He looks at the screen. A dialogue box pops up. Inside it reads: "Impact Update. Click for details."

Sure, let's see it, he thinks, clicking.

The dialogue reads: "April's projected deaths: 75 million."

In the abstract, at least, that's not so hard for Jeremy to swallow. Just more game theory and simple probability. An attack in, say, San Francisco, triggers a counterattack, then reprisals, then the dominoes fall. The program is taking into account the hundreds of parameters and key variables that, Jeremy's research at Oxford determined, can be used to predict the length and intensity of war.

He looks at the map.

Red, red, red. The only difference between the rendering of the future on this map and on the version of the map he saw six hours ago is that attack is six hours closer. That, he notices, and it looks like the red is spreading. Meaning: whatever conflict this computer has foreseen will go from hellacious to worse. The countdown clock shows 66:57:02. Hours, minutes, seconds.

Jeremy looks up at the guitar player. It crosses his mind that if the guitar player is looking at him, Jeremy's going to advise the guy on the problems with his chord-hand position. Just a little jab, one that will come across as possibly well-meaning and hard to interpret. But the guitar player is buried in his world, unavailable to hear unsolicited advice.

Jeremy pulls out his phone. He's trying to remember Evan's cell phone number. Trying to think what he's going to say after: Hey, fuckface!

He pauses. Never go into a fight unarmed. He needs more evidence. He can check the inputs.

On the phone, he calls up Nik's number. Taps out a text: "notice anything strange?" The corpulent assistant is either asleep or glued to an infomercial. But if he does see the text, it might jar him; Jeremy doesn't ask questions like this, not open-ended ones, not even of Nik.

From his backpack, Jeremy pulls an external keyboard.

Is the data coming into his machine, the data that some-how adds up to impending doom, accurate? Has it been al-tered?

Jeremy rolls his neck, pre-computing calisthenics. He looks at the key fob, enters six numbers, then his password, then he begins tearing his way across the keyboard, causing symbols and lines and numbers to appear in the window. It's less fancy than it looks. Jeremy's simply creating a category of all of these data points—all 327 inputs—collecting them into a single file, then writing a code to send out the numbers, all of the data points, and check them against their sources around the world, and then to double-check the data points.

Most of them largely irrelevant. In the grand scheme of predicting conflict, they are modest measures, weighted lightly relative to the handful of big ones: troop movements, demographics (specifically, concentration of males age eighteen to thirty-five), changes in income distribution (the wealth gap), weather, arms shipments insofar as they can be inferred by production and profit from companies in the military-industrial complex, and, powerfully, a "rhetoric" measure. It looks at changing use of language by politicians and media around the world but, with more emphasis, in hot zones. How are powerful "entities," whether people or media outlets, describing their relationship to the rest of the world? Internet spiders can easily comb through mountains of publicly accessible commentary to look for phrases like "we will never surrender" or "vanquish the enemy" or "date which will live in infamy." Algorithms Jeremy has developed and forfeited many nights of sleep perfecting can compare them with previous utterances by those politicians or outlets, looking to see if the rhetoric had been more conciliatory, and so forth.

Those are the key variables for understanding more conventional war. But predicting and understanding localized terror attacks, insurrection, jihad, guerrilla warfare that has, in effect, become war in the 21st century, that's even tougher. It relies on narrowing the search to a region in question, even a city or mountainous area, to the spot where a group of insurgents are focused. It relies on looking at an additional key variable: the formation and concentration of small groups capable of carrying out attacks and creating instability. These are, in fact, mini-armies, the modern analogue to the massive buildup of troops and a war machine before the outbreak of World War II. What, the Soviets never saw it coming?

And Jeremy's been monkeying around with other ideas, ways to refine the conflict algorithm. Over the last several months, since everyone severed ties with him, he's been playing with a particularly wild-eyed effort. It's an attempt to identify a specific person whose actions, or words, are singularly important in igniting conflict. The program measures the relevance of a person's influence to potential hostility based on that person's network of connections. It aims to mine the mountains of data on the Internet to connect people to one another, a version of what Facebook does when it draws connections between potential friends.

Jeremy calls it "Program Princip." It's named after Gavrilo Princip, the nineteen-year-old who shot Archduke Franz Ferdinand, igniting World War I. Jeremy's idea is that he'll go beyond being able to identify someone like Ferdinand as a potential influence in an impending conflict, to identifying the tiny needles that will ignite the conflict haystack. In some ways, it's not so far-fetched. A handful of startups have gotten big venture capital to develop software aimed at combing the Internet to determine who is most influential in, say, business or art. So why not conflict? But so far, Jeremy has only beta-tested it, showed no one, only really muttered about it to Emily.

Jeremy finishes his latest iPad query in about twice the time it ordinarily would've taken, because he's got to type so carefully in order not to make mistakes and because he's tired. He hits "enter" on his command.

Is the data accurate?

If so, what data set changed? When?

He should know in the next six hours. It's well past 1 A.M. He pulls the iPad to his chest, folds his arms around it. Pulls it back off his chest. He opens a browser. Googles: Evan Tigeson.

Lots of hits. He clicks on the web site for SEER, Evan's latest thing. And then a mission statement about not merely predicting but driving global trends using proven, patented algorithmic technologies. Yeah, Jeremy thinks, my fucking technologies. He clicks on Evan's bio. Sees the picture, a black-and-white photo, square features, an almost seductive eyebrow raise undercut with a geeky subtext that Evan can't bury. To Jeremy, he's a "51 percenter"; just on the other side of slick. Like so many in the Valley, he's just shy of fully slick, geeky enough to come across as authentic. This type of businessperson in Silicon Valley is like the do-gooders from college who go to Washington, D.C., and it becomes impossible to tell the difference between their ambitions for the world and for themselves.

Jeremy clicks back to the home page. Sees an infobox that catches his eye. "Sign up for SEER 2013, an initiative for the future." A conference, the typical way to jump-start a new business, a networking opportunity. He clicks for more information. None comes up, other than a list of current conference partners. It's impressive, Google, Intel, Sun Microsystems, Apple, Cisco, Hewlett-Packard. The very biggest tech companies. Slick Peckerhead.

And there's an email: InfoSEER@seer.com.

Jeremy closes his eyes, pictures one of his last meetings with Evan, at least the last one with any pretense of civility. Down in the Valley offices, where Jeremy visited with increasing in-frequency, he ducked into Evan's glass-walled office to find his partner playing around on the conflict map. At first Jeremy blanched, but then he realized Evan wasn't actually inside the guts of the algorithm, not changing it or able to, just running various scenarios: what if this business were located here, or this one located there; what if flat-panel television manufactur-ing plants continued to decline in profit margins, blah, blah.

"What happens if Walmart gets into the widget business? I hear that's going to be huge," Jeremy said. "Get that one right and you can move to Atherton."

Evan managed a smile. He always could. Nothing seemed to ruffle him, something he'd point out in speeches was owed to his upbringing in northern Minnesota, where twenty below was balmy. He'd say that his quaint upbringing in Moorhead, population forty thousand, was like the Internet: if you tried you could connect to everyone, live a more intertwined life.

"This is the future."

"Business applications are my passion."

"It's so much more than that, Jeremy." A slight hint of edge in his voice. "Look what happened when they developed Ireland and rural China. Huge economic prosperity. What if your machine could be more powerful than you ever even imagined?"

"Whatever, Peckerhead."

"Don't take my word for it. Ask Harry."

This one stopped Jeremy in his tracks, a rare comment for which Jeremy didn't have a quick retort.

"You've been talking to Harry?"

"It's impolite to have lunch with someone and not talk."

It was the moment that Jeremy learned that Evan, the business partner he was learning to loathe, had cozied up to Harry. Jeremy became instantly convinced the pair were conspiring behind his back. Maybe they were just two people interested in the world, Emily said, and she tried to broker a peace.

She arranged a picnic, held at the log cabin, a beautiful setting in San Francisco's Presidio, in the shadow of the Golden Gate Bridge. The setting was also intended as symbolic; the Presidio was a former military base turned gorgeous public sanctuary. A place where the machinery of war, its essence, turned decidedly tranquil. And a favorite place of Harry's to come think big thoughts about peace and conflict.

But so much for symbolism: no sooner had Harry and Jeremy arrived than they went right to war, each firing rhetorical ICBMs turbo-powered by his immense ego, each accusing the other of disloyalty and stupidity. After all Harry's generosity over the years, Jeremy spat the ultimate insult—all the while, Harry was seeking to discredit Jeremy and his computer so that Harry, and Harry alone, would be the ultimate authority on conflict and its causes. Harry, Jeremy was saying, was little more than a power-hungry conflict-monger himself.

And here Jeremy sits now, in the café, ties severed from Harry, and Evan—and wondering if the two are somehow in league against him.

He stares at Evan's new web site. He pulls up his phone and scrolls through old emails until he finds a phone number for his ex-partner. He pushes a button to dial. It rings and rings. Voice mail picks up. Jeremy hangs up.

His eyes are glazing over. He closes the browser, pulls the iPad to his chest.

He thinks back to what Evan had said in their last conversation at the office: "Your machine can be more powerful than you ever imagined."

What had he meant by that? Something Jeremy didn't realize?

The words and ideas blur and jumble together as Jeremy falls asleep.

CHAPTER 8

"TWINKLE, TWINKLE."

He feels someone kick his foot. "Twinkle, twinkle."

Jeremy cracks open his eyes. "Twinkle, twinkle little fart," Jeremy manages.

"How I wonder where you fart."

Standing before him, a boy with light brown hair, spilling out unkempt from the sides of his red wool hat with earflaps. He's got black rain boots and the trendy puffy blue ski jacket that Jeremy had given him at the beginning of the school year. Kent bobs his head and torso side to side, herky-jerky, as if moving to some unheard music, the rhythm of an energetic boy.

"You look like a collage," Jeremy says. He's getting his bearings. He's sitting in a beanbag, arms wrapped around an iPad.

"Did you sleep here? You seriously smell like a fart. Seriously."

Jeremy inhales. Boy's got a point. Kent and Emily must be here on the way to school and work. How many times has Jeremy told Emily to make coffee at home to save the money;

and pastries aren't good for the boy: even the raisin bran muffin brims with sugar.

Still, he smiles. His last interaction with Kent was the worst they'd ever had. Some stupid disagreement as they sat on the living room floor, trying to make sense of the strewn pieces of a rocket ship puzzle. Jeremy suggested looking for the corners first.

"I have a better idea," said Kent. He was sorting the pieces by color, looking for the ones that might go together.

"Only if you want to be here all day," Jeremy said.

"Get your own puzzle." Kent said it absently, something from the mouth of a babe. But Jeremy laughed haughtily. Something cruel. But he at least was able to check the counter-attack that nearly spilled from his mouth, even though the bad taste didn't leave Jeremy for days.

Kent turns and Jeremy follows his gaze to the counter. With a modest smile, Emily orders coffee. She's got high black boots and a long black skirt and a light purple blouse, her shoulders covered by her near-black hair, and Jeremy can practically taste the pheromones across the café. He thinks: Emily, something bad is happening. Someone's messing with me.

And, then: But just in case no one's messing with me, just in case something really bad is happening, get away from here. Take Kent to your brother's house in Reno.

Emily tilts her head toward the guy standing next to her at the counter, listening to him. She laughs.

The guy is tall and wiry—built not unlike Jeremy, fuller brown hair suggesting he's younger. Brownish skin, one of those hybrid ethnicities, half something and half something else. Is he seriously wearing a stone-washed jean jacket?

He puts a hand on Emily's shoulder, friendly, close to inti-mate, maybe not quite there.

Kent says: "Ready?"

Jeremy looks at the boy.

"Old McDonald Had a Fart."

Part of their ritual, turning Mother Goose rhymes and songs into potty humor. Relief washes over Jeremy; whatever tension is long since past.

"Eee-eye, eee-eye-oh. And on that farm he had a cow," the boy continues, off pitch, a little self-conscious. "With a poo-poo here and a poo-poo there."

Emily looks over. Jeremy watches the cascade of analysis and emotion: why is my son talking to this strange man un-furled on the beanbag chair; oh shit, that's not a strange man. Her face turns to puzzle pieces. One looks like anger, one like pity, and one like fear, not from the threat of a stranger but of the familiar.

She turns and says something to the guy she's with—the guy she spent the night with?—then clears her throat and begins her last-mile walk to Jeremy.

Jeremy represses an urge to stand to meet her. Realizes he wants to save that movement for when it might really count. Before Jeremy can look down, in an effort to communicate his fake nonchalance, the old flames lock eyes.

"We're late, bunny. Let's get a move on." Emily's balancing her coffee and a juice and a couple of pastries on a compostable brownish takeout tray. "What are you doing here, Jeremy?"

"You can't be serious," Jeremy says. He juts his chin toward the guy. "The 1980s called. It wants the denim jacket back."

"Let's go, bunny, we're late." Then to Jeremy: "Let's do this later."

"There isn't going to be any later."

Typically obtuse for Jeremy; he must be setting up some

line of attack. But Emily senses that it's dramatic in a way that Jeremy usually avoids until he's launched his final verbal offensive. Which is why moisture glistens in her brown eyes, sympathy, yearning for understanding, not recrimination. His heart thump-thumps, a drumbeat urging him forward into an embrace or confession. He clears his throat.

"Kent, bunny, can you go wait by the piano while I talk to Jeremy." She extends a raisin muffin to the boy. He holds it, but doesn't move. Emily grits her teeth at this impossible situation, her stubborn son and stubborn former lover. "It's not healthy for you to be here."

"Not healthy?"

"Jeremy . . ." She knows the essence of what's coming, if not the exact words.

"What's not healthy is that raisin bran muffin. Tons of sugar. What's not healthy is bringing home some strange man. It's in all the literature. You've got to be sure he's the guy. It's sending Kent really confusing messages."

"I'm right here," says Kent. "She didn't bring him home."

"Not healthy, Jeremy? Like starting a fight in front of Kent? Like showing up at a café blocks from where we live; there's a café every half block in this city. Like . . ." She pauses. She looks around, happy that no one seems to be paying attention, but still lowers her voice further. "I'm not doing this."

"He's definitely not Jewish." He's looking at the guy who was with Emily and who now sits in a ratty high-backed chair near the front trying hard to pretend he's flipping through a broadsheet.

"That's sheer desperation, and obnoxious, and neither, for that matter, is Kent's dad, or you." She pauses. "But you do need a coping mechanism."

He's fighting for footing. "Did you notice his shoes?" Emily looks at the guy for a lingering second, looks back at Jeremy.

"You are brilliant, Jeremy. I'm not disputing that. You are so kind when you want to be. Kent cherishes you. But you have the biggest blind spot of anyone I've ever known. You only see trees."

"The shoes and the jacket don't match. Something's off about that guy. There's a lie in him. I'm guessing he picked you up at the gym, or after work. You fell for his apparent goofiness. You like a project. But this guy is a charade. He's using you for something."

"All trees. No forest." She shakes her head. She's practically seething. Enough so that Jeremy lets himself look at her directly, another move he tries to avoid when in a heated conversation because it also can send the message: okay, I'm listening; you might have a point.

"You can't see the big picture, Jeremy. It's pathological. You nit and pick and nitpick and nitpick. Challenge and refute. Then, when you finally let down your guard, whenever we got so close, you'd nit and pick and then go nuclear. You destroy everything in your path, tree by tree by tree."

Jeremy has to pause before responding. He's impressed by her reasoning, flawed though it is. Usually, she's led by succinct, true emotion, famous for such profundities as "I'm feeling sad." It's how she prefaced the final breakup with Jeremy, after lovemaking on the futon in her living room that was, on its face, intense, but in which Jeremy sensed her absence.

"I know you're bitter about how things turned out," Jeremy says, which is true but also ridiculous because Jeremy's equally bitter.

She ignores his bullshit. She looks up to see, thankfully, that Kent has receded to the piano bench, where he's munching his muffin.

"It's not me, Jeremy. It's everyone. Jeremy, to be blunt, I don't think you've got a friend left. Not a single ally. Not that people wouldn't help you. You won't let them. Remember the log cabin?"

"Harry's messing with me, Emily."

She laughs. She bursts out. It's a genuine laugh, a honey drip of irrepressible amusement.

"Harry didn't want to fight with you. He wanted to help you, and you just attacked him. Get out of the trees, Jeremy. And probably you should stay out of this neighborhood. It's really not healthy for you." She looks at Kent. Unstated: It's really not healthy for Kent. He loves you. You know how much he loves you.

Jeremy feels a vibration in his pocket. He extracts his phone. It's a call from a private number. He's about to send the call to voice mail. A call from a private number. He remembers what's going on with his computer. Who is calling?

He swipes his finger across the screen. "Hold on," he says into the phone. He cups his finger over the microphone.

"Kent is the forest, Jeremy," Emily says. She looks him in the eye, draws him in. He wants to put his head on her lap. "Please don't bother us."

Jeremy's arm shoots up. He holds up his hand as if to say: wait, please. With his other hand, he cups the phone against his chest so that whoever is on the other end of the line can't hear what he's going to say. He looks at Emily, the slight cherub in her cheeks, the emerging crow's-feet around her deep brown eyes, a picture of softness and beauty, someone he, when he's feeling charitable and condescending, likens to the Giving Tree in the book by Shel Silverstein that he often read to Kent. She gave, Jeremy took, and it seemed to work for everybody.

She senses something powerful in him. "Is everything okay?"

Now is the moment, he thinks. Now he can tell her that he needs to tell her something.

"Where were you last night?"

She raises her eyebrow. Are you kidding me?

"I was on a date. I didn't spend the night at his house. He came by this morning to take me to coffee. He's a nice guy, a friend, and nothing more. For now. And you are not entitled to know anything further about my life, Jeremy. If not for Kent, please, do it for me. I need to be able to live without fighting."

She shakes her head and starts walking away. Jeremy feels his heart thump, unable to respond. So he switches his attention away from it, and to his head. "Hello."

Chapter 9

"WHAT'S WRONG, ATLAS?"

The sound of the voice sends electricity shooting through him.

Jeremy watches Emily usher Kent out the front door without a look back. Trailing behind, Emily's suitor. He peeks back at Jeremy, seems to smile. Does he look familiar?

"Why are you calling me?" Jeremy demands.

Andrea Belluck-Juarez laughs. "Just as hostile as I remember. Do you wake up that way or does it usually take enough caffeine to fell an elephant?"

"Calls from blocked numbers make me hostile."

"You're the one who answered, Atlas." Her moniker for Jeremy, deriving partly from an inside joke between them that Department of Defense contractors deserve code names and partly because, she told him, he likes to think he believes he can carry the whole world to safety; he, she jokes, and he alone.

"What's up?" He's trying to sound nonchalant, feel her out. But his antennae are bristling. It's a big coincidence that she'd call mere hours after his computer warned of impending doom.

"I should be asking you that question."

"What's that supposed to mean?" Andrea laughs again. Then explains: "Usually your hostility comes thick with sarcasm and witty repartee. Maybe you really haven't had your caffeine."

"Hanging up now."

"Easy, Atlas. I'm calling because you're a week late."

Jeremy swallows, still getting his bearings.

Every two weeks or so for the last eighteen months, Jeremy has called Andrea to ask one question: are you ready to admit I was right? It's a question referring to his predictions—or, rather, the predictions of his conflict machine—about the length and intensity of conflicts in Afghanistan and Iraq. Ever since the military brass there dismissed him as a quack, he's regularly hounded Andrea to own up to the fact that they somehow duped him. They promised at one point to send him overseas so he could do a real-time test, pitting his algorithm against reality on the ground in Iraq, but the trip never materialized. It was further evidence to Jeremy that they were afraid to allow him to see firsthand the breathtaking value of his technology.

"I was worried you'd lost faith in yourself," Andrea says.

He looks down at the iPad, swerves his finger across the screen to awaken it, sees the map covered in red.

"So was I right?"

"That's the Jeremy I know and have some grudging appreciation for."

He doesn't answer. On his iPad, he looks at the countdown clock: 59:15:32.

He swallows thickly, flicks away the map and pulls up a window from the background. It shows the calculations he was running overnight, the requests for whether the list of 327 global parameters was accurately reported. The screen reads: "Action complete. Would you like to see the results?"

"No," Andrea says.

"What?"

"No, you were not right."

"You want a prediction I'm absolutely one hundred percent correct about?" Jeremy says into the phone.

"Sure."

"I'm hanging up."

He pulls the phone from his ear to end the call, hears: "Wait."

Something in the intensity of the plea causes him to pull the phone back.

"I'm in town. Visiting another asset. Let's get a drink."

He rolls the logic around in his mouth, the change in data, the statistical significance of this call. And of the proposition. A drink, from the woman who seduced him into service.

He pictures Andrea, an unlikely cocktail: born in Mexico City of a local and an American doing executive kidnap recovery work for insurance companies, then raised in Idaho, forged with a kind of quiet and abiding patriotism. And undeniably beautiful, and quirky; encyclopedic about the nearest karaoke bar, blessed with a powerful soprano and no fear of showing it off. To inform his standard holier-than-thou worldview, Jeremy wanted to dismiss her as an affirmative action hire, some favor to her father—the kidnap specialist with CIA ties. But she just kept proving herself too smart for that.

After an introduction by Harry, she recruited Jeremy to the Pentagon, got him to let his guard down, put him and his computer in a position to be humiliated. The flash passes and he's back to his head, wondering why in the world he's hearing at this moment from a case officer in the Department of Defense.

"Andrea, do you know why they made me your asset?"

"Why?"

"Because they suspected I was a hack, a blowhard. You're a junior case officer, an affirmative action hire, an effort to doll up an agency, a skirt they could send to low-level meetings on the Hill. They figured they could waste your time with me."

"You're an asshole."

"Ta-ta."

"But you are right."

He doesn't respond to her vague provocation. She clarifies. "You're right about why they hired me. I'm good at dealing with assholes."

"Ta-ta."

"Does tonight work? It's too small of a world to burn bridges. You never know when we might need each other."

He grunts something noncommittal, which she takes as assent. "Not the usual spot. Let's try somewhere new. I'll call you later." She hangs up.

He had deliberately chosen the most provocative, childish, offensively sexist language to infuriate Andrea, test her, and still she didn't hang up or even challenge him. Why not? Because she's used to dealing with him and has tuned out his bullshit, or for some other reason?

Is she part of some scam?

He's had his questions from the start, that night she recruited him, consummated his commitment. The government had flown him to Washington, which didn't seem so odd. Everyone was flying Jeremy everywhere at this point. Consult on this, speak at that, Jeremy finding himself at the gooey center of the world of peace and conflict studies. At his hotel in Georgetown, there was a knock on the door and there stood Andrea, so in opposition to what Jeremy had expected. He'd let down his guard. At a swanky restaurant downstairs, they'd eaten oysters and drunk martinis, which she could put away. She was neither overly flirty nor remotely shy in showing him the edges of the bird tattoo above her left breast. She didn't mention a thing about the algorithm, his reason for visiting, the thing they'd ask him about at a briefing the next day at the Pentagon.

So when she went to the bathroom, he felt suddenly nervous. He patted his pockets, discovered he was missing the key fob, the access code for the conflict program. He left the table before she returned from the bathroom, rushed up to his room. There was the fob, on the desk, right next to the computer.

He exhaled, felt a kind of shame —not because he'd freaked but because of something in this woman's power. When she showed up at his door, she'd caused him to forget himself, forget to take his precious fob. Thereafter, he'd worn it around his neck, an amulet, a veritable locket.

After that, over the months, he'd alternately opened himself to Andrea and protected himself from her. Did she like him or was she just recruiting him? Their last in-person interaction, the last time they'd had a drink, was at the usual place, South of Market. She was hemming and hawing about another last-minute cancellation of a trip to send Jeremy to the Middle East. *I'm doing my best for you, Jeremy. I believe in you, and it.* His computer.

So much brown in her eyes and promise in her voice. Jeremy wondered if this was the night Andrea would finally invite him back to her hotel, allowing him the pleasure of declining, or deciding whether to decline. Then, a surprise interloper: Evan. The slickster happened into the same bar, with a twenty-something date. An awkward moment among the three of them, shattering the rhythm of the night. Andrea petering out, professing to share Jeremy's distrust of his MBA backer, but whatever momentum he imagined had been there, totally lost.

Back in the present, Jeremy remembers himself, his habit of getting lost in his head, especially lately. He can't stop puzzling through so many little moments the last few years, these Hansel and Gretel crumbs that have led him to this isolated place. He looks up. The café bristles; a man in a fashionable red rain jacket chomps half a donut in a single bite, then looks around furtively, suggesting to Jeremy that the man's guiltily wondering if someone might catch him eating too many carbs of the inorganic variety.

Fucking San Francisco. Maybe it should get nuked.

He looks at the phone, then hits the cursor. Yes, he fucking wants to see the results from the program he ran the night before. Just how full of shit is his conflict algorithm? He hits enter.

The screen reads:

327 variables checked.

327 variables accurately reported.

Jeremy feels a painful pulse in his clavicle. The computer has based its results on accurate information.

So that means that the problem isn't what's being fed into the computer. It might be that the algorithm itself has been tinkered with, not the inputs, but the equations. The guts.

Jeremy looks up, scans the café. He's looking for faces that might be looking at him. Some trickster, someone getting even. That, weirdly, he realizes, is his first impulse at this moment.

He doesn't quite put it together that there's something else compelling this action: he's feeling humiliated. This fucking computer, this life's dream turned nightmare, might just be out-and-out wrong. It's like the Pentagon all over again. Worse than that; a realization not just that his computer is screwing up, but that someone is messing with it, just like messing with the inside of his own brain.

At least that's got to be the working assumption, that someone is messing with the computer. Who? How?

He looks at the countdown clock, then below it. At the bottom of the screen, Jeremy sees a query: *Would you like to see a list of the variables?*

Jeremy clicks yes. Yes, he wants to see which variables have changed such that this computer is predicting the end of the world.

CHAPTER 10

A LITTLE OVER AN hour later, and poorer by eight dollars spent on a ham-and-cheese croissant and coffee and the bus, he looks up from the iPad and watches a raven-haired woman apply makeup to her pale face with help from a pocket mirror. Pale like his mother on that last visit, her head rolled to the side, dry lips, Jeremy wondering whether someone is going to say something, anything, something conciliatory, or maybe one last twinkle-eyed parry on her way to eternity.

The bus slows. It mostly emptied on the circle through downtown. Just two stops now until Jeremy's condo. To-do list: shower, change clothes, get a backup battery, walk to the office, go deeper into this list of variables.

He looks down at the iPad to see what it's already given him: a list of 327 parameters that the computer used as a basis for predicting an attack.

A column on the left on his iPad window lists the name of a particular variable; then, in the next column, the variable is quantified, like the number of oil barrels shipped or produced. Next to that, one column shows how much the variable has changed in the last day and another column shows how much it's changed in the last week. Finally, a column on the far right shows the extent of the change.

Jeremy scrolls up and down this dense, text-heavy list. Three of the lines of variables are blinking. The blinks signal that the variables in those columns have seen a significant change.

When he first built the program, he'd look every few hours at the variables, looking for changes, like a hopped-up day trader or, Emily once observed, like a psychology student who, a few days into class, starts imagining that he and everyone around him has everything from clinical depression to multiple personality disorder to attention deficit disorder. Jeremy was seeing conflict everywhere.

But he quickly realized that changes to the variables, even the most weighty ones, did not mean imminent war. Much more important is the combination of changing factors, their relative and combined influence in waging war. The precise right amount of sugar and butter and chocolate makes delicious cookies; the wrong amount, combined with arsenic, makes something that tastes like shit and kills you.

What he's looking at, even if the data is accurate, still is likelier to be a predictor of a hoax than a war. Jeremy looks at the blinking columns. One is Tantalum. The second is Conflict Rhetoric. The third is the Random Event Meter, known as REM.

The bus slows again. Jeremy glances at the countdown clock: 57:40:00.

57:39:59.

57:39:58.

He looks up. The raven-haired woman applying makeup, sitting two rows ahead, is looking at Jeremy in her tiny hand-held mirror. Isn't she? As the bus comes to a stop, she hastily stuffs her makeup kit into an oversize purse and exits out the front.

Jeremy looks down at the variables. Rhetoric. The computer is programmed to see changes in language, to see nuances even in hyperbole. But from the column, Jeremy can't tell exactly what has changed in the language of conflict, or where in the world it has changed. That level of abstraction will take more research, another command to the server, easily enough done when he gets upstairs. He'll be able to tell if the language of conflict has intensified in, say, the Baltics, or among Greek bankers, or in Iran.

All Jeremy can tell from this column is that there has been a sharp uptick, 14 percent, in the last few days, of the collective language of conflict, material enough for the computer to care about.

There's been an even sharper rise in the Random Event Meter. It's up 430 percent. Jeremy shakes his head, mostly annoyed, vaguely curious. The meter measures whether there has been some event or series of events that, in historic terms, would seem far outside the standard deviation. And the event can be anything. An alien landing. All Major League Baseball games being rained out, or being decided by more than 30 runs. Statistical anomalies unconnected to any of the other variables.

Jeremy clicks on the line. He sees a story from the Associated Press. The headline: "Lions Freed in Three Zoos, Leaving Man Dead."

He glances at the article. Lions loosed over the last twenty-four hours at the San Francisco Zoo, and in Oakland and in San Diego. Outside the San Diego Zoo, an old man found dead from claw wounds. Police speculate the man was responsible for freeing the lion. They speculate further that this is some effort coordinated among animal rights activists but acknowledge the theory is for the most part conjecture.

An off-duty cop shot the lion in San Diego. Animal control managed to dart and subdue the one in Oakland. The one in San Francisco remains at large.

It's all Jeremy can do to stop himself from rolling his eyes. Fucking computer, fucking nonsense. Maybe the three lions were planning to get together to cause the apocalypse.

He turns to the third variable, tantalum. That's up 4,017 percent.

The precious metal is integral to the making of cell phones. Tantalum, Jeremy recalls, comes from refining a raw material called coltan, which, in turn, is found in mines in Uganda and Rwanda.

Jeremy knows this not because he knows a bunch about how cell phones are made. Rather, he knows it because he knows how wars are made. And the battle for coltan once set off a rash of insurgencies in Africa. Simply: demand for coltan, which sold for $100 a pound when Jeremy was studying the conflict region in 2001, fueled efforts to control the mines and the municipal governments by guerrilla bands. It was a great place to explore localized conflict, even inspiring a visit once by Jeremy, then a graduate student, to try to put a human face on the variables measured by his computer brain.

Jeremy looks at his phone, sensing this might be further evidence of a hoax. After all, what difference could tantalum make in the possible onset of conflict? The sharp rise in shipments of tantalum, 4,017 percent, is certainly material, at least to the brokers and buyers and suppliers of the metal. But it could hardly, Jeremy imagines, have anything to do with tip-ping the balance of massive global conflict. He can imagine himself talking to some news blogger explaining he thinks that there's going to be a nuclear holocaust because of an increase in the shipment of some precious metal. Oh, and the release of some zoo lions.

You don't say, Mr. Stillwater? And for a follow-up question: are you still taking your meds?

The bus slows. Jeremy hears the doors open. He hears the rain. As he stuffs his iPad into the backpack, he sees the slick streets and smells the wet air.

How long has it been raining? How come he hadn't noticed? Is the rain the forest, or the trees?

Fucking Emily. And that guy, there was something about him that didn't add up. Something deliberate. A too on-point jacket, like a costume, but with shoes from an entirely different circus trunk. No, that's too simplistic. Was he too handsome, too deliberate in some way? Jeremy can't pinpoint what nags him.

Outside the bus, he walks against the foot traffic to his apartment complex cum condo, all steel and sharp corners, modernity that is San Francisco's version of urban renewal. The high-rises near the ballpark are beautiful. What twenty-something could resist? Perfect for the Trustafarians and stock option babies able to throw down 20 percent of $1.2 million for nine hundred square feet that serves as nest and résumé. The elevator ride is a networking opportunity and a speed date.

He takes the elevator to the eleventh floor. Feels a sense of relief as he reaches his floor, maybe a chance for a catnap. He slips his key into 1117 and opens the door.

He sees the innards of the couch. They're strewn all over the living room. Someone has gutted his sofa.

He peers to his right. Papers tossed on the counter that separates the kitchen from the living area. A stainless-steel spatula, an egg beater, lying beside their ceramic container, upside down on the counter.

Magazines on the floor.

Someone has overturned his apartment.

Someone still inside?

Jeremy backs out and shuts the door. He catches the eye of a young woman coming out of the apartment next door. He hates this woman, a bubbly, friendly, sycophantic thing, working at a startup in South Park. Actually, he once made an overture. When she first moved in. She rejected him in such an indirect but insurmountable way that it infuriated Jeremy. He has slipped several notes under her door asking her to turn down her music and, one night when particularly piqued at the sounds of sex coming from next door, anonymously warning her that it will set a bad precedent in her relationship if she fakes orgasms. Lies beget lies, he warned her. The building manager got involved but nothing could be proved, quiet warnings issued; the thing blew over.

"Excuse me, Tara." He sees that her umbrella, while it isn't unfurled, has Mickey Mouse prints.

"Hey."

"Strange question. Have you seen anyone coming into my apartment? Anyone not me?"

Her mousy face, beneath a bob haircut, registers a genuine concern.

"Did someone take something?"

He shakes his head. "I'm not sure. I might have had an unwanted visitor. Did you see anyone? Last night?"

"Did you tell Aaron?" The building manager.

He's starting to get irritated. Just answer the question, pixie. She must sense it.

"No," she says. "I went to bed after *Idol*. It was quiet last night."

He looks at the lock. No signs of forced entry. He opens the door.

CHAPTER 11

H E SLIPS INSIDE the doorway. He inhales, smells something, an alien presence. Wonders if it's gas but only momentarily. A perfume of some kind, heavy, no, a cologne. Like inhaling the Polo counter at Macy's.

He can hear Emily's voice inside his head and, for a second, he can clearly see the difference between the forest and the trees or, rather, tree. The tree is his desire to kill whoever was in his place, who overturned it. The forest is his safety. Call the cops, Jeremy, or the building manager. Get out of here.

He takes a few steps inside.

"I've called the police!" he yells. He paws his phone. He listens. Nothing, no sound. False bravery, he's realizing; of course no one is waiting for him. It would be a tactical error of the utmost stupidity, ransacking his apartment and then waiting around to get caught.

How did someone know he wasn't home last night?

What could someone want from him?

He feels the weight of his iPad on his back.

He takes in the condo, an open kitchen and living area with a fifty-inch Internet-connected TV hanging on the far wall. A massive window that would look onto the drizzle-shrouded bay if the curtains weren't pulled shut. Jeremy knows that's not his doing; he rarely remembers to shut the blinds; if people can see inside and don't like what he's doing, that's their problem.

The condo is mostly empty of furniture, edging on desolate. Jeremy hasn't had a chance to furnish the place; at least he tells himself he hasn't been able to afford the time, but it's more that he can't afford the cost of the things he'd like. He takes his furniture as seriously as his haircut. He likes things just so. And now they're ransacked.

The TV hangs askew. Someone looked behind it. The stuffing in his one couch unstuffed, jigsaw lines cut through the leather. And the knife, his own knife, lies on the throw rug. The implement of destruction, one of a set of three matching Wüsthofs, black riveted handle, razor edge. "To cut to the truth, and also for food prep," Evan had joked about his housewarming gift, back when Evan didn't fully grasp that Jeremy had no problem cutting to his version of the truth.

Jeremy picks it up, sees the leather-bound notebook, open to a middle page, lying beside the fireplace. Eyes ahead to the hallway and bedrooms, he kneels, glances at the notebook, flips. It's a backup system, phone numbers, scribbling of ideas. A page is torn near the front, torn but not torn out. He glances at the phone numbers.

Evan; Andrea; the guys at Intrinsic Investors; a few old friends from grad school; a hacker Jeremy likes who started a travel price-comparison web site acquired for hundreds of millions of dollars; Nik; two women Jeremy met at cafés, identified only by their initials so Emily wouldn't see them; Emily's brother, in case something ever happened to Emily—written in her loopy cursive—and, of course, Harry.

He pats his iPhone, pulls it out of his pocket. He's still holding the knife. He looks at the phone numbers. Already knows where he's starting, knew it hours ago, actually.

He's got to call Harry.

He's got to swallow his pride, or appear to, and hear what's in Harry's voice. Were Jeremy even half honest with himself, he'd admit he doesn't really suspect Harry; Harry might be tough and ticked off, but he's likely not malicious. And were Jeremy fully honest with himself, he'd admit he'd like Harry's help. But he's not—honest. He won't ask for help. He's going to ask Harry what the hell is going on, and then go from there.

He fingers the number into his iPhone, hits send, stands, begins walking to the back of the condo. The phone rings. He peeks into the bathroom. It's largely intact, but the medicine cabinet is opened and the handful of prescription medicines are uncapped.

The phone rings again.

Obviously, Jeremy thinks, an intruder left no bottle unturned. But also made, apparently, no effort to hide the intrusion. Unless the woman was somehow interrupted. Why, he wonders, does he think it was a woman?

He'll have to ask the building manager. That guy notices anything with a vagina. Rumor has it that the cops once got called and hassled him about whether he had a weird habit of lurking around the underground parking garage when a particularly attractive young woman would come home at night, and offer to help her carry her things upstairs.

The phone rings. C'mon, you duplicitous motherfucker, Jeremy thinks, making his way to the bedroom.

Ring.

More of the same. The mattress sliced open, presumably with the same knife Jeremy's holding. The closet tossed, and the bathroom.

The phone picks up. "You've reached Professor Harry Ives . . ." Jeremy clenches his teeth; he'll have to try another number.

Before he can hang up, it picks up; a voice comes onto the line.

"If it isn't James the Seventh." Harry's powerful lecturer voice booms over the phone. It causes Jeremy to withdraw the phone from his ear, and raises an image of the wizened professor, the sagacious codger, the scraggly gray beard and unkempt curls pasted onto his forehead with a light perspiration. He's doubtless clad in a checkered red flannel vest over a long-sleeve blue T-shirt, baggy khakis. He always looks like he spent the night somewhere other than a bed.

Jeremy feels an instant of pity and a filial affection for this combination of father figure and an outdated, slightly crazed Santa Claus, a mythical figure that isn't nearly as mythical as his legend would tell it. At least not to Jeremy.

"I know," Jeremy spills.

"I doubt it. Or you wouldn't make the same mistake over and over."

"I know, Harry. Cut the shit."

"So let's hear it. Who is James the Seventh?"

Jeremy looks around the splattered room, feels the knife clenched in his hand. He's hit by a realization: the fact that Jeremy's house was attacked suggests that he and his computer are being punked. This is about him, somehow. Not about a computer, or the apocalypse. Someone is definitely coming after Jeremy.

"Battle of Auldearn," Jeremy says. "Why, Harry? Why in the hell . . ."

Harry interrupts. "That was 1645. Not bad. Almost the right decade. But I'm referring to the Battle of the Boyne, which took place fifty years later. James the Seventh, flush with cash and arms supplied by Louis the Fourteenth, aimed to regain his crown."

Jeremy laughs bitterly. Typical haughty Harry, condescendingly making his point through a conflict metaphor. Fine, old man, you want to play it that way. "He landed in Ireland where he had Catholic supporters."

"But not the element of surprise. King William of Orange sussed out his plan and met him with thirty thousand men. And sent James and his invaders packing."

Just like that, Jeremy's found his opening, the admission. "You knew I was going to call you. I'm under surveillance. I know. I know, Harry. Do you really want to spend your last days teaching peace studies in prison?"

"What? No, Jeremy. I'm just saying: in the end, preparation and superior know-how will win out against your ill-conceived venture-backed capital dreams and your supercomputer. So I accept."

Jeremy, fuming, still knows goddamn well better than to ask what Harry accepts, mostly because, despite how furious Jeremy is, he's not so out of control as to miss Harry's request for an apology. They've not talked since the picnic at the log cabin when Jeremy went nuclear after Harry had the audacity to say that the algorithm could "use a little tinkering." Jeremy threatened to publicly expose Harry's "academic fraud," whatever that meant.

In the silence in which Jeremy calculates a response, Harry says: "What the fuck do you want?"

Both the tone and substance catch Jeremy off guard. He knows that Harry, as disheveled as his appearance tends to be, has a reputation for civility. A graceful lion. Jeremy can't ever remember hearing him use a curse word. He feels himself being manhandled when he's the one with the axe. And he's in an odd spot to begin with; he's called to confront Harry with circumstances he's not fully prepared to explain, not yet, and he's called a man Jeremy recently threatened to ruin with public disgrace.

Is Harry taunting Jeremy? Did he hack into Jeremy's computer and plant the idea that an attack is imminent, and is he now making vague references to it, baiting Jeremy, by mentioning his failed venture-capital backing?

Is the old codger toying with Jeremy? Is he capable? Maybe not on his own? How?

"I'm not closing up shop, Harry. You won't shut me down."

"Oh, I thought this was the *Missouri*. I shouldn't have bothered to iron my vest." Sarcastic; of course Jeremy's not shutting down; the USS *Missouri*, where the Japanese signed an unconditional surrender on September 2, 1945. "Jeremy, the market has spoken. First the marketplace of ideas, and then the actual marketplace. Besides, the government experiment didn't work. Look at the bright side: without funding from France, James the Seventh wouldn't have even been able to be in a position to get his ass kicked."

A clean shot, bare-knuckle, jaw, smack.

"Yeah, that worked out beautifully for Ireland in the end."

Harry chuckles. Then a pause, and "Listen, I've got to go."

"You set me up with the government, Harry, right? You hooked me up with them, then watched them humiliate me. This is all about making sure no one challenges your wisdom."

Silence from Harry.

"You're up to your ears in this. What's the game?"

"Goodbye," Harry says.

"Wait!" Then Jeremy lets himself say: "I need to talk to you."

"Need," a big word for Jeremy. Even if Jeremy means it in a threatening way. Harry knows it.

"Are we through, Jeremy?"

"Harry, something's gone wrong."

There's no response.

"Tell me, Harry. You owe me that."

Silence.

"Harry, goddamn it. Someone broke into my house. They broke into my . . ." He doesn't want to say about the computer, his digital brain. It's too incendiary, vulnerable. "Someone is following me."

Harry says: "Statis pugna."

"What?"

Silence.

"C'mon, Harry."

"Not over the phone." Practically whispered.

"What can't you tell me over the phone? Harry?"

Click.

"What? Harry? Fuck."

Chapter 12

A WOMAN KNOWN BY many names, but whose given one is Janine, runs her fingers up the back of the high-tech executive's leg. He emits a low sound, deep from his throat, a guttural murmur that predates mankind, the reptilian linking of the primitive brain and the reproductive organs. She trails a fingernail over the crest of his buttocks.

He swallows hard and pulls his head from her shoulder to look at her eyes. She smiles, telling herself she shouldn't. Not this smile. In her eyes, the look: you soon will burn. He sees the blue eyes twinkle, a startling contrast to the brown skin the color of wet beach sand, an irresistible modern beauty. But rather than exciting him further, the smile for some reason makes him shiver.

She watches his eyes leave hers, then trail down to the deep scratch along her neckline. She's told him that her cat went bananas on her, something he clearly didn't believe but chose not to think too much about. In fact, she wasn't totally lying. Her scratch did come from a cat, a feline. A lion. The extraordinary beast she loosed from the zoo.

The man buries his head and sinks into her. She generates a moan. She clenches her fist behind his back, feeling her nails dig into her palm.

Her phone rings. From her purse on his dresser. Not any ring.

"Redemption Song." Bob Marley.

Have no fear of atomic energy. None of them can-a stop-a the time.

She's programmed that ringtone to indicate an emergency call. That she's been away too long. The Guardians need her.

She shouldn't have spent the night. But why can't she get her kicks? Besides, she can't take any chances. No complaints, no inquiries. Not when they're this close. Even if he yields no further intelligence. Maybe this guy doesn't know where the scions of Silicon Valley will hold their gathering. Maybe word hasn't trickled down to this relative minion. Maybe he's too smart to tell her.

Now she needs something else: she needs him to be done with her, even if it leaves her unsatisfied. Easy enough.

Redemption Song. Redemption Song.

"Do you need to get that?" he whispers.

"Mais, no." She forces a giggle. "I need this." She tugs his shoulder and urges him on his back, a move about which he will only later remark to himself: she's quite strong. Straddling him, she puts her head back, squeezes her muscles, looks at the ceiling, reaches between his legs and runs fingernails lightly over him. That's all it takes. He's done with her.

And, predictably, up and off to shower and work minutes later. She doesn't care for the money on the dresser. What she wants is information. Dates and times. A location. Names of others in the network. Where will they hold the big meeting? The one that will become ground zero for the return of the Messiah.

But she got none of it. Nothing of value in his glove compartment. Nor in his closet. Nor from his phone.

She listens to the water in the shower. These technology moguls must know what they're doing or they wouldn't take such precautions. They would join forces to bring their soulless tools to modernize the Holy Land. *Modernize*? Do they have a clue at what cost? Can they possibly know how backward their notions are?

Regardless, they will soon know what they've wrought.

They will know the error of their ways, along with the adherents of modern, liberalized religion—the practitioners of contemporary versions of Islam and Christianity, Catholicism and Judaism. These groups think they can pick and choose from God's teachings. They have made their devotion selective, based on their Earthly yearnings, based on *their* understanding of how the world works, not the Word. And they, like those who make an idol of capitalism, have jeopardized eternity for everyone. Not without a fight they won't.

She opens her eyes and spies her bulky black purse sitting on a low bookshelf filled with business tomes. She can imagine the powerful knife nestled inside her purse. Should she unsheathe it and use it to pull any information from the heretic in the shower?

She shakes her head.

The man appears at the edge of the bathroom, wearing a towel.

"I . . ." he stammers. "I've got a conference call. I should go."

So should I, thinks Janine. Though the idea of whatever spontaneous thing she might do to this googler fills her with shivers of excitement.

Twenty minutes later, back at her room, she turns on the fax machine. A few minutes later, it rings. She sits on the bed, stares at the slowly emerging pixelated image, sips lukewarm jasmine tea, calming her stomach.

The first quarter of the page is indiscernible, a dark, jumbled mass, the product of an antiquated machine using outdated technology. But fax machines are an occupational hazard; for the most important commands and messages, there can be no use of computers, no sent or saved files, no digital traces, no signatures or key words that are searchable by the vast government surveillance machine. Sure, the Internet chat rooms and virtual worlds allow for basic communications, the first level of recruiting. Not for heavy lifting. The weapons of mass destruction are more sophisticated than ever. But planning to use them is typically and necessarily an analog exercise.

She looks out the wide picture window in this fetid rented room. Fog covers the top of the distant Golden Gate Bridge. Weather. *Merde.* She doesn't want to worry about weather. So many variables she can't control, too many unknowns. She's hearing rumors inside the group: They've still got to identify the location of the attack. The near vicinity will not do the trick. To make this statement, it's got to be precise. How can they not know that yet?

Is the answer in the fax machine?

As the paper begins to emerge from the fax, she sees that the bottom half of the image, the dark morass, is a big, bushy beard. And as the paper falls to the floor, she can make out the rest of the face. Predictably pronounced nose, soft eyes looking to the side, huge beard. She thinks the man has an old face but the wicked soul of a three-year-old boy who hates having his picture taken. At the top of the page, three scrawled words: "your better half."

Then, in small, fine script: Oakland Port, tonight.

Her better half.

She winces at the cruel joke.

Not a location, an ally, another one. A key one. It's a joke because he has the visage of a historic enemy. He's a Slav, worse, a Jew.

But a Guardian too.

She calms herself: we're all on the same side now. There is a much bigger picture. Only through an unholy alliance, only through the Guardians, can we bring holy peace.

She strikes a match and lights the edge of the picture. It gives her no solace to watch the hairy visage burn.

She turns and looks at the door of her small closet. She can picture the suitcase inside it, packed with the precious piece of metal, smooth, seemingly so innocuous. Her half of the bargain.

NOW JUST MILES away, the bearded man listens to the voices in the corridor. "Adam."

"Come out, come out, wherever you are. Adam."

Adam. Hearing the name, the bearded man grits his teeth. He hopes he didn't kill someone named Adam, a holy name.

This Adam, the bearded man thinks, now packed beneath piles of socks, destined for some low-cost retailer.

Outside, the waves have stopped. The storm has passed. The

bearded man closes his eyes, presses himself in the dark between the containers, tries not to make any sound that would alert the searchers to his presence. He calms himself with the knowledge of his purpose, the *purity* of his purpose. I am, he reminds himself, a Guardian of the City. He wonders: How many others have faced much worse peril with much more courage? How many have acted on the basis of such faith, anonymous contacts and dead drops and unseen allies? He considers the rumors, the whispers: that there are now so many allies, the belief and wisdom multiplying beyond any previous comprehension.

How many others like me are out there, right now, en route to undo a century of calamity, *millennia* of political folly? Are they enjoying this much good fortune?

CHAPTER 13

WIKIPEDIA DESCRIBES TANTALUM as deriving its name from the Greek mythological hero Tantalus. He was the son of Zeus, condemned for eternity to stand in a pool of water beneath a tree of low branches bearing sumptuous fruit that is just, just, just out of reach. The son of God, relegated to an eternity of suffering with satiation just out of reach. Jeremy feels like he can relate.

He's hoofing it down the Embarcadero, reading his iPad, impervious to the drizzle, trying to focus on substance, not his suffering. He can add his building manager to the sources of it.

The asshole actually took a look inside Jeremy's apartment and shook his head. His head, clad in a fucking *beret*.

"Who else has a key to your place?"

"Does it seem like I'd give the key to a crazed samurai?"

"Are you saying they were Asian?"

"That they did it with a knife. This knife."

"Your knife."

"Are you seriously being hostile with me? Condo board's gonna love this."

"I'd call the police."

"I could call the police. I was trying to involve you in the process."

"What are you asking of me, Mr. Stillwater?"

"Security tapes."

The building manager gets it. "I'll make a backup."

"We should call the cops."

A few minutes later, Jeremy sat in the manager's office while the guy did paperwork and called to back up the security tapes—kept on some server somewhere—but he wouldn't access or let Jeremy see them without getting the proper permissions. The fat jerk seemed reluctant to call the police but promised to do so; Jeremy dismissed a momentary suspicion this guy might've attacked his apartment and remembered the manager just generally doesn't like the police, having once been questioned by the cops about a resident's harassment claim.

Jeremy, anxious to get to Harry, buries himself in his iPad, lost in the latest feedback from the computer, biding his time. Getting his homework done so that when he confronts Harry face-to-face, he'll be armed with all the material, about the computer, the alleged changing variables. Aware of the clock, counting down.

56:30:00.

56:29:59.

But counting down to what? An attack, or something else? Nothing at all?

He's not fully admitting to himself that he's going to get answers from Harry but, maybe, depending on what the old man has to say, he will let himself ask Harry for help. Or maybe he doesn't need to. He thinks he knows Harry well enough to understand the message. *Not over the phone.* Translation: get over here. Harry knows something.

Jeremy remains marginally puzzled by the other thing Harry said: "statis pugna." A pidgin of ancient Greek and Latin that he's heard Harry say before and that reflects an underlying philosophy of the old codger. Means, more or less, constant state of tension. Harry, while he has devoted his life to sniffing out war, holds that the stability of the world requires a constant, low-level state of conflict. Too much calm in an environment creates a power vacuum, he argues, one that will be volatile until the natural foes gain equal footing and create a balanced state of low-level conflict.

Harry says that it's how we live our lives—constantly on the edge. We are contained, but barely so, in the way we deal with authority figures, like the meter maid, the opposing player in a pickup basketball game, our bosses and wives. Even basic forms of life, like the single-cell organism, find themselves in a life-or-death struggle against other organisms for precious resources. Up to a point, the best survival strategy is cooperation among organisms, but conflict, certainly its threat, is never far beneath the surface.

Taken to the extreme, détente, the Cold War, two massive nuclear powers, equally armed, mutual assured destruction.

And, for the geeks in the room, wordplay. Ancient Greek and Latin in a verbal tussle.

Was Harry trying to tell Jeremy something else? If so, Jeremy can't fathom what.

Fifty-six hours, the countdown clock tells him, plenty of time to unearth the joke, figure out what's going on, be the guy who shoves it up the ass of all the doubters.

Sitting in the manager's office, Jeremy read about tantalum. The computer had previously told Jeremy that tantalum shipments rose 4,017 percent in recent days, a number that Jeremy assumed extraordinary. But what, if anything, could a sharp rise in shipments of tantalum have to do with impending global conflict? Or a practical joke, and who is behind it.

He ran a handful of Google searches for "tantalum and 4,017%," and "tantalum demand," and "tantalum markets."

He got tens of thousands of hits. None of them seemed to point to any recent conflict news, most old documents about the tribal violence in the mid-1990s, when African gangs fought for control of the lucrative coltan mines.

Then, even in a few minutes, he learned more than he thought he ever cared to know about how the precious metal is used as a conductor in high-tech electronics, notably phones. But not what he really wanted to know: Who is shipping tantalum, who is demanding it, and why? And does that have anything to do with how someone messed with Jeremy, and how?

Adhering to the mantra "Follow the money," he visited Yahoo Finance, a web site he learned about in his academic studies as a way to look for companies involved in particular businesses, namely, at the time, arms dealers and their subsidiaries. He needed their names to plug into the conflict algorithm so the computer would know what to search for. In the manager's office, he searched for companies in the tantalum and coltan industries.

He found a list of a handful of specializing companies. Discovered something odd about one of them. A major tantalum supplier called Elektronic Space Suppliers PLC (ESS), an international company with Turkish headquarters, had seen its share price spike 600 percent in the last week.

Shares in the company, traded on an obscure secondary European stock exchange, rose to $1.50 from 25 cents.

Seems huge, or not so much. The company is a mere penny

stock. The share price was so low to begin with that a 600 percent price rise seems much less interesting than it would be were the company a heavily traded blue chip, like Apple or General Motors. That would be astounding. But a spike in the price in some penny-ante company with Turkish headquarters could be, far from astounding, merely anomalous.

He found the company's web site. It was, predictably, in English, the international trading language. And predictably, uninformative. It said that it specializes in trading precious metals, particularly tantalum, in southern Europe, the Middle East and the Organization of the Black Sea Economic Cooperation, a trading group made up largely of Russia and formerly Soviet states.

Jeremy set up an alert so that he can get an update if any news breaks about the shipments of tantalum. It'll come right to his phone.

"Tape backed up," the manager said. And police report made. Jeremy could check back in a few hours. "You can go upstairs but try to keep your fingerprints to yourself."

Back up in his condo, Jeremy showered; put on clean jeans, T-shirt and a plain gray, light wool J.Crew sweater; filled his backpack with a bunch of survival gear: snack bars, a change of shirt, a backup battery for the iPad, umbrella stuffed tightly into its outer casing.

His phone buzzed. A text, from Nik: "Yeah, maybe." A response to Jeremy's text from the night before: noticed anything strange?

Jeremy texted back: go on.

MOMENTS LATER, AS he walks out of the building, Jeremy looks at the countdown clock. Fifty-six hours. He pictures

Kent, Emily. Then the guy who tagged along with her at the café. Something about him.

Not an apocalypse, he reminds himself, a personal vendetta. Right?

En route to the subway that will take him to Harry, Jeremy pops into his office, which is on the Embarcadero, not even a few steps off his route to the train.

First thing he notices is that the papers on Nik's cubicle desk, usually stacked so neatly, look disheveled. On the top, there's a copy of the *San Francisco Examiner* with a picture of a zoo cage, empty, and a headline: "Lion on Loose." With a subhead: "Prankster Frees Jungle King."

On Nik's computer, a virtual landscape, hills and valleys, a vibrant sun in the background. In the foreground, some oblong green creature with a hammer. World of Warcraft. Jeremy leans in. Along the screen's side, inscrutable chatter. Someone asking a question of "Commander Perry." Nik's given name, Perry, a sidekick in real life, somehow a leader in this nonsense world of virtual, perpetual combat.

The door to Jeremy's office is closed. Outside it, lying on the ground, the two envelopes that had previously been stuck under his door, from the law firm of Pierce & Sullivan. Two envelopes Jeremy had previously ignored and then, the day before, summarily smashed with his feet on the way out the door.

One of them has been opened. And closed again, sort of, its flap loose. Maybe it unsealed on its own. He bends down, cautiously at first. He looks around the little room. Opens it.

He nearly dismisses it without a close glance, assuming it's another reminder to attend a deposition at such-and-such a time and place. It has that look and feel. But he finds himself struck by the words in bold, "cease and desist." He reads the two paragraphs more closely. This is a letter telling Jeremy to stop contacting Evan, to leave Evan alone. That Evan wishes to cut off all further communications.

Jeremy shakes his head. Confused. Hadn't Evan been hounding Jeremy, and now he wants to be left alone?

Jeremy looks at the date; it's from three weeks earlier. Around the time Jeremy was doing a last round of fuck-you calls and taunting emails.

He scoops up the other envelope, same thing, but from two weeks earlier.

Whatever, Evan, you want to disconnect from me, have it your way. The more material value of these letters, at least the one that was unsealed, is that it might suggest possible intrusion.

Jeremy turns his attention to the door of his office, listens carefully, hears nothing from inside, still is cautious as he opens the door.

Sees Nik.

Sitting at Jeremy's computer. He turns his head and blinks heavily, half man, half big dog.

"Someone turned it on." Nik wears cargo pants he bought online for eleven dollars and a gray wool sweater with nothing on underneath it. It is standard-issue ascetic. Jeremy once bought Nik some fashionable khaki shorts and a golf shirt and Nik reddened when he opened the package. Never wore them.

"How do you know I didn't leave it on?"

Nik shakes his head, like he's gotten hit with a light jab, smacked in the nose with a rolled-up paper. "I thought you always turn it off." He pauses for a second. "Lately."

From someone else, a jab back. Not from Nik.

"I didn't leave it on," Jeremy says. "And you didn't turn it on?"

Nik shakes his head. He swivels in the chair. A few books have been tossed on the short gray carpet; the Pepsi can is overturned on the desk, dribbling out the bottom of its contents. Someone spent some time looking around in here.

"How did they get in?"

"Maybe the same guy," Nik says.

"Same guy as who?"

"My place, last night. Got home late and some cat was banging on the window from the fire escape."

"Cat?"

"Burglar." Nik has bags under his already puffy eyes, and a question mark in them. Would Jeremy like to explain what's going on?

"Rosa just sat there."

Takes Jeremy a second to make sense of Nik's reference to his dog, big and lumbering like Nik. Rosa. In full: Doggy Dolorosa. Worthless orphan Nik picked up from a Spanish exchange student back in the day. Nik seems to connect more with animals than with people.

"The usual suspects taking a nail gun to our coffin, trying to," Jeremy says, pauses, then continues. "What's up with Evan? Can you find out about his company, some conference he's holding? I thought Evan was trying to sue for my ideas, not push me away."

"You don't read your mail."

"Why didn't you tell me?"

"I can bring the mail to water . . ."

"But you can't make me drink. You know I don't read that stuff unless you tell me to."

Nik looks down, clears his throat. "With everything going on, I didn't think it was worth—"

"Never mind." Jeremy cuts him off. "Find me Evan. Fuck his lawyers. I need to talk to him. Let's use the Yahoo email account to communicate, the old one. And Harry I'll take care of myself."

Nik shakes his head. "Harry?" As in: Harry did this?

"I'm going to find out."

"You're going to talk to Harry?"

Jeremy half nods. He wonders whether he even trusts Nik. Where did he come from, this abjectly loyal hangdog? Half British, half American, he appeared one day at Oxford, referred by a professor of conflict studies. He stood at the doorway to the lab, wearing a secondhand black sport coat—looking like a cast-off waiter—staring at the earliest version of the conflict map, a prototype, blinking on the wall. A child of sorts but with a talent for making things orderly, so Jeremy gave him a minimum-wage administrative job he'd gotten grant funding to fill. A few weeks later, one of the graduate assistants saw Nik playing around with the conflict program, messing with the columns, and dragged him in to Jeremy to get fired.

Jeremy asked what Nik was doing.

"This predicts war," Nik said of the algorithm. "So I wondered if it could predict peace."

Jeremy laughed. So innocent. Nik. PeaceNik. The son of missionaries, who had traveled the world humbly preaching the word. Nik. First and last guy ever to survive an unauthorized intrusion into the software. The son of well-traveled missionaries, monkish in his own right, devoted to Jeremy the way some people are to a monotheistic God.

"What did he look like?" Jeremy asks.

"Who?"

"The cat."

Nik shrugs. "Scampered away."

Jeremy glances at the computer monitors, lit up, but blank, showing only the log-in screens. Whoever had been here, whatever they wanted, they couldn't find it without the key fob and the password buried inside Jeremy's brain.

"Sure it wasn't a lion?"

Nik blinks. "What?"

"Not a cat burglar. A lion. Escaped from the zoo."

Nik shakes his head, looks hurt. "It's ridiculous."

"What is?"

"Opening a lion's cage. That's just courting disaster."

It's Nik at his most animated. Jeremy laughs. "Not everyone shares your sense of decorum, PeaceNik." Jeremy pauses. "Email me that stuff, pronto. Not from here." Another pause. "Go to the gym. Lay low around some guys with big jabs."

Jeremy starts walking to the subway, more convinced now someone is fucking with him. Rattling Nik too, or looking for something, business intelligence. Harry will enlighten Jeremy.

One of Jeremy's phones buzzes. He pulls both from his crowded pocket. It's the iPhone, with a reminder: dr.panckl.

He stares at it. He feels the tightness in his left pectoral, where the pain has been intermittent, sometimes severe. Coupled with night sweats and tired bouts during the day. Might be stress, his doctor tells him, but, just in case, she orders tests. His phone is reminding him to call and schedule the MRI. He's told no one, not even Emily. She knows, of course, that Jeremy's dad died young from the bad kind of Hodgkin's lymphoma, but that was before you could treat anything under the sun. And that his mother, notwithstanding the wrenching chemo near the end, lived to be fairly ripe.

He pockets the phone, looks up, sees the woman. Thin, perfect. And definitely familiar. From the café the night before, and then again from the bar.

CHAPTER 14

"H EY!"

She looks up.

Jeremy starts to run. "Hey!"

He picks up steam, steps into the bicycle lane on the edge of the street to avoid a half dozen colleagues walking, spilling out from under two shared umbrellas.

The woman slips around to the driver's seat, hops in. The car starts to peel away. It's something bland, Jeremy thinks, a blue-gray Hyundai. He's in the street now, fully unleashing healthy, practiced legs, decent lungs, and DNA that made him a sufficiently capable track athlete to win a Rhodes. Not sufficiently capable to catch a sedan, accelerating. He recognizes the woman, right? Same person from the night before?

He hears the horn. From behind. Another car approaching. It swerves, splashing rainwater onto Jeremy's jeans.

It dawns on him he might want to get a ride from the car passing him, try to chase the sedan. Instead, he finds himself yelling: "Watch it, asshole!"

Brake lights go on in the car, a BMW. The driver slides down his window, then thinks better of it. Takes off. Jeremy yells: "The prom queen called. She wants her low-end Beamer back!"

Ten minutes later, damp, furious, Jeremy descends into a packed BART station to head to Berkeley. Discovers train delays. Thirty minutes due to some refuse on the tracks near City Center in Oakland.

Jeremy forces his way onto a bench in the tunnel and pulls out his iPad. He looks at the map. Red, red, red. He opens a new window and clicks on a link that will let him delve further into the variables that, allegedly, have prompted the computer to predict war. Chief among those variables: changes in conflict rhetoric, language that presages war.

While the computer whirs, calling up the data, Jeremy marvels at this particular capability—the one that allows him to track the language of the world. It is, to Jeremy, one of the most powerful tools afforded by the Internet. It is the equivalent of giving the world a blood test, taking its temperature, assessing its mood. Or, rather, it will become that. Eventually. For now, the Internet is remarkable at capturing what everyone is saying, and even organizing that data—by region, topic, media (Twitter versus blog versus newspaper), communicator (politician versus CEO versus activist).

It was amazing for Jeremy to watch the Arab spring and the protests in Russia, organized around Twitter feeds, and social networks, spontaneous calls to action in which the language elicits, organizes and stokes conflict. An amazing nearly one-to-one relationship between words and thoughts and action.

More broadly, Jeremy thinks that this development of mining and sifting the world's conflict rhetoric could help answer an age-old philosophical question about the relationship between language, thought and action.

Philosophers and linguists have for millennia debated the relationship. To what extent are the words we choose insights into what we think—not what we want to communicate but what we really *think*? On one hand, of course, it is very easy to lie about what we're thinking, making words fundamentally untrustworthy. Clearly, Hitler did intend to invade Russia, despite his protestations otherwise, and George W. Bush did not believe Iraq had weapons of mass destruction. Words, not true thoughts. To that end, Plato and others who engaged in the most powerful early analysis of communication thought of language in terms of rhetoric: not what do we think but what do we want to communicate? Or, put another way, what do we want other people to think we think, or what do we want to persuade *them* to think?

But where Jeremy thinks the Internet is so powerful is in the way it creates such a huge sample size of language that it betrays what we, the human race, think. All the linguistic data, unprecedented insights into the human psyche, a global inkblot test, a linguistic prism into our collective subconscious, where we've been emotionally and where we're going, a digital augur, or, as Jeremy sometimes prefers, the Freud machine.

Part of a larger embrace of Big Data, aimed at predicting the stock market, of course, but also forecasting political tastes, weather, consumers' susceptibility to pricing changes and their shopping desires.

Just before Jeremy's fall from grace, there was a party held in his honor at a two-tone mansion off Fillmore. It was hosted by one of the handful of Silicon Valley socialites with that knack for convening, at a moment's notice, fifty interesting and smart people, along with journalists. The evite heralded: "Make PC, Not War." Computers, not conflict.

Partygoers came mostly for the interesting cocktails, using pomegranate juice or fresh leaves picked from such-and-such garden. But also to connect to, or stay connected to, Jeremy, just in case he became the next Zuckerberg. His own vertical, his little satellite world, opportunists, but also, given the highly politicized nature of the quest, ideologues, academics, curious government officials domestic and international and, of course, venture capitalists with military backgrounds—a staple in Silicon Valley going back to the creation of the region by the military brats who started Hewlett-Packard.

What they didn't know, or some may have only sensed, was that Jeremy soon would be not the next Zuckerberg but, rather, the next *Hindenburg*. A week before the party, the Pentagon had told him the conflict algorithm had failed. He was waiting for Andrea to call to tell him when he could get on an airplane to Iraq, or Afghanistan, to check the results for himself, do the field research. He'd already packed a bag so, per Andrea and the Pentagon's admonitions, he could pick up and climb on a plane at any moment.

Meantime, he pacified himself with figs and goat cheese and high-potency frozen vodka.

Drunk, in the shadows, he overheard the half dozen late-night stragglers descend into an argument about whether Big Data could be used to predict individual behaviors, like the likelihood of suicide. For instance, could someone's communications or movement patterns—as measured by a mobile phone—be a predictor of whether the person is getting depressed or uncommunicative, suggesting eventual suicidal ideations?

Could it predict whether someone is becoming hostile, or even homicidal?

Jeremy heard one of them say: "I have a prediction. Sometime soon, Stillwater will let loose with a hostile outburst."

Another said: "You don't even need a calculator to tell you that."

Lots of hushed laughter.

Jeremy, unseen, receded to the basement, to a guest room. He called Emily, who told him to calm down. He hung up and slammed the iPhone down on the bed. *I'll fucking show them.*

He passed out that night, furious, with an idea, the seeds of "Program Princip," the algorithm named for the assassin of Archduke Franz Ferdinand. Jeremy's idea was to try to go deeper than merely understanding when a conflict might start, to understanding who might spark it. Not the obvious person—like an aggressive and politically motivated President Bush—but someone lesser known. Could Jeremy take all the increasingly public information about the connections between and among people and figure out who belongs at the center of a conflict?

Another brainstorm, a terrific one, marketable, at least. But personal too. At its heart, Jeremy wondered if he might be able to use the program to figure out who was lying to him—Andrea, Harry, Evan. Who, even then, was undermining him? Who is Jeremy's enemy? Or who is his most central enemy?

It never dawned on Jeremy that night that the very problem might be Jeremy.

In the present, his computer beeps. It is returning the data. Unfolding before him, the report on where the rhetoric of the world has changed so much that the computer now projects Armageddon. T minus three days. Fighting off fatigue, he takes in the screen, a menu at the top. It reads: "five entities."

Jeremy purses his lips. There has been a material change in the language of conflict in five different categories. The categories materialize:

```
North Korea (related), + 14 percent
Moscow (related), + 9 percent
Mexico (related), + 46 percent
Congo (related), + 6 percent
Fertile Crescent (related), - 12 percent
```

He taps his right toe on the ground, nervous energy. With an index finger, he points at the word "Mexico." His finger is so close it nearly touches the screen. Forty-six percent—a veritable explosion in conflict language coming from Mexican authorities or from other figureheads around the world relating to Mexico. Something's going on to the south.

He calls up another window with the map. It's seething red, pulsing around the globe. He runs his mouse over Mexico. A pop-up box shows: 112,336,538, 8.8 percent. The population and its annual growth.

He looks on the bottom right of the map, at the countdown clock. 55:19:27. Hours, minutes and seconds.

Jeremy startles at the buzz in his pocket. Private number. He picks it up from the desk. "I'm on the Do Not Call Registry and have retained a legion of rabid plaintiff attorneys to enforce it with threat of lawsuit and execution."

He hears nothing on the other end of the phone. Then a sound in the background, a horn or loudspeaker, maybe a hint of breathing from a caller. Then the line goes dead.

He recalls the list of regions with changing rhetoric: North Korea, Moscow and Congo experiencing rising tensions. Might mean something. The Fertile Crescent, the Middle East, experiencing dulling tensions. That's at least one variable he can toss out.

He slips the phone into his pocket. On his tablet, in the window with the Rhetoric statistics, he swipes the line about Mexico, and discovers a place consumed by the language of war.

Chapter 15

J ANINE FEELS THE Earth move. The San Andreas
Fault. A nuclear blast. Judgment Day.
Her phone.

She opens an eye.

She's been dreaming. She's drenched. There's a vibration, something deep. Where is it coming from? Not the end, not yet. It's from beneath her pillow.

"Okay, okay." She reaches underneath the sweaty pillow and feels the vibrating phone. She registers the darkness. How long has she been asleep?

She flips open the phone. It's 12:17. There are two texts. That's very bad. One text is bad news. Two, worse.

Both from a private number. The first reads: "Rouge."

She doesn't let herself acknowledge it, or its meaning. She reads the second: "Maintenant. Hier."

Red.

Now. Yesterday.

She picks up the pillow and uses it to wipe the sweat from

her face. She searches for images from her dream, something about a boy shooting a dog in a field. She flips on the light. She swings her jeans-clad legs over the bed and stares at the fax machine. *Maintenant*. It won't be long.

She takes a voracious slug from the tea next to the bed. It both quenches her thirst and prompts a gag. No training, no will, she thinks, can allow the body to work if it gets only a few hours of sleep each day. She places the tea back on the worn copy of *The Killer Angels*, which she picked up for the title and discovered had nothing to do, really, with murderers or angels. But was about the Battle of Gettysburg. She can't put it down, and it is in some minor part responsible for her insomnia. Brothers fighting brothers, courage, but all the blood spilled in vain, by a godless nation. This is her guilty pleasure. The last few years, emotionally isolated, often out of communication with anyone she can trust, traveling from one bed to the next, the only common thread her books.

Of course, there is only one book, the Bible, the word.

She thinks back to how the Guardians first enlightened her about The Book, when they found her, covered in filth, starving, a child of war, in ruins on the border of Lebanon. She couldn't have been twelve years old, and she'd been in a terrible fight with two older boys, and routed them—over ownership of a water bottle. Just another day in the refugee camps; she'd been raped, her mother too, among the other daily indignities. Then a man lifted her from the dirt. He had bad teeth, smelled of American cheese but had an angelic face, a thick cross around his neck, and a Bible. She flailed and kicked at him too. And he took her attacks, and smiled, what's the word, "beatifically," and he filled her water bottle. And then, trite as she'd come to think of it, he filled her soul.

He was a Guardian, of course. And he eventually trusted her enough to tell her the truth about him and the Guardians. Their secret work, how the network was sworn to protect the Holy Land, The City, Jerusalem. To keep it from being "compromised."

That was the word the Guardians found most distasteful, evil—compromise.

If there is compromise, if the God-fearing do not truly adhere to the word of God, then the Messiah will not return.

She knows by heart the passage the man read her from Genesis:

> I will be with you and will bless you, for to you and to your offspring I will give all these lands, and I will establish the oath that I swore to Abraham your father. I will multiply your offspring as the stars of heaven and will give to your offspring all these lands. And in your offspring all the nations of the earth shall be blessed, because Abraham obeyed my voice and kept my charge, my commandments, my statutes, and my laws.

But, she asked: aren't the enemies the Jews, the deadly army of the Israelites, the Muslims, and the other heretics?

He smiled.

Of course not, he said. Not the true believers, the ones who favor and follow the true word of God.

Think of the biblical passage, he told her: all nations on Earth will be favored if the Bible is truly adhered to. When he explained the meaning to her, she immediately understood the equation. Israel must be reestablished as a Holy Land, one in which the God-fearing descendants of Abraham embrace the covenant. Only then will all the nations be blessed. Only then will the Messiah come. Only then will there be no more hunger, no more rape, no more fruitless tribalism.

The Guardians gave her truth, meaning, safety. Hope.

And, over the years, deadly training.

She shudders with awe when she thinks of her transformation. She was raised to trust only Syrian Christians. But what good did they do her? Weren't they just as responsible for the rape of her dusty village, her rape? Weren't her supposed brothers and sisters just as culpable as the Muslim hypocrites and the pious but heathen Israeli army? All the generals and politicians, all the king's men.

Not so the Guardians. They are not one ethnic group. But they are connected in their belief. They are a true family, *his* children. Her siblings.

She will do anything to protect them, help save them. And now they ask a new task.

The woman called Janine closes her eyes and allows herself to imagine she's got one big eye on the top of her head, like a Cyclops. She's mere hours from helping to open up the Earth. Throw the ugly parts into it, like the Cyclops, scrape things clean, then let God, the one and only, sort things out.

The fax machine beeps, answers, begins to print.

Janine reaches beneath the bed. She pulls out a small suitcase, a flee bag, she calls it, just enough stuff to let her survive
if she has to go on the lam. She pulls out her last clean shirt,
her last clean not-whore shirt, a green blouse she made sure
was loose enough not to accentuate her breasts or attract attention. Still, she thought, almost too flattering. She pushes
it aside, finds a long-sleeve gray T-shirt with a University of
Arizona crest.

She lifts and smells it. Not clean but dry.

The fax is halfway through its printing.

She takes off her shirt, pulls out a bra from the flee bag,
clasps it, pulls on the gray T-shirt. She opens the first text. She
responds: "And a good morning to you too." She knows any
vague response will suffice to acknowledge receipt.

Rouge. Red. Blood. A simple, juvenile code. Kill.

Maintenant, hier. Now. Yesterday. Translation: No time to
plan. Act.

And, within that, an unstated implication: Something is
going wrong. Very, very wrong.

The printing is three-quarters done. She begins to make out
the face coming through on the fax. She begins to recognize
it. She whispers: "No. Gracias." Not this man, this fierce indi-
vidualist, with a big brain and a divine spark. He takes no side,
other than his own, and his truth. Still, there are no noncom-
batants.

This is the target and this is her job. And this man, the one
appearing on the fax, is, apparently, the source of sudden and
acute trouble. He's doubtless begun to piece it together.

The face fully appears, the fax near complete. And now,
with a tight, bitter smile, she thinks she understands the dream

she just awoke from. This man is the mongrel shredded by bullets. She's the boy with the gun.

At the edge of the facsimile, a scrawled note: Make it amateur.

She feels new sweat beads on her brow. On top of everything else, it needs to be messy.

Chapter 16

La Prensa (Mexico City). Hector Gonzalez, secretary of the National Action Party: "We may not yet declare victory, but with drug war casualties falling for the first time since 2006, we may say we have this menace in our sights. Now we go for the kill."

La Prensa. Unnamed drug cartel executive: "The corrupt right wing has soaked this nation's poor and downtrodden while we have employed and fed and clothed them. The government wants war, then it shall have war."

Economista, cover: Hector Gonzalez murdered. WAR!

@ForthePersonas (Twitter): Rise Muertos. It's the SPRING of the dead. Rise and retake our land!

La Opinion (Veracruz): Garden Rodents Chewing Lawns; Mayor Declares War on Varmints.

Jeremy shakes his head, making sure he is reading this correctly, then leans back and laughs. The algorithm, sensitive though it has been programmed to be, can't distinguish a rhetorical attack on drug lords or politicians or terrorists from one on weasels.

It's merely looking for a broad-based increase in the intensity of language as measured by use of hundreds of keywords identified as either threatening or conciliatory.

He looks up at the packed subway car. Hears the moans. People somehow shocked that a quasi-governmental transit system could be stuck in a tunnel under the ocean, awaiting the re-clearing up of problems on the other end that had been solved and now need resolving. He'd be among the haters but he finds it easier to dismiss his disgruntled fellow commuters than the transit system. Besides, the guy next to him smells like a fucking fish sandwich.

He glances down the list of phrases the program has identified as material from Mexico. In the last few days, the words and phrases have grown so intense as to sound comical: "war," "eradicate," "threat to our way of life," "purge," "terrorist," "scorched earth."

As the words begin to blur together, Jeremy starts to get the picture. He sees the rhetoric spark catch and spread into wildfire; the right wing renews its pledge to end the drug war, the cartels strike back and reinforce their words with attacks, begetting more arrests, tougher language, cycle of violent language. Then the left wing kicks in, condemning the violence, but also, at first, tacitly accusing the United States of fostering the drug market, failing to police its urban demand; then the cartels weigh in, taunting America and, by proxy, the right-wing politicians who ally with hard-liners in the United States.

Cartel: "The United States has jailed our brothers and enslaved our sisters in menial shit jobs. You have feasted on Mexico too long. Beware the riders from the south. We can take down your towers too."

Jeremy isn't quite sure if he's got the exact language, given the fact it goes through a translation program. But, even if it's close, it's both insane and loosely cryptic, and the "towers" clearly a reference to 9/11. In fact, the computer has picked it up, highlighting in bold the word "towers."

He looks closer at the citation. It comes from *Diario de Morelia*, a small daily in Michoacán. The location strikes Jeremy as mildly noteworthy because it is such a central feeder of cheap labor to the United States. He looks for more on the person quoted. It refers only to an anonymous high-ranking captain in Los Negros, the armed contingent of the Sinaloa drug cartel, involved in the border wars.

Jeremy looks at the screen, feels his exhilaration trumped by a wave of exhaustion, perspiration. He wipes his forehead, feels the glisten.

Jeremy looks back at the garble of intensifying language from Mexico. He does a Google search on the threat about the "towers." He's wondering if it elicited any response. It materializes slowly, the bandwidth being sucked by the frustrated subway companions.

He finds, in a communiqué from the U.S. State Department, that an undersecretary of state's office has put out a short press release condemning the use of "inflammatory and irresponsible language." The release thanks the Mexican government for its "forceful efforts" to shut down the drug trade, which the release characterizes as a "cancer" attacking North America and Central America and their free people.

Jeremy's seen hundreds of such releases in the past. This one seems unremarkable in every way. It feels like a response the U.S. government was required to make, given the inherently inflammatory nature of the "towers" language. It's like the geopolitical version of the "n-word" to describe black people. Always gets a response. And, he suspects, American journalists saw the State Department release as perfunctory and nothing more. No one has written about this.

Rather than setting off bells for Jeremy, the lack of interest by the American press confirms a suspicion that he is harboring. The flare-up in physical and rhetorical attacks coming from Mexico might well be insignificant—not insignificant to those involved, but insignificant as a predictor of global conflict. After all, Jeremy thinks, looking at the texts of the carping Mexicans, the drug war on the border there has raged for a decade. A slow-materializing Wikipedia search tells him that casualties started to grow around 2001, then escalated until the late part of the decade and then, after hitting more than thirty thousand total, began to decline.

This, Jeremy wonders, might actually be a conflict that has peaked. Or, more to the point, it's a conflict that has been going on for some time. And that means, Jeremy is nearly certain, there have been linguistic flare-ups in the past that have far exceeded what he's looking at right now.

He opens his palms and puts them against his forehead. He feels a grudging appreciation for Harry, even as he is headed to confront the motherfucker, the transit system willing.

There is no one on Earth better equipped than the eccentric Berkeley professor to put into perspective the rhythm of this Mexico conflict or, for that matter, the rhythm and pace of any of the other conflicts in the world. Harry War is like a dog and conflict a whistling sound no one else can hear. Harry can tell its tenor and decibel level; he can tell if the sound is shrill or normal. He's spent a lifetime listening to the different pitches of conflict.

Harry is to war what Warren Buffett is to finance. Just as Buffett seems to be able to see the financial landscape like no one else, Harry can see the geopolitical landscape like no one else.

That's why they were such a great team, Harry using his gut and Jeremy using his processor. At the same time, Jeremy knew, or believed—in Jeremy's case knowledge and belief are two inextricable states of mind—that his computer could do far better in the long run at understanding and predicting conflict than could Harry's brain. To Jeremy, it's a simple matter of math: Harry's brain can hold and process only so many different streams of information, whereas Jeremy's computer can be programmed to hold and process innumerable streams.

And, so, in the end, Jeremy wanted to prove he was his own man, mostly sticking to his own ideas and framing. And he did. After the article came out, Harry called him and, Jeremy can never forget, told him: "Brilliant, young man. You'll put me out of business. And I'm glad," he had said with a laugh. "It's a lot of pressure being wrong most of the time."

"You're right more than most."

"Jeremy, when it comes to this stuff, you can't afford to ever be wrong."

Harry War told him: That's why I'm a tenured professor, with inviolable job security. If I had to test my stuff in the real world, in the private sector, I'd be fired within weeks.

Jeremy mutters: "You're fucking with me, old man."

Looks at the spread of red on the map.

He swipes to read about the fall in conflict rhetoric in the Fertile Crescent, as Harry insisted on referring to the region—fecund, Harry said, with ancient seeds of conflict.

The Israeli prime minister, in "off-the-cuff" remarks to reporters, says regional peace remains a distant dream given the radicalized factions in the region, but, he adds, Israel will continue to invite sincere efforts at partnership.

No remark, Jeremy knows, is off the cuff. And it's hard to believe these remarks constitute cooled rhetoric. So too, is it hard to take too much heart from a recent comment by the Palestinian president saying that Israel must break down the economic barriers and grant his people full economic freedom or else the region could "fall back into a state of chaos."

Only in the Fertile Crescent, Jeremy shakes his head, does "fall back into a state of chaos" represent things looking up. Beats, he supposes, people threatening to nuke each other back to the Stone Age.

Jeremy's thoughts are interrupted. "We'll be moving again shortly," the subway conductor announces over the intercom. "But expect further delays."

A murmur in the train. It lurches forward. Jeremy's phone buzzes. He pulls it from his pocket. Discovers a voice mail. He's missed a call, from a blocked number.

Something prompts him to look up, that feeling of being watched. He looks halfway down the train, to the connecting cars. Sees the corridor of standing-room-only passengers, arms forced to their sides by the tight quarters. Ordinarily, a midday commute would be mostly empty, but the train delay created a backup on the platform.

Jeremy puts his head down, then looks up quickly. Now he finds his mark; a tall man pressed against the corridor has stuck out a long neck. Intention in eyes that bulge slightly, like someone blew too much air into his head with a pump. This time, Jeremy gives him a smile. If you're a stranger, accidentally looking my way, I'm deranged. If you're following me for dark purposes, then come and get me. The guy recoils his neck and then melts into the adjoining car.

Jeremy presses the screen of his phone to hear the voice mail.

"Tonight at five, Atlas. At Perry's."

Andrea. Instructions on where to meet. Her voice brings back her intonation and the invitations it carried: *so can you come to Washington; want to meet for a drink at the hotel; I'm up for chatting tonight if you're free; up for a last-minute trip to the Zagros Mountains to do field work?*

It's not the words she used. Nothing special about the semantics. It's the tone. The almost imperceptible buzz of a hummingbird outside the window that you've got to look at. And that, remarkably, hovers right at eye level, buoyed by a seemingly effortless frazzle of its tiny wings. And then, when you wonder if a magical connection is coming, it darts off.

Sure, he'd come to Washington and meet for a drink, and have those late-night phone calls. She was his ally, dinnered with him and his investors, gently mocking Evan, wondering what they mix into the sports drinks at Stanford business school to make students become obsessed with making everything more efficient. She never asked about Emily; didn't that suggest romantic interest?

And she could spar. Fun, intense, wordplay, flirtation, or was it just her way of relating to the world? Sometimes, it seemed, she was on the verge of sharing a secret with Jeremy, a part of herself, maybe an official secret, something. She was just out of reach.

Jeremy agreed to go to the mountains of southern Iraq. She put him off. Then another trip to Afghanistan that materialized and evaporated overnight.

All the while, though, she insisted: his computer was wrong; Jeremy was wrong. So why did she stick with him?

Tonight at five at Perry's. Too coincidental. She knows something. Harry knows something.

The train roars out of the bottom of the bay, rattling into the East Bay. Just a few stops to City Center, the transfer to Berkeley.

He looks down at his iPad.

"We want freedom, of course. We want to promote freedom. But chaos, no. We must be on the side of order, for the sake of our own society and the furtherance of our values. And I will fight with you, side by side, to preserve those values."

The words belong to Vladimir Putin. From the rhetoric, it sounds like it could be a speech to the Russian parliament. Or he could be speaking on television to the masses tweeting to insist on greater power for the middle and lower classes, and mobilizing through social networks. But he's not. The phrase comes from a speech two days earlier at the groundbreaking of a new campus of the Rosoboronexport State Corporation.

Jeremy's heard of it, Rosoboronexport, this huge arms hub. Long government controlled, then quasi-government controlled. A veritable munitions Walmart, building and serving every deadly product under the sun.

So what?

Jeremy studies the intensifying rhetoric from Russia. The

computer's report shows a collection of commentary from politicians, newspapers, tweeters that the algorithm has identified as most influential as denoted by the number of their followers and the number of times they've been retweeted.

```
@reformredsquare: putin coddles military-ind-complex,
    a deadly partnership that must be toppled.
@restoreorder: CALM! The real danger comes
    from anarchy, WMD leaked from a sieve of
    democratization. Save us Putin.
@onemanonevote retweeting @restoreorder: Puppet!
```

Jeremy scrolls through pages of the report, tweets like these, headlines and op-ed pieces, blogs, a speech from Arkady Rybhorov, a Russian billionaire who made his money in land development and who is now challenging Putin for power. The speech refers to Putin's cozying up with the military-industrial complex, calls upon Putin to do more than support a sterile and humanity-less machine that arms nations and dictators and to do more to police the leaking of dangerous weapons of mass destruction from rogue scientists and soulless entrepreneurs. Well-oiled political bullshit.

Jeremy starts to get the picture. This narrative, this explosion of conflict rhetoric from Russia revolves around the role of Rosoboronexport in influencing both Russia's internal politics and its geopolitical stance. An op-ed mentions, for example, that 45 percent of Rosoboronexport's sales go to China, which, the editorial states, obviously markedly impacts Russia's dealings with its neighbors.

Jeremy digs a bit deeper. The origin of this flare-up seems to be a news story written a few days earlier in a small online-only newspaper from a town outside Moscow. In the story, a local reporter claimed to have interviewed a former Rosoboronexport engineer who said the corporation was enjoying growing profits from selling nuclear-grade materials on the down low to terrorist cells. The engineer in the article was quoted anonymously. The article was largely dismissed but it also set off a debate about the role of Rosoboronexport, which was one of those topics that occasionally flare up.

"Twelfth Street/City Center!" The voice comes over the speaker inside the subway. "Transfer to the Richmond line. Please expect some delays."

The words echo somewhere in Jeremy's brain, pull him from his iPad. It's his stop, the transfer to Berkeley. The train slows. Jeremy realizes he must hustle if he's going to get at the front of the line. He slings his backpack over his shoulder, palms the iPad and tucks it under his arm. He stands.

Starts walking to the doors sliding open, thinking about Russia. Like Mexico, and its own explosion of rhetoric in the drug war, it's hard to see Russia's linguistic wave as anything more than just one more cresting in intensity in a society engulfed in constant low-grade tension. Cresting, crashing, calming, repeat.

Just one thing sticks in his craw about Rosoboronexport. An article in a small newspaper refers to the leaking of nuclear-grade material. A bomb that got away? Jeremy thinks: Could that be true? Could it be nuclear material?

Jeremy's struck that this is a bit of an aha moment. Maybe the bomb is key information, perhaps misinformation, that is so material to his computer's apocalyptic projections?

Someone who was screwing with Jeremy—if anyone was— might be capitalizing on actual events to do it.

He's so locked in his thoughts, scrambling through the sardines to catch the connecting train, that he doesn't see the long-necked man taking him in from the subway platform. The man extracts his phone.

CHAPTER 17

*A*RE YOU MOVING YET?

Janine nearly laughs when she reads the text. What a geek. It's the stilted formality of someone so outside the norm of modern world communication. Not: R U moving? Or: allgood? Or: cool?

They've got a veritable Boy Scout running Operation End-of-the-Earth. An increasingly desperate Boy Scout.

Janine pulls over. She texts back: *check*. She thinks: I'll see your arcane, 20th-century vernacular, and raise you.

She breathes deeply, metabolizing chaos. Changing plans, a new checklist: get the bearded Jew, but first, strike against the infidel. With her hands. What she was born to do or, maybe, *shaped* to do. Nature, nurture. A foolish distinction. All part of the big plan.

She sees a sign for underground parking. Can't risk getting caught in there, having the car encased, or so easily found by the cops, should it come to that. Then she sees a space on the street, just behind her. She puts the car in reverse and speeds to the opening, narrowly beating a car coming the other direction—the correct direction. Its driver pounds the horn.

The driver pulls alongside Janine. The car's window rolls down. The driver, a student in a hooded sweatshirt, says: WhatThe-Fuck. Janine rolls down the window of her aging Toyota. She smiles at the young man and shrugs, then, still smiling, nearly flirtatious, channels her go-to thought: your flesh will soon burn. The young man flinches, and he drives away.

A parking spot. In Berkeley, in the rain. You take your miraculous signs where you can get them, Janine thinks. Her grim purpose confirmed. The chaos be damned.

CHAPTER 18

D WINELLE HALL, A rectangular three-story building with red roof tiles in the center of Berkeley's campus, would be ordinary, certainly unspectacular. But it seems to have gobbled up and embodied the spirit of the yells and protestors and one-man showmen who mount soapboxes and spew ideas or juggle them, or balls and knives—actual and linguistic—the quintessence of the stereotypical Berkeley politicized catcaller. Now absent.

The Dwinelle plaza stands eerily empty, something Jeremy barely registers along with a distant thought: must be spring break. His pause is instantaneous, just enough to take in the condensation coating the walls of the storied hall, and to feel the pain near his sternum. He's missed his MRI. He thinks: I wonder if my mother felt this sensation before she got her diagnosis.

He strides forward.

"You want war, Harry," Jeremy mutters, "you've got it."

He descends to the basement, walks to the far right of the building, hearing his feet clop on the ratty tile floor. He's got a full head of steam when he knocks on the door at the end, the one with the sign. "Harry Ives."

No answer. The knock reverberates down the hallway. In an unusually self-conscious moment, Jeremy glances down the lonely corridor. He sees a man with floppy hair and a backpack exit an office at the far end of the building. Grad student or associate professor, Jeremy thinks, as the man looks his way, then turns and heads down the hallway and up the staircase. Feeling pity for the man, all these academics.

To Jeremy, there's something deeply corrupted and corrupting about an environment like academia, where success is so purely subjective. Success depends on selling ideas, which requires convincing people of their merit but not actually asking them to spend money or hard-earned capital to purchase the ideas. It is, to Jeremy, the highest order of rhetorical gamesmanship.

And so, while the idea oppresses him, it also exhilarates him. It is a forum for endless potential conflict, debate, one-upmanship, backstabbing and, better yet, the barely disguised front stabbing.

And none a better foe than Harry, thinks Jeremy, as he nestles his knuckles on the old wise man's door. He raps again, louder than the first time, and the brown door creaks open. It's been left slightly ajar.

After modest hesitation, he pushes the door open.

He hears a footstep in the hallway, a cough. Peers back out, sees no one.

He sees that he's got his iPad in his hand, and that it's damp from sweat. He opens the cover, sees the countdown clock.

52:03:35.

He stuffs the computer into his backpack, and peeks back into Harry's office. Rather, he's looking into a classic anteroom of a professor of the highest esteem at a state university, meaning: drab and small and, to Jeremy, pathetic. It's smaller than his own Embarcadero office, barely big enough to hold a cheap metal bookcase against the opposite wall, and, against the wall to his left, a desk, probably belonging to Harry's graduate assistant. On a metal shelf attached to the wall over the desk, he sees a thick rectangular book that he identifies even though he can't read the words on the spine: *Conflict: A History*. It is Harry's well-worn and traveled bible on the subject. Piled on it, three books with titles Jeremy also can't read, though he thinks he makes out the word "Mesopotamia."

Next to the bookcase, another doorway, with a frosted square glass window, the portal to Harry War.

"Harry."

No answer.

Another clop-clop of feet in the corridor.

On the desk, there's a neat stack of folders, a blue plastic cup with the Cal Bear logo, holding a circle of pens. A laptop. Maybe the computer that Harry and some partner—a grad student, or Evan—are using to scam Jeremy.

He hears a thump from inside Harry's office. The sound of the old man dropping a book or slamming down the phone.

It's wartime.

Jeremy turns the handle, opens Harry's door.

The smell hits him first. Sweet, sticky, fresh. His brain flashes on a piece of conflict trivia, the battle in the early-mid 1800s in South Africa in which ten thousand Zulus fought

Voortrekkers. So brutal was the battle that it turned the Ncome River red.

The Battle of Blood River.

Blood. Rivers of blood. He's standing in rivers of Harry's blood.

CHAPTER 19

H ARRY!"
The aged professor, plopped in his chair, slumps over the desk, folded, like a soggy towel. The old man twitches. Doesn't he? Hard for Jeremy to tell. Too dark. Lights off, shades down.

Without taking his eyes from Harry, Jeremy reaches behind him on the wall, feels for the light switch. Turns it on, gets a blast of red and terror, an image of Harry turned into a jigsaw puzzle, wounds to neck, and chest, back. A weapon, a knife, protruding from his shoulder.

Jeremy turns off the light.

"Harry. Jesus. Harry." Quieter this time, self-conscious. The only light now from between the shade slats covering a window over the cot across the small room. Wall-to-ceiling bookshelves, a scattering of folders and files, some in stacks, a tomb of wisdom and learning. And Harry.

The old man twitches again. Jeremy feels something sticky under his shoes. Blood. Horrified, he lifts a sticky foot, nears the desk. Sees Harry's head is flopped in the other direction, looking away. He touches Harry's shoulder. No movement now.

Jeremy pulls out his phone. He swipes the screen, tries to, can't steady himself.

Harry lifts his head, turns to Jeremy, drops his head again.

"Harry. Hang on, Harry. I'll get help." Jeremy reaches for the knife. Pauses. Will it do more harm than good?

"L . . ." A sound escapes Harry.

"Harry?"

"Lo . . ." Sounds and gurgles. Blood trickles from the professor's lips, his eyes glazed and intense, determined.

Jeremy lowers on his haunches. He rests his chin on the edge of the wooden desk. Looks into dull eyes.

"I'm getting help. Who did this, Harry? Say a name."

Harry swallows. Jeremy fingers 911. The touchscreen phone takes only the first number. The sweat, nerves, momentarily locking up the screen. He wipes it against his shirt.

"Is it Evan?"

He dials 911. "Andrea? What are they up to? Why?"

Jeremy looks around, for some sign, some explanation. A neat desk, office intact, the phone knocked from the hook, Harry's near-lifeless elbow, a protruding knife.

The knife.

Jesus.

He knows that knife. The riveted black polymer, the fat carbon-steel blade.

"They're setting me up, Harry."

"Emergency services." It's a woman's voice.

Jeremy says: "Um . . ."

"Hello. Is everything okay?"

"Ambulance. Hurry."

"Calm down, sir. Is someone hurt?"

"A stabbing. At Dwinelle Hall."

He doesn't say: a stabbing with *my own knife*. Just like the one someone stole the night before from Jeremy's apartment.

A look of excruciating pain crosses Harry's face, like he wants to say something but can't make words; distant, forever eyes.

Jeremy reaches around and into his backpack. Does he have anything? Water? He yanks off his backpack and plops it onto the desk. He rummages inside. Shit, didn't he have water?

Across the desk, Harry, eyes intermittingly closed, taps his finger. Tap, tap, tap. Jeremy wonders: is it Morse code? Another tap, tap.

He looks down where Harry taps. A desk calendar, stained by Harry's life. Where Harry taps, something scrawled. Words? Letters?

He wants to turn on the light. Doesn't want to. Can't. Looks at Harry. If he pulls the knife out, what? The blood pours out? He saves Harry? Kills him?

"Are you there? Sir?" The emergency operator.

"Ives, Harry Ives. In the basement."

Jeremy puts the phone in his pocket, but doesn't hang up. They'll find him, trace the signal. Within seconds, be here in minutes. Harry taps again, twice urgently, once slowed. Jeremy walks around the left side of the desk to see the calendar from Harry's vantage point. He makes out an image. It's a V, or an upside-down triangle without the line connecting at the top.

On each point, there's a number. At the top left of the symbol, "972." On the top right, 970. Along the right side, more numbers: 7, 41, 212. Along the left side: 986, 86. At the bottom, more numbers still, and then the numbers trail off, leading to Harry's index finger, shaking.

Bloody scrawl, lowercase, running together. Jeremy clenches his teeth. Begging his brain to make sense of it.

"What is it, Harry?"

"Lo . . ."

"A victory sign?" Jeremy says, exclaims: "Will there be war?"

"Logca—"

Harry tries to shake his head. "Logcab—"

"Log cabin?!" Jeremy blurts.

Harry blinks.

"The argument at the log cabin? *V* for victory. You . . . what does it mean?"

Harry sucks in a labored breath. His beard quivers. Jeremy puts a hand on the old man's back. Withdraws it to the knife handle, wondering whether to pull it, feels the sensation like it's submerged in Jell-O. Feels hot tears in the corners of his eyes.

Harry spits something, a word. Jeremy leans down. Harry repeats: "You."

"What? Harry, what about me?"

Harry doesn't react. It's not what Harry means or not clear what Harry means. Jeremy's inches from his face.

"Please, Harry. Please tell me what to do."

Harry's eyes suddenly open. It's an adrenaline burst, perhaps unknown to him in this moment why: his dying body recognizes that Jeremy, his proud protégé, his unyielding son, is begging, near tears.

Harry wheezes: "AskIt."

"What?"

Harry extends a finger, points to the backpack sitting on the desk.

"Ask it? Ask the computer? Harry, I'm supposed to ask the computer?"

Harry reaches out and grabs Jeremy's hand. Jeremy recoils, leans back in. He hears footsteps coming. Nearing, nearing, entering the anteroom. The ambulance?

A voice from outside. "Dr. Ives?" A woman.

"What?" Jeremy implores. "Harry."

"Peace. Peace . . ."

The thick fingers squeeze Jeremy. Hold them on to the calendar. Harry catches his eye. "Beware Peace . . ." He flinches, jerks, his eyes open quickly, then begin to close.

Jeremy looks up. In the doorway. A woman, drops the book in her hands, screams.

CHAPTER 20

"I CALLED 911."

Tall woman, black sweat suit, a student-athlete maybe, one hand over her mouth, now pointing at Jeremy. Some primal accusation.

"Help!" she screams. Wails. "Heeeeeeeelp!"

"No," Jeremy says, repeats: "I called for help."

"Heeeeeelp!" She steps backward.

Jeremy looks at the scene, sees what she sees, a suspect covered in blood.

He looks down, then at the woman, and back down. Yanks his backpack toward him, and, as he does so, pulls the calendar, tears it, obscuring the part with the blood scrawl. Hoping to scramble the coded message, if that's what it was. He looks at the woman.

"I called 911." He repeats, implores.

Harry emits a low, feral moan. The intruding woman blinks, calculating, her reboot nearly finished, coming back to life.

"I'm going for help," Jeremy says.

The woman steps forward to Harry. She's going to take some action, Jeremy thinks; she took a lifesaving class.

Jeremy looks at the calendar, the message. He rips the top page of the calendar, sliding the torn top page from beneath Harry's evaporating life.

He runs.

Past the woman, into the anteroom. Hears the bloody squeak of his own sneakers. He scrambles off the shoes and socks. Folds and stuffs the calendar page and the bloody scrawl into his back pocket. Takes off out the door, curls into the hallway, suddenly slows when he sees several students, hand in hand, quickly approaching, drawn by the sound they thought they heard of someone yelling for help.

"Dr. Ives is hurt. I'm going for help."

The students start to jog forward. Jeremy walks past them, a half jog, and, when he's past, jogs. Looks down, sees his feet leave no marks. Runs.

When he reaches the stairwell, he pauses. Heads down the stairs to the back.

Seconds later, he's outside, in a lonely parking lot. He sees a short building to his right, Dwinelle Annex. He hears sirens.

His heart slams in his chest. He could turn around; it's not too late to go back and explain to the police that he went looking for help and has returned. He has an alibi, right, evidence someone broke into his condo, the surveillance tape with the building manager, logical explanations. Justice will be served.

But there are Jeremy's fingerprints, on his own knife, in Harry's back.

He looks ahead, sees the grove of ancient, leafy trees that surround a creek-side path leading to the south of campus. Over the path, the trees converge, their leaves intermingling, taking a shape, something circular.

A clock.

The countdown clock.

Jeremy shakes his head. Blinks. Just trees.

The log cabin.

Ask it. The computer.

Is it right? There will be war. Is that what Harry was telling him? Maybe Harry thinks there's going to be a conflict and he wants Jeremy to ferret it out on the computer. Maybe Harry thinks the computer knows something. Everything?

Ask it.

Not if he's in jail.

And something nags him, a factor in this instant algorithm his brain is running: what if the computer's right, partially right, about the apocalypse? Ask it.

He puts his head down and walks to the grove, the path. When he hits it, he sprints.

TEN MINUTES LATER, at a drugstore on Shattuck, he spends $6.95 for flip-flops. He walks outside, peers across the street in the drizzle to the entrance to the subway, the way to San Francisco. A beat cop stands outside, eyeing people descending into the escalator to the subway tunnel. One tall fellow, thin, wearing a hoodie, passes the cop, gets stopped, questioned.

Jeremy curls back into the drugstore. He buys a red rain slicker, with a hood. He retreats into the bathroom. He pulls on the slicker, looks in the mirror. Sees the smear. Blood, turning brownish, stains his cheek beneath his left eye. He must've scratched himself. He looks at his hand. Both hands. Stained. With Harry. He rinses them in the sink.

He rubs his hands on his pants to dry them, feels the phone

in his pocket. The phone. Still connected, presumably, to the police. Shit. He yanks it out. He swipes to disconnect the call. Then thinks the better of it. He turns off the phone.

They can't track him. Not with the phone off. Can they?

Back at the door of the drugstore, he watches the officer. Watches, watches. He hears a screech. The driver of an SUV approaching the nearby light has slammed on his brakes. A bicyclist shouts, unhurt, unhit, but spilled. The officer shakes his head, annoyed at the little things, begins a reluctant walk to the intersection. Jeremy bolts for the subway entrance.

Inside, downstairs, another cop, chatting with a heavyset woman inside the ticket box.

Jeremy walks unnoticed through the turnstiles.

Minutes later, he sits in the empty train, regretting that there are few commuters this time of day, little cover. But he's made it through the first, most crucial line of defense. The officer at the mouth of the subway will tell people he saw no thin man without shoes trying to escape west.

Likely, Jeremy thinks, he'll face curious officers, even a dragnet, at the other side of the trip. The subway exit providing a perfect bottleneck through which potential murderers will have to pass.

He exhales, expelling stale air, his senses returning, slides lower into the filthy fabric of the subway seat, stares at the grubby carpet beneath his flip-flops.

Log cabin. What does that mean, Harry? A code? Who else would know of the symbolism of the log cabin, the day when the last pieces of Jeremy's life fell apart. He pictures it, the day, the group: Emily, Harry, fried chicken and white wine, and Jeremy. Sitting on a blanket under a tree, the Golden Gate

Bridge in the distance, Harry casually asked whether the algorithm might be improved and Jeremy, without missing a beat, said, "Are these your suggestions or the ones Evan gave you when he had his puppet hand up your ass?"

Harry just looked at him. Then said: "Early in the day to go nuclear against your last ally."

And that's just what Jeremy had done. Without warning, he'd severed ties with his last ally. It was, Emily said, so plainly self-destructive, an act by Jeremy to distract himself from the fact he was no longer in control, no longer the center of attention. Or worse: that when it comes down to it, Jeremy feels more comfortable in a state of conflict than in anything approaching vulnerability.

Or, as Harry put it that day at the log cabin: Jeremy, you prefer fighting.

"To what?"

"To truth," the old man said, shook his head and walked away. He was done fighting.

What truth?

What did Harry mean when he said: "Beware Peace." And "Statis pugna." Same thing, really. Something is too calm. Is that what Harry means? Things are too calm? It was one of Harry's landmark theories that the world actually is safer when there is a constant level of low-level conflict. In fact, while Harry hated war, he did not hate conflict; he thought conflict was a simple way of life, a reality of a world filled with competition for limited resources. The key, he said, was to accept it and manage it, allow it to simmer, just not boil.

Was Harry saying things are getting too peaceful? And thus poised to boil and explode?

Ask it.

Jeremy glances at the two other passengers in his car, a stringy-haired man with a cane standing near the door, bent at the waist, neck craned, eyes downcast, defeated. And another man, seated, locked in a mass-market paperback, wearing a mass-market prefab, no-wrinkle blue shirt.

Jeremy extracts his iPad. He clicks it on. As it comes to life, he paws cautiously at the message in his back pocket. He looks around, pulls the hastily folded paper and shifts it between his legs, outside anyone's view. He unfolds the deadly origami, glancing up and down, furtive, making sure no one sees. He can make out the message, sort of; the blood has smeared. Jeremy tastes vomit.

Forces himself to look at the symbol, the message. A shape, likely a *V*, but not totally clear, with numbers on the points; 972, 970 on the top points, and 218-650 at the bottom.

Along the sides: 7, 1, 41, 212, 986, 86.

He finds scratch paper in his backpack and uses a blue pen to copy onto it the symbol and the numbers. He shoves the calendar, the bloody evidence, into his backpack. He looks at the symbol.

A code, obviously. A riddle? A taunt?

218-650 at the bottom.

Not binary. Not computer language, probably. Harry didn't talk that language, didn't like anything about computers, even argued they made the world more dangerous by diminishing in-person contact.

And what of the symbol. Is it a letter, or a shape?

Harry was never much into the code-cracking part of war and conflict. He found it boring—the Enigma machine, the efforts by the Allies to crack Nazi and Japanese codes, the use of encryption schemes and misdirection and words born of adding together the first letters of various sentences or paragraphs, dead drops and back-alley whispers.

Is this a message for Jeremy, or for anyone?

Jeremy, feeling intensely self-conscious, looks up, sees his iPad is alive. He looks at the time. It's just after 4 P.M. It takes a second to pinpoint the significance of the time. He's supposed to meet Andrea shortly. He pictures the meeting place, Perry's, an eatery cum pickup joint on the Embarcadero.

He clicks down to the countdown clock. Fifty-one hours, and a half.

Ask it.

Ask it what, Harry?

Who attacked you? Will there be a war?

The computer beeps. Beep, beep, beep. An update. Jeremy doesn't have to ask it anything. The computer has something to tell him.

CHAPTER 21

THE SHRILL UPDATE-BEEP is one of those features that Evan had insisted on including in the product. The feature announces any changes to major data points, the key parameters that affect the timing or gravity of impending conflict, like weather or troop movements or major leadership changes.

"Think of it as our version of IM," Evan would say to prospective customers over lunch at One Market or some other trendy downtown restaurant. Often, he'd be speaking not to prospective buyers in military or government procurement but to executives from the private sector, like the insurance or wireless industries. They were interested in the business applications of the digital oracle but they couldn't help being sucked in by the sexy lure of the conflict algorithm. And that was the point, really, Evan would tell a chagrined Jeremy: the conflict machine is our brochure but business intelligence is what will make us rich.

"IM?" one of the lunching executives would invariably ask Evan. "Instant messaging?"

"Instant Menace," Evan would say. "It tells you when there's been a change to a variable that could change the world."

They'd laugh, invariably.

"Of course, I shouldn't joke," Evan would continue. "Not when it comes to predicting global conflict. And not even when it comes to your business. You've got to know when a market is moving, or might move, or a competitor is transforming. It's a cliché, but business is war and you can't afford to be a second behind, not a *millisecond* behind, or you wind up on the defensive, maybe in an irreversible position."

Jeremy looks at the bottom right of the screen. He sees four little flags, all red, meaning four key parameters have changed. Four of the 327 variables have shifted. More data, or more lies.

A voice comes over the train loudspeaker. "City Center. Transfer to San Francisco."

The train slows, wheels screeching on the track. Outside Jeremy's window, the passing of blurry walls at the station entrance. He shoves his iPad into his backpack and puts the rain slicker over the top.

The train whines to a stop. Jeremy stands, looks out the window, sees the cop. She's descended the stairs at the far end of the platform. Then he loses sight of her as the train lurches ahead to its next destination.

Jeremy's pectoral aches, pounds. Just to the left of the key fob hanging on the silver chain. He looks down at his flip-flops, calculating. Is this a cop-cop, or a subway cop checking to make sure passengers have their passes—a routine measure at the first of the month? He pictures the conflict map. Red, red, red. The first of the month. Just a few days away. April 1. Armageddon or system bug or joke. He looks up. It's a cop-cop.

The subway doors open. Across the platform, a train, Jeremy's train, right there, spitting distance, sprinting distance. Its doors open too. He has to get on that train.

He pokes his head out the door. The portly cop, only fifteen feet away, has her back turned, looking at a handful of commuters making their way from one train to the other. She turns in his direction. He recoils.

A horn sounds. The other train set to go. He sucks in his breath. He peers out the doors. The cop is one car down, entering his train.

He runs.

Seconds later, he slips into the closing doors of the westbound train. He feels like he's got a scarlet letter, telltale flip-flops and a bright red slicker. But none of the half dozen commuters seems to take notice.

He sits in an empty row, yanks out his iPad. He clicks on the first flag. A dialogue box pops up. "Mover-shaker update re: Russia. Click for details."

"Mover-shaker." That's the program's vernacular for news involving a leader, someone with enough clout or importance to potentially have a material impact on the timing and nature of conflict. To move markets or shake up geopolitics. It could mean something as extreme as an assassination, or the change of a lesser ingredient, like an outspoken hawk in some inflamed area losing an election, or winning one.

Before he clicks for details, he runs his cursor over the second flag. A dialogue box pops up: "Rhetoric. Decline. Re: Fertile Crescent. Click for details."

A fall in hostile language. A further decline in the semantics in the Fertile Crescent. That's only good news. Would that all the world's conflict rhetoric would decline.

He clicks on the third flag: "Weather update. Click for details."

Jeremy tastes bile. Weather, a major factor in the onset of conflict; better weather can allow troop movements or beach landings; clear skies can permit air attacks. He clicks on the box for details.

There is a link to a web site called AccuWeather. The page is for the Hawaii weather forecast. On top of the page is a satellite image, clouds swirling above the Hawaiian Islands. Below that, radar images showing incoming weather and short forecasts for the individual islands, Maui, Oahu, Kauai, and so on.

In the middle of the page, he finds what looks to be an update. It reads: "Tropical Storm Serena downgraded. Westernmost islands, Pacific fisheries spared heavy rains as low-pressure system dissipates."

That's it. On this page of links and charts and graphs, a single sentence that might or might not be pertinent.

So what? What could the computer be inferring from this? He scrutinizes the page again, unable to make any clear associations or inferences.

He clicks on the fourth flag. Inside the dialogue box: "Update, Random Event Meter." And he mutters: lemme guess, more lions. A *Washington Post* headline pops up: "Three More Lions Set Loose."

Kooks have freed lions from zoos in Seattle and Portland and one from a traveling circus act stationed in Reno, serving a casino there. The article says police continue to investigate the acts as potentially involving animal rights activists. The article notes that the vigilante acts have left one person dead, an older man in San Diego who apparently was responsible for the freeing of the lion there. An unnamed official from San Diego said the man had on his back a curious tattoo: a lion standing on its hind legs, its tail up in the air.

"Thanks, computer," Jeremy mutters under his breath. "Let me know every time someone in San Francisco takes their dog for a walk."

But he can't help wondering. Something about the image pulls at him.

Harry, is this what you want me to ask it? About lions?

He moves his cursor onto the other flag, the one about movers and shakers, clicks for details. A new window pops up. In it materializes a link to an Associated Press story with the headline "Russian Arms Exec Arrested in Paris."

Marat Vladine, a billionaire who was former chairman of Russia's state-controlled arms dealership, was detained in Paris today by French state police. The French said that he'd been held at the request of the Russian government investigating charges of tax evasion and money laundering.

However, one French authority said that Mr. Vladine's detainment was instead related to an intensifying domestic political squabble inside Russia.

In recent days, Russian politicians at the highest levels of government have been in a public spat about the heavy foreign-policy influence played by the state-backed munitions dealer, Rosoboronexport State Corporation. Mr. Vladine was the longtime chairman of Rosoboronexport until earlier this year but is still thought to be heavily involved in the company's strategic direction.

Opponents of the current government say the multibillion-dollar munitions corporation has encouraged policies that are in the interest of its shareholders and political backers, not the nation at large.

These opponents have seized on rumors that Rosoboronexport allowed nuclear-grade bomb materials to escape in recent years into terrorist hands—or sold such materials to rogue elements. Rosoboronexport vigorously denies the charges and dismisses them as political misdirection and, thus far, there has been no independent verification that such dangerous materials ever were sold or wound up in the wrong hands.

Erik Soliere, a Paris-based attorney retained by Mr. Vladine, declined to comment on the detainment of his client.

Jeremy scrolls down but discovers that he's read the full article. He reads it again, feels a pinprick of disappointment at the lack of direct or helpful evidence. Where's the smoking gun—an assassination or an attack on a capital city or something. Something that would make sense of the dire predictions. Something that would explain what's happening—to him, to Harry. To his computer.

Looking at the AP news story, he's wondering why the computer bothered to update him about such minutiae. Then he remembers. It is designed to report any new information, small or large, related to the larger variables that may be contributing to impending conflict.

Previously, the computer had reported changes to the level of conflict rhetoric in Russia and related to Rosoboronexport. So, Jeremy reasons, the computer is sending what it determines to be a related update, however tangential. The feature was Jeremy's brainchild; the algorithm uses artificial intelligence to make decisions about whether two ideas are sufficiently related to send an update. But now Jeremy is mourning an update about one more seemingly meaningless data point.

"Say something useful," he mutters to his iPad.

The computer, as if in response, beeps. Another different sound, or, rather three beeps, in quick succession, brief and shrill. And, at the same time, a box materializes in the middle of the window on his iPad. In the box, big letters, "Conflict Clock Reset. Click for details."

It's a feature that, as much as he chided Evan for demanding it, he quietly relishes. It provides an alert that the computer's basic prediction has changed. It could mean that conflict is less likely, or more likely, or, if conflict is already ongoing, that the computer now predicts it will last longer or be more quickly resolved.

As Jeremy clicks on the dialogue box, he feels an eerie calm. He's sure that the computer will rescind its dire prediction, the jig will be up, the dire prophecy revoked or revealed as a hoax.

A new box appears.

"CONFLICT TIMETABLE ACCELERATED. 27 HOURS, 17 MINUTES."

Without moving his head, he glances at a woman in a Giants cap chewing her nails, looks down and taps his index finger against the screen, on the warning in the dialogue box. He puts his finger on "27 HOURS." Some part of him wants to feel that this is real, not just some virtual, ethereal thing, the digital ranting of a box that Jeremy helped create, his cyber-subconscious taunting him.

He does the math. Previously, the computer had projected

the outbreak of conflict in less than three days. As little as ten minutes ago, that was the prediction. Now, suddenly, it's down to little more than one.

He taps the edge of the countdown box, bringing up another infobox. It shows the longitude and latitude of the project attack, the *ostensible* project attack. Still San Francisco. Right here, Jeremy thinks, tomorrow night, just after 7 P.M.

Then he realizes what's bothering him. It's no longer projecting April 1. If this is an April Fools' joke, someone has mixed up the dates.

"What can it answer?" he mutters.

"Are you talking to yourself?"

The voice belongs to a boy in the aisle, little more than four years old, jacket zipped up to the bottom of his lip, holding his mother's hand, staring intently at Jeremy. The woman looks at Jeremy with a sheepish smile, as if to say: from the mouths of babes. Jeremy looks down at his iPad but all he sees is the face of Kent. Dissolving into bullet points:

```
A computer warning about the end of the world.
    Here, in a few hours.
Log cabin: a rustic and homey setting for a final
    clash of wills between him and Harry
A message from Harry, symbols and numbers
A break-in at his apartment, at his office.
    Everything strewn.
Someone, more than someone, following him. Setting
    him up?
AskIt
```

In sum, clues left by an inscrutable computer and a genius

ally turned foe. Can it add up the clues for him? What can he ask the computer that it can answer?

The train screeches into San Francisco. It's 4:20. Should be crowded on the platform, thick with commuters, but easy enough for a cop to stand at the top of the escalator. Jeremy stuffs his iPad into the backpack. He looks at the mom, holding hands with the child, absent a wedding ring, in her early thirties. A *New York Times* tucked under her arm, the right audience.

"Caught in the act," Jeremy says to the woman. "Talking to myself. I promise it's not habitual. Something I only do in public places."

She laughs.

CHAPTER 22

D RIZZLE COATS EVERYTHING, street, his cheap red slicker, the newspaper boxes and lampposts, the awnings. It pastes the pages of a torn real estate magazine to the sidewalk. An afghan of gray, just the cover Jeremy's looking for. Makes people lazy, dulls them, puts mud into the machine, why military campaigns work so much better in sunshine.

But, now, the foul cover makes Jeremy feel that one less thing is going against him. He was able to file through the turnstiles with the irritable masses, the two cops a little less motivated, and probably dissuaded from wasting energy on the man interacting with the woman and the boy, talking flirtatiously, happily. He parted ways with Ivory and Johnny at the top of the escalator, their smiles holding a promise of an exchanged Facebook friendship, but not really, since they exchanged no last names or other personal identifiers. Just a little shared walking daydream.

He stands at the corner of the Embarcadero and Mission, looking out onto the Bay Bridge, strewn with wall-to-wall lights of people who mistakenly thought they could beat the commute.

He's hunting.

Just around the corner, within easy sight, the valet stand for Perry's. In the next ten minutes or so, he can watch Andrea arrive. He can decide on a course of action. At this point, all bets are off. Maybe she'll show up with the general and a three-headed alien.

He extracts a phone. Not his iPhone, not the one he used to call 911, but his backup, a flip phone, an old standby that is something you just carry in Silicon Valley, like, because. It's like being a soldier and carrying an extra ammo magazine.

Jeremy holds his finger over the on button. He wants to believe that the cops, if they are tracing his other phone—totally a possibility but far from a certainty—might not be tracing *this* phone. But he also knows that if they're tracing the whereabouts of one, using simple triangulating technology, they're likely tracing both.

Not if he keeps it quick, doesn't let them get a handle on the signal. He turns on the flip phone. He calls his voice mail on his other phone. There are two messages. The first from Emily: You can't do that to the boy. It's not all about you.

The second one also from Emily: Are you okay?

He enters her phone number and taps her a text: "Take Kent to Eddie's." He looks up, sees a black sport utility vehicle pull into the circular entrance of a swanky downtown hotel. Looks back down at his device, wonders whether he should add "I love you," which he tells her only in the dark. Will that get Emily to drive Kent to his uncle Eddie's house outside Reno?

No, it'll just engender a cascade of calls and texts from Emily. Or she'll ignore it as spam or the work of a manic version of Jeremy. Maybe she won't even recognize the phone number of the second phone.

He pictures her the morning they broke up, after making love on that futon. Or trying to. A rare instance in which Jeremy couldn't finish. Couldn't keep going. It's okay, Emily said, brushing his cheek with the outside of her hand. Without warning, he started in about the bowl of half-eaten raisin bran that Kent had left on the floor, how much the boy needed to start acting his age.

"You're upset over cereal."

"You're not listening."

And then, before Jeremy could do his thing, Emily said: "I'm done."

It was like a rifle shot. Cold, true, hollow-point rhetoric. You'd have to have a magic cape to stop the power of her words. And the stuff that came after, the tears and the explanation, really unnecessary. Something had changed, she told Jeremy, in the preceding few days and leading up to them, an even more confrontational Jeremy, as well as a feeling Emily couldn't shake that he would undermine every beautiful thing.

"You are right. You are right more often than anyone gives you credit for. It doesn't scare me that you're almost always right, Jeremy. I like it that you speak your truth. What scares me is that being right isn't ultimately what it's about for you. That's a means to an end. To burn it down."

She'd had enough. All the while, Jeremy kept thinking about Kent. For days, Jeremy could think only about the boy and the argument they'd had over the rocket ship puzzle—whether to put the borders first as Jeremy suggested or group the pieces by color. Life had been teetering on the precipice, worse than that, Jeremy being held from plummeting by Emily and Kent—all the others having already abandoned him, or he them, and then, splat. Down he went.

In his phone, he texts: "Please." That should get her attention. She used to beg him to try to learn the proper use of the word "please." It became almost a joke between them. He'd ask for something and Emily would say "What's the magic word?" And Jeremy would say: "'Abracadabra'?"

Jeremy looks at his text. He taps: "I love you and Kent." He erases it. Taps it again. He feels the sting of tears. Wipes them away. Hits send.

He's poised to turn off the phone when, instead, he pulls up the calculator. He's thinking of Harry's admonition: AskIt. Ask the computer. Is that what Harry meant? If so, ask it *what*?

At the least, Jeremy finds he's asking *himself* a question: do I believe the computer's prediction?

For some reason, he just can't get his head around an answer. He, and his computer, have been so discredited, by so many people close to him. Part of him desperately wants the computer to be right; he will be redeemed; he will show the world; he, alone, will *save* the world. But what if he can't? What is the cost of being right?

And what is the cost of being wrong? How much more egg can his face withstand? On the corner, he sees a line of newspaper dispensers for the *Chronicle, Examiner, Guardian,* and one of those free real estate throwaways. Is that my play? Call a newspaper, or maybe that local TV reporter who a while ago mentioned Jeremy and his algorithm as part of a bigger story on a new generation of business ideas attracting venture capital?

And say what? *My iPad thinks there's going to be a war!*

Proof. I need some proof, he thinks. He knows what he'd like to ask the computer:

1. Who is responsible for this alleged attack on San Francisco, the one that will ignite a global conflict?
2. And what can Jeremy do about it?
3. If none of the above, who is fucking with Jeremy? Why?

He's already investigating who might be fucking with him, so he focuses for a moment on the first two questions. They are simple inquiries, at least on their face. But how to ask such questions is another matter altogether, a remarkably complex matter. In fact, it might prove impossible, even for a very good programmer like Jeremy.

The trouble is, in the first place the computer wasn't built to answer such questions any more than an automobile was built to, say, make a breakfast smoothie. Sure, in theory, both an automobile and a blender are machines, and the car probably could be disassembled and its parts used to build a blender. But not in an eyeblink. No more can this computer, which was built to predict the timing, extent and length of conflict, be easily programmed to divulge who is responsible for an attack, and why.

Maybe he can get there indirectly.

"What if . . ." he says aloud. Then pauses, and looks up to see a woman stride by under an umbrella emblazoned with a Gap logo. She's glancing at him—the man in the red slicker mumbling to himself. She quickens her pace.

The computer projects that war is imminent because of a change in the world's circumstances—in a range of different variables. But, Jeremy wonders, would the computer still predict conflict if only one of those variables changed, or several, or a different combinations of variables? Or would the computer still predict conflict if a single variable were removed from the equation? For instance, Jeremy is asking himself, if the conflict rhetoric in Russia hadn't intensified, would the computer still prophesy Armageddon? What if there were no increase in the shipments of tantalum?

These are questions that he can ask this computer, at least indirectly. He can, he realizes, ask it to run simulations that remove a particular variable. He can ask it to remove two of the variables. He can mix and match and change the circumstances to see which of the variables are most instrumental in the computer's projection of conflict.

And then, he can make a key deduction. If one variable stands out, he'll know where to focus. It's an idea, at least, a way of taking back some control from this suddenly inscrutable computer, from the conspiracy that has overtaken his life.

The computer has identified nine different potential variables, including the six different changes to rhetoric, tantalum, weather and the arrest. Jeremy does a quick computation of the number of simulations he's got to ask the computer to crunch. Nine variables, a factorial of nine. Into the calculator on his phone, he does the math: 9 times 8 times 7 times 6 times 5 times 4 times 3 times 2 times 1 = 362,880.

362,880 different combinations of events.

Nothing. Not for a computer with any kind of horsepower.

Might take a few hours. That's the easy part. But Jeremy's got to program the computer with the question. How long will that take?

Would it even work?

He grimaces. First, he's got to deal with Andrea. He glances at the clock. Still a few minutes to go. He's about to turn off the phone when he sees he's got a notification. He clicks. It's a news flash about tantalum, the precious metal that has seen an explosive rise in shipments.

He clicks and discovers not a news story but a press release. It's from a company called Elektronic Space Suppliers. Jeremy recalls that's the company in Turkey that ships tantalum, the company whose stock price has soared. According to the company's press release, a mere three lines, it has secured a long-term contract to deliver tantalum to a consortium of Silicon Valley companies, including Hewlett-Packard, Google, Intel and others.

On one level, it's compelling. Very much so. Not that Silicon Valley companies would buy tantalum. Everyone's in the mobile space. But the fact they'd do so in concert. Why cooperate on something so competitive?

But what could that possibly have to do with war?

He shakes his head, willing away cobwebs and dust and exhaustion, turns off the phone, pulls himself closer to the side of a restaurant behind him. Wants to blend in, a red-slickered object of what he assumes must now be a manhunt.

Jeremy, feeling intensely self-conscious, looks up. His eye again catches the tint-windowed sport utility vehicle, the kind you see all the time in Washington, D.C., a heavy, dark power machine.

The passenger door opens. A man gets out and jogs into the hotel lobby.

No way. Jeremy shakes his head. No way.

CHAPTER 23

T HE DOCK CREAKS and groans. Light waves rock the gigantic anchored ships, nothing compared with the powerful sounds produced crossing the Pacific, but then the churn and purr of the engine had covered the clash of ocean and steel.

The man with the beard and the backpack crouches. So much of his life is spent crouching. Hiding, scurrying, the posture of the Lord's work is not a proud one, not in the era of heretics. In this case, he crouches behind containers at the Port of Oakland. Not far to his left, he can see the ship he stowed away on, which landed hours ago, and now he's watching the police hustle about.

They've found the young man whose neck he broke, whom he ushered into the next life. He had no choice.

And his righteous certitude has been reinforced by the ease with which he escaped the ship onto the dock—safely and with his deadly backpack by his side. God must be here or he'd be in handcuffs right now.

He pulls the backpack close, waiting for the Guardians to find him.

He hears a policeman "comb the place," and the words take him back to the beginning. He pulls close to the shipping container and thinks about the story, how long his people have been hiding while heretics comb the world for them.

"Your grandfather, Fishl, he knelt and he waited," his father's story would begin.

Always the kneeling, always the waiting. He could imagine his grandfather's beard, and see his father's own commanding beard, a towering upside-down cone, wisdom in the form of facial hair. The story was always the same. His grandfather knelt, and waited, and listened to the onrush of furious Russian villagers, literally wielding pitchforks, literally on horseback, like a cliché of the horsemen of the apocalypse. If only the world could've been so lucky. It wasn't the end of days, just the end of another poor Jewish village, its inhabitants persecuted because they did exactly as they were told: helped the nobility tax and manage the peasants. Jews, wanting only to be left alone to pursue their beliefs, by happenstance gained middle-class status, upward mobility.

But the Russian peasants didn't understand that. And finally fed up with the inequities that governed their society, they turned on the Jews, the partners of a noble class that were themselves untouchable with pitchforks. Just another deadly ebb in the ebb and flow of the Jews in European culture. A boatload of pious refugees subject to the waves of change, awaiting final redemption.

His grandfather could hear the wails of the murders on the edges of the village, the shouts and cries of the mothers begging for their babies' lives. And then, his father tells him, his grandfather heard another voice telling him what he must do.

"Was it . . . ?" the boy would ask. He'd know he couldn't say "God," but how could he ask if his grandfather had heard a divine voice?

"No, Moshe," his father said, understanding the unspoken. "It was the rebbe," in his devout sect, a divine intermediary, a prophet. "He said, 'Go that we might live.' Your grandfather begged to stay. But he was commanded."

And so, the story went, his grandfather leaped from the window, escaped and eventually became a seedling planted in the verdant valleys in the north of Palestine. And from him sprouted the bloodline, his father, like his great-grandfather a pious man, committed to the word and the ancient code, the Talmud, and not wayward convenience. And certainly not to Israel.

Israel, a heretical concept. At least a secular Israel. In fact, little could be more heretical. Its establishment would, in effect, institutionalize, formalize godlessness. The Messiah might well never come.

"So it is bad that Grandfather came here?" the boy would ask.

"Quite the opposite." Of course, his father always had the answer. "We are here for a reason, an important reason."

His father tells him, again, about the Guardians. In ancient times, Rabbi Judah the Prince sent emissaries to inspect pastoral towns. In one, these rabbi emissaries asked to see the city guardian and they were shown a municipal guard. The emissaries said this was not a guard, but a city destroyer. The townspeople asked who should be considered a guard, and the rabbis said: "The scribes and the scholars."

The Guardians of the City. Neturei-Karta. From Aramaic. The Jews who would keep this land pure, who would not allow a secular weed to take root. His father, among their leaders, was hunted for seeking to disrupt the Zionists in 1947 and 1948. So hunted that he was forced to disappear, or maybe the hunters got him.

"Our own people," his father told him before he packed up a small sack of belongings. It was the last time he saw his father, and that majestic beard. "Tracked down by our own people so that they might do the work of Satan and create a goyish land. Take care of your mother, Moshe. Guard the city."

The boy thinks of the old words; the Zionists combed the northern valleys for his father, as these heretics surely will comb the belly of the ship for him, the boy, the grandson, now bearded himself, carrying the mission. Neturei Karta. And the stakes so magnified. Otherwise, he wouldn't be called to such purpose.

And, as always, such risk, and uncertainty. Seeming happenstance that left him with his half of this deadly suitcase, a treasure bestowed by unlikely authorities, inert though it is in its current state.

And then a contact from the Old City, and another contact, calling his tiny cell to action. Giving him clear but incomplete directions, codes, instructions to find an unlikely—even impossible ally—a woman, a Syrian, a Christian. The Guardians, he's told, are no longer merely Jews, as the world's mythology heralds. They are Christians, Rastafarians, a secret network, zealots, in the best sense of the word. A simple, abiding, core belief: for the Messiah to come, they must cleanse Jerusalem of the infidels. The nonbelievers.

And the nonbelievers have become so powerful. They hold the key to forever undoing the eternal peace.

Can it be that he and a Christian from Syria, and white men from America, are not enemies but share a common enemy?

These are, anyhow, the rumors. He will believe it when he sees it.

And then he does—he sees it. Rather, he sees her.

A woman like a shadow moves through the open platform, unnoticed, and then scurries between two containers. She is dark-haired and dark-skinned. And soon, she is nearly beside him. How did she find him?

He pulls the backpack tight as she inches near.

She whispers: "Have no fear of atomic energy."

"Shalom," he says.

"Salam," she says, then repeats: "Have no fear of atomic energy."

The bearded man keeps his back to the voice. "None of them can-a stop-a the time."

"Redemption Song," by Bob Marley, the code.

The man looks directly into her face and sees her bright eyes, breaking into a smile.

He recoils. Her smile, it is not joy, but tightly controlled fury, the look of a bloodthirsty animal before a fight, anxious to kill, and eat what it has killed.

"You are Janine," he stammers.

"That works."

"The Guardian."

"No, I am not *the* Guardian. Merely a guardian, as it were, a foot soldier, like you. You will meet him soon. Come. We are in a hurry."

"There's a problem?"

By way of an answer, she ushers him with a gentle hand on

his elbow. Moments later, undetected, they've made their way into the port parking lot. She opens the door to a dark blue van, loosing from the inside stale air. She gestures him inside.

She eyes his backpack.

"You have done a wonderful thing. Now we have our divine tool."

"How long before . . ."

"Mere hours." She guns the engine, accelerating the van out of the lot. "But, first, we have urgent work."

CHAPTER 24

JERFMY PRESSES HIMSELF against the building, wants to withdraw his head into his slicker, turtlelike.

Alternatively, he wants to sink his teeth into an attack, a drooling, take-no-prisoners, savage attack.

He knows he wasn't imagining things. Knows that cocky gait, the too-cool for an umbrella or a jacket, the iPad case tucked under his arm.

What the hell was Evan doing climbing out of a sport utility vehicle across the street?

But that's only the setup. Jeremy's staring now around the corner of the building at the punch line.

The SUV dropped off Evan, then sped off, and seconds later appeared around the corner and parked at the valet stand at Perry's.

The door opened.

One sheer leg, the hem of a knee-length skirt, the other leg. Deliberate, practiced, careful, seductive. Andrea.

He's watching her now, as she hands the keys to the valet, curtsies a flirtatious little thank-you. All while looking around, swiveling her head, craning her neck to look inside.

I'm right here, Andrea, Jeremy thinks. Watching you lie.

She was the one driving the big sport utility vehicle that dropped off Evan. He's almost positive, but not *positive* positive. The big car dropped off Evan and sped around the block, out of sight. Then it, or one virtually identical, appeared at the front of Perry's. Hard to imagine, almost impossible to imagine, it was two different cars.

Andrea opens the rear door, pulls out a handbag off the backseat. Which for some reason makes Jeremy think: handgun. She's licensed to carry. She once flirted with him by suggesting she'd purchased a pink holster bra.

"Packing a concealed gun is like wearing lingerie," she told Jeremy. "Even if you're the only one who knows you're wearing it, it still makes you feel different."

"What if you're wearing both—a gun and lingerie?"

She laughed that syrupy laugh. "Exactly my point."

She walks into the restaurant. Jeremy looks at the revolving doors of the hotel, then back. Evan barely knew Andrea, right? And what little they knew of each other, they professed to hate.

"We call someone like him an instigator," Andrea once told Jeremy of Evan. Meaning: he tries to disrupt things so that he can find market opportunities in the rubble. "A business terrorist."

Jeremy's not sure of the time, but can safely assume it's a little past five, the hour of his planned meeting with Andrea.

The rain is intensifying, not yet a downpour but now a challenge to the limits of his cheap slicker. A bus passes, flush with passengers, including one woman Jeremy can see with a cheek matted against the window in a post-work nap. Behind it, a taxi. Its driver reaches the intersection just in front of Jeremy and makes a sharp U-turn. On any other day, Jeremy lets the driver have it, threatens to call 911, maybe does so.

The driver pulls into the circular entrance of the hotel. Seconds later, Evan slips through the revolving doors. He's not alone. Next to him, two people: an elegant man in a gray suit, wisps of gray hair to match, tall but slightly bent at the shoulders, weathered, dark-hued skin; and a woman with a pink suit and short, fast steps. Jeremy recognizes them, sort of. People in the high-tech world, big dogs. He pulls himself into the building, close as he might. Wishes for invisibility. Evan and the pair climb into the taxi, and it speeds away.

Jeremy takes a deep breath, looks down, inhales deeply again.

He reaches behind him, feels his backpack. It's damp but not soaked. He sees the coffee stand across the street, an awning shaking in the wind and three tables beneath umbrellas. Mild shelter but the vantage point he's looking for.

He decides he must stop thinking. There's too much to think about, and not enough: not enough data to conclude anything. He must act. He needs more data.

He sneaks a look at the iPad, the clock.

26:40:40.

He shoves the device back into the bag.

Two minutes later, he stands against the side of the coffee hut across the street, a vantage point from which he can look right into the front of Perry's. He can see someone standing right inside the door, beside the maître d' stand. Might well be Andrea, a woman almost certainly, given the person's height, but hard to be sure it's her because of the drizzle on the windows. He can see the woman glance at something in her hand, probably a phone. She noodles with it—dialing; reading a text?—then puts it to her ear.

Jeremy scrambles to pull his phone from his pocket. She's got to be calling him, naturally; that's what you do when your friend is late. Even if the woman at the front of the restaurant isn't her, even if Andrea's sitting at the bar, or at a table, she's got to be calling him, or she will soon. He turns on his iPhone. He'll keep it brief, he promises himself, hoping to forestall anyone tracking him as the device comes to life.

The screen flickers and so does a hard truth. Jeremy can't go to the police, not to Harry, or Evan or Andrea. The media? Who can he turn to for help?

"You want a coffee?"

Jeremy looks up to see a short man with a mustache and an East Indian accent, gleaming teeth in a crescent smile, holding out a coffee in a tall white to-go cup.

"On the house," the man says in a high voice. "I'm done for the day. Take a pastry, too. Even the pigeons aren't buying in this shit."

Jeremy looks at the counter, with a spread of pastries, crumbly muffins, a gooey lemon bar wrapped in plastic, croissants, a half sandwich. "Take a couple," the man says, cleaning the nozzle of the milk steamer on his industrial espresso maker.

Jeremy pockets the tuna sandwich, bites into a muffin, tasting cranberry, turns to look back at Perry's.

"A simple thanks would be nice," the man mutters.

Jeremy almost says: I thought you said they were free. Instead he looks back and says: "I really appreciate it." But stops short of a completely human truth: I'm having a really bad day. That would be tantamount to an apology for not saying thanks.

His phone rings. With a mouthful of half-chewed muffin, he fumbles the phone and looks at the screen. A 202 area code. He answers.

"You're late, Atlas."

He swallows, a strategy forming. "You know how it is."

"How what is?"

"Having the weight of the world on your shoulders."

She laughs. "It never fails to amaze me, even surprise me, how you communicate. It's like Ping-Pong," she says. "Volleys, deep shots and chip shots, spin, things that keep the other person off balance, even in the most innocuous exchange. Then the occasional overhead smash. Maybe it's more like Ping-Pong meets chess meets javelin throw."

"New plan, Andrea."

"Case in point." She hesitates. "I like spontaneity."

"It's a little weird."

"Even better."

"I want you to come outside but stay on the phone with me."

Finally, silence. Then: "It's raining."

"When you get out here give the guy your valet ticket."

More silence. He can hear her brain clicking and he can guess what she's thinking: how does he know I parked my car with the valet? It's a logical assumption that I did so, but still. For his part, Jeremy wants to make sure she stays on the phone, that she can't alert someone she might be in cahoots with, whoever that might be, or for whatever reason.

"I'm watching you," Jeremy says.

"What?"

He lets loose a small laugh, to keep her off balance. "I know, Andrea."

She clears her throat. "Okay, you're right."

"About what?"

"This is weird. It's downright kinky."

He has to smile. She's good. She's not giving an inch, just like his mother.

"What happens after I give my ticket to the valet guy?" She pushes open the door at Perry's. She had indeed been the woman at the front, near the maître d' stand. He takes a big slug of coffee, looks around. Is there a place to hide? If not, he'll soon be in plain sight when she starts looking around.

She walks outside, takes a step, then steps back against the building, remaining mildly protected by the blue awning.

"Is that you, a vision in red?"

"I'm down the block, to your right, around the corner."

"Bullshit, Jeremy. I'm looking right at you."

"Are you packing?"

She holds her hands up in the air, the phone away from her head, looking in his direction, as if to say: what the fuck? She brings the phone back to her head.

Jeremy says: "You're not wearing cargo pants so I'm guessing it's in your purse."

"I can't carry a gun on an airplane."

"All the same, I want you to give the valet guy your ticket, put your purse in the trunk and then climb into the passenger seat. Tell the man that he's going to give the keys to your husband."

"Okay, enough. What the hell is going on, Jeremy?"

"Andrea, I know you're lying to me. And I know you want something from me. And if you want it, you're going to have to do it my way."

She hesitates, looking his way, shaking her head.

"I'm leaving," he says.

She sighs. "You're an asshole, Jeremy. You know that. I deserve to be treated better. But then, so do you."

"Meaning?"

"I owe you one. I'm here to pay my debt. But after that I'm done." She gestures to a valet who stands beneath the awning, arms crossed. He hustles over and grabs her ticket, says something into a walkie-talkie. She walks back into the restaurant.

Mere seconds later, the sport utility vehicle with the black tinted windows pulls up. Andrea walks to it, opens the back, puts her purse inside, waves the man off when he offers her the keys and points to Jeremy, who is walking across the street.

She climbs into the passenger seat. Jeremy, having reached the other side of the street, scopes his surroundings, unsure what he's looking for, clicks to power off his phone. He takes the keys of the car, pulls off his rain slicker and hands it and his nearly drained coffee to the bewildered valet, and climbs inside.

Chapter 25

"Y OU'VE CHANGED," Andrea says.

Jeremy adjusts to the light inside the car. He sees the long hair, the preternaturally smooth skin, the overall look of someone who doesn't have to take too many pains to rise from attractive to irresistible but takes pains nonetheless. He tastes her perfume in the back of his throat. She's got a half smile, knowing, practiced, showing perfect white teeth against light brown skin. But her discomfort is betrayed by the tight cross of her arms against her chest, the way she's pulled back against the door, as far as she can get from him. Beneath her blouse, he can picture the blue tattoo. Tipsy, one night, she showed him, a jagged knife starting just above her left breast, pointing at an angle toward her heart and cleavage.

"Not the patsy you remember."

"Your hair. Longer. Nice. And, it's true, you were always more of a counterpuncher. Usually, you'd wait for the slightest provocation before going on the attack. I'd heard through the grapevine that you'd gotten more aggressive but this is an impressive display by any standard."

"Grapevine." He puts the keys into the ignition. Does she mean Evan? He'll draw her out.

She ignores the edgy comment. Just another Jeremy trap. "Where are we going? I don't have all night."

He looks in his hand and discovers he's holding a plastic key, a fob, one of those newfangled deals that let you start the ignition not by inserting it but by merely pressing a button on the car. He presses, and the car purrs to life.

"You owe me. Besides, it's a nice night for a drive."

Jeremy takes in the decked out dashboard, a built-in nav screen, a CD changer, the radio tuned to NPR but with the volume so low it creates only a hum of background chatter.

"Sweet rental for a low-level bureaucrat."

She shrugs, uncrosses her arms. "I'm rolling my eyes. Are you really planning to drive wearing your backpack?"

Blood rushes to his face. Rookie move, so clearly betraying his attachment to his device. And without realizing he'd done it. He slips out of it and nestles it between the back of his legs and his seat.

He pulls into thickening traffic, eliciting a honk. "You were saying."

"What was I saying?"

"You owe me."

"So no foreplay, then. I was hoping we'd have a drink." She clears her throat. "Jeremy, we've always been honest with each other. We talked, and it was real stuff. I always told you what I knew." She pauses. She shifts, sitting straight back but looking out the window into the rain, a faraway look. She turns back and meets his gaze. She has clear blue eyes, their power under-cut with the slightest puffy redness, sleeplessness.

Jeremy turns away, feeling an adrenaline burst he tries not to show. She's going to lay it out for him, whatever it is. Maybe. Something in her voice sounds far less than revelatory. It sounds sincere, even kind. He remembers their rapport, that handful of conversations where he stretched out on the couch in his sleeping gear—boxer shorts, T-shirt, socks—and got lost in the banter. Work talk turned to personal chat, the edges of flirtation, light pokes around the edges of personal matters. He picked up bits of her failed relationships and a childhood that had a painful core she was careful to guard with thick yellow police tape. He felt kinship with her, liked that she was protecting him amid the brass, but also felt an uneasiness. It's not that he didn't trust her intentions, or maybe he did. It was more that he couldn't get comfortable with her emotions. The playfulness excited him, left him feeling challenged, but feeling that he always had to be on, that low-grade intensity was the price of admission in talking to Andrea. With Emily, by contrast, he could be completely at ease or, rather, as much at ease as he could possibly be.

"No foreplay," he says. They've hit a stop light at Howard. Jeremy, eager to get out of the bumper-to-bumper traffic, puts on his blinker. He reminds himself that Andrea lied about Evan. Urges himself to be careful.

"What I'm about to tell you I didn't know. I swear that to you."

He doesn't say anything. He glances in the rearview mirror at the car that followed him onto Howard. A fancy black sedan. Doesn't look suspicious. He sees Andrea glance in the passenger-side mirror. Following his gaze? Suspicious herself? Hoping someone is tagging along?

She continues. "I found out a few weeks ago, or that's when

I began suspecting. But this was my first chance to come out without eliciting a fuss. I came out to—"

He interrupts. "Visit another asset." It's what she'd told him earlier on the phone. He wants to remind her of her lies. Keep her off balance, keep piling up chits.

He hits a patch of cars, guns the powerful engine and slips into the right lane then back into the left. Buys himself half a block of clear sailing. He passes Third Street. Were he to take a left, he realizes, he could soon be at home. He could query the building manager. Needs to. Was it Andrea who will appear on the surveillance tape, busting into his condo?

"I'm sorry," Andrea blurts out.

A sizzle burns through him. Jesus, he thinks, it's the government. They're the ones who have duped my computer and she's here to fess up.

"The maps, the warnings. Unbelievable. Harry."

She shakes her head. She's not understanding him.

Harry. Dead. He's holding that back. Does she know? Will she tip her hand?

"Let's just start with basics. Was Harry involved?"

"With what?"

"Harry introduced us."

"Okay, so?"

"Why?"

"He consulted for us. He helped us understand patterns of conflict. He said you could do the same. You and your computer."

"He wanted to see me go down, right? He felt threatened."

"Jeremy, Harry cherished you, like a son."

Jeremy feels a terrible twitch, grief. Harry, in a pool of his own blood.

"And Evan is involved too. Don't lie to me. I know about you and Evan."

Jeremy flashes on a theory: Evan, starting SEER, a new company that crunches Big Data in order to predict the future, creates the illusion of an impending conflict and then swoops in to save the day and, in the process, lend a helping hand to Jeremy, the mad and incompetent genius with Harry in league. A proof of concept and a marketing coup?

What is SEER? What's Evan up to?

The half-baked theory makes no sense, clears Jeremy's brain as instantly as it appeared. Why would they kill Harry? Had he realized the folly and was he threatening to tell Jeremy the truth? It's all so far-fetched.

"I'm not jockeying for position in this conversation, Jeremy. We can drop the dance. Just hear me out. As it turns out," she starts, pauses, picks up again, "you were not wrong."

"About what?"

"Don't play stupid, Jeremy. This is embarrassing enough. About Al Anbar. And the skirmish at the Afghani-Russian border. Both of them. I had no idea."

He looks at her, then out the window, eyes glazed at the skewed light of urban neon coming through the prism of drizzle. Al Anbar, the Afghani skirmish, the two mini-conflicts that the U.S. military used as a test of the validity of Jeremy and his algorithm. They told him that he and his computer were wrong, that they had miscalculated the length and nature of the conflict.

"You weren't wrong," she repeats. "Put another way, Jeremy, you were right. Your computer was right. You, it—your computer—correctly identified when those conflicts would end, with, frankly, eerie accuracy. Almost like you had a crystal ball."

He realizes he's holding his breath. He blinks, hot tears in his eyes. He repeats the words in his head. Did he hear right? He forces himself to pick out an object through the window. It's an umbrella, being unfurled by a tall woman in a long, shiny raincoat standing next to an ATM.

He feels a pulsing around his clavicle. He puts his hand on his shoulder, suddenly, momentarily, grateful for the pain. It says to him: you are here and this is not a dream.

"Jeremy, we had our reasons. . . ." She pauses. "Not me. I didn't know. I suppose *they* had their reasons. That's a lot of power you had that we didn't understand. It was, is, a potential game-changer. Understandable enough, right? That's what I thought too. But I think it's something else."

She's not making sense. But it doesn't matter. Jeremy's finally getting a grip on the conversation. He turns to her. "I was right? I was right?!" Not a question; an accusation.

"I shouldn't have said anything. I just—"

"Bullshit!"

She puts up her hands, surrender, and a primal show of defense.

"I know things haven't worked out for you. But I thought you should know what happened. Maybe there's some way we can work together in the future. I don't know. I'm in way over my head here."

Someplace, in a faraway corner of his brain, he hears a piercing noise, a honking. He looks down at his white-knuckled fists gripping the wheel. Honk. He's at a green light, cars piling up behind him. HOOOONKK.

He puts his left hand over his right because it keeps him from reaching out and grabbing Andrea. I was right?

"When I started to piece this together I figured they just

didn't want a computer nerd to know more than they did but it's not that. It's something else. To be honest, I'm not sure they ever gave a damn about you and your computer."

He waves her down with a hand. Shut up, shut up! If the computer was right before, then is it right now?

"It's about something else? Like what? What do you mean they didn't give a damn about me and the computer?"

"I don't know."

"I don't believe you," he roars. "It's a trap, a game."

Jeremy pictures Evan coming out of her car. Too many co-incidences; how can he now, suddenly, take her confession at face value?

Honk. Finally, he punches the accelerator. She continues: "Why would I make up something this embarrassing? Jeremy, please, I can appreciate the skepticism. You've gotten the run-around. So have I. Believe me."

The sound of her voice makes him want to scream. He paws his pocket, feels his cell phone, making sure it's there. He pictures Emily, her hair half covering her face, sees Kent. What's he supposed to do; call her? Warn her? Say what? *Emily, you and Kent should arrange transport to the moon, just in case.*

In case of what, Jeremy?

The end of the world.

Or maybe, for whatever reason, the government is playing with him—piling lie on lie. Does it have the capacity to mess with his algorithm? Probably, but why? What could its incentive possibly be?

"Give me your phone," he says.

"Um, no."

"Fuck you. Log cabin."

"What?"

"What's the log cabin?"

"I saw him, Andrea. Evan. I saw you and Evan."

"What?"

He looks at Andrea. She brings a thumb to her mouth.

"Everything connects together, somehow, all of you. It's in the V, on Harry's desk, with the numbers. In the computer."

"It's in the computer? What is?"

"Harry's dead. But you know that."

"What?" Pause. "Harry Ives?"

Jeremy spits a foul half laugh, opens the door. He starts running.

Chapter 26

HEAD DOWN AGAINST the wind, he dashes away from the car and into the oncoming drizzle. Navigates a handful of damp commuters coming the other way. He runs on. Brain searing, like an iron pan that's been too long on the stove. Too hot to be useful. One thought predominates: keep the backpack out of the rain, protect the iPad from the wet and cold.

Hence his direction. Into the wind.

The iPad, the computer, the algorithm. It was right.

He glances over his shoulder and sees Andrea's big car heading in the opposite direction, or trying to, absorbed in traffic, stymied. Good, right? He had to get away from her but, if only he could've kept his cool, he had a captive audience, someone who knew something. He needs to look her in the eye and go point by point, assertion by assertion, lie by lie.

Does she know what the computer is telling him? That the whole world explodes in, what, twenty-four hours?

Is that the real reason why she's here?

"Easy there."

The voice belongs to a pedestrian he's nearly collided with.

He skids on the brakes, does a half spin, stopping short of three smokers huddled outside the bar, impervious to the chill. He catches eyes with another smoker, guy with droopy jowls. Guy flicks his cigarette, coughs, half nods, emphysema-laughs. "You okay, pal?" Adds: "You know it's a rough day when a smoker asks if you're doing okay."

Jeremy starts running again, his legs churning in erratic rhythm with his frantic mind, shuffling and tossing puzzle pieces. Harry, dead; Evan, mysteriously appeared; Andrea, conceding his computer was right; log cabin; AskIt.

At the end of the block, Jeremy passes a shuttered sandwich shop, turns left, leans up against the concrete, barely registering the fact that, far from protecting himself from the weather by pressing up against the wall, he remains exposed to the direction of the wind and wet. The drizzle has intensified, now just shy of real rain. To his right, a tall man in a long jacket comes across the intersection, walking Jeremy's way. The man's face is down, shadowed. At the corner, the man looks up and Jeremy flinches, a threat in every glance.

Jeremy looks left, sees an opening between the building he's leaning against and the one next to it, an alley, a refuge.

He slips inside it, sidestepping a homeless man who seems fully passed out, wrapped in a sleeping bag, covered in refuse. The man mutters something, rolls over. Jeremy winces at the stench of spoiled milk and dry leaves. He steps backward, bumping into the bottom rungs of a fire escape.

He closes his eyes. All the questions and disparate pieces of evidence fall away and he pictures Emily. Just at this moment, he can see her putting the broccoli crowns in front of Kent, cajoling him to eat *just one, just one, please,* allowing him to talk her into letting him instead eat only mac-'n'-cheese for the four-hundredth night in a row. Then he hears her voice, talking to Jeremy. I'm done. He knows she means it. Done with his nonsense. He instantly feels why. As soon as something gets close to great, even just good, he attacks it. Not just with her, with Kent. The fight they had, over the puzzle. Why was he trying to outflank a little boy in a conversation about how best to solve a cardboard puzzle of a rocket ship?

What's the point of saving the world?

Jeremy shakes off the pointless image, and question. He opens his eyes. He pulls his phone from his pocket. He needs . . . who? Nik, the police? Demand answers from Evan? Isn't that Peckerhead's office nearby? So what? Would he even be there? Jeremy goes to the list of his most recent calls. Presses Nik's number. It rings and rings. No answer. Into his assistant's voice mail: "I need your help." Click. He looks up, sees in the distance a foggy horizon, vapors and mist swirling around the apartment complexes on the skyline, near the ballpark. He thinks he makes out his own apartment building in the mist.

Was it Andrea who busted into his apartment? Evan?

Took his knife and stabbed Harry.

Jeremy paws in his back pocket for his wallet and pulls from it a business card, the one belonging to his building manager. He dials the number on it.

After the first ring, a pickup. "Aaron Isaacs."

"Did you get the security tapes?"

A brief pause, the fuckface getting his bearings. "Glad you called, Mr. Stillwater."

"Did you get the tapes?"

"I got permission to go through them. I'm not entirely sure what to look for but I started looking." He pauses.

"Hello?"

"A lot of people go in and out of the building—"

"Anyone in the middle of the night looking like they might want to play Jack the Ripper with my couch?" Jeremy asks.

"I don't much like the tone."

This is actually, Jeremy realizes, exactly what he's hoping for.

"Are you sure you were looking at the security tapes and not just spending another afternoon eating Cracker Jacks and watching Oxygen?"

There's a silence. Then, calmly: "Mr. Stillwater, why don't you come down here and check them out for yourself? Maybe you'll be able to find what you're looking for."

"I just insulted you by saying you watch girl TV in the afternoons and eat junk food. Did I mention I suspect you jack off watching women on the front-door security camera?"

"Look, I know you're frustrated—"

"The cops are there." Must be following the evidence, looking for Harry's killer.

A tiny silence, then: "You're being very paranoid, Mr. Stillwater."

"Tell them I didn't do it."

"What?"

Click.

No cops.

Something compels Jeremy to look up. He sees the woman.

She's standing across the street, at a bus stop, covered by a thick plastic shell, bathed in the murky yellow neon of a McDonald's. She's thin, shapely, arms crossed, familiar. It's the woman from the bar last night and the Embarcadero. His stalker. She's looking at Jeremy, not making the slightest effort to hide her interest in him.

He bellows: "What the fuck do you want?!"

The words barely register. They get swallowed by the wind and a bus pulling up across the street, its broad side momentarily blocking Jeremy's sight of his stalker. On the bus's side, a lengthwise ad shows a woman sitting in an expansive plain, surrounded by exotic animals, a zebra, wildebeest, elephant, monkey. She holds an iPad. The ad copy reads: "With an iPad, you're King of the Jungle."

"Jesus." It's the homeless guy, turning over in his refuse. "Find your own spot."

Jeremy stuffs his phone into his pocket and steps out of the mouth of the alley. He waits for a car to pass on his side of the street, then begins sprinting as the bus departs. When it disappears, Jeremy sees the woman has too.

He's standing in the middle of the street, looking around, as near as he can be to being frantic. He looks in the parking lot of the McDonald's. A roadster pulls out, an old Fiat. It's not the woman. Nor does it appear she's in the window of the restaurant. Nor up and down the block. She could've gotten onto the bus. She could've slipped into a car. She could, Jeremy thinks, be a figment of my imagination.

He puts his head back, looks up into the drizzle. He hears tires skid on the pavement. From the far corner of the McDonald's lot, a midsize car appears, a dark tinted sedan.

Gaining speed.

Heading right for Jeremy.

The car swerves out of the McDonald's lot. Twenty feet away, ten. Jeremy dives left. A full sprawl. The car misses him by inches. His body smacks into the wet pavement, skids. Brakes screech. Jeremy rolls. Springs up, swivels. Ready to dive again. Sees the sedan drive off.

He tries to shout, or wants to shout: "Stop! Police!" But he can't get anything out. The car takes a left. Jeremy wants to run. His hands ache. Is something broken?

"I got the license plate."

Jeremy turns and sees that the voice belongs to the homeless guy who'd been sleeping in the alley. He looks half bent at the waist, a lifetime of tragedy bearing down on him. He's got wet newspaper stuck to his body.

"F-L . . . something. It started with an F and an L. And then . . . . there was a seven in there." He shakes his head. "Sorry, man. It's bullshit out here." He turns to the alley.

"I've seen it before."

The same car he saw outside the subway earlier in the day, driven by the same stalker, the thin woman.

"Are you okay?" he hears a voice say.

A handful of people have trickled from McDonald's, peering at the guy in the middle of the street having narrowly avoided a hit-and-run. Jeremy somehow recalls that San Francisco has the state's highest rate of accidents involving cars hitting pedestrians and bicyclists; it has something to do with San Francisco being both a driving and a walking city.

This was no accident.

He brushes himself off. His hand burns, skid marks, embedded gravel. He can feel eyes on him, bystanders. But he's lost in thought. A thousand inputs pouring into his brain. That woman at the bus stop, the car, and, oddly, the image on the side of the bus—a woman with an iPad turning into the king of the jungle, a lion.

Something about lions. The computer said something about lions. That's important. He reaches for the idea, can't grasp it.

"Sir, you want me to call an ambulance?"

Jeremy shakes his head at the distant voice, no. I'm okay. Ideas, images are circling his brain, his brush with the pavement jostling things together in a new way. AskIt. The computer? He's struck with an idea, something he can ask the algorithm. He needs a wi-fi network. Someplace to pull out his iPad and keyboard.

He wipes away drizzle from his forehead, ambles to the sidewalk, sits on a bench at the bus stop.

A stout black car takes a left from the street, kitty-corner. The car pulls in front of Jeremy and stops.

CHAPTER 27

THE WINDOW OF the black car slides down. Andrea leans over from the driver's seat.

"Get in, Jeremy."

He stands.

"Jesus, Are you okay? What happened?" Now she's looking him up and down.

Jeremy's palms burn with embedded gravel from his dive and skid.

"Country codes," he says.

"What?"

"They're country codes!"

"Did you hit your head?"

Jeremy says: "Get out."

"I'm sorry, Atlas. I should've told you earlier . . . I didn't know. I didn't realize that you'd—"

"Get out!"

He reaches for the door handle. He sees Andrea recoil inside. He pulls on the door. It's locked. He reaches inside. He can feel the interest of a small crowd. He hears someone call for the police.

"I'm driving," he says.

"What just happened? Your shirt . . . your face . . ."

He reaches inside for the door lock, groping.

"Please move over and let me drive. You owe me."

"You're right."

"You told me already," Jeremy says. "Move over. You owe me."

"You're right. Harry's dead." She says it in a loud whisper, suggesting her awareness of the crowd. "It's on the news now. No details. Heart attack?"

He glowers at her, doesn't answer. He turns his back, bee-lines for the sidewalk, starts walking. Ten steps later, she's pulled up next to him.

"Get in," she says through the rolled-down passenger window.

He's still walking. She inches along with him. "You're in no condition to drive."

He hears sirens, maybe someone called in the near hit-and-run. He laughs. "Fine." He stops and turns to her. "But I am in a condition to use the phone."

"What?"

"You drive. I get your phone."

"You don't have a phone?"

"Battery's dead."

She grits her teeth. She reaches into a compartment be-tween the seats and pulls out her smartphone. She tosses it onto the passenger seat. She presses a button to unlock the door as Jeremy climbs inside.

"What just happened?" she repeats.

"You tell me." He looks in the rearview mirror, sees the small crowd, losing interest. "First and Howard."

She hits the accelerator. "Which is where? And what?"

He squints his eyes, thinking, trying to remember something. Evan's office; there's one on the peninsula, obviously, and one nearby.

"Straight ahead and then left. The offices of SEER, but you know all about that."

"Jeremy—" After a pause, she says: "Who are you calling?"

He doesn't answer. On her iPhone, he does a Google search: "Country codes." As it loads, he pulls from his back pocket the piece of paper onto which he's copied Harry's symbol and the numbers: 972, 970, 7, 41, 212, 986, 86, 218-650.

He looks at the list of country codes delivered him via Google. The numbers correspond:

```
Israel
Ramallah, the West Bank
Russia
Switzerland
Morocco
Syria
China
```

"I figured something out."

"What?"

"Country codes. All but the last one. 218-650. The one at the point of the V."

"Again: what?" Less frustration in her voice than resignation; she's long since been accustomed to Jeremy's communication style, working things out in his head as he goes, chess in every exchange, the stuff of a halting, sparring conversation.

"It's the important one, I think. The connection. The Middle East at the top." Jeremy looks at Andrea, stuck in thought. Country codes. So what? What does the symbol mean?

Andrea says: "You realize you only figure things out when you're in a screaming match."

He blinks again.

"I used to get you riled up when we talked, prick at you, get you fired up. You'd have searing insights. Conflict suits you, Jeremy."

"Take a right."

"It's how you communicate, like the other person is simultaneously foe and sounding board."

She turns onto Howard. Traffic's decidedly thinned, downtown, the business district, closing for the night. A lone taxi hurtles in the other direction. Jeremy can't believe what he's thinking: Harry was involved with something, instigating something? A conflict? Why? So he could then predict it, stop it, be the hero, prove that he's the world's greatest conflict sleuth.

C'mon, Jeremy, he thinks to himself, even you can't be that egocentric.

"What's 'log cabin'?"

Andrea swallows. She says: "We had an affair. But you know that."

"You and Evan."

Andrea blinks. She looks up at the long block ahead.

"Where are we . . ." She pauses.

"I assume you're familiar with Evan's offices. Pull over."

The building is on the right side of the street, taking up nearly half the block. It's a checkerboard of dark and light, three-quarters of the offices shut down, mixed in with squares of workaholics, crashing and caffeinated entrepreneurs and litigators. Without further prompting, in silence, Andrea pulls up in front of the maroon-hued structure, with a marblelike exterior and revolving doors leading to a grand entrance, like the hallway to a train station. Inside, behind a desk, a lonely security guard, reading.

"Okay." Jeremy's response, finally, is distant, noncommittal. As if to sarcastically say: whatever you say, Andrea.

"Not an affair. One night. After one of those ridiculous parties, where you played the reluctant straw-that-stirs-the-drink. But Evan couldn't let go, that night. Regardless, it's irrelevant, one night. And not your business."

Jeremy looks up at the building. Not sure which office is Evan's or if he'll be there. Getting past the security guard is tougher than it looks, Jeremy knows. Condensation obscures the heavy glass windows and doors.

Andrea puts her hand on Jeremy's knee, withdraws it. "Please listen."

Jeremy half looks at her, acceding, looks away.

"Why are you here?"

"To tell you the truth." She pauses. "And because I'm feeling used."

He feels suddenly, totally exhausted. How long has it been since he slept, or slept well? He glances at her phone in his hand, wanting to restart. He paws the list of "recent calls."

He can see that she received several calls earlier in the day from Evan, placed several calls herself to both Evan and Jstillwater, received several calls from blocked numbers, placed a handful to a number in the 703 area code. He hits the number. Puts the phone to his ear.

"I have nothing to hide from you but this is beyond inappropriate."

Ring, ring, ring. Voice mail picks up. "You've reached Lavelle. I'm unavailable." Then a beep.

Jeremy racks his brain.

"The big shot," he says.

"Lieutenant Colonel Thomson."

Andrea's boss, the big boss. The guy who sat at the end of the table at the Pentagon and told Jeremy that his technology didn't work promised Jeremy he could go overseas to test his technology against real, battlefield conditions, and then never followed through.

"Lavelle is an odd first name." An instinctive jab. "You're pretty anxious to reach the boss. He's not picking up."

She doesn't answer.

"I'll need the car keys."

"Why?"

"Because I don't want you to leave me here and I need to go tell Evan that I'm going to the press and the police."

"You're the one that told me to get in touch with Evan."

"What?"

"Your email, earlier today, after we talked."

He looks at her: no, I didn't email you.

"You asked me to contact Evan. Said it was important."

"Bullshit." Then: "Someone's been inside my computer."

He looks at her again. She shakes her head. Great acting or she has no idea what he's talking about.

"Jeremy, we're allowed to have lives of our own."

"What?"

"A lot of people gravitated to you because of your work; that much is true. I know that was heady, being in the middle of a big conversation. The investors and entrepreneurs and military folks and academics. But we were allowed to have our own lives, our own conversations."

He's feeling plainly mystified. It dawns on him, clearly, he's got to establish some common ground with her, some vernacular. He's got to overcome his instinct to keep her off balance. Even if she's lying to him—presumably she is lying to him—he's not grounded enough with her to understand how to even poke around for the truth. They're conversing on different planes; the pronouns, even, may reference different people.

"What's Evan doing? What's SEER, the new venture?" Jeremy recalls looking earlier at Evan's web site, seeing his partners, big names, like Google, Intel, Sun Microsystems, the major hardware and software players in the Valley, a who's who. Something about the list tugs at Jeremy, but he can't figure out what.

Andrea shrugs.

"The same companies buying tantalum!" He exclaims it, and then wishes he hadn't.

"C'mon, Jeremy. Make some sense."

"Tell me the truth, about your sudden reappearance in my life."

The glass doors of the office building revolve. Two women stride out, forcefully, ambitious strides of strivers. No umbrellas, impervious to anything but the market forces, which they can fully appreciate.

From here Jeremy can see if Evan leaves the building. Or if he goes in, which is more likely. Maybe he's still at that mysterious meeting downtown. Maybe he engineered Jeremy being run over; why? Nothing makes sense.

He reaches into his backpack. He pulls out the iPad and he pulls out the attachable, external keyboard.

"I'm telling you: I've been used too, Jeremy."

"Cute." He doesn't even look up. He's connecting the keyboard. The iPad comes to life. He withdraws to the door and glances, privately, at the map, the clock.

24:25:00.

"Spare me the sympathy ploy and tell me the part about how and why the government lied to us."

Andrea furrows a brow, not getting what he means, then sees he's typing on the computer. Us. He and it.

"I didn't know, Jeremy. I swear to the ends of the Earth."

"Curious word choice. Expecting the world to end?"

"Focus, Jeremy. Let me answer your question about why I'm here." She pauses, inhales, exhales. "When your paper came out, when you got all that notoriety, what, a couple of years ago, my bosses asked me to look into the validity of your findings. I made a report. Told them it seemed interesting if nascent. You joined the list of various conversation topics at various meetings. Y'know, Lavelle, the lieutenant colonel, would run down the agenda items, and every few months he'd check in with me about whether you seemed legitimate and whether you'd made any more progress with the technology."

Jeremy waves his hand. Meaning: speed forward. Something catches his eye. He looks up at the building's revolving doors. A man exits and gets slightly bent back by the wind.

"You know that distracted driving kills thousands of people each year," Andrea says.

"We're parked."

"You can't focus on two things at once, let alone three. I'm laying it out for you. Least you could do is pay full attention."

He just smirks.

"Eventually, they asked me to make contact."

Andrea tells Jeremy what she's told him several times before, in their early meetings. They told her they wanted to know if this kind of Big Data analysis—the latest new, new thing in Silicon Valley—might be applicable to war modeling. Could they predict conflict? Its onset? What might a computer see that gaggles of West Point studs, armed with mountains of historical analogues, could not?

"They warned me you were prickly."

"Was I as prickly as your other assets?"

"If you're trying to test my truthfulness, you already know you were my first asset, such as that word really means: guy who might be able to help us. This is not spy shit, Jeremy. It's bureaucratic shit."

Jeremy again turns the iPad so only he can see it. Eyes the map, sees the red appears to be spreading. The initial attack begetting others, a domino effect in a nuclear era. He swipes away the screen and calls up the algorithm menu, the heart of the conflict algorithm software. It asks for a password.

Jeremy reaches a finger beneath the silver chain hanging around his neck and pulls it over his head, freeing the key fob. In the process, he gets a whiff of himself, the ripe scent of stress and exhaustion. It triggers his awareness of the pulsing in his temples. He needs caffeine if he's not going to get sleep.

The key fob changes its nine-digit number every ten seconds. It shows a new number now. Jeremy types it in, followed by his password. An hourglass appears on the window, the algorithm innards materializing.

"The rest is what meets the eye, Jeremy. I recruited you, we had you in to talk, we ran the tests, they didn't work out, we parted ways."

He looks up at her.

"You were after my computer."

"I told you that."

"No." He's eyeing the device, touches the fob.

"You tinkered with the computer. When I first came to Washington to meet at the Pentagon. You and I had a drink, remember? In the hotel."

"Yes, but, no. I didn't tinker with your computer."

"When I got back to my room, someone had monkeyed with it."

"You're making this up as you go."

"Yeah, maybe. This is totally unwieldy."

"What is?"

"I can't work here." He taps his fingers on the tablet. He needs Nik. Where the fuck is Nik? He should be up at this hour watching infomercials and snacking and waiting for Jeremy to call with an inane administrative request. Jeremy suppresses a moment of panic: what if they've come after Nik too?

He looks at the computer, and realizes he's ready. He knows now for certain what he wants to ask it, what he's fairly sure it can answer. It's the idea he heard earlier—about asking the computer to delve deeper into the conflict variables and tell him which are the ones most likely leading to an attack. He thinks he knows *how* to ask it.

"I want to assure you of something, Jeremy."

"Which is what?"

"We promised you we'd run a field test, then strung you along. I can tell you, with complete and utter confidence, they worked their asses off to make that happen. I got the calls myself, once in the middle of the night: 'Call Stillwater tomorrow and tell him we're a go for this weekend.' They were damn serious. Or they gave me that impression . . ." Her voice seems to trail off.

Jeremy turns back to his computer. Starts to, then notices a rectangular plastic card standing on its edge in a small open compartment in the dashboard, next to the left edge of the radio, the place you'd store parking quarters or mints.

She says: "Yes, I have a hotel for the night. The International. Not far from here. I lied. I don't have a flight."

"So you have a flight, or you don't have a flight. You hated Evan, or had an affair with him. We were wrong or we were right. You are Santa. Or are the Easter Bunny."

She half laughs.

He looks at the screen, the control deck of the algorithm. The guts. He thinks: I've got a question for you, my friend. He puts his fingers on the external keyboard and taps rhythmically.

"I don't think they were ever serious."

He blinks, trying to sort out too many inputs with a tired brain. "About sending me on a field test."

"About you or your computer. I don't think they gave a damn about some wonk and his algorithm. I think it was about something else. Maybe they were testing me. Maybe he was testing me."

He looks at the hotel card, back at the computer.

"Lavelle," she clarifies.

"I know what else I can ask it."

"What are you talking about?"

Jeremy's thinking of Program Princip, his latest innovation, represented by the icon in the top right of the algorithm's menu.

Could Jeremy use it to identify who to trust? Could he plug into it the names of Andrea and Lieutenant Colonel Lavelle Thomson, Harry Ives, Evan Tigeson? Could Jeremy discover which of them is the functional equivalent of Gavrilo Princip, the bit player turned assassin who ignited World War I?

Could it identify which of the bit players in Jeremy's life is dangerous, even deadly, maybe contributing to impending apocalypse?

He puts his fingers on the keyboard. Tap, tapping them.

"I need to use your room."

CHAPTER 28

TWENTY MINUTES LATER, they've parked and settled into the International. It's vaguely Japanese themed, stone and marble, reds and blacks, double-tall glass revolving doors that lead to an expansive lobby, more marble, wood carvings and sculptured bonsai trees.

In the elevator, there's a television—screens everywhere—showing news headlines. A surfer with a permit to carry a concealed weapon shot the zoo lion walking along an ocean beach.

"Crazy story," Andrea says. "Tragic."

There's a related news nugget: bloggers report that a man found dead outside the San Diego Zoo, alleged to have set free a lion there, had two tattoos: one, previously reported, of a lion standing on hind legs, and a second tattoo. One word: *Custos.*

"It's Latin," Jeremy says.

"What?"

"Guardian."

Andrea's not following. "I'm all for animal rights. But give me a break."

The elevator door opens to the twelfth floor. In the room on the twelfth floor, Jeremy asks for her phone but she scoffs.

Jeremy says: "I can't have you calling in my coordinates for a strike."

"You're right that Evan's a peckerhead. But *he's* right that you not only think there's a target on your back, you keep pasting one there hoping people will shoot."

She plops on the bed. In spite of himself, everything, he watches the black skirt inch up above her knee when she sits down. He sits at the desk. His back to her. Stands again and settles in a stiff armchair, paisley patterned, near the window. As he pulls out his iPad, he catches her giving it a look.

It's remarkable to him that she's been this pliant, going along with him. Hard to believe that she'd be this accommodating just because she feels guilty for having lied to him. There's something else going on. She wants something.

On the car ride over, she'd told him that, over the last month, she'd grown suspicious, broadly, about something going on in her office. Lots of chatter, quiet meetings, she'd been left out. She did a little snooping around. She recalled for Jeremy one particular meeting where she asked if she was being left out because she'd somehow messed things up on the conflict algorithm, her one big assignment. A midlevel military manager had laughed. No, he told her, that wasn't a big deal. It hadn't been a serious attempt to predict the future. In fact, the guy said, Jeremy had been right, his computer dead-on accurate. But there'd been no point in going further with it. Really, the guy had smirked, you think we were going to entrust our war modeling to some angry geek with an iPhone?

She told Jeremy she'd been seething. It had been an affront to him, and her. What had been the point, she'd asked the guy, of going to all the trouble? He shrugged. "We spend money on stuff."

She said she'd marched right into the lieutenant colonel's office. She demanded to know why she'd been used, forced to lie, her time wasted. Simple, he said: not everything here works out, and the lies had a simple, brain-dead origin: no sense in giving an angry Silicon Valley know-it-all the sense that he understood war better than the Pentagon. In a world like this— where everyone can make a case on the Internet, and every case made on the Internet can affect funding and congressional decisions—it didn't pay to have a second-guesser like Jeremy running loose.

In the hotel room, Andrea fluffs a pillow, puts it behind her back, so she's sitting upright, looking at him.

"Lavelle is like a father to me," Andrea had said.

Jeremy's trying to focus on the iPad screen.

"You hated your father." Jeremy remembers she'd had a mixed relationship with her father, a fire-and-brimstone blue-collar worker in northern Idaho.

"Loved him but questioned what drove him. Same with Lavelle. Look, Jeremy, I've been forthright with you. It's your turn."

He doesn't dignify it with a response, not at first. He wants to talk to his computer. Finally, though: "How have you been used?"

"I'm honestly not sure."

It seems sincere.

"What do you know about tantalum?"

She shakes her head.

"It's a precious metal used to make cell phones."

She shrugs.

"How about Rosoboronexport?"

"Russia's state-controlled arms dealer?"

"It's a big deal."

"General Electric plus Honeywell plus Lockheed, and then some. Why?"

"It's been in the news lately."

She nods. "One of their former execs, the chairman, got arrested in Paris."

"You follow this stuff closely."

She gives him a look: gimme a break. It's her job, like someone at Morgan Stanley following the Dow Jones Industrial Average. Then she says: "Tax evasion. But I wouldn't buy it."

Jeremy perks up. "He was arrested for some other reason?"

"I honestly have no idea. Rosoboronexport is scary as hell. The company makes and sells massive amounts of weaponry, traditional and nuclear. In a sense, that was once relatively comforting, the idea that a big authoritarian government had everything under one roof. But as Russia has ebbed and flowed between authoritarian and quasi-democratic-slash-capitalistic, this huge company has sprung leaks. Individual entrepreneurs have emerged, taking pieces of the technology, selling off assets, even aligning with rogue nations."

For a moment, Jeremy is caught up in Andrea, substance and style.

"Maybe the former chairman has gone, to use your word, rogue." He sees her eyes briefly go to the backpack.

She looks up again, flushes. "Is that what your computer thinks?"

"Why do you ask that?" Pointed.

"Don't start, Jeremy."

He doesn't respond.

"We're finally having a real conversation. I'd rather not start sparring again."

"Then just tell me why you're here, plainly."

"I've told you. I owe you the truth."

Jeremy straightens; something passes over his face. He looks dead at her. "Get naked and start to do jumping jacks."

"I beg your pardon."

"You know you wanted me, someone like me, to dominate you. All those nights on the phone, jockeying, flirting. You were waiting for me to take charge."

She grits her teeth.

"Just topless and push-ups."

She blinks.

He shrugs. "I'm seeing how much bullshit you'll endure," he says. "You want something and until you tell me what and why, I'm going to play my iPad close to the vest. And until then, we can go along like we always have, with one of us in bed wondering when and whether the other's going to join in." Momentary pause. "Give me your phone."

"No."

"Have a nice nap."

He stands, takes his gear and walks to the bathroom. Turns around, walks to the minibar, grabs a handful of shit, nuts and cookies and an orange sugar drink. Back inside the bathroom, he locks the door, settles in on the marble floor. Screw Andrea. He can cuddle up with his computer. In the guts of the algorithm, he clicks on a command line: "nstd.exe." He hits copy. Then he clicks and drops a copy of the program into a box at the bottom right of the screen labeled "rmt server." The remote server. Jeremy hates putting a copy in the cloud, in the storage space he rents in some Google data center. He doesn't like anyone, even as secure a company as Google, having access to his secrets.

But he's got to make sure he's got a clean copy of his algorithm's brain before he starts doing surgery.

A message bar appears: "copying. Est time: 9 minutes, 22 sec."

Jeremy minimizes the box, then decides to wait until the copying is done before he tinkers. While he waits, he thinks about what the computer has already told him.

War is imminent because of a change to: weather; shipments of tantalum; lions loosed from zoos; arrest of a Russian arms dealer; changes to conflict rhetoric in Russia, North Korea, North Korea, Mexico, Congo and the Fertile Crescent.

Now he has time to ask the questions he'd been thinking about earlier: Which of the variables is most telling? If the weather had remained constant, would the computer still predict war? What if the conflict rhetoric in Russia had remained steady, not worsened?

He can ask the computer those questions. He can ask it to run simulations that hold some variables steady and allow others to change, just as they've changed in the real world. Mix and match and change the circumstances to see which variable stands out, which is allegedly the one responsible for the projection of war.

Nine variables: heightened conflict language in five regions, diminished war talk in the Fertile Crescent, increase shipments of tantalum, changing weather, the arrest of the Russian billionaire arms dealer.

The number of possible outcomes: 362,880.

Child's play.

The computer is done copying the file. He sets the iPad down next to him. Stands up, glances in the mirror, nearly recoils. Hollow eyes, sunken cheeks, an Edvard Munch painting.

He splashes water on his face. Rubs the towel hard to dry

himself, spur adrenaline. He opens the bathroom door and peeks outside.

Andrea's eyes are closed, arms crossed over her chest. Asleep. Asleep? She's beautiful. He wants to be next to her, but not in sweaty entangle; asleep too.

He closes the door, locks it, sits back down. Puts his fingers on the keyboard. And he becomes a blur. He's typing and thinking at equal speeds, lightning.

Ninety minutes later, he looks over his creation, the product of a nonstop frenzy of human processing. It's a sea of hash marks and commands, brackets and if-then statements. He looks at the blinking cursor at the bottom. "Not fucking bad." He hits enter, initiating the inquiry.

He stands, wants to wash his face again. Wobbles with exhaustion. Sits back down. It's nearly 1 A.M.

He checks the door of the bathroom, makes sure it's locked. He pulls out the bloody scrawl.

A V, an upside-down triangle, numbers.

Log cabin.

AskIt.

Beware Peace.

Or Beware the Peace.

What did Harry say?

Beware Peace, and then it seemed that he was going to add something.

Jeremy feels his eyes closing. He forces them open, rolls his neck in a circle. He stares up at the vent on the ceiling, wishing for a blast of cold air. He looks down at the computer, does a search on Google News for "tantalum." He's looking for the press release that explains how Silicon Valley companies, some consortium, have bought up a bunch of future tantalum contracts. He finds the link to the story. Clicks on it. It reads: link broken.

"What the hell?"

He searches again, tries other search terms, related ones. Nothing comes up. The story is no longer there.

He stares at the screen, disbelief and exhaustion. His head lolls to the right. The next thing he sees is Kent. Unkempt hair, footsy pajamas, a puzzle piece in his hand.

CHAPTER 29

"IT'S A NINE." The boy holds it up in the air.

"Why not a six?"

The boy shrugs. "Well, let's just put all the numbers together and we can figure it out later."

Jeremy looks at the jumble of puzzle pieces on the shorthair carpet. It's not a rocket ship. It's nothing, just pieces.

"Look for the corner pieces, Kent. And the ones that go along the sides. Pieces with straight sides."

"I want to put the numbers together, and the letters. They go together. I figured out the dinosaur puzzle all by myself. You were wrong about the rocket ship. We should also find all the colors and put them into a pile."

Jeremy puts the toe of a scuffed brown loafer into the pile of pieces, moving them about; he can't recall a puzzle this complex. Where's the top of the box? He needs to know what picture they're even trying to create. He looks at the base of the reddish armoire; it's not there. Where is Emily? He thinks he hears voices in the other room. One sounds so familiar but he can't place it.

He looks down a darkened hallway. Someone standing in the darkness. Something. A creature.

He looks at the boy. "No point in grouping by color. Almost all the pieces are red. Corners and sides."

"Why do we always have to do it your way?"

He looks at Kent. The boy now has a mustache and stands nearly six feet. He blinks and Kent is himself again, adorable and boyish, red and blue pajamas with baseballs.

"Kent, we don't have to do it my way. We have to do it the right way. If you want to do it the wrong way, then you may as well do everything the wrong way. Good way to get a great fast-food job. You can put the Kent in Kentucky Fried Chicken."

"The world doesn't have corners. It's a circle. Besides, I'm the one that recognized the colors of the bridge."

Jeremy looks near the boy's pajama-clad feet. A pile of puzzle pieces with letters, combining to make words. One of them combined into an arch. Wait, no, the span of a bridge?

"Bad logic. Just because something doesn't have corners doesn't mean it can't have sides."

"For goodness' sake, Jeremy, why can't he be right?"

Jeremy startles at the sound of the woman's voice. Seized with fear of recognition, he turns slowly around Emily's living room to find out where it is coming from. He turns his gaze from the armoire to the futon couch, the scratched end table bought at the secondhand store from that woman with the vulture's pose. He stops on the antique chair next to the front window.

He sees her, holding a box in her hand.

"You're dead," he says to his mother.

"Oh really," she says, and smiles. "Then how come I'm looking right at me?"

Kent lets out a hysterical laugh.

"She thinks you look like an old woman."

"That's not what she—" Jeremy pauses. Looks at his mother, her flowing gray curls, the blue hospice gown. "You have the puzzle box."

"I do."

"Show it to me."

She looks at the cover. "That won't make you happy."

"Mom, this is serious. This is about the end of the world. This is about—"

There's a low growl. It's coming from the other side of the room. In the darkened hallway. Jeremy looks up. Something in the shadows.

"A lion."

"Calm down, Jeremy."

"Mom, listen!"

"You're losing your cool."

"Give me the fucking box."

Kent laughs. "Mom, Jeremy just said 'fucking'!"

"Let yourself love them, Jeremy."

Jeremy sighs. He hears a pounding noise. It's the front door. Someone frantic to get in.

"Wake up, Jeremy," his mother says. "You're almost out of time."

"To save the world?"

His mother smiles. It's so tender, angelic, a smile he's never in his life seen from her.

Bang, bang, bang.

"I've seen that bridge before."

"Wake up!" she implores.

Jeremy startles. Bang, bang, bang. He's awake. A succession of thoughts. The numbers, the bridge.

He knows where he's seen that bridge. Exactly that view.

Dry air courses into his nostrils, a shrill feeling bordering on painful from having slept inhaling recirculated air. How long did he sleep? The sharp artificial light in the bathroom burns his eyes. He vigorously shakes his head, willing the blood there.

He hears the voices. Outside in the hotel bedroom. He's still locked in the bathroom. Andrea, presumably, is still outside. The TV, or is she no longer alone?

CHAPTER 30

E LI, RISE."

He's been dreaming. The van smells like warm bread, freshly cooked in a brick oven in a bazaar back home. The bearded man is ravenous.

"Challah?" Janine says. "Do I pronounce it correctly?"

Tears fill the bearded man's eyes.

"We're here," says the raven-haired women with the perfect teeth and the soft pink lips and the evil glow in her eyes. She looks tantalizing, like *treif*, succulent nonkosher food.

How long has the bearded man been asleep? Not long.

"Where are we?"

"Border of Oakland and Berkeley. You've heard of Berkeley?"

"It is the dawning of the age of Aquarius," he says. He looks up, stunned at what he sees on this ramshackle street. "Is this a temple?" he asks.

He's looking out the van window at a modest street-level establishment, no windows, but ornate doors. Hebrew scrawl, four Stars of David. A temple? It is sandwiched between an apartment building that looks abandoned, with a rusted metal jungle gym on the lawn, and a barbecue restaurant that looks like it should be abandoned.

"No. Not an actual temple. It is, what's the word, a front. We would not do you such an insult by using a holy place. Keep your head covered, Guardian, please," Janine says. She hands him a prayer shawl.

He clenches his teeth. Who is she to give him such a garment?

"I ask humbly, Guardian," Janine says. "It is to protect your identity. Because you are a terrorist."

He looks at her.

"Like me," she smiles tightly, and opens the door to the van.

INSIDE, SECONDS LATER, his heart bounces, a rabbit in a warren in his chest. Two dozen people sit in the mock congregation, or stand and mingle. When he enters the surprisingly cavernous sanctuary—its size hidden from the street—all eyes turn to the pair.

His first thought: melting pot.

His second: sacrilege.

White faces, light brown ones, a few dark.

Some with yarmulkes, others crosses. One man kneels on a mat, facing his left. Moaning in Arabic, from the Koran.

"Not the tiny cell you imagined," Janine says.

"Guardians?" gasps the bearded man.

Janine nods.

"Ange," comes a voice from the back.

"Curatore." Another.

"Guardianna." A woman in the back. Mexican accent.

Tears again sting the bearded man's eyes. It is as he's heard. A mélange of the most faithful. Brothers and sisters.

The man on the mat stands, he pulls up his pants leg. On his ankle, a tattoo, a lion on its hind legs.

There is rustling at the front of the congregation, a man in all black going up the stairs to an ark.

"The covenant," Eli says.

The covenant.

What was agreed upon by God and Abraham. Only through adherence to the word of God will all the nations of the Earth be blessed.

The covenant. No compromise.

Eli looks at the ark, which the man in all black has opened. Sitting inside on soft purple felt is not the Bible, not the Torah, but a metallic cylinder. It is hollow in the middle. A hole that could contain a very large Tootsie Roll or a loaf of freshly baked sourdough bread.

He knows that shape. It's the shape of the black object he's been carrying in the backpack. The insides, the guts of the atomic weapon.

He turns to Janine and he sees that light in her eyes, the demonic light. He holds the backpack tight and thinks he might run.

The man who had been kneeling on a mat muttering from the Koran rises. "We don't have much time, Eli."

Janine clears her throat. The assembled look in her direction. Clearly, she is a leader here. *The* leader? It's not clear to the bearded man.

"We have work to do," Janine says. "There are complications."

There are murmurs.

"Guardians!" she commands them. They pause and take her in. "I have a puzzle for you, a question: what do you call a black man flying?"

The assembled seem struck, confused. Is she telling them a joke?

The answer comes from a stout woman, hearty, dressed conservatively in a handsome pants suit. "A pilot, you racist."

It is a joke, and a few of them get it, and laugh.

"Please remember that we are united, Guardians, by our faith, and united we will succeed. Each here knows his or her job. So let us get the divine weapon where it belongs, and put the rest of the pieces in place. You know where to gather, in that beautiful park."

A voice says: "The Presidio."

Janine continues but now she quietly addresses Eli. "Join me. I am told we have a particularly special task."

Her rare combination of beauty and cruelty, a devil's charisma, causes him to take a step backward. And then follow her out the door.

CHAPTER 31

J EREMY SWALLOWS, COUGHS, throat dry to the point where he feels like he might choke, presses his ear to the door. He hears at least three sounds: the television and two voices.

Then just the television. Is he imagining things, more than one voice?

He looks next to him on the cool, smooth stone floor, finds his iPad, fingers the screen. It is 4:25. He's been asleep, he calculates, a little more than three hours.

He looks at the map. Red, red, red. The countdown clock: 14:10:07.

14:10:06.

14:10:05.

He shakes his head. Where did the hours go?

14:10:04.

And there, in the upper right-hand corner, a notification. The results have come back from the test he programmed before he fell asleep. His finger hovers over it, poised to click, even as he tries to make out what's going on in the bedroom. He can't make out what's being discussed on the TV. The tenor and vibe sound like news, maybe the CNN early report.

There's a knock, knock on his door. A hard rap, not the work of a hand, but a book, an object intended to make a lot of noise. It startles him and he almost topples forward. It must've been what woke him. He pictures the dream, his mother, frail but unyielding, Kent, boyish in his pajamas, then unyielding too with his mustache. The puzzle.

"Are you listening?"

Jeremy recognizes Andrea's voice. He clears his throat. Craves water. "I fell asleep."

From the other side of the door, Andrea says:

"*Harry W. Ives, a renowned professor of conflict studies, was found dead last night from multiple stab wounds. Police said the esteemed scholar was discovered in his office on the Berkeley campus by a student. They have identified and are seeking a suspect described as a white male in his early thirties believed to be an acquaintance of Dr. Ives.*"

Jeremy leans his head against the wall. He looks up at the ceiling, sees the air duct. Thinks: I need a trampoline to get into it and a tiny stunt double to slither through the canals to my escape.

"I told you," he said.

"You didn't tell me he'd been murdered. Get out here, we need to talk. I know. I can help you."

"I need to wash up. Give me a second, please."

He opens his phone, turns it on. While waiting for it to power up, he clicks on the iPad for results from his test. An hourglass appears. In seconds, he'll know which of the variables is most important in predicting the impending conflict. Or, he thinks, as words begin to materialize, he'll know the variable or variables most material in predicting the *alleged* conflict.

On the screen, a header: 362,880 results.

Damn it, Jeremy thinks. His chin falls. Why didn't I think

of it before? This is nine factorial. I'm going to get an endless
stream of results, combining and mixing and matching all the
different influences. How am I going to wade through the different permutations to determine which is the most telling? It
will take a veritable infinite number of monkeys sitting at an
infinite number of screens to go through all this shit.

Punctuating his concerns, the results begin to scroll. The
first few look like:

CHANGED PARAMETER(S)	COUNTDOWN CLOCK	MAGNITUDE DELTA
Mexico rhetoric constant	28 hours, 55 minutes	0%
Mexico/Russia constant	28 hours, 55 minutes	-9%
Mexico/Russia/ Tantalum	28 hours, 55 minutes	1%

The list scrolls and scrolls and scrolls. At first, he's able to
see only the swirl, the unfurling of the data, a ghost whir of
returning results.

"Jeremy, do I need to call the front desk to tell them that my
husband has locked himself in the bathroom?"

"One sec."

He forces himself to focus on the first three results to remind
himself what he's looking at. The first column describes which
combination of parameters has been held artificially constant by
the computer. In other words, in the test represented in the first
line, the world is precisely as it is today except that the conflict

rhetoric in Mexico was not intensified. Under such a scenario, the countdown clock is unchanged—as represented in column two—and the magnitude of the conflict is unchanged, the number of people projected to die, as represented in column three.

It tells Jeremy that Mexico alone, the rising conflict rhetoric there, is not where he should be focusing his investigations.

But the second line offers a different insight. It says that if the conflict rhetoric is held constant in both Mexico and Russia, then the attack still happens but its magnitude falls. And measurably. The projected deaths drop 9 percent.

What does Mexico have to do with Russia?

In the third line, the shipments of tantalum are kept constant. The countdown clock remains unchanged. The projected deaths rise 1 percent.

He begins scrolling down the list, even as it continues to grow and grow. One permutation after the next. One catches his eye:

CHANGED PARAMETER(S)	COUNTDOWN CLOCK	MAGNITUDE DELTA
Mexico/Russia/ Tantalum/Fertile Cresc/Arrest	N/A	-100%

Jeremy feels himself stop breathing. A delta of 100 percent.

Meaning: under the scenario in which the computer artificially holds constant the conflict rhetoric in Mexico, Russia, and the Fertile Crescent, and also holds constant shipments of tantalum and the arrest of the arms dealer, there is a 100 percent change in the prediction.

There is no attack.

A clue. Way more than that. The key. It's in here. Somewhere in here.

"That's it," he mumbles.

There's a vigorous knock on the door.

Jeremy feels the perspiration on his hands, hears a veritable echo inside his head. He's so tired, can't tell if he's understanding her.

"What?"

"I just need to clean myself up."

The computer was right.

"Lavelle. The lieutenant colonel . . ." Her voice trails off.

Jeremy doesn't respond. He's got an idea. He starts clicking on his keyboard. He's regrouping all the results, the hundreds of thousands of results. He's grouping them in terms of which results have the highest "magnitude delta," in other words, which ones wind up with a set of variables under which there will be no predicted attack.

Within seconds, he's found what he's looking for. There are eight such scenarios. He looks down the list of them, looking for the common theme. Until it strikes him.

"Impossible," Jeremy mutters. He leans in close to the computer. "You've got to be lying to me." He tilts his head. "Or you're very, very good."

He stands up, gently pushing the iPad on the floor. He lets pass a lightheaded wave, feels the creases uncrease in the jeans he's been sitting in, sleeping in, the blood drop back down into his numb feet. He shuffles to the mirror, sees the ragged face looking back at him, can't help noticing the same pointy chin as his mother, the hawkish eyes, but the nose that came from somewhere else altogether. He thinks of her taunting presence in the dream, purporting to hold all the answers in her hand.

He thinks: Screw you. Screw all of you. I'm holding the answers. He glances at the iPad. Impossible. But possible. The country codes, Evan, the Pentagon, they must fit together some way.

And now this, a powerful message from the computer: the chief parameter leading to the prediction of war is that tensions have cooled in the Middle East.

Jeremy flicks on the cold water, lowers his head to the sink, splashes and splashes.

Out of more than three hundred thousand scenarios, there are eight under which there will be no attack whatsoever. Under all eight scenarios, the conflict rhetoric in the Fertile Crescent doesn't go down. It remains unchanged or, possibly, goes up.

Meaning: the one variable that Jeremy has dismissed as irrelevant—the Middle East seeming more peaceful—is the one most influential in triggering war. Singularly influential. Makes no sense, none. Things have been getting *more* peaceful in the Middle East, at least from the standpoint of the language of war.

The language of war has been intensifying in so many other places—up sharply in Mexico, moderately in Russia, North Korea, Congo—but it has been falling in the Fertile Crescent. According to the computer, it's fallen 12 percent in intensity. The collective hue and cry from Israel, Iran, Syria, Egypt, has taken a turn in a positive direction. This is presumably what the world wants. Right?

There's another basic pattern, one that completely stands to reason: the magnitude of the projected war rises and falls depending on how many of the other conflict parameters are included in the calculation.

For instance, if the rhetoric in North Korea does not intensify, the magnitude of the conflict gets smaller. Fewer people die.

If the Russian arms dealer is not arrested, the magnitude of the conflict gets smaller. Fewer people die.

Same thing if the Mexican conflict rhetoric is held in check. Or if there is no rise in the Random Event Meter: in other words, if the lions aren't let loose from the zoos.

And if more than one of those parameters is held in check, the magnitude falls even further. For instance, if the dealer is not arrested and the conflict rhetoric stays constant in Mexico and North Korea and Russia, then the magnitude drops precipitously.

And, in the most extreme case, if all the parameters are held in check *except* the drop in the conflict language in the Fertile Crescent, the magnitude seems to be limited to a single attack: one projected to take place in mere hours, right here in San Francisco.

The computer is telling him something absolutely essential: the most important parameter is the falling conflict rhetoric in the Fertile Crescent. It alone triggers the attack in San Francisco. Without it, no war. And if it is the only change in the last few weeks, then the conflict gets limited to San Francisco.

Is everything else a red herring? Does the tantalum or the arrest of the Russian arms dealer mean nothing? Jeremy senses otherwise; they're all connected, somehow. But with varying degrees of significance.

Knock, knock on the door.

He towels off.

On his phone, he looks at the time. Nearly 5 A.M. Sees a text. "How can I help?" From Nik. At two in the morning.

He'll be waiting for a response. Jeremy thinks about his dream. The bridge, the view. The puzzle. Harry's end-of-life warnings.

Jeremy taps back a message. He tells Nik what to do.

He slips the iPad into his backpack. Puts the backpack on, pulls the straps to tighten his swaddled baby on his back. Pulls open the door. "Let's play chess," he says.

No sooner has he cracked the door open than he feels a violent push from the other side. Jeremy begins to fall backward, thrown by the tremendous surge. Instinctively, he pushes back, throwing himself against the door, Jeremy in a nutshell, reacting to a push with a pushback of equal weight, greater, his nature fueled by fear, no, terror.

A reverse tug-of-war, bodies pressing and pushing the heavy wood door. Jeremy losing ground. He sees hands grope inside, not just two, not just Andrea. Another woman's hand.

"Jeremy, we have to talk to you."

We.

He pushes, strains, feels his feet slip on the stone. He can't hold this. He sees hair, a face begin to slip through the widening opening of the door; can't believe his eyes. Her? He pushes back, a surge from his legs and trunk, a last effort to close himself in. The door begins to yield to his will. It's closing, closing and, then, he can't find any more reserve. The momentum begins to turn back.

He suddenly thinks: let them come.

He gives one last grunt, a push, but a feint, waits for the inevitable heave back at him. When it comes, he lets go. The door swings open, the women—two women—fly past him, careening, bowling pins in reverse, spinning, slipping forward toward the bathroom counter.

Jeremy leans down and picks up his backpack. And he runs.

CHAPTER 32

"CAN YOU FIND a secure line?"

Janine reads the text on her phone. The bearded man cringes; they are driving fifty miles an hour over the Bay Bridge, heading to San Francisco. Janine, steering with a knee, texts back: "Um, yeah, this one."

Seconds later, her phone rings. She presses a button and a voice comes onto the speaker.

"I won't repeat this," the voice says.

The audio quality is bad, choppy, with static. But the bearded man feels a moment of awe. This must be the master Guardian, the one calling the shots.

"We have access to the code."

The bearded man doesn't understand. The code? He looks at Janine, who seems to blink rapidly. Processing, troubled.

"Didn't we always have the code?" she asks into the phone.

"Sabra, there was no point in telling you we didn't have it when we knew we'd get it."

She smiles, willing herself to find some external expression that doesn't match her fury. What was the point of going through all this, the months of prelude—the years—if they didn't have the code in the first place? I'm not your fucking Sabra. That's Hebrew, not the right language. I'm Syrian, Christian, Arabic, and no less righteous.

"Actually, we don't have it," says the quiet, patient voice.

"What?" She thinks: Wasp. But she senses he's so much deeper than that. Calmly: "We know where it is. Exactly?"

"Look up!" the bearded man says.

Janine, who had been focused on the conversation, notices she has drifted into the lane to her right. She swerves back.

"Hello, Eli," says the voice on the phone.

"Hello."

"We must have the code," Janine says.

"That's why I have called you. It is your time."

The bearded man sees Janine grimace. "You are a Guardian. Since my father found you. We are like siblings, Sabra."

He tells her what they need to do.

She hears a click.

The van has nearly passed over the bridge. The bearded man marvels at the magnitude of downtown San Francisco. The massive man-made kingdom. Not long for this world.

"The code?" he asks.

"For the weapon. It needs a code. So it can go bang. And apparently we don't have it."

"But . . ."

"It will be easy to get. The one who has it—he's a . . . tortured fellow, pathetic, lost in the things of this world. Easy enough to get his cooperation."

Chapter 33

OLD LINGUINE.

Jeremy flies down the hallway at the Mandarin, past a cart, a housekeeper's cart, pushed against the wall. Towels and soaps, and on top, a haphazardly balanced plate of half-eaten pasta. He hears footsteps behind him. Urgent whispers of his two stalkers: Andrea and a tall, thin woman, a shock but not a complete stranger. He saw her the night earlier at a café, then at a bar, then on the street.

Then in the car that tried to run him over.

Now at his heels.

"It's pointless, Jeremy!"

He passes the housekeeping cart and swoops his arm around the edge, trying to push it behind him into the hallway. Slow the women. His aim is true; the cart topples behind him, giving him maybe an extra second.

His legs explode off the swirls of red and black on the carpet.

He hears a click. A click. A gun?

Finds the extra gear. Reaches the elevators, pauses, hears the women leaping over or crashing through the toppled cart.

The elevators are a trap, a cage. He keeps running, toward the end of the hallway, a sign: exit. The stairs.

An urge strikes him to yell, what, "Fire"? Bring people out of their rooms, their dawn beds, create more chaos. Something prevents him, pride, maybe. He wants to confront, not run. At the stairs, he turns back, allows himself to look. They're coming, Andrea and the woman, no longer sprinting, hustling, confidently. They've got Jeremy in their sights, a helpless gazelle.

He scans for a fire alarm; shouldn't there be one right here on the wall? Not to be. He opens the stairwell doors.

Up.

Steps echo as he bounds. Two steps at a time, three. The twelfth floor, thirteenth, fourteenth, thighs burning, lungs tight, stairs looming endlessly. A cavern with a dead end.

One of the women says: "Take the elevator to the top."

He keeps on, hearing the door open on one of the floors. They're maybe two floors behind him, feet chasing sound. But now one of them has gone for the elevator bank, heading, where, presumably the top floor so she can come down. One will be behind him, the other in front. Unless he hurries. To the top, and then what?

"Jeremy!" Andrea is the one behind him.

He sees a sign: "Nineteenth Floor," and, beneath it: "Roof Access."

He reaches for the handle. He pushes down. It opens. He pauses. Andrea, alone, is beneath him. Surely he can blow past her, shove her out of the way, one-on-one, and were this Pamplona, he'd be the bull.

What's he running from?

A gun? The unknown?

Do these women want to kill him?

He opens the door to the roof. As he does so, he sees the fire alarm. Reaches for it; not yet. He needs Andrea. She needs him, but he needs something from her, a truth, a story. An idea surfaces.

He shoves the door closed and spills onto the roof. Darkness, a twist of neon in the distance, from the side of a building. Coca-Cola. He feels frigid air, foggy drizzle, tarry gravel beneath his feet. He blinks, willing sight. Looking for a foe; has the other woman made it up here?

He sees no one. Just the expansive roof, scattered storage units, a rectangular cement room, probably for electrical equipment, Internet, locked off by a heavy metal door.

He hears the door open behind him. Looks back and sees both women, purposeful, but not sprinting. He starts walking to the side of the roof.

"I know," he says.

"What do you know?" Andrea asks.

"About the attack. Why?"

She and the woman look at one another.

"It's on here," Jeremy says. "All of it. In here, my backpack. The future foretold, all the evidence." He blinks. He's trying to piece something together, anything. Trying to sound like he's holding cards. "It has to do with the Russians, a rogue executive." He pauses. "A missing bomb."

The women step forward.

"Bomb?"

"Stop lying!"

"Jeremy, I can help you. You're a brilliant man, brilliant. But you're lost in an alternate reality." Tiny pause. "You killed Harry."

"No."

"I saw the . . . I saw the stains. The blood. I'm only looking out for you."

"You're not telling me something."

No answer.

"I can give you what you want."

"Which is what?" Andrea looks at the woman. Something silent passes between them.

"But first you have to tell me what you know, Andrea."

"I'm telling you. I am. Telling. You. The lieutenant colonel was missing." She clears her throat. Her arms are crossed. She juts her chin toward the tall woman, the dangerous fawn with the gun.

"Okay."

"What do you know about it, Jeremy?"

"So he's no longer missing."

"What?"

"You said he 'was' missing. So he's no longer missing."

"He's dead, Jeremy."

Jeremy takes it in. He watches the women circle. "I know."

Andrea takes a deep breath. "You know who killed him."

"You did."

"Very funny."

Jeremy looks at the taller woman, the mute gun toter, circling around to his left. She's practically silhouetted by the darkness.

Jeremy says: "You tried to run me over in the car. Last night, outside the McDonald's."

Andrea: "She wasn't trying to run you over. She was trying to scare you."

"Why?"

"So you'd get into the car with me. So you'd help me. She's with me, a trusted colleague."

"She's helping you to do what?"

"Figure out what's going on. With Lavelle, the lieutenant colonel. He mentioned you. He warned me."

Jeremy shakes his head.

"Before he disappeared. He was nervous. He mentioned you. You have a vendetta, Jeremy. You hate him, us, for ruining your dreams. It's about you."

"And Harry?"

Andrea shakes her head. "I don't know."

"He was working with you too."

"Yes, I told you."

"Doing what?"

"I told you: helping us to understand the world, how conflict works. I showed you mine, Jeremy. Show me yours."

"See for yourself," he blurts out. He takes off his backpack. "If I show you, you'll let me live."

"Of course. Jeremy, I'm not a—"

"The future foretold."

Jeremy throws the black backpack in the direction of the tall woman, roughly, more toward the corner of the roof. It spins, like a Frisbee, lands, and slips and slides toward the corner, the edge of the hotel. She starts loping toward it and as she makes her break, Jeremy makes his. He's heading right for Andrea.

Within steps, he's on her, then past. She reaches out an arm, but he shakes it. Steps later, he pulls open the door leading to the stairs. He ignores the sounds behind him. He knows they'll be preoccupied, but for only the briefest second.

Minutes later, after an elevator ride, he's sprinting down.

He feels the iPad and keyboard. They're tucked awkwardly between his back and his shirt, which in turn is tucked into his pants. In his pocket, the tiny wireless mouse. Portable Jeremy. The women have doubtless realized now that they were left empty-handed. Wonders how they feel having discovered *The Complete Idiot's Guide to Dating*.

Why would they want the computer?

He feels relief, then a thrill. There's the beat-up Toyota, on the corner. Inside it, Nik, the dutiful Nik; should Jeremy expect anything less?

He sprints to the car to discover his assistant mouth deep in a donut. A half-eaten dozen between the two front seats. Jeremy paws a maple-frosted and stuffs it into his mouth. The smell mixes with a sanitized odor of dog, Nik having done his best to spray away the scent of Rosa, his dog. On the floor of the passenger seat, Nik's old leather bag, which Jeremy nudges aside as he climbs in.

Jeremy points ahead on the road and Nik puts the car in drive and accelerates.

"Youliedtome." Jeremy's words—You lied to me—get swallowed by a mouthful of donut.

Nik shakes his head: what? The corpulent assistant points to a coffee in the middle compartment.

Jeremy swallows a thick chunk of half-chewed donut, follows it with coffee.

I said: "Let's go save the world."

Nik looks at him, blinks. Is this sarcasm from his boss? Drama? Not the kind of thing that Jeremy ordinarily would say.

Jeremy tells Nik where to drive.

Chapter 34

I S THIS ABOUT the break-in? At the office, and my apartment?" Nik asks.

"Nik, did you know about Evan and Andrea? You knew. I know you knew."

"So much for pleasantries."

Jeremy points left, directing Nik onto Broadway, a four-lane thoroughfare that travels from the Embarcadero—downtown—through North Beach, toward the Golden Gate Bridge. The bridge. That view.

It's drizzling, dark, the barest hint of morning, pre-morning, predawn.

"This is what it's going to be like, Nik."

Nik turns left, doesn't respond. He's used to Jeremy brainstorming aloud, using Nik as a silent sounding board. He's not sure what Jeremy means, which is: this is what the world will look like when it's been darkened by nuclear weapons.

"Kind of peaceful," Jeremy says. "I really need to fill in the blanks, Nik. Did you know about them?"

"You remember that party, the one with the theme?" Nik's response, spoken quietly.

Jeremy nods. The Binary Bash; come as a One or a Zero. Another cocktail party, not in Jeremy's honor, but he was one of the signature guests mentioned on the evite. "Andrea wasn't there," Jeremy says.

"I heard Evan on the phone. Arguing, trying to convince someone of something, laughing. I thought it was Andrea."

Jeremy doesn't say: why didn't you tell me? That's just not Nik's style.

"Another thing I'm wondering: Has anyone messed around with your computer? Any sign of hacking?"

Nik takes his eyes off the road—also not Nik's style—and turns to Jeremy. No driving risk, really; the only car on the street is a taxi, and it's parked in front of a twenty-four-hour corner food mart. Nik looks back at the road. He passes through a green light, cresting a hill. Jeremy can see the gateway to North Beach, announced by the neon from Larry Flynt's Hustler Club and the more traditional Condor Club on the right. Classic San Francisco: new-money nudity and old-money nudity right across the street.

Jeremy's thinking about something Andrea said: that Jeremy had emailed her about Evan. Was she lying? If so, wouldn't that be the strangest lie? Obviously, Jeremy would know whether he emailed or not.

Wouldn't he? Not if Nik co-opted his email. But why?

He's struck by the strangest thought, which he expresses aloud. "What if my computer is doing something on its own?"

"Still straight?"

"Not possible. Yes. Right on Van Ness." He opens the cover on his iPad. He looks at the map. Red, red. Countdown clock at just around thirteen hours. He thinks back to the Binary

Bash. Nik wound up talking to that woman from CNET, the reporter with the limp and the thick glasses.

"Remember that reporter you dated?"

"We just went out a couple of times."

"I'm going to need you to do something for me. I need you to tell her, and others."

Jeremy opens Yahoo mail and zips an email to Nik: *The conflict machine predicts there will be an attack. Tonight at 8 pst. In San Francisco. It will lead to nuclear war. Nik, tell the reporter you know. Tell them Jeremy Stillwater will stake his reputation on it. And that they should not hesitate to tell the world—before it is too late.*

"Nik, I sent you an email. It explains something very important. I need you to spread the word. For now, it is better that it comes from you than from me. I'm persona non grata. But frankly, that doesn't matter. The press, such as it is, will eat this shit up. It's a 24/7 news cycle, a cycle that needs filling. So even if they think this is nuts, they'll print it and spread it, and link to it. It'll light up Twitter. Even if people think it's nuts, they won't be able to ignore it."

"Is this about Evan and Andrea?"

"No. I don't know. Then I need you to find Emily, and Kent. You have to take them somewhere."

Just ahead, a traffic light turns yellow, and Nik slows. At the light, he turns to Jeremy.

"I do a pretty decent job keeping your affairs organized."

"I know."

"So I must not be a complete idiot."

Jeremy turns to look and Nik looks away, back to the road. Jeremy takes his meaning: stop treating me like a child.

"I think there's going to be an attack, Nik. That's what this thing is telling me. I sent you an email with the details. You're the only one I've told. But there are a lot of variables. With your permission, I'd like to think about it for a second."

"An attack." Nik accelerates through the green light. The car makes a whining noise. Jeremy sees Nik wince. His assistant takes care of the little things, like making sure his car, tattered though it might be on the outside, is kept up, the oil changed, the dash dusted, the handful of compact discs kept in their cases and stacked neatly in the center console.

"An attack."

"Then all-out nuclear war. Tens of millions dead."

Nik swallows. Jeremy sees him pull a hand from the steering wheel and touch his chest, the shirt above the cross that hangs around his neck.

"Maybe it's wrong."

"It was right, Nik. The computer was right. About the Middle East, the stuff with the Pentagon."

"I thought—"

"Andrea came clean. The government lied. They manipulated me. I'm not sure why. But I'm sure they did."

"You haven't told anyone?"

"About the Pentagon?"

"About the . . . the attack, the thing the computer is telling you."

Jeremy sees Nik glance in the rearview mirror. Jeremy looks over his shoulder. A dark car has materialized. No, a van. Its windshield wipers rapidly dust away the drizzle, obscuring the face of the driver. A woman, short hair?

Nik takes a right onto Van Ness. The van and its driver continue straight.

"Left on Bay," Jeremy says, not answering Nik's question. "Go past the Safeway. I need a minute."

Jeremy looks at the iPad, and his eyes glaze over. He's trying to add everything up—the clues, the computer's prediction, the murder, or is it murders. He doesn't doubt that Harry is dead, but Lavelle, the lieutenant colonel. Is he? And if so, so what?

He's the guy who oversaw Jeremy's visit to the Pentagon, who approved it, who made it a lie. At least according to Andrea. They told him they wanted to test his technology, then told him it didn't work, then offered to send him to the Middle East to see for himself. Then pulled the plug. A dog-and-pony show. Were they using his technology? Are they using it now? How? He's the only one who can get inside the machine, right?

He thinks about Harry's cryptic messages. A note, a symbol. V, victory, or something else. Country codes, Israel, the West Bank; and superpowers, China and Russia; and Morocco, a crossroads, a land of great insignificance, at least in the larger scheme.

All the codes coming together at the point of the symbol with numbers that don't correspond to a country code, that don't correspond to anything obvious.

He thinks about cooling conflict rhetoric in the Fertile Crescent, which includes Israel and Ramallah, both represented in the country calling codes. The computer has told him that this softening language is the most pointed evidence of an incoming attack. How can that be? Could the softening language from that region be a trap, a deliberate showing? Might the leaders of, say, Israel, or the Arab nations be lulling people to sleep and then planning an attack? That makes no sense; cooperation between these eternal enemies?

He makes a mental note to look into the details of language from the Middle East. Who is saying what to whom?

And what of the intensifying language of war from around the globe—Mexico, Russia, North Korea. The world is heating up. It's a tinderbox. Isn't it always?

Where do the Russian arms dealers fit in, if at all? A missing bomb or a red herring?

Maybe there's going to be an attack; maybe the computer is lying. Maybe someone messed with the computer. But there's no doubt that Harry is dead.

"At the least, it's a murder mystery."

"Which way?"

"Toward the right, past the courts."

The volleyball courts. And the marina, down by the waterfront, the Golden Gate Bridge looming ahead. In silence, they drive down Bay, passing between the water on the right and, on the left, the high-rent fitness-centric businesses: the sporting goods outlet catering to the overzealous exercisers, the indoor rock-climbing facility, even, for the kids, a house of jumpy castles so that San Francisco's toddlers can get their cardio on.

On the grass that leads to the beach, someone has erected a placard with a picture of a lion on its hind legs.

"The Lion of Judah."

Jeremy feels the car swerve. He looks up. Nik seems transfixed by the protestors.

"Nik!"

He jerks back the wheel. "Sickening."

"You're really broken up about the lions."

"Of course it's going to get shot."

Poor Nik. So boyish. "You know much about the Middle East?"

"My parents, obviously."

They'd been missionaries all over the world, including in Jerusalem.

"So you know the lion is the symbol for Jerusalem," Jeremy says. "The Lion of Judah." Then Jeremy shakes his head. He takes in Nik. Studies his pasty sidekick. Looks back out the window.

"All roads lead there—to Jerusalem." Almost under his breath. Then: "Where do Harry and Evan fit in? They fit in. It's all connected."

"Evan's not reachable. He's out of town."

Jeremy blinks. He just saw Evan. Is Nik lying to him?

"You asked me to find out and so I called his office and his assistant told me that he's out of town on personal business through the weekend. I told her that I was someone's assistant too and so she felt comfortable."

"A rare bit of manipulation."

"And she said he has an important meeting. Something top secret. Even she didn't know what. She said, 'You know how important bosses think they are.'"

"Hmm."

"Where are we going?"

Jeremy points to a sign. There's an arrow. It reads: "Log Cabin."

"He left me something."

"Who?"

Jeremy doesn't answer. He's thinking not only about Harry, and the admonition: log cabin. He's thinking about Emily, who tells Jeremy that he misses the forest for the trees. She means that Jeremy always thinks about winning, confronting every little battle, rather than about the big picture. When it comes to Emily and Jeremy, it means that he doesn't think about the overall health of the relationship; he thinks about scoring one more point.

In the case of the "log cabin"—and Harry—Jeremy kept thinking it was a reference to the fight. Maybe that is what Harry was referring to. But there's another possibility.

Harry came all the time to the log cabin. It was where he did his thinking, wandering in the grassy knoll of the Presidio, a former military base that symbolized war and came to symbolize the transition to peace. And, Harry would prick Jeremy, no Internet access, so Harry could think in peace, let his brain roam without interruption or digital crutch.

From the edge of the grove next to the log cabin, there's a view of the Golden Gate Bridge. The view represented in the puzzle in Jeremy's dream.

"Not the trees, Nik, the forest."

"What forest?"

"Peace. Nik."

They wind up in the darkness, climbing toward the log cabin. Jeremy looks out and sees the very beginning of light, and the tip-top of the bridge. It's the same view from his dream, the puzzle.

The road veers to the left. A few more turns to the log cabin, answers.

CHAPTER 35

I DON'T SAY PLEASE much, do I?"
The wheels of the Toyota crackle a last time and the car comes to rest at the cabin. Surrounding it, enveloping it, a grassy knoll and then trees. Just a few of the grand eucalyptuses that dot so many of San Francisco's landmarks, even here in the Presidio. More of them here are mutt trees, short and tall, bushy, a little Hansel-and-Gretel forest of makeshift paths and hollows with the cabin at the gooey center.

Occasionally, the spot gets rented out to wedding parties or for corporate bonding functions. More often, it's just one of those landmarks where locals in the know picnic, or let their kids roam, or, in the case of Harry, come to think big thoughts.

"I also tend not to ask questions," Jeremy says.

"Do you have a question?" Nik lifts a chocolate frosted and takes a fat bite.

"If you were a secret, where would you be?"

"In bed."

Jeremy almost lets himself laugh. He takes in his assistant. Is Nik a simpleton or canny? Quiet because he's shy or deferential or for some other reason? Always in the shadows, with access to everything, all Jeremy's contacts.

"I just asked a question, and now I'm going to say please."

Nik looks at him.

"Please drive the car over there." Jeremy points to the far end of the gravel driveway, where the road, such as it is, resolves into a grove of trees. The car should be hidden there from the road. "Please keep your cell phone off, and then please help me start looking."

Nik, mid-bite, looks up.

"I have no idea for what." Jeremy opens the car door. He looks at the iPad.

12:32:48. Hours, minutes, seconds, until attack.

He closes the cover. He looks for his trusty backpack, remembers he's sacrificed it to dupe Andrea and her statuesque henchwoman.

"Can I use your bag?" Jeremy reaches down and lifts Nik's worn leather bag with the long strap Nik slings over his shoulder, looking like a corpulent bike messenger.

Nik eyes it. Shrugs. "You might want to pull out the library books."

Jeremy does; sets on the floor a book with a title about defensive boxing; some fitness book, *Build Your Body in God's Image*; and something about foreign-language phonetics. Nik, always reverent, and quietly trying to better himself. A humble sidekick and nothing more. Right? Jeremy with mild disgust moves aside a hooded orange sweatshirt, almost stiff with perspiration, Nik's boxing jersey. In its place, Jeremy stuffs his iPad and keyboard into the bag and slings it over his shoulder.

His eyes roll over Nik.

"Academics are not nearly as clever as they'd like to think.

They overcomplicate things, they go for cheap symbolism, their ideas aren't nearly as sophisticated as they'd have you think."

"Isn't Harry dead?"

"I'm not speaking ill. I'm being frank about how to find what we're looking for."

"Did Harry tell you about the attack? Why aren't you telling someone?"

Jeremy, standing at the door, no longer facing Nik but looking at the outlines of the cabin in the darkness, pauses. It's the first time someone other than Jeremy—or his computer—has taken seriously the idea that there might be an attack.

"And like the sign says, no talking. Go where I'm not. Please." Jeremy closes the door, takes a crunch step onto the gravel, eyes the sign stuck in the grass near the trees to the left. He can't read it in the dark but he knows what's on it: a phone in a circle with a red slash through it, and words underneath: "This is a peaceful place."

He makes a beeline for the cabin, endures an intruding memory, he and Emily and Harry sitting across the grass, the far side of the knoll, sandwiches and ostensible celebration. Harry looked like particular shit that day, khaki cargo shorts and a wrinkled button-down shirt, patterned with colorful checks and tucked in tight.

"Have you been diagnosed with Pastelsheimer's?" Jeremy prodded him.

"Alzheimer's?" Emily asked.

Harry laughed. "I think he means that, at a certain age, you develop clothing dementia. Paisleys and Hawaiian shirts become the order of the day."

"Props to old Dr. War for self-awareness."

Laughter. Things had started well enough, Jeremy, abandoned by the investors and Pentagon, celebrating solidarity with the last of his loyal band of partisans. These guys, and Nik, they'd help him make his way back to conquer the known world or, rather, prevent its conquest by nefarious antagonists, Huns toting nuclear suitcases.

It was shortly thereafter that Harry made the offhand remark when Jeremy glanced at his phone. Jeremy can't remember the exact comment, something about Jeremy missing the forest for the phone. Jeremy blinked, then, without another beat, said: "It can predict envy too."

Jeremy felt Emily's hand on his leg, a squeeze.

"It's dehumanizing. It can't fully comprehend conflict and might even contribute to it, Jeremy," Harry said.

"Careful, Dr. Ives," Emily said. "You're talking to a man who has much better relationships with computers than people."

She laughed when she said it, a joke of course. But no matter. That was that, a land war. The thing that Jeremy objected to most of all wasn't the content of Harry's statement, which didn't totally make sense to him. Rather, what most bothered him was the pointed way Harry said "Jeremy" at the end of his admonition, like a parent to a child, or a sagacious professor to a not-sagacious student.

Jeremy looks out into the darkness.

What's here, Harry?

The dimmest light shines from inside horizontal windows running along the sides of the log cabin's tall wooden doors. It's the only spot of even modest visibility. Maybe the product of a night-light plugged in near the floor inside the door, some modest effort to discourage thieves or high school pranksters or whoever might stumble into this place at night.

The light proves sufficient for Jeremy to make out the one

part of this log cabin that is decidedly modern, the heavy industrial lock on the front door. He thinks, Gonna make it hard to get inside, if it comes to that. That's suddenly not a priority. "The tree," Jeremy mumbles. Not the proverbial forest, he's thinking, an actual tree. He hears footsteps crunching on the gravel behind him. Nik. Apparently getting with the program.

Jeremy starts walking purposefully, a near jog, across the native green-yellow grass, lumpy, pocked with tiny dirt mounds and, literally, molehills. His walk becomes a hundred-yard dash. Dead ahead, the spot where Emily unfurled the picnic blanket. No Kent that day, Jeremy remembers remarking, because the boy had been on a sleepover. "A grown-up thing," Kent had said, a comment that, for some reason, irked Jeremy. What's wrong with staying a kid, Kent?

Harry stood at a tree, drawing some kind of diagram with his finger, a professor at a wooden chalkboard, outlining some theory about the superiority of the human mind and how Jeremy might better incorporate feelings and emotions into the war machine.

In the dull black morning, Jeremy finds himself at the same tree, a fat, knotty pine. He walks close, puts a hand on the cool trunk, feels the bumps, makes out some adolescent's carving. He shakes his head; what am I looking for? He runs a hand around the back, feeling for, what, a hole in the tree that holds a manila folder, magic eight ball, cryptic hologram of Harry explaining the world?

A joy buzzer and a popgun with a flag that says: gotcha?

No, this is not a joke. Harry is dead. The computer was right. People with guns are chasing Jeremy.

He falls to his knees. He starts digging at a lump of soil to the bottom right of the tree. His hands quickly muddy with the wet ground, his fingers cold and stubbing against dense ground just inches below the surface.

Self-consciously, Jeremy looks behind him. Even with the edges of light of dawn, he can't see across the field. He thinks he hears his loyal assistant's footsteps somewhere to the right, maybe on the other side of the building. He finds himself suppressing the urge to call out (Found anything?!), partly because even now he doesn't want to betray his desperation and vulnerability. And he's not sure how much to trust Nik. Partly, though, it's too peaceful to shatter this moment with a shrill cry.

Peaceful, he thinks. Ask it. Harry hates the computer.

Jeremy stands up and starts running. A dead, anxious sprint, his feet slipping beneath him on the damp, fog-drenched grass, that dull ache in his clavicle. But still picking up speed until, less than a half minute later, he stands at the sign. The little one near the grove of trees, not far from the car. He practically slides into the base of it, a baseball player trying to beat the throw to home plate. He pats the lumpy soil and grass around the bottom of the sign, fingers making their way in deliberate but frantic concentric circles toward the base of the sign itself.

He feels the metallic ring.

It's smooth, maybe an inch beneath the topsoil. On his knees, he paws away scoops of dirt, fingers full of cool, grimy soil and tiny rocks. He frees the top edge of the metallic ring, now realizes that it's attached around the sign, like a little collar. And he can feel something beneath the ring, attached to it, buried snugly beneath the soil.

He pops up his head, and looks around. Instinctually, hoping for a shovel to materialize from the dark, damp air. Where's Nik? He must be around the side of the cabin.

Jeremy looks at the sign telling him not to use a phone. "Get over it. It's the future." He reaches into his pocket and pulls out his clamshell phone, his backup. He pushes it into the ground, a makeshift shovel, an app of the pre-civilization variety. Digs, digs, digs, discovers what he's been expecting: the ring around the base attaches to a little lockbox, just like the kind that real estate brokers put on the homes they're showing.

On the front of the box, there are numbers, like those on a rotary phone, and then a larger black button. Inside, something, a secret, a treasure. The answer? Jeremy pushes the black button. Of course, it doesn't open.

"What's the code, Harry?"

Jeremy grits his teeth until his whole head pulses. Closes his eyes. Log cabin. AskIt. Beware the Peace. What did Harry say?

Is it one of the numbers from the symbol?

Jeremy puts his hand against the base of the pole. Shoves. Digs his feet into the ground, pushes at the sign. It won't give, it won't budge. Jeremy closes his eyes, mustering rage, not having to look hard for it, pushes, feels himself tiring, his hands cutting on the edges of the post.

He lets out a deep grunt, a visceral yell of a tennis player laying into a forehand. He shoves mightily; the sign begins to give. Another big heave and it topples, the bottom popping from a good foot beneath the soil. Jeremy drops down, feels the sharp, ragged tip of the sign. He pulls the metallic ring off it. Free. He's got it. What? Something. It, a piece of evidence, a key.

"What is it?"

Jeremy turns, sees Nik walking, about halfway across the field.

"Something."

Nik trudges, trundles, really. Jeremy can hear the scraping of his big legs against one another.

"It's locked. I need . . . do you have tools?"

Nik pauses, his typical deliberation. "I might."

Nik starts walking to his car.

Jeremy focuses on the locked box, fingering it, feeling damp grass against his jeans. He poises a finger over the number pad. Harry wouldn't send him here, not from his deathbed, without some clue as to the code. He thinks back to the numbers on the calendar, most of them country calling codes, all but one. 218-650. The one at the bottom of the V. What is that one?

Into the lockbox, he fingers 218-650.

Waits a second.

Pushes the black button to open the box.

Doesn't open.

He puts his neck back and looks up at the sky, such as it is; so much low-level, wispy fog, windblown, that the actual sky seems that much more unattainable, blocked. "Give me a sign, Harry War." He feels his voice catch in his throat. Harry, dead.

What did the codger say:

AskIt.

Peace.

Those aren't numbers. They could be numbers, Jeremy supposes. He could translate numbers from letters using his phone, in the same way that phone numbers used to be expressed in letters, or the way 800-numbers are often done. He looks at his phone; the word "peace" would start with the number 7, which corresponds with "p."

He listens to Nik fiddling in his trunk. He decodes "Peace" into 72323.

Punches it in.

Doesn't open.

"Would this work?"

Jeremy looks up to discover Nik just ten yards away, wielding a crowbar.

"What is it?" Nik asks.

"I doubt it," Jeremy says, absently answering Nik's question about whether the crowbar would work. A crowbar. "We need a time machine to go back to talk to that cryptic old cryptographer. You got one of those?"

Nik walks purposefully forward. Heavy metal tool clenched in that thick boxer's paw.

"Is everything okay, Nik?"

"Huh?"

Jeremy inches backward as Nick shuffles forward.

"Have you been to the zoo lately?"

"The zoo?" He steps closer. "What did you find?"

"You're obsessed with the lions."

"I don—"

Nik's response is cut off by the approach of a car, an explosion of tires on gravel. They look up, trying to make sense of another dawn visitor to the log cabin. Just as Jeremy recognizes something about the van.

"It was behind us."

"Where?"

"On Broadway."

"Is this about Harr—"

They hear the first gunshot before he can even make out the person firing.

"Run, Nik."

"What?"

"Away from me. Run!"

Chapter 36

B EHIND THE TREE." Jeremy spits out words at Nik, who runs a few steps ahead.

Jeremy glances over his shoulder. They've got a good seventy-five yards on the person who exited the van and started shooting. Rather, took one shot. Intentional? Now seems to have paused, looked at Nik's car, and then is heading their direction. A woman, Jeremy thinks, slightly built, not Andrea or her tall, thin adjunct, and hustling not sprinting.

Could shoot again at any second. But would have to be a hell of a shot to hit someone in this low light, at this distance. And with a handgun, not a rifle.

Jeremy lunges forward, giving a slight shove to Nik to propel him. It's unnecessary, it dawns on Jeremy; his sugar-fed assistant has surprising speed and dexterity, those hours in the boxing gym.

"She doesn't care about you," Jeremy rasps.

Nik keeps going, just a few feet from the big tree, the one where Jeremy and Emily and Harry picnicked, the one at the edge of the Hansel-and-Gretel forest. Beyond it, the Presidio, more tree groves and open space, a maze of hiding places, or a fine place to get shot and not found for weeks.

Jeremy glances over his shoulder. Hears a click.

"Her gun might be jammed." It's Nik.

The pair jump behind the tree, huddle.

"Split up?" Nik isn't even out of breath. He's read Jeremy's mind.

Jeremy almost smiles with filial affection.

"She doesn't care about you, Nik. She needs me." Spewing his plan, no longer any filter between his thoughts and mouth. "I'll draw her away. You circle back and tell the reporter and—"

BOOM!

The gun's report rips through the air. Thwack. A bullet smacks into a tree, their tree, another one?

BOOM!

Leaves and dirt spray at Nik's feet.

Jeremy falls toward Nik, hoping to blanket him. Push him aside.

" . . . tell the reporter there's going to be an attack, and also that chick from CNET, arrange for us to talk. I'll try them too when I figure out—" He pauses, allows himself to glance around the tree. The woman has stopped midway across the field. She's trying to get her bearings. She's short, confident, legs apart, stable, moving like someone with some kind of specialized training. Looks right in the direction of Jeremy, not that it's certain she can see him.

Jeremy pulls on Nik's arm, zigzagging, guiding him farther back into the trees.

Nik whispers: "You want me to take that?" The lockbox Jeremy clutches.

"Take the crowbar and smash up her engine. Meet me in

two hours at that café with the statue and the view, and . . .
218. Two eighteen!"

"What?"

"Find Evan."

"Jeremy—"

"Do you understand, PeaceNik. Two hours. And—"

They both pause, hearing the sound of their stalker, deliberate steps, faint, but feet on grass.

Jeremy: "I'm sorry I doubted you. Do you understand?"

Nik whispers. "Reporters. Two hours. Evan. I tried. I don't . . ."

"Find him!"

With several jabs of his finger, Jeremy points to the right, into the forest, showing Nik where he wants him to go. And without another word, Jeremy runs in the other direction. At least at first, then zigs from behind bushes and up a slight embankment so that he heads directly at the big tree, in the direction of the woman with the gun.

He stops, in a modest clearing amid the foliage and pines, a single eucalyptus to his right. Dawn upon him, the world. The first light. He can see the outline of the woman, and she him. Less than fifty yards apart. The gun held just in front of her with her right hand, steadied with her left. Not yet in firing position.

She raises it. Jeremy runs.

BOOM!

Thwack.

His legs explode, feet spitting bark and grass behind him.

"Arrêtez!"

Stop, French. Or die. And die. Now he can hear her following, as he'd hoped. He hits a second gear, third, clavicle pumping, heart shouting at him for air, alive. A voice in his ears: It was right. I was right.

He crests and slides down a treeless embankment, briefly exposed for want of trees, but then encircled again. Dodging left and right. She's behind him. He can sense it, still with the decided advantage of the gun, but she can't keep up and she's getting farther from Nik, his car, Jeremy's trap. He imagines his pursuer, for a second, in the greenish gray uniform of the Jerries, Germans trying to fight on two fronts, Jeremy and Nik, spreading her too thin.

Nik will tell the world and Jeremy will unlock the evidence in his hand, put the puzzle pieces together. Redemption.

He churns through this demi-forest, serpentines around a bush to his right, then one on his left, watches a squirrel fly up a tree, thinks: I will save you, all of this. Takes two more steps, and stops. Dead. At the abrupt end of this grove of trees. Before him, a wide-open field. He pictures Gallipoli, nearly half a million killed running at one another's trenches, conflict at its most extraordinary, the frailties of men—cowed by peer pressure and cowardice, driven by arrogance and dreams of immortality—mowed down by machines powerful well beyond the understanding of those who wielded them.

To Jeremy's left, more groves he could skirt through and around. He hears the woman, maybe fifty yards behind, picking her way through the trees.

He steps onto the open field, and he sprints, screaming across it. Digging his feet into the grass so he won't slip, willing his shoes to develop cleats, hearing the crowds at Berlin in the European championships and a fifth-place finish and a Rhodes scholarship. Step, step, run, over a hill, slipping only slightly on the downside, gaining distance between himself and the woman, until at last he reaches another grove of trees, a mess of big and tall and bushy, light emerging above, but in front of him, a veritable forest, far-reaching, the kind of thing that hid the Polish underground from the Nazis. He lets himself turn back. In the middle of the field, she stands. Stopped. Heaving breaths. Gun now at her side. She's a quarter mile from her car, and Nik's, defeated.

He puts up his fingers in a V.

Victory.

He turns and begins jogging, picking his way through the grove of trees. He hears Emily's voice: you're exhilarated, you're enjoying this. He shakes his head to make the admonition go away. But no sooner is it gone than he hears Andrea's voice telling him that conflict crystallizes his thinking. That he's prone to revelation when under duress and amid competition. Blink, then a vision of his mother, an image from his childhood, she and he squaring off over which movie to see. He's only eight or nine, wants the grown-up movie. You're just a child, his mother tells him. They debate the pros and cons; she's hassling him and he just wants to see the movie about the cars and she wants to see a different one. The more he digs in, the more she smiles, enjoying this sport, and her power.

Up ahead, a small building, made of native redwood, a sign above the door on the near side. Men. A public bathroom. Jeremy sprints the last twenty-five yards across a field, head swiveling, not finding another soul. No parking lot or pavement, no easy access if a would-be killer is circling, just the caw of morning birds and the smell of dew.

Inside the bathroom, he relieves himself. In one of those murky public restroom mirrors, he glances at himself and looks away. He splashes cold water on his face. Palms braced against the chipped wood at the edge of the basin, he thinks: Andrea might be right, and Emily; this conflict, this intensity, has allowed my brain to find answers, fueled me.

Get out of here. Too easy to get trapped.

Back out the door, Jeremy jogs in the direction away from the log cabin, toward the marina, another eighth of a mile, across more open field, then into a patch of trees that feels like it might be in the middle of nowhere. He's slightly elevated, a mild hump in the landscape, a molehill, but elevated. He thinks of Assisi, in Italy, a city surrounded by plains but set on a hill so that its inhabitants and zealots could see the attacks coming miles away. He pulls out his phones, makes sure that they're off. Any signal would just draw attention. So too, he checks his iPad to make sure that he's not connected to his own account, which someone, in theory, could triangulate. He discovers, with relief but not surprise, two different unsecured wi-fi networks. He chooses the one "PresidioX145."

He calls up the algorithm on the server, logs into it with the key fob, lets it begin to materialize.

First, though, the box, Harry's treasure. He holds it in a palm, notices the sweat and condensation, feels a chill. Pokes into it: 8773.

T-R-E-E.

What did Harry and Emily say? Jeremy lost the forest for the tree.

Jeremy pushes the black button. Click. It opens.

Onto the ground spills a computer disk. Jeremy half smiles; really, Harry, a computer disk?

He glances around, pulls the keyboard and iPad from the leather bag, attaches the thumb drive. A box appears on the screen showing the contents of the drive. A single document, named "Surrogate.doc."

He touches it. A note appears: "Do you wish to open this document?" He knows what his computer is really asking him. Could this document have a virus? Does Jeremy know its source?

Jesus, he thinks, what if, after all that, Harry's sent him some poison pill, some nuclear warhead aimed at the conflict computer?

He scrolls back to the browser, the conflict map. The clock.

11:05:12.

11:05:11.

He returns to the document left by Harry. He taps on it. It opens.

CHAPTER 37

PROJECT SURROGATE

ALPHA CLEARANCE

BACKGROUND: IN SEPTEMBER 2011, IRAN AN-
NOUNCED THAT IT WAS OPENING ITS FIRST NUCLEAR
POWER PLANT, BUSHEHR REACTOR 1. IT ALSO AN-
NOUNCED PLANS TO DEVELOP A 360 NW NUCLEAR
PLANT IN DARKHOVIN.

IRAN'S NATIONAL LEADERS HAVE SAID PUBLICLY
THEY ARE CONTINUING TO DEVELOP MIDSIZE URA-
NIUM MINES. IT IS BELIEVED THEY ARE RECEIVING
HELP FROM THE RUSSIANS IN DEVELOPING THE MINES
AND POWER PLANTS. EXISTING MINES, STILL WITH
URANIUM CAPACITY, WERE BUILT WITH HELP OF THE
UNITED STATES UNTIL 1979 AND THE FALL OF THE
SHAH.

Jeremy hears a sound, startles and looks up. It's a squirrel
scampering up a tree. Jeremy rubs his eyes, with both palms,

trying to infuse himself with enough energy, enough focus, to make sense of this. Iran, Russia, please tell me this leads somewhere, Harry. He delves back in.

IN NOVEMBER 2011, THE INTERNATIONAL ATOMIC ENERGY AGENCY CONDEMNED IRAN FOR FAILING TO DISCLOSE THE EXTENT OF ITS RESEARCH. FOR THE FIRST TIME, THE IAEA'S BOARD OF GOVERNORS EXPOSED IN SOME DETAIL THE EFFORTS BY IRAN TO DEVELOP AND TEST NUCLEAR WARHEADS AND TO TRANSFORM ITS DOMESTIC NUCLEAR POWER GENERA-TION INTO ATOMIC WEAPONS.

THOSE EFFORTS HAVE BEEN INDEPENDENTLY VERI-FIED BY OUR OWN ASSETS AND TWO ALLIED AGENCIES.

PREVIOUS EFFORTS:

SMALL-SCALE, SURGICAL STRIKES HAD SUCCEEDED IN SLOWING AND HAMPERING FULL-SCALE DEVEL-OPMENT OF A NUCLEAR ARSENAL BY IRAN. THIS SABOTAGE, INCLUDING ASSASSINATION OF LEAD SCI-ENTISTS, AND, POINTEDLY, CYBERATTACKS, WHILE EFFECTIVE TO A POINT, HAS, IN FACT, ULTIMATELY FAILED. WE NOW BELIEVE THAT THE IRANIANS HAVE THE CAPABILITIES AND RESOURCES TO BUILD AT LEAST ONE AND MAYBE SEVERAL FULLY CAPABLE, ARMED NUCLEAR WARHEADS.

THIS INTELLIGENCE IS CONTRARY TO PUBLIC AND MEDIA ACCOUNTS SUGGESTING IRAN HAS BEEN DISARMED AND HAS BEGUN TO ALLOW LEGITIMATE

INSPECTIONS BY INDEPENDENT AGENCIES. (PUBLIC
ACCOUNTS HAVE BEEN MANUFACTURED TO MAXIMIZE
POLITICAL AND MILITARY FLEXIBILITY BUT HAVE
NOT DIMINISHED THE URGENCY FOR DISARMING IRAN.)

THE OPTIONS FOR DISARMING IRAN HAVE BEEN,
AND REMAIN, EXTREMELY PROBLEMATIC. A DIRECT
ASSAULT CARRIES CATASTROPHIC CONSEQUENCES, NO
LESS SO A DIRECT ATTACK BY OUR ALLIES IN THE
REGION.

Jeremy pauses, fighting frustration, exhaustion. What does
this have to do with anything? It's not news that Iran wants a
bomb and America and others want to stop it. He lets himself
picture Emily, feeling adrenaline surge. He reads:

PROJECT SURROGATE:

IN NOVEMBER, 2012, EAGLE 1 APPROVED CLAN-
DESTINE PROJECT SURROGATE TO BE RUN FROM THE
PENTAGON OFFICES FOR PEACE AND CONFLICT.

THEIR CHARGE ENTAILED DESTROYING IRAN'S
NUCLEAR CAPABILITY WITHOUT ANY CONNECTION TO
THE UNITED STATES GOVERNMENT OR ITS ALLIES.
AND WITHOUT ANY CONNECTION TO WEAPONS USED IN
SUCH AN ACT OF SABOTAGE OR THAT COULD CONNECT
THE WEAPONS TO ALLIES.

THEY WOULD FIND AND DEPLOY A SURROGATE.

THE INITIAL STAGES OF PROJECT SURROGATE
SUCCEEDED. ASSETS WORKED THROUGH UNDERGROUND
CONTACTS OBTAINED A "SUITCASE NUKE" FOR AN
UNDISCLOSED SUM (TAKEN, AGAIN, OBVIOUSLY, OFF

THE BOOKS) FROM A FORMER EXECUTIVE OF RO-
SOBORONEXPORT STATE CORPORATION. THE WEAPON
HAD THE NECESSARY CAPABILITY OF DESTROYING
IRAN'S WEAPONIZED FACILITY, EVEN WERE IT NOT
DETONATED PRECISELY ON A HEAVILY ARMED AND
DEFENDED TARGET.

PROJECT SURROGATE ALSO SUCCEEDED IN FIND-
ING A HANDFUL OF FRINGE INDIVIDUALS AND VERY
SMALL CELLS IN THE REGION TO COORDINATE THE
STRIKE. IN PARTICULAR, TWO GROUPS, WITH HIS-
TORIC ENMITY TOWARD THE IRANIAN SHIITE GOV-
ERNMENT AND THEOCRACY.

THIS PLAN CARRIED ENORMOUS RISK. BUT PROJ-
ECT SURROGATE PUT IN PLACE TWO IRONCLAD FAIL-
SAFE MECHANISMS. FIRST, THE TWO PARTNERS IN
THE REGION THEMSELVES HAD A LONG HISTORY OF
OPPOSITION TO ONE ANOTHER. ONE WAS JEWISH
EXTREMISTS AND THE OTHER CHRISTIAN EXTREM-
ISTS. EACH WAS GIVEN ONE-HALF THE NUCLEAR
SUITCASE—IN EFFECT, THE EXPLOSIVE ITSELF AND
A DETONATOR COMPONENT. FOR THE PLAN TO SUC-
CEED, THEY WOULD NEED TO COOPERATE, AND COULD
NOT USE THE DEVICE AGAINST ONE ANOTHER OR THE
COUNTRIES THEY PURPORT TO REPRESENT.

BETWEEN THE TWO LOCAL "PARTNERS," THE LEAD
WAS GIVEN TO THE SMALL CELL WITH ARAB TIES.
THAT WAY, IT WOULD IDEALLY LOOK TO IRAN LIKE
THE ATTACK CAME FROM ROGUE ELEMENTS IN THE
REGION, RATHER THAN ANYONE WITH TIES TO ISRAEL.

BUT THERE WAS A MUCH MORE CRITICAL FAIL-
SAFE: THE UNITED STATES ALONE MAINTAINED THE

LAUNCH CODE FOR THE WEAPON. IT COULD BE DETO-
NATED *IF AND ONLY IF* THE CODE WERE PROVIDED,
WHICH WOULD HAPPEN ONLY MOMENTS BEFORE AN
ATTACK AND ONLY IF THE AMERICANS WERE 100 PER-
CENT SATISFIED OF THE LIKELIHOOD OF SUCCESS.

WITHOUT THE LAUNCH CODE, THE SURROGATE
WOULD BE INERT.

Jeremy's eyes begin to glaze over. Not with exhaustion or
boredom, but as a product of analysis; he's reading and trying to
make sense of this. There's a secret project to undo Iran's nuclear
capability by nuking it, and doing so using some secret group
or organization, *cells,* two groups that are not affiliated with the
United States, and that are not historically affiliated with each
other. He's struck that it's totally far-fetched and also totally in
keeping with the kind of weird stuff he'd come to expect from
people in the Pentagon. So these cells would be armed with a
nuclear suitcase and sent off to bomb Iran but with some kind
of secret detonation code provided by the United States. And
this connects to the end of the world how exactly?

CONCLUSION OF SURROGATE:

AFTER THE INITIAL SUCCESSES IN ACCESSING
AND DEPLOYING TWO SEPARATE PARTS OF AN INERT
NUCLEAR WEAPON, PROJECT SURROGATE RAN INTO
NOT WHOLLY UNEXPECTED AND NONTRIVIAL CHAL-
LENGES. COORDINATION BETWEEN THE CELLS GREW
DIFFICULT. THE LOCAL PARTNERS CLEARLY SOUGHT
TO BARGAIN AND PARRY THEIR NEWFOUND RELATION-
SHIP. THE OFFICE OF PEACE AND CONFLICT SUC-

CESSFULLY OVERCAME THIS OBSTACLE AND THE LOCAL PARTNERS REALIZED THE WEAPON COULD SUCCEED ONLY THROUGH COOPERATION.

SEPARATELY, THE OPERATION FELL INTO MORE BASIC, AGE-OLD CHALLENGES INVOLVING LACK OF CLEAR INTELLIGENCE FROM IRAN AS TO THE LOCATION OF THE WARHEADS. AFTER THE LOCATION WAS IDENTIFIED TO A SATISFACTORY EXTENT, TWO NEAR LAUNCHES WERE ATTEMPTED, BOTH THWARTED BY SIMPLE BUT NOT INSUBSTANTIAL LOGISTICAL CONSIDERATIONS, INCLUDING ONE OPERATION ABORTED DUE TO INCLEMENT WEATHER THAT PREVENTED DELIVERY OF THE LAUNCH CODES TO LOCAL PARTNERS COORDINATED ON THE IRANIAN BORDER.

ULTIMATELY, THE DECISION CAME DOWN TO SCRAP PROJECT SURROGATE. THE LOCAL PARTNERS PROVED EVEN LESS RELIABLE THAN EXPECTED AND SOME CONCERN AROSE IN THE OFFICE OF PEACE AND CONFLICT THAT SAID PARTNERS WERE EXHIBITING AN UNEXPECTED LEVEL OF COOPERATION.

FURTHER, ORDERS CAME DOWN THAT A BILATERAL DIPLOMATIC OR MORE FORMAL MILITARY RESOLUTION MIGHT SUFFICE (INCLUDING A LATE-GAME TURN IN THE RUSSIANS' POLITICAL CLIMATE THAT SUGGESTED THEIR OWN OIL INTERESTS MIGHT WORK IN FAVOR OF THEIR EXERTING FURTHER PRESSURE ON THE SHIA THEOCRACY).

A SMALL EFFORT WAS MADE TO RECOVER ONE OR BOTH PIECES OF THE SUITCASE NUKE OBTAINED FROM ROGUE RUSSIAN AGENTS. BUT, IN THE END, IT WAS DECIDED THAT THESE TWO ISOLATED PIECES WERE

```
NOT JUST INERT BUT ULTIMATELY AND COMPLETELY
UNUSABLE WITHOUT THE LAUNCH CODES.
```

Jeremy pauses, struck. There isn't much of the document left, but something is finally clicking for him. He reads again the phrase: "the suitcase nuke obtained from rogue Russian agents." Russian agents, suitcase nuke. The computer's been telling him to pay attention to the Russian arms organization, something with access to nuclear weapons, or material. Is this the connection, or one connection?

There is little to satisfy him in the last few sentences.

```
    PROJECT SURROGATE WAS DISBANDED IN MARCH
2013. IT IS CONSIDERED NEITHER A SUCCESS NOR
A FAILURE BUT A WORTHWHILE RISK IN A DANGER-
OUS WORLD.
```

```
OFFERED INTO THE RECORD.
-LT COL. LT
```

CHAPTER 38

J EREMY LOOKS UP and stares the rabid creature dead in the eye. The squirrel, beady, bulging black eyes, tail frayed from disease, sniffs the bag near Jeremy's feet. Jeremy's struck that he must've been so entranced, so still, that the squirrel felt safe enough to approach. Or maybe Nik has left inside some irresistible chemically enhanced snack food.

The squirrel scrams.

Jeremy, struck by a hunger pang, reaches into the leather bag, rummages. Finds a bag of Cheetos, rolled up, mostly eaten. He opens the bag, bites into a stale snack, spits it out. Hangs his head. *I'm sorry, Nik. I was beginning to doubt you. Beginning to wonder about your constant presence, loyalty, your access to all my contacts, strange habits, your network of virtual warcraft friends. Still waters running deep. And your weird fascination with the Lions.*

But you nearly got killed too.

Is there no one I can allow myself to trust?

No time to think about that.

Project Surrogate.

A top-secret effort to attack Iran. Using a bomb siphoned from Russia.

At once audacious and, in part, no surprise at all. Such clandestine efforts must be, if not commonplace, continual and ongoing.

Jeremy goes through the content, the logic, more slowly, making a few basic inferences and connections. Project Surrogate was run from the Office of Peace and Conflict Studies, a small part of the Pentagon run by Lieutenant Colonel Lavelle Thomson. The guy whose initials appear at the bottom of this memo.

Andrea's boss.

The guy who oversaw Jeremy's recruitment and the use of his computer.

A guy who Andrea claims disappeared a few days ago. And now purportedly is dead.

Could the lieutenant colonel have switched sides?

Or could he have been killed and forced to divulge key information about Project Surrogate? To whom? To what end?

Jeremy tries to keep himself from making the leap that he, a milli-instant later, makes: somehow, the bomb provided by the United States to attack Iran is about to be used to attack San Francisco.

And it's a bomb tied to Russia, to Rosoboronexport, a connection that somehow his computer pieced together. Or was the computer just making leaps in logic involving the sorts of influential entities—companies, executives, politicians—likely to affect the fate of the world?

Jeremy shakes his head. There's no way to know, exactly, what the computer was "thinking." It might have connected the dots between the arrest of a Russian munitions executive, unrest at Rosoboronexport, and a potential conflict. Or it might have simply added those developments to a larger body of evidence, creating more weight behind the computer's pre-diction of conflict. Regardless, it is seeing connections the rest of us don't see.

He thinks: The rest of us, except Harry. He must've pieced this together. He got hold of the top-secret memo. How?

Of course, Jeremy thinks. He worked with the government, was a consultant.

Harry put the pieces together, just like the computer, maybe more ably. More quickly?

And he died for it.

Harry, I'm sorry.

Jeremy feels pain pulse near his neck, now excruciating, at the bony protrusion of his clavicle.

Jeremy has a sudden urge to pace, to walk. To think and move, to synthesize. He looks at the clock. It's just after seven in the morning. His legs are wet from the damp ground, his joints aching from exhaustion, but he's alert, coursing with adrenaline.

Just after 7 A.M. There's an attack coming, tonight, here. Where? Nik will alert the media, and Jeremy will follow suit. The media, in turn, will alert the authorities, the cops, the army. They'll watch the airports and the ports, guard the land-marks. Ten hours, an eternity. *It was right. I was right.*

I can stop the attack. Redemption.

He starts to stand, when he realizes there's one more thing to do on the computer. Jeremy glances around, calls up a browser. Puts in "area code" and "218." He gets northern Minnesota.

He looks at a map of the area. There's nothing up there, except Duluth. Places called Hibbing, Moorhead, Fergus Falls.

His eyes trail back to the western edge of the state, Moor-head.

Evan.

It comes back to Jeremy. That's where Evan grew up. Jeremy recalls that, after high school, Evan attended Carleton College, in southern Minnesota, studied engineering, interned at some big data center there, went to Harvard for his MBA, then Silicon Valley, a couple of IPOs.

218-650.

"A phone number, the start of a phone number," Jeremy mumbles. He recalls that Harry's blood trailed off after the last number. The dying professor was trying to write more, trying to point Jeremy to Evan without showing his hand to someone else. Figuring Jeremy might figure it out.

He blinks, thinks, nice theory, but that's it. No endless number of Google searches under "218-650" will yield an exact phone number, presuming Jeremy's right. He pulls out his external keyboard, pops it in, and indulges in one search for "218" and "Tigeson," Evan's last name. He gets a hit. It's for Eileen and Frank Tigeson, an address in Moorhead. Must be Evan's parents. There's a phone number starting with 218 but the rest doesn't match.

No matter, further confirmation. He's got to find Evan. That seems to be the key to connecting the dots on the message from Harry, the V. A whole bunch of country codes and then, connecting them together, 218, Evan. The Peckerhead. Identified by Harry Ives, Harry War, the greatest conflict prognosticator in human history, as the fulcrum.

And, now, Evan connected to Andrea.

Could this be less an attack from the outside than one from within?

Evan, Andrea, Lavelle Thomson, Harry.

A brainstorm rocks Jeremy. His hands begin blazing across

the keyboard. Seconds later, he's entered his password and gotten himself into the guts of the conflict algorithm. Clicks until he finds a subdirectory, Program Princip. Clicks on it.

On the tablet screen materializes a beta, beta, beta program, an alpha program, the product of a forty-eight-hour creative binge. Jeremy drawing on research he commissioned from an intern from Berkeley, a protégé of Harry's. Jeremy trying to create a living example, or a dead one, of what he believed eminently possible in the Internet era: a machine to predict not just the onset of conflict but the seemingly insignificant actor pulling the trigger.

On the top right corner, he clicks a pull-down menu, then "New Test." The Princip web disappears and a spiderweb appears, absent names and faces and places. In the center, a blinking cursor. And a command: "Enter Name(s)."

No harm in trying.

In the command line, he types: Andrea Belluck-Juarez. Even before the word is finished, a panel opens on the right. In it, the results of an evolving Internet search. With each letter Jeremy types, the search engine, using keystroke intelligence, tries to keep up with, even anticipate, his search.

Are you looking for:

Andre Agassi

Then

Andropov, Yuri

Then

Andrea Bocelli

He manages to get her full name typed.

"For Andrea Belluck-Juarez," the search engine reads. He hits enter. In the panel on the right, beneath the name "Andrea Belluck-Juarez," a dozen or more options to people with the name. Third on the list is Andrea Belluck-Juarez, born in Mexico City; raised in Coeur d'Alene, Idaho; resides in Bethesda, Maryland; referenced on Facebook, LinkedIn, Tumblr, Twitter, WashingtonPost.com, dozens of others. Network: 10,000-plus connections.

Jeremy pridefully takes it in. This part of the algorithm is telling him that it can draw lines between Andrea and many, many people and ideas using publicly accessible databases and an underlying technology built from a search engine kernel. The special sauce, Jeremy's brainchild, is that it does the search in a context of conflict. How, if at all, do Andrea's connections bind not just to bad actors, or suspect ones, but to ones that themselves are connected to a prospective conflict?

Jeremy clicks on her name and it appears on the panel in the left, in the middle of the spiderweb. Next to her name, in the center of the web, a new dialogue box opens with a question: connect this person to what event?

Shit, he hasn't input the conflict predicted for mere hours from now.

He works in a flurry, clicking and typing, telling Program Princip which part of the larger conflict algorithm to tap into. Within less than two minutes, the command is complete: the computer will ask whether Andrea has some connection or connections that the naked eye can't see to an impending attack in San Francisco.

It's almost as if he's asking the computer the most human of questions: can I trust Andrea?

He feels a gust of wind. Looks at the clock. It's 7:37. He calculates he's got just more than an hour to find his way to Nik, who, in turn, might be able to help find Evan.

Into the spiderweb he enters Lavelle Thomson, discovering, at first, hundreds of potential matches for the name. He narrows it down by refining the search to the Washington, D.C., area and West Point, from where, he vaguely recalls hearing, the lieutenant colonel graduated.

Next, into the spiderweb Jeremy enters Harry Ives. Even as he does so, he doubts that Harry could be the culprit. Harry was warning Jeremy, not duping him. Then, on a whim, he enters the president. He's about to click on the button at the bottom of the web to start Program Princip from doing its thing, when his computer beeps and an icon appears at the bottom. Incoming mail. He runs his cursor over it. A message from the office manager at his building. He ignores it, returns to the algorithm.

He enters Evan's name.

Looks at the screen.

Enters Nik.

And, finally, he clicks on a pull-down menu and chooses from it "Computer-generated Princip."

This, in effect, is asking the computer to attempt to identify a person or persons most responsible for the potential attack, to draw connections between all the variables—rising and falling conflict rhetoric, arrest of an arms dealer, and on and on—with specific individuals. It's a complete wild-eyed effort. But why not?

He puts the curser over the button to launch the query. Something nags at him. What's he forgetting? Then it hits: he needs to give Program Princip some baseline against which to measure the potential threat posed by Andrea, Harry, the lieutenant colonel, the president, Evan, some random individual the computer divines. Otherwise the program can only compare their threat potentials against one another. That could be useful, but not necessarily, not positively, not if, for instance, they're all implicated in some way.

Who can he pick? Donald Duck? Emily? Who is the most innocent person he knows?

Of course. He puts himself into the spiderweb. He hits enter. He watches the web begin to whirl, doing its calculations. Will this add any evidence? He has no idea, not the slightest fucking clue. It's another appendage of his digital self, this computer that he feels he can't fully control, that is bigger than himself, so much more powerful, but so mysterious. A savant that can communicate only results, not the emotions or even the reasons behind its predictions. It's a brilliant black box, but still, a black box. And it leaves Jeremy feeling an instant of hatred. Is he like this box? All analytics, no ability to really connect—assessing people at a distance, performing some kind of game theory on them without really understanding them? Or they him?

A last computing stroke. He asks the algorithm to email him when the results come back. That way, he won't have to log on to the program every fifteen minutes to see if the results are back.

He throws all his stuff into the bag, and he starts jogging.

Fifteen minutes later, he stands behind a eucalyptus, looking out onto one of the main roads that wind down and through the Presidio. He swallows hard and peers behind the tree, wanting to make sure that a van toting a killer isn't among the cars dribbling by. Or among the three cars he can see parked fifty yards down on a gravel outcropping where cyclists pull their high-tech bikes from the top of the Subaru and burn two thousand calories before work.

A couple, already finished with their morning workout, load back up.

Jeremy pulls out his iPad, looks both ways, jogs down the side of the road. When he gets within ten yards, he waves his hand, the one holding the iPad.

"Pardon me, fellow travelers."

They look up. Windbreakers, spandex, short haircuts, wedding rings.

"What's up?" the man asks, glances briefly at his wife, closing the hatchback, and then glances back at Jeremy.

"Made a huge mistake on my morning hike," Jeremy says.

"Got lost?"

"Took my . . . this . . . albatross, wound up under a tree and lost track of time surfing for who knows what. Some story about Putin." Jeremy sighs. "Just looking for a lift down the hill so I can get to the office at some reasonable hour."

A pregnant pause. Enough for Jeremy to panic. What if the guy has heard reports of police seeking someone looking like Jeremy for the murder of a Berkeley professor? Then, he thinks: would that be so bad—to be in police custody, where he could show evidence of the attack, work in protected confines to discover the who, what, when and where?

The guy shrugs. "Could drop you at Divis."

Ten minutes later, Jeremy stands at the corner of Divisadero and Bay, then minutes after that, goes into the Starbucks at the Safeway, where he scrounges enough for a supersize coffee and, when the barista turns her head, pockets a banana and some chocolate cookie thing from the counter.

Then he hops an inbound bus and waits for the caffeine to

take effect. And waits. But the act of sitting, ensconced among jacketed commuters and dulled by the putt-putt sound of the bus engine, seems to have only the opposite effect. He can't think, let alone process and synthesize. He's down to a few basic mantras:

Find Evan.

Call the media. Call the police. Report the attack.

Of less significance:

Debrief with Andrea. What does she know? Is she even part of this equation? She knows what Harry knows.

Near Geary, the bus door opens. A wholesale exchange of commuters. Exiting is a group of a half dozen twenty-somethings wearing blue scrubs beneath their jackets as they head out to the handful of medical clinics. Getting on, khakis and pressed shirts, social climbers in North Face outerwear, heading downtown.

Jeremy presses himself against the window, still waiting for the caffeine buzz, vaguely aware that the neurochemical cock-tail that his body is delivering him to keep him awake and let him cope with the stress is way more powerful than anything even Starbucks can cook up. He remembers overhearing some study about how a growing number of people check email first thing when they get up in the morning, even before downing coffee, thus getting a mild buzz, a contact high. Maybe the conflict machine will wake him up.

Or is Jeremy just rationalizing an urge to look at the clock, see what news his gadget has delivered him?

The lumbering vehicle circles left on Geary, bodies sway-ing with the turn. Jeremy pulls out the iPad and pulls it close. Thinks better of it. Puts the device back into the leather bag and pulls out his iPhone. He'll be able to see if there's an email telling him Program Princip has finished its business; if he turns the phone on for only a few seconds, he can't imagine anyone could triangulate the signal and find him.

They're nearing Japantown, not far from the café with the view, a running joke, the place where he's supposed to meet Nik. It's got no view at all, the worst view for a café in the whole world. They used to meet here, sometimes with Evan, to talk business, a coffee shop outside the orbit of cool coffee shops, where no one could overhear, at least no one with any business acumen.

Jeremy pulls the plastic wire to signal the bus to stop.

He glances at his email. No update from the algorithm. But another email from the office manager at his building. "Asswipe," Jeremy mumbles, climbing off the bus.

Ignoring drizzle, or, rather, too tired and distracted to realize it's drizzling, he starts walking south on Fillmore. Behind him, the faux glitz of Japantown, a few-square-blocks commercial tribute to an ethnic community with deep visceral ties to this city. And on the sidewalks next to him, just ahead, liquor stores, a pawnshop, a Laundromat, a descent into one of the remaining yet-to-be-gentrified neighborhoods. And, in a block, the café with the view.

Jeremy swivels his head, looking for Nik, any followers. Then back to his phone, and the message from the office manager. It says, simply, "See attached (fuck the pigs)." The building manager, an unlikely ally, probably feeling harassed himself by the police. There's a file, .mov. A video clip.

He clicks on it. As it loads, he looks up to sees Nik standing in front of the shithole café, under a torn black awning.

Jeremy looks down at the device, the grainy video. It's a snippet from the surveillance cameras in the entry to his building. There's a time stamp. The middle of the night from two nights ago, when his apartment was broken into.

He sees the doors swing open, then the interloper looks for a second up at the camera. Jeremy feels his clavicle burst with pain, dopamine surging, his eyes physically bulging. Can't be.

He puts his finger over the phone to show the face again. Hits pause. Looks at the image.

At the top of his lungs: "No!"

CHAPTER 39

"WHO LIKES SUNSHINE?"

Emily closes the front door, unlatches the chain, opens the door. Feels the bristle brush of damp air.

"You're a persistent one," she says.

"You think I'm persistent. What about this fog?"

Emily takes in this new friend, met, what, ten days ago, two weeks? One date, a few phone calls. Charming, sure, walking a very careful line between being too aggressive and trying to communicate his interest. That's not novel for Emily. She's a magnet, even though she doesn't fully recognize it in herself. But she's usually a magnet for the wounded and angry, the eventual drug user who will lose a job and spend a year packing fat bowls on the couch, not this self-possessed, put-together entrepreneur. There's not a speck of dirt inside his car, the CDs arranged in the middle compartment alphabetically, as if he showers twice a day and then gets professionally vacuumed—him and his car.

And then there's Jeremy's warning about him, about how his jacket didn't match his shoes. Probably envy, right? Probably just Jeremy taking a shot. But, the thing is, Emily knows that what makes Jeremy so dangerous, so potent, is that even his offhand jabs are based on a whiff of truth. It's like the best comedy; it's funny because it's true. When Jeremy insults the guy behind the counter of the pharmacy, or at the café, he's articulating something frank and fair, even if it's totally socially awkward, wholly inappropriate. Like a child, like Kent, trying to get his mother's attention. And Jeremy saw something bad in this guy. Jealousy, truth, or both?

It makes her think, secondarily, about how much she misses Jeremy. This suitor, this slightly odd, nice guy, feels so inauthentic by comparison.

"You can make the fog go away?" Emily asks him.

He laughs. "I can put it in the rearview mirror. I took the audacious risk of packing a picnic lunch for the three of us. There's a spot on the other side of the bridge where the Marin County supervisors have outlawed fog."

She almost laughs. "You're serious."

"Kent's not in school today, so I thou—"

She cuts him off. "Deal, Liam."

He smiles.

"Do me a favor. I could really use a cup of coffee, and I'd like to get Kent ready, which will require some reorientation of his expectation that we're spending the day playing board games in the fog. Would you mind picking me up a coffee on the corner, and some sugar snack for Kent?"

"Ten minutes enough time for you?"

She smiles and shuts the door.

She moves to the window, watches this suave caller walk up the street, hands stuffed in his jean-jacket pockets, so nonchalant.

She thinks about Jeremy's hysterical messages. Almost

rants. *Get out of town*. And, again, about her ex-lover's instincts about her new suitor. She turns and looks at a picture frame over the mantel. The frame is empty. Until three weeks ago, it held a picture of Jeremy and Kent, the pair of them caught smiling together, an unposed, even haphazard image taken on a hike on the cliff above Seal Rock.

She sighs. She walks back into Kent's bedroom, finds the boy on the floor encircled by puzzle pieces. Standing beside him, a multicolored robot, whose arms move by remote control, something she picked up at a secondhand store on Geary.

"You're dressed. Good."

"It's cold."

"Sweetie, I've got a surprise for you."

Kent looks up skeptically. His sandy brown hair flops over his eyes and she shoves away a feeling of such love it might crush her insides.

"Come on, I'll show you."

He reluctantly rises. "Is it a pony?" An inside joke.

She leads him down the stairs, into the ratty garage, past the musty old mattress and the cans of paint. She opens the back door. "You're wearing your pajamas," he says.

She pushes him out the back and shuts the door.

"Can you climb the fence, Kent?"

"Mom, what—"

"We're climbing the fence, Kent. Do you understand me?"

Kent blinks, recognizing something like terror on the face of his mother.

Chapter 40

S LOW DOWN. PLEASE."

"You're not listening to me, Nik."

Nik's blinking, but impassive. He nearly steps backward because Jeremy's rushed in so close. Next to the café, a woman blanketed with newspapers and a sleeping bag, attended by a large stuffed brown bear, stirs from slumber, mumbles.

"Emily. Kent." Jeremy now talks through his teeth, a kind of hysterical whisper.

"You want me to call them, and the police."

"No!"

The woman by the wall rolls over, moans. Jeremy puts his hand on Nik's shoulder, inviting a rare flinch from the portly aide-de-camp.

"No. No police. Don't call that reporter."

For just an instant, Nik looks down. Looks up and sees horror on Jeremy's face.

"I just left a message, saying to call me and that you had an interesting story. Why—"

Jeremy sees the bandage on Nik's right wrist.

Nik whispers: "I can't tell if it was from bark, or a rock, or—"

Bullet graze.

Jeremy takes Nik by the arm, glances over his shoulder and walks into the café. It reeks of ammonia and glares orange from the shitty paint job that matches plastic flowers kept on vases on the faux wood tables. Behind the counter, a man with a scarf wrapped around his head doesn't look up.

Jeremy leads Nik to the one booth, in the corner. The pair slide in. Jeremy taps on his phone, drawing Nik's gaze.

"You've seen him?"

Nik takes in the grainy image of a man in his late twenties, dark hair. The surveillance camera has caught the side of the man's face, accentuating a pronounced nose.

"Does he look like the cat burglar?"

Nik looks at him, like: what the hell are you talking about?

"From the other night, your apartment? You told me a guy tried to break into your house."

Again, a clueless look from Nik, then "No." The assistant shakes his head. "I didn't get a look at him. Dolorosa scared him away." Nik's dog.

"He was masking an accent, sounding almost too American," Jeremy thinks aloud. "I need your phone."

Nik swallows, clears his throat. He slips a hand between his corpulent belly and the table, paws at his jeans.

"You left it in the car."

"I found a spot a couple of blocks away. I can—"

Jeremy waves him off. He opens his dialer and punches in Emily's number. Ring, ring, ring, ring.

No answer.

Jeremy puts down the phone. "We'll have to split up."

"Something happened to them?"

Jeremy lets himself look at Nik. The sweaty forehead, the mismatched sideburns, one nearly a lamb chop and the other a quarter inch shorter, the curl of unkempt hair behind the ear. Jeremy slowly looks up into Nik's eyes with something plaintive, vulnerable, sees that impassive gaze coming back, locks on to it, shivers. So alone.

Jeremy's phone rings. He scoops it to his ear. "E!" For Emily.

"We have to talk, Atlas." It's Andrea. Not Emily.

"You have her."

"Who?"

He doesn't have her. Jeremy puts his hand on Nik's thick arm.

"Listen, Andrea, goddamn it," Jeremy starts, and then his phone beeps again. He looks at the screen. He recognizes the number. Without missing a beat, he switches the call over.

"Are you safe?"

"What's going on?" It's Emily.

"That guy, the one from the café. Bad news. Worse than that. I'll come get you. Where are you?"

"Seal Park. It's not called that—"

"What? Where?"

"At the park, across from Seal Rock. Y'know, with the big tree in the middle and that place where we talked about—" Emily pauses; the stone deck overlooking the Pacific where they once fantasized they'd get married. In the pause, Jeremy looks at Nik, pins the phone against his ear with his shoulder and uses his hands to simulate a steering wheel.

Nik shakes his head, not getting it. Jeremy says into the phone: "Wait for us at the restaurant."

"What?"

"Wait, like in the trees—Kent's with you?"

"Of course. Restaurant?"

"Seal Rock Café. Wait across the street. You'll see us in twenty minutes. Me and Nik."

Nik is already scooting out of the booth, getting the plan: he'll run to get the car and come back to get Jeremy. On his way out of the booth, he pauses, reaches into the back pocket of his Dockers, pulls out a folded piece of paper.

"What's going on?" Emily asks.

Jeremy reaches for the paper, unfolds it. Sees two names and phone numbers. Something Nik has dug up for him but Jeremy can't focus on yet.

"I don't know. You've got the plan about where to meet?"

No response.

"Emily!"

Both Nik, who is halfway to the door, and the guy behind the counter look up at Jeremy.

"Emily," he repeats in his seething whisper.

"I'm here. Listen—" She pauses. "We love you, Jeremy. Kent . . . I—"

"Be careful. Twenty minutes." He's not sure what to add, then is startled by another beep from his phone. He pulls the phone from his ear, glances at the screen. A notification: the update from the conflict algorithm, Program Princip. The latest results are back. He paws over his shoulder to the leather bag, feeling his savior and burden.

"Twenty minutes," he repeats to Emily and hangs up. Across the room, he sees a woman nestle down at a table and pull out a laptop, open it, punch in a password. He looks out the window, beneath the neon sign: "Coffee Made Your Way." Outside, it's damp with fog, no sign yet of Nik. Maybe another three or four minutes the way he waddle-jogs.

Jeremy yanks out the iPad. Opens it, the browser springing to life. Looks at the clock.

9:30:15.

9:30:14.

9:30:13.

9:30:12.

He's mesmerized, tears himself away, swipes away the screen and calls up the log-in to get to the guts of the algorithm.

"You gonna order?" It's the guy behind the counter.

Jeremy nearly responds: "Large cup of coffee for me and a shave for you." Says: "Large coffee."

On the laptop screen, the guts of the algorithm appear. There's an icon in the center, the thumbnail of dark-eyed Gavrilo Princip, the face of a beta test. It's blinking. Another answer from this inscrutable computer. Jeremy looks out the window. No Nik. He clicks on the icon.

An hourglass whirls for just an instant and then a list of names and numbers materializes in the computer window. It's a list of all the people Jeremy asked the program to assess, to connect to the impending attack, and to determine who among them is most material in bringing about the apocalyptic events in less than ten hours.

One name stands out, at the top, blinking.

Jeremy squints. He's got to be reading it wrong. He brings his nose close to the screen. "You're fucking with me again."

He hears a honk. He startles, looks up to see Nik pulled up outside.

He looks around the café, sees the woman, bent over her laptop, typing away, the man standing at the counter, arms crossed, steam rising from the giant to-go cup on the counter in front of him. For the first time since this ordeal began with his computer, Jeremy's wondering not whether his computer is wrong or someone is fucking with him, but, more than that, whether he's going insane.

"Your coffee."

Jeremy barely hears the words from the guy behind the counter. He scoots from the booth, jeans tacky on the scummy vinyl upholstery, tucks the iPad under his arm. He scoops up the piece of paper left by Nik, hustles to the door.

"Your coffee!"

The words barely register as Jeremy flies out the door. Seconds later, he's inside Nik's car, inhaling that clean smell. "Stat," he says.

"Outer Richmond?"

Jeremy doesn't answer Nik, an affirmation in and of itself. Unable to come fully to grips with what he's seen on his iPad screen, he looks down at the piece of paper Nik left for him.

"Phone number?"

Nik says: "VOIP number. We had it in one of our databases. He doesn't seem to answer. But you asked me to try to reach them. Maybe you'll have better luck."

The piece of paper reads:

Evan: 218-293-2254.

Jeremy feels his face burn, pulsing with adrenaline and recognition. Harry's death scrawl, the clue. A symbol, looking like a *V*, connecting a bunch of country codes, and, at the bottom of the image, "218" and "650."

The 218 confirmed. Evan's phone number, the start of it, at least. The "650."

"How could I not have seen it?"

"What?"

"Area codes."

"Evan's area code—218."

"Okay."

"What's the area code for Silicon Valley?"

"I guess there are two, 408 and 65—"

"650!" Jeremy cuts him off.

An alliance; Evan and Silicon Valley.

Is that what Harry meant? Connecting the world?

"Evan, at the center of it."

Nik takes a left on Geary.

"At the center of it," Jeremy repeats. He looks up as they pass a bus, coming face-to-face with an advertisement for Google, and the smiling face of the company's youthful founder turned CEO imploring people to search. But in Russian: искать.

"I'm at the center of it too."

Nik doesn't answer, not atypically. He's accustomed to listening to his boss work things out, think aloud. He slows at a yellow light at Masonic, a complicated intersection, four-way lights, beginning to clog with morning traffic, medians thick with trees separating the sides of the street.

"Blow it."

"What?"

"Blow the fucking light!"

Nik looks at Jeremy and then around, and then accelerates through the red light. A driver pulling into the intersection lays onto the horn. And then Jeremy hears the siren. A single burst. He looks over his left shoulder and sees that they've just blown a red light in front of a police car, or, rather, a cop who has just passed through the intersection heading in the other direction.

"He has to turn around!"

"What?"

"Gun it, take the first right, turn off the car, duck."

Nik lays onto the accelerator. Jeremy looks over his shoulder, sees no sign of the police car. The cop, Jeremy realizes, faced daunting logistics finding a place to turn around, given the medians and the thickening commuter traffic.

Nik turns right at an intersection between a tire store and a single-screen art movie theater.

"Go up another block, then left."

Jeremy sees Nik's knuckles grip the steering wheel. He might be pushing his unquestioning assistant with these mercurial demands. "I'll explain everything. We just have to find Emily."

Nik glides to the end of the block, turns left, pulls into an empty driveway.

"Smart," Jeremy says.

The pair duck down. Jeremy looks at the screen of his iPad. The near high-speed chase has pumped him even more full with dopamine and cortisol, the fight-or-flight cocktail. He knows now that he's awake enough to be seeing these results clearly.

He turns the screen to Nik. The hefty assistant tilts his head, a gesture indicating he's trying to make sense of this.

"Gavrilo," Jeremy says.

"Princip. What about him?"

"This computer. This . . . thing."

Nik waits for Jeremy to explain.

"It thinks I'm him."

"Gavrilo?"

Jeremy looks at the results from the beta test, Program Princip. It shows the list of names Jeremy had asked the program to connect to the impending attack. At the top, one name.

Jeremy Stillwater.

"I'm the triggerman."

"Of what?"

He puts the cursor over his name.

"I'm the one who is going to cause the world to end."

"Jeremy—"

Jeremy looks up. He feels hot tears, a salty question forming in his eyes. Not a specific question, just a spasm of wide-open yearning.

"It doesn't make any sense. I have nothing to do with these people, this . . . this plot. But the program, it put it all together, all these disparate pieces of data, and it says that it's me. Tell me it's wrong."

Nik swallows. "I joined you, I followed you, stuck with you, because it's never wrong, it's never been wrong. You're not wrong."

It's more than Nik ever says, serving to shake Jeremy, maybe dumb luck on Nik's part, maybe a powerful instinct that these are the words that will shake Jeremy back to his impervious self.

"We can't call the cops. Not until we get Emily and Kent. Until I get some time to try to piece this together. Even then . . ." He pauses. "It's safe to go. We've lost him."

Nik starts the engine and pulls out.

Jeremy looks at the iPad, his mind flooded by a cascade of images: dead Harry, the numbers and the V; Andrea seducing him to work for the Pentagon, cornering him on a hotel rooftop; Andrea and Evan at odds, or perhaps not; Project Surrogate discovered by Harry at the log cabin.

All of it somehow adding up to Jeremy himself.

Nik speeds down California, barely pausing at stop signs, just a few miles to go. Jeremy looks at the piece of paper with the phone number for Evan. Another call first.

He dials Emily.

The phone rings. And rings. Jeremy's clavicle pulses in pain as Emily's voice mail picks up.

"Something's wrong."

"Another update from the computer?"

No, Jeremy thinks. My gut.

"Gun it."

Chapter 41

Sitting on a rock, surrounded by bushes, Emily and Kent can see through branches to the side of the Seal Rock Café. Inside, they can make out a man spooning something from a plate to his toddler.

"Was I that small?"

"Even smaller." Emily squeezes her arm around Kent's shoulder, taking advantage of the discomfort of the moment for physical intimacy, which her son seems less and less willing to allow.

He pulls in close.

"He got so mad at me," Kent says.

Emily turns and looks at her son, noticing a tiny blemish of skin above his lip; she wonders if it might be an early sign of pre-adolescent hormones.

"About the puzzle," Kent clarifies. She looks away from him, toward the street in front of the restaurant. A sedan pulls up to the stop sign but then rolls off.

"Jeremy doesn't always know how to explain what he's feeling. He thinks more than he feels."

"Sometimes I wish I was little again, like that."

"How come, sweetie?"

Kent swallows, doesn't answer.

"Jeremy liked me better when I was little."

"Don't be absurd!" But the protest is too instant, aggressive. She pulls it back. "He's adjusting. He's trying to adjust."

She frowns. She's losing Kent at a key moment but it's hard to explain, let alone understand, causing her to choose inaccessible words that lack precision, meaning.

They hear rustling in the bushes behind them. They turn, startled. Hear a voice: "Here, Binky. Here dog."

The bush rustling gets closer. Mother and child turn around. In their little enclave of bushes stands a big-boned man with a frothy black beard and a heavy coat.

"Did you see a little dog?"

"No." Emily instinctively recoils, begins to stand, pulling her son up with her.

"I'm sorry," the man says, his thick accent nearly swallowing his words. But the tone sounds so sincere, out of place, that it pauses Emily.

Then she takes two steps backward with the boy. Watches with a feeling of inevitability as the man pulls a black metallic object from his jacket. A gun.

He says, quietly: "Don't scream or I'll kill him."

CHAPTER 42

"WHERE?" NIK SLOWS a block from the restaurant.

"Out front. I'll . . ." Jeremy doesn't finish his thought, which he's expressed on autopilot. He's looking at the iPad screen, the results from Program Princip.

At the top.

> **Princip (most relevant):**
> Jeremy Stillwater.

Then, below it, other headings and names:

> **Potentially highly relevant:**
> Lavelle Thomson
> Evan Tigeson
>
> **Potentially relevant:**
> Andrea Belluck-Juarez

In other words, Jeremy understands, the computer has determined that he is most responsible for the upcoming attack, but also that the other names have relevance too. Potential relevance.

"This is not helpful."

"I don't see them."

Jeremy looks up to discover they're in the middle of a U-turn. Nik steers the car into a red zone in front of the Seal Rock, a motel with a restaurant of the same name. Jeremy sees a man walk out holding the hand of an ambling toddler wearing a red hat with earflaps.

"The problem is that it doesn't show its work."

Nik turns the ignition off, waits, ever the sounding board, for Jeremy to finish the thought.

"It draws connections, using probabilities and algorithms which, while I wrote them, I'm not totally sure how they work. Just that they work or that I've told people that they work." Jeremy doesn't add, but thinks: *It was right. I was right.*

What if it's right now?

"Unless the computer's been manipulated, or is somehow being used as part of the scheme."

"What?"

Jeremy turns over his shoulder and looks across the street into the park, such as it is, really a vast area of multifaceted terrain, pockets of trees and bushes lining and buffering the outside, a wide-open grassy area in the middle, then, beyond view from here, a stony outcropping that overlooks the ocean. Somewhere in the trees, Jeremy thinks, hide Emily and Kent.

He reaches for the door.

"No one had access to it. And what would it tell them, what could it tell somebody? When the world is getting so hot, so confrontational, that an attack would cause a domino effect; when the world is ripe for war."

He looks at Nik.

"Or when it's getting too peaceful."

Nik blinks. "Was this where they were supposed to be? Where are they?"

Jeremy: "We get them safe and then we get Evan. He's the key." Doesn't add: not me. Instead: "C'mon, Emily!"

Jeremy flings open the door and takes off, leaving the iPad on the seat. He makes a beeline for the phalanx of trees and clumps of bushes on the edge of the park. As he does so, he passes the father struggling to strap his son into a car seat in one of those mini-SUVs, this with a surfboard strapped to the top.

Jeremy runs his eyes along the trees and bushes until he comes to a gap halfway down the block, a narrow stone staircase that leads to the innards. He half expects to see Emily and Kent materialize, but they don't.

"Emily!"

He starts to run, stops. Turns back to the man and the boy, their car.

"Did you see a woman?"

The man, having succeeded in strapping in his son, walks around the back of the car, nearing Jeremy, who stands in the middle of the street. "Did you see a woman. She was with a boy. I'm supposed to meet them. It's an emerg—the boy is hurt and I'm his . . ."

"Kind of flip-flop hair?"

"Kent. You saw them?!"

The man pauses from zipping up a formfitting black jacket, suddenly appreciating some gravity. "I saw them through the window, of the restaurant. The boy's okay, I think. He looked okay."

"I didn't ask for your medical opinion. I asked you where they went. Where?"

"I . . ."

"Please."

"With . . . with the guy with the beard."

"Who?!"

The guy takes two quick steps toward the driver's door, clicks it open. "I'm with my son."

"Then you're obviously smart enough to see when a father is scared out of his mind." Implied with tone: you dipshit.

"Hey, bud, this isn't my business." He climbs into the door, says before he closes it. "They got into a van. The boy and the woman and some guy with a huge beard."

"Beard?"

"Like Moses or Abraham, but black." He shuts his door.

"The guy was black?!"

"The beard!" The man shouts through his window. "A woman with black hair was driving." The man peels away. But hardly any faster than Jeremy starts sprinting back to Nik. He finds the car door still open, flings himself inside, pauses, nearly sitting on the iPad, allowing himself to register a thought: he'd left this here to see if Nik might open it, tinker with it, glance inside, a test. Nik passed. The tablet and phone remain right where Jeremy left them, seemingly untouched.

"They went that way." Jeremy points behind them, toward the ocean. "No police, Nik."

"But—"

"No police!" He pictures Emily and Kent dragged away, stowed in some van, terrified. His clavicle bursts in pain; he squeezes his leg with his hand, willing calm.

"Let's get them."

Jeremy puts his hand on the keys, holding them in place.

"No! No . . . They're safe. They have to be. In danger but, for now, safe. They want me, something from me. They'll want to trade them. So we have time. If I get the police involved now, there will be no one left to ferret it out, and there can't be even nine hours left."

"Nine . . ."

Jeremy looks at the countdown clock. Under eight hours and thirty minutes. He needs to do something. Take some action.

He picks up his phone, then reaches into his pocket and pulls out the phone number, the one for Evan.

He dials Evan's number. Ring, ring, ring. "Pick up, Peckerhead!" Ring. No answer, then a generic "The person you are calling has a voice mail that has not yet been set up. If you'd like to—" Before Jeremy can leave a message, his phone beeps with an incoming call. It's the very number he's been calling, Evan.

Jeremy picks up. "What have you done with them?"

"You have received our correspondence, Jeremy." Evan's voice, even and handsome like the man himself, carries mostly charisma, but the fact the businessman doesn't start with a pleasantry, an overture, betrays stress.

"I know, Peckerhead. I know. I'm stopping it. I'm crushing you."

There is a silence. Evan clears his throat. He nearly laughs, recovers.

"My lawyers have sent no fewer than a dozen letters asking that you maintain a distance from me and my efforts. I understand that you're angry over the dissolu—"

"Cut the shit! I want to know where you've taken them. I know about Harry, all of it. You and the high-tech consortium, the tantalum shipments," He's just riffing, bluffing, stacking blocks, trying to stack them. "I'm taking you down."

"You are a dangerous man," Evan says, then adds, quietly, "You are not going to fuck this up."

"I—" Jeremy, a stalking beast, pauses, taking in some new information he can't quite read, a tacit admission. Evan's involved in something, all right, the center of it, just as Harry said.

"What do you want from me?"

"Goodbye, Mr. Stillwater."

"Meet with me!"

"Goodbye."

"Or I'll expose everything."

"You're a discredited zealot, Jeremy. Enough. Goodbye."

"Hello, CNN. Hello, Marines. Hello, 1600 Pennsylvania Avenue."

There's a pause. "You don't have a clue what you're meddling with."

"The end of the world."

Evan exhales. "I'll text you a place."

"Where? When?"

Evan disconnects.

"They want me, they don't want me, they use me, they discard me."

Nik says: "I guess at this point it's not too much to ask what is going on." His eyes fall to his wrist, the bandage, then quickly return to Jeremy.

"Maybe they got what they wanted from me, and my computer."

Nik raises his eyebrows, a silent question: who got what they wanted?

"Andrea, Evan, maybe both of them. Remember when I flew to Washington, the Pentagon, all that horseshit? Never mind." Jeremy thinks: too much shorthand. "You drive and I'll try to make sense of it."

Nik starts the engine, takes Jeremy jutting his chin as a cue to head back down on Geary. He again pictures Emily and Kent, blinks it away.

"They have planned an attack but they're missing something."

"Pronouns."

"I don't know who 'they' are. Maybe Evan, maybe someone connected to him, somehow connected to us, to me. Closely. The computer tells me that I am playing a role in the attack, that I'm instrumental, the trigger. But unless I'm insane, truly certifiably insane, I don't know anything about it. And unless the computer is truly, certifiably insane—" Jeremy pauses. "Unless the computer is wrong, then I have some role that is unknown to me."

Jeremy's eyes come to rest on a diner a half block ahead, next to a tire store. He pictures himself on that first trip to Washington. He remembers returning to his hotel room after drinks with Andrea, thinking something was amiss with his computer. What was it?

"Let's eat and think. Can you turn off your cell phone?"

"It's off."

"If they didn't need something, they'd have killed me already."

Nik pulls the car to the curb. "You realize this sounds—"

"Forget about the computer. Even without its predictions, Harry's dead. The guy who was with Emily at the café is the same one who broke into my apartment. Andrea and some henchwoman chased me at gunpoint—"

"Who?"

"There was a secret buried at the log cabin. Project Surrogate. For goodness' sake, Nik, you were shot at yourself. We were nearly killed in the Presidio. And now Evan admits he's involved in something, maybe the attack itself. There's a mass of evidence that doesn't just portend something terrible but, by extension, suggests that the computer is right."

It was right. I was right.

I am Princip.

Nik pulls the keys from the ignition. Jeremy, lost in thought, climbs from the car. The pair trundle into the diner, impervious to the drizzle. At a table beneath an autographed picture of a drummer for the Grateful Dead, who apparently once ate at the diner, Jeremy drinks coffee and Nik water.

"Surrogate?"

"An American plot to destroy Iran's budding nuclear arsenal." And with that, Jeremy is off and running, explaining about the bomb, segregated into two parts so that the fringe groups could not detonate without cooperation from one another and from the Americans. He opens the iPad, stares at the bloodred map.

"You want my guess?" It's rhetorical. He continues. "Harry was involved, somehow. Of course. He's the leading authority on conflict, its resolution, consulted by governments. He must've been involved in conversations about Surrogate, planning, advising. Another guess: they killed Lavelle Thomson, the lieutenant colonel, whoever 'they' is, trying to get hold of the bomb or figure out how to detonate it.

"But I still don't get why they're attacking San Francisco, now. It's . . ." Jeremy pauses, struck by a thought, just as a waitress arrives with two plates of food; the omelet Jeremy ordered and the same for Nik, who simply said: "ditto." Jeremy asks the waitress if he can borrow a pen. On the paper tablecloth, he draws the symbol from Harry's calendar.

"What does this look like, Nik?"

"A V, the letter."

Jeremy holds up his right hand, then folds into his palm his thumb, ring and pinkie fingers. It leaves his index and middle finger standing. He parts them, creating a V.

"What does this look like?"

Nik clears his throat. "Richard Nixon, or . . ."

"A peace sign." Jeremy simultaneously says it and lets it sink in. He takes a bite of his food, then pulls his iPhone from his pocket.

"We're getting a tacit message," Jeremy says.

"What?"

"My phone's been on for thirty minutes. If they wanted to find me, they'd have done so already; they could've tracked the signal. Why aren't they coming for me?"

Nik holds a fork in his hand, his food untouched. "Because they have her, and . . ."

"Kent."

His phone buzzes. There's an incoming text. Jeremy calls it up, stands, and without a word sprints for the car.

CHAPTER 43

L EFT ON MASONIC. Did you help coordinate my trips with Andrea?"

Nik goes through a yellow light, eliciting a honk from an oncoming Jeep with its top down.

"Now where?"

"Veer right at the corner." Jeremy and Nik are cruising up a hill, passing a grocery store on their left. In the distance, to the right, downtown, the sunnier part of the city, emerges from the fog. "Then left, past the JCC for a few blocks. The trips to Washington and the Middle East?"

Nik says: "When you didn't feel like cooperating."

"No need to be defensive. I'm trying to understand what they wanted from me, what she wanted from me. They didn't want the algorithm to predict the future of conflict. She said so herself. They weren't taking the computer seriously. Did you deal with her or anyone else?"

"Her, briefly. She—"

"Left. What?"

Nik turns. "You remember a board meeting we had, a retreat, at the house by Muir Woods?"

Jeremy pictures it. Harry went on some diatribe about the coexistence of the coho and silver salmon in Redwood Creek. "What's that have to do with Andrea?"

"I came back to the office, and she was there. Late at night."

"So."

"Here?" They're across the street from the Jewish Community Center, slowing. Jeremy watches Nik stare at the large, elegant building with a private security guard standing out front.

In his mind's eye, Jeremy pictures the Lion of Judah, the symbol for Jerusalem. What was the news report? A man dead with a tattoo of a woman, and a word in Latin: *Custos.* Guardian.

So what?

"No, two blocks ahead, and to the right, there's a park. Kids and stuff. Evan says he'll be there. But I want you to drive past it, see what we see, then decide. So Andrea is at our office, and . . . ?"

"Inside our offices. The ones where we are now. She tells me she's been trying to get hold of you and that they've scheduled one of those trips. She's there to pick you up."

"Inside my office or inside the outer area?" The publicly accessible part.

No immediate answer. Nik turns right, pausing to let a hearty dark-skinned woman with a double stroller pass through the crosswalk. Nanny central. Nik swallows, trying to remember. "Your office. She said it was open and she was trying to leave you a note. She said the trip was imminent."

"How did she seem?"

Nik doesn't answer, lightly shakes his head, not getting it.

"Stressed? Calm?"

"Not like a burglar, if that's what you mean."

Jeremy takes it in. "You never told me."

"She called you that night. I watched her make the call, listened to her."

"But the trip didn't happen." Jeremy sees the outskirts of the hillside park on the block ahead. "There were a few of those—close scrapes with last-minute Middle East trips." He can't remember this particular call or another trip that didn't materialize. "They told me I was going to be able to field-test my algorithm, first in southern Iraq, then in . . ." He can't remember the places, all right in that region. "Right around Iran." He pauses. "Stop, please. Let me out here."

Nik looks at Jeremy, like he'd prefer a little more clarity. It's a look frequently elicited by Jeremy, someone who often divulges little, speaks in fragments and clipped ideas, often in challenges or rebuttals. Even now, maybe especially now.

"I'm just saying that none of the trips happened, not to Iraq or any of the surrounding areas. Lots of head fakes. I don't know what to make of that. I don't know who or what to trust." Jeremy looks down at his phone. It's 11:48. "Peckerhead is not going to be here for a few minutes, if he's really coming."

Jeremy looks up, sees they've stopped a half block from the park, in front of a trendy Italian restaurant and a five-and-dime liquor store. Across the street, an artsy movie house and a café featuring organic pastries made by "local artisans."

Walking up the street, some doofus in a lion mask and a sign: "The end is near."

"Have people no shame?" Nik mutters. He looks ashen.

"You're really taking the lion thing hard." Jeremy puts his hand on Nik's shoulder, causing his assistant to flinch. If Jeremy's ever touched him with such a gesture of intimacy, it was accidental and after several pomegranate cocktails, maybe when Nik helped carry his drunken lean-to boss to the car. Nik allows himself to look at Jeremy, take in a glance filled with paternal responsibility.

"You're remarkable, Perry."

Nik laughs. "I knew I had a real name."

"You never stopped believing. You have been a stalwart, PeaceNik. The only one, really." It's a statement containing an unspoken question: why?

"It was fate," Nik manages, still half smiling, then clears his throat, fidgets, sees Jeremy's powerful gaze, then manages: "I never lost my faith."

Jeremy sees Nik absently scratch his rubbery neck. Sees the chain that holds the cross around Nik's neck. Jeremy, in an act of subconscious mimicry, feels beneath his shirt, pats the key fob. He puts a hand on Nik's shoulder. "Don't worry, I'm not just buttering you up. This is a pep talk. We're going into . . . battle, forgive the cliché, and I need to know I can count on you, completely."

Nik stares straight ahead.

"I'm going to meet with Evan but it may well be a trap. In fact, I suspect we're being watched now. I've had my phone on forever, so, at the least, Andrea's probably somewhere around here, maybe . . . who knows who else."

"Trap?"

"He wouldn't meet me if he didn't want something from me. Guy never in his life took a meeting that didn't serve him."

The pair falls silent. Jeremy opens the car door, pauses, looks at the liquor store they're parked near. In the window, a large blown-up rubber bottle of tequila, a kind of kitsch you might see in Las Vegas. "It's out of place here."

Nik follows Jeremy's gaze.

"But I guess even the trendiest neighborhoods have alcoholics, the real purists." Jeremy shakes his head. "I'm a conflict-a-holic." He smiles sadly. "And prone to the non sequitur. You've done a hell of a job listening to me all these years. Drive to the other side of the park. Leave your phone on. I'm going to text you and tell you where to pick me up. If you see me running—I'll head in that direction—drive by and throw a life preserver."

Jeremy looks down at the countdown clock. It's just under eight hours.

"Should we pick a place to meet?"

"Good plan, Nik. If we get disconnected, let's meet at CPMC."

"The hospital?"

"Right down at Cherry and California. Close enough for me to walk. There's a lot of chaos at hospitals, which could come in handy. I'll come bearing answers, the kind that you can rely on only a human to get, not a computer."

Nik takes in his boss; he's unable to put a finger on what is strange about the man he's shadowed for years. "You sure you don't want me to stay with you?"

"No one knows me better than you do . . ." Jeremy opens the door, pulls out the bag, slings it over his shoulder, leaves his thought unfinished. "Off with you, Nik." He shuts the door, watches Nik drive off.

He peers at the park, suspecting Evan's not there yet, if he's planning to be there. Knowing that Evan, while he's generally punctual, is also cautious. He'll wait until he knows Jeremy's arrived, or maybe someone is scouting the area.

Jeremy, like a computer juggling if-then statements and what-if scenarios, settles on an idea and sprints across the street to the café advertising itself as an organic haven. Lost in thought, he pulls open the door, perhaps a little abruptly, causing heads to pop up to see the zealous interloper. Gazes drop again. Jeremy makes for the back of the café, bypassing the counter, sees a sign for restrooms and stairs leading to a handful of tables in a loft, being mounted by a woman toting a steaming mug and a laptop bag.

He falls in line behind her, climbs the stairs and, seconds later, finds himself in the restroom. To Evan's number, he texts: "Running 15 minutes late."

He washes his face, starts to look in the mirror, looks away, stung by a momentary fear that he'll look up and see the bony, ruined outline of his mother's face, her judgmental, knowing eyes.

He pokes his head out of the restroom door, seeing nothing particularly suspicious. To his right, an emergency exit, a heavy door, evidently leading to stairs or a fire escape, some waste of money required by the overly bureaucratic building codes.

Jeremy looks back onto the loft, sees that the woman he'd followed up the stairs has her face buried in her work. She's bundled around the shoulders in a fluffy black coat. He starts for the stairs, nearing the woman, sees her, animal-like, stiffen. She's using her own fob to log into her computer, settling in.

"I'm very sorry for interrupting," Jeremy says. "I made a huge mistake."

The woman looks up with a round face and eyes, mid-thirties, no wedding ring, a jogger's tan, still keeping in shape, fighting age.

Jeremy half smiles. "I only put seven hundred dollars in my parking meter."

"Seven hundred dollars?"

"Gives me six minutes. If I don't add another seven hundred in quarters, I'll get a ticket, then probably arrested. It's getting draconian. You don't by chance have quarters for a seven-hundred-dollar bill."

She laughs. "Been there. You want me to see if I have quarters?"

"I got 'em." He widens his smile. "I just want to put my stuff down and establish squatter's rights on this excellent table. Would you mind watching it while I feed the meter? I promise, when I come back, I'll not interrupt your work again." A flirtation that suggests just the opposite.

"Are you okay?" the woman asks.

"The idea of a ticket fills me with dread."

She laughs. "Feed the meter. I'm not going anywhere."

Jeremy puts down the leather bag.

He jogs down the stairs, pausing at the door to look back at the woman in the balcony loft, lost in her work. He feels the iPad tucked into the front of his shirt, still with him, the bag empty but maybe serving a purpose that Jeremy's percolating. He looks left at the park, sitting on a hillside, sloping downward in the opposite direction. He takes a right, heading away from the park, considering his two assumptions: that Evan will be late, or cautious, having received Jeremy's text; and that Evan will approach the park from the high side, the peak of the park, not the bottom of it. A basic tenet of war, seek the higher ground.

He looks up to discover that he's right. A block away, on the other side of the street, head down in his device, Evan turns the corner. Jeremy starts running. A plan coming together. He wants to reach Evan before his old Peckerhead partner gets near the park, out of its view, or maybe Evan's reinforcements. Jeremy passes the movie theater on his right, watching Evan still facing down over his gadget, sees him passing in front of the liquor store, then crosses the street so that he's now behind Evan.

He hustles behind his ex–business partner and takes him by the elbow.

"What the . . ."

"I need a cold one."

"A cold . . ."

Jeremy tries to guide Evan into the liquor store. Evan pulls away, then, after several rapid eyeblinks, follows Jeremy inside. Behind the counter, a man looks up, his head wrapped in a red and white kaffiyeh. Jeremy keeps walking to the back of the store, Evan a few steps behind. Then stops. "Jeremy."

Without looking back, Jeremy reaches under his shirt and pulls out the iPad, holds it over his head, keeps walking. He hears Evan's loafers click on the cheap liquor store flooring, following.

Seconds later, Jeremy pushes through the doorway marked "Emergency Exit" and finds himself in an alley.

He turns around. Takes in Evan, that smooth skin, the face of commitment, part of the crop of entrepreneurs who believe it when they say their technology companies make money incidentally but are really aimed at changing the world.

Jeremy shoves Evan against the wall.

"Where is she?!"

"Stop!"

Jeremy holds his hands against Evan, the pair looking at the iPad lying on the ground.

"We're going to do it," Evan says. "Just like we said."

"What?"

"Change the world."

Jeremy swallows, loosens his grip.

"What I'm going to tell you must remain between us."

Jeremy laughs. But he's listening.

CHAPTER 44

"P EACE," Evan says.

Jeremy drops his hands. Evan brushes his chest, smoothing out a royal button-down, lightly starched.

"The final frontier."

"Spare me the soapbox. How does war bring peace?"

Evan shakes his head. "I have five minutes. You can listen or you can do your usual thing and waste your life and my time with confrontation. I think, anyway, you've way crossed the line this time. Let's walk to the park."

"No."

Evan looks up and down the alley, a wide berth between businesses and restaurants on each side, lined with plastic blue and green and black recycling, composting and garbage cans. Gathering dusty drizzle.

"You're going to be part of it. You deserve credit." Evan's change in tone, right from the management manual, the supportive uncle, makes Jeremy want to barf. "The last few years, I ran a million scenarios with the algorithm. I was looking for business outcomes; the next great business sectors, the most

economical and efficient regions to start a business, put manu-
facturing, mine new markets. Looking for specifics and proof
of concept."

Jeremy waves his hand; he knows all this.

"I discovered a fascinating by-product, maybe one that
wasn't all that surprising. In regions where business got hot—
say, if we hypothetically located a semiconductor plant in a city
in Thailand—there was a concurrent outbreak in peace."

"Thailand isn't at war."

"Actually, it's facing terrible unrest. By peace, I mean: a re-
duction in variables associated with war, like economic growth,
harsh political rhetoric, especially that. Of course, this comes
as zero surprise—"

"Morocco."

"Exactly." Evan's face lights up, one of those outbursts
not just of genuine enthusiasm but also showing how quickly
these two men can connect. "By all rights, Morocco has a
terribly volatile demographic mix: urbanites, barely educated
desert people, religious Muslim, secular Muslim, the vaca-
tioning Europeans. Yeah, they've had some Al Qaeda attacks
but, well, that's kind of the point. The extremists can't stand
the fact that, on balance, Morocco is a fairly sane place, at
least relative to say, Syria."

"So what?"

"So I tried like hell to persuade you to make this an economic tool, to try to build both business and political prosperity, a democratizing tool. But you wouldn't hear of it."

"Bullshit . . ." Jeremy rolls his eyes.

"Jeremy, you never wanted to do anything that wasn't ex-
pressly your idea. Not that your ideas were bad, far from it.

It's just that others also just might have something valuable to contribute."

"Keep talking." Jeremy hears a noise, looks down the alley, sees that a car has turned into it. Something small. Evan pauses for ten seconds to let the Smart Car pass, a man behind the wheel, his dog in the passenger seat. As it passes, the car nearly sprays the men with a puddle.

"Don't flip him off, Jeremy."

"What does that have to do with what's happening today?"

"I took your technology to a few execs, big-time folks, initially hoping, like I told you, to use it as a business tool."

"And?"

"You know Andres Potemkin?"

Jeremy nods. Of course. A cofounder of Sky Data, one of the biggest makers of large-scale servers, the guts of cloud computing.

"Russian by birth," Evan says. "A Russian Jew, which is relevant." In Silicon Valley, unlike the East Coast, people apologize if they ever identify someone by ethnicity, this place considering itself a color-blind meritocracy.

Jeremy feels a buzz. But so what?

"He got immediately jazzed. Well beyond my imagination. He asked if he might run some scenarios himself, and a few days later, he got back to me with some ideas."

The grimy sweat of uncertainty and revelation forms on Jeremy's forehead. He listens as Evan starts to explain, a semi-ramble: he explains that Potemkin went to Carlos Fox, the billionaire Mexican chip manufacturer; and Raj Arooth, the venture capitalist; and a very tight group of high, high-level executives at the biggest companies, and, together, they began exploring whether they could use the algorithm to work backward. Meaning: rather than putting business first—to emphasize profits—they'd discover what economic models would lead to peaceful outcomes in imperiled regions.

"It was heady stuff, heavy stuff, incendiary, in an intellectual sense, as I said, a new frontier." Evan's voice is going high the way it does when he's very excited. "This handful of huge thinkers, coming together, competitors, looking not at predicting the future, but . . ." He pauses, realizing he's about to use his own buzz phrase ("but shaping the future") and realizing too that this conversation is too real for bumper stickers.

"They're all immigrants," Jeremy mutters, a kind of whispered revelation.

"Foreign-born, the preferred term. But, yeah, right, Silicon Valley itself is their model. Peace and prosperity, economic growth through intermingling of cultures. Morocco was a trading crossroads, the place where East and West and North and South once traded. That's a little bit like Silicon Valley today. Walk into an office and you've no idea what color or religion or orientation you'll be trading with."

Jeremy says: "So they got together, made a secret plan to join forces, reverse-engineer peace."

"Couldn't have said it better myself. They want to join forces to bring an intertwined business community, to build an irrepressible technology economy in the most volatile region in the world."

"The Middle East."

Evan nods. "You're never far behind." He smiles.

"Mobile phone technology. Semiconductors? A massive joint venture."

"Impressive. Maybe that computer does work. How did you—"

"Tantalum." Jeremy's thinking of the increased shipment of tantalum, used for mobile phones; might be related, a lucky guess. No, more than that, concrete evidence ferreted out by the computer. Tantalum isn't a red herring after all, not ancillary. The computer has somehow picked up and put together these seemingly disparate developments: a Russian arms dealer arrested, perhaps responsible for selling a bomb; the explosion of conflict rhetoric around the world; the relative calm in the Middle East; the surge in demand for tantalum. Does the computer know they're connected or is it doing some mystical probability?

"You've signed some tantalum contracts, a bunch of them, for use in this . . . venture."

"Yep."

"You sought out Harry. He started helping you form alliances. Make some sort of pact among these businesses. To do what—exactly."

"Seriously?" A rare hint of condescension from the very political Evan.

"You're not going to tell me."

"No. I just . . . I've told you, a thousand times. At least in general terms the last eighteen months. You haven't listened. The idea is to bring big companies, their leaders, together and, as you say, reverse-engineer peace by creating economic hubs in places with the deepest traditions of conflict. The promise of technology isn't being able to predict the future of, say, conflict. It's being able to use the tools you've created to shape the future. Determine what factors are most likely to bring war and then create the conditions that would least likely lead to it—war, conflict."

"A peace machine."

"Nice." Sincere. "Say what you will about the wonky entrepreneurs driving the world's economy, innovation, computing, but they're not all about money. Yeah, they, I, don't mind getting rich. But at some point, there's a bigger legacy. Besides, it's an enlightened self-interest. The world gets safer, wealthier; we've got a better place for our kids to live and—"

"A lot more consumers."

"Make e-commerce purchases, not war." Evan shakes his head lightly, understanding he's being too cute by half. "The biggest tech executives in the world are about to announce a future of peace and prosperity, peace through prosperity. They're all immigrants, a multicultural society that runs Silicon Valley, that drives it, and they've pulled off the single greatest act of diplomacy the world's ever seen."

Evan pauses. In the last few minutes the temperature has dropped half a degree, the fog turning to a light drizzle. Jeremy's head is down, his neck near his chest, wincing at a pulsing of pain.

"Israel, the West Bank, will get so peaceful they'll make Morocco look like Gettysburg in 1863. We're building it in the image of Silicon Valley, not imposing our ideas, just giving rise to economic interdependence in a way that the world has never seen. Not just words, but billions in investment. A production center for mobile technologies, the next generation of devices and software, a digital trading post. We're going to change the world starting at the cradle of civilization."

"We. The business leaders?"

Evan smiles. For him, another of those punch-line moments that he lives for. "And the leaders of the stakeholders in the Middle East. Key officials from Israel and the Palestinian territories. We'll break ground in two days on the road to Ramallah. And everyone is here to meet this afternoon, then announce it tonight."

Jeremy feels his heartbeat pick up, not in terror, for the moment, but in lockstep with Evan's enthusiasm, a physiological recognition of the sales power of his former partner.

"We're going to shock the world. No one knows, other than the highest-level group of stakeholders. We've kept the whole thing off the grid." Evan half laughs. "Cloak-and-dagger stuff. No emails on the subject, personal contact, code names, all the bullshit."

Evan smiles, continues: "Blood brothers, we all swore not to share the particulars, where, when. I don't think a single person on Earth knows about today's meeting, and announcement. Hell, I've told everybody I'm out of town."

"At the JCC? Is that why we're here?"

"No, what? Too public. We've chartered *The Idealist*."

Jeremy shakes his head.

"A boat. Most of them are already on it. Safe from any public view. We'll make peace beneath the Golden Gate Bridge. Like an armistice."

There's a pause. Then: "Who doesn't want peace?" Jeremy suddenly asks.

"What?"

"Harry's dead."

Evan doesn't say anything.

"He's dead! They took Emily and Kent."

Evan winces. "They're looking for you."

"Who?"

"The police. They tell me you've snapped, finally. Totally lost it. Jeremy, I want to help you if I can . . . I'm here because I owe you a lot. I know you mean—"

"You have no idea what's going on, do you?"

Jeremy leans down and picks up the iPad. He wipes from the cover a coat of drizzle.

"Jeremy, you're a genius, I grant you—"

"You're so fucking clueless."

"Listen to me!" Evan's tone. "You are . . ." He doesn't say the next words: fucking clueless. Instead: "A genius, but you've been used. Over and over again. I admit. Everyone around you: me, Harry, Andrea, hell, even PeaceNik, Nik, thinks about peace. All of us. You think about conflict. You never really saw this as a peace tool. But it couldn't exist without you. You were like the sun, the center of this extraordinary, embryonic universe—people and institutions interested in understanding conflict and promoting peace. But, like the sun, you can be dangerous and, to stretch the metaphor, scorching. We all coalesced around you— the government, the academics, the entrepreneurs—but we realized we needed to give you a wide berth. We, if I'm honest, we used you. Let you lead us, in a way, but also took advantage . . ." He pauses. "There's something so predictable about your urge to conquer, to win. If . . . if something happened with you and Harry, I'll do what I can to help you. I . . ."

"Took advantage." Muttered.

"Huh?"

"Look!"

Jeremy's tone shakes not just Evan, but the alley, echoing down the opening.

"I was right. *It* was right." Again, muttered. It somehow pieced together these disparate elements: the Russians, the tantalum, the volatility in general of the world, and, most of all, the likelihood of peace in the Middle East.

Jeremy opens the cover of the iPad. He swivels his finger on the screen, bringing to life the conflict map, drenched in red. No sooner does it materialize than a series of dialogue boxes pop up. A shrill chirp. Updates.

Evan reaches for the iPad. "What's this?"

He's looking, not at the screen, but at something on the back of the tablet. Jeremy looks too. He sees a little nodule, a tiny metallic tick.

"Are you bugging me?" Evan bellows.

Jeremy shakes his head. "No. You're missing the point. Look at the screen." He turns the iPad back to display the map.

"Is that . . ." Evan doesn't finish his thought. Instead, he turns his attention down the alley, to a car turning inside, rambling slowly onto the gravel of the bumpy alley.

Jeremy sucks in sharply, clicks on the dialogue box. Countdown clock update: 2:36:12. Two hours, 36 minutes, 12 seconds.

Jeremy shivers. "It's supposed to be seven hours away, not until tonight."

"That's the conflict map?"

"Peckerhead."

Evan looks up. Sees what Jeremy sees: a steel rod, a barrel, sticking from the driver's-side window of the oncoming car. A pistol.

"Down!" Jeremy dives toward Evan's legs, tackling him to the pavement.

Splat. Splat. Splat.

"Evan!"

Jeremy feels his partner's heavy weight collapse over him, hears screeching. Van tires on wet pavement. It slides ten feet ahead, to Jeremy's left, skids and stops. Jeremy scrambles. "Evan!"

No answer, dead weight on him, dead. Dead?!

Evan!

His face, his head. A hole . . .

Car doors open. Voices, urgent, woman and man.

Jeremy, no distance between thought and action, movement and instinct, scoots from under the body, sees the back door of the liquor store, dives for it. Into the cove of concrete protecting the door, a little entryway and a concrete overhang.

Splat, splat, splat. Bullets slam into the wall next to him. Splat. A searing pain in his calf.

"Go around front!" A woman's voice. Glances, sees her shape, a blur, something familiar.

Jeremy yanks open the door, sprints. Adrenaline trumping the pulse in his leg. Doesn't look down, tumbles, knocking over a cardboard cutout, some marketing thing, hears bottles tumble.

"Hey!" The man behind the counter.

Jeremy flies by him.

"Hey!"

"Police!" Jeremy says. It's out of his mouth before he can take it back.

In seconds, he's out the door, head swiveling. A stroller, a delivery truck coming up the street, rain, no bad guy, yet. An idea. It's been with him. *I am right. It was right.*

I am Princip.

He keeps sprinting.

CHAPTER 45

"D ONE, COMMANDER."

"And you got Jeremy?"

No answer. Silence. Assent. Nik looks out the car window at the drizzle, the playground at the park, a mother pushing a boy. Nik's heart picks up, adrenaline, then something so beyond sadness. He's glad he didn't hear the sound of bullets.

"What next, Nik?"

Nik doesn't answer.

"Nik?"

"Janine, call me Perry." Perry, known to so many as Nik, PeaceNik, looks at the boy on the swing. Hopefully destined for a better place. Nik wonders if it would solace the boy to know that Nik himself will join the pile of ashes and dust. The price, the promise, of being Neturei-Karta. The price of being not just a Guardian, but, for this operation, *the* Guardian, the sentry at the top of this show.

They know where the meeting is now, the target. What made Nik think they'd be able to execute the plan without terrible bloodshed? And, yet, a few deaths somehow feels more painful than the impending apocalypse. Each life an expired spark.

"We need to make sure we get the code," he says absently. "Lose the body."

He hears his voice. This is not how he ever talks aloud, just online, in World of Warcraft. Where he's Commander Perry. An alter ego, or his real ego. What's the difference? Online he can connect with other Guardians, command, collect other believers, help manage and guide, unseen and unnoticed in an online world filled with code and conflict.

"Of course." There's a pause; Nik hears a phone ring. "Hang on," says Janine, then, "Uh-huh."

"Perry."

"What?"

"Small hiccup."

"What?"

"Small. We'll take care of it."

Click.

Chapter 46

J EREMY SPRINTS BACK across the street, scanning the street. Doesn't yet see his pursuers.

He reaches the café. At the doorway, wipes off his brow. Slows, stops. Dead stops. One deep breath, looks down, sees the tear in his jeans, over the left calf.

A bullet brush, an ache, like a burn, not pulsing blood. He puts his hand on the spot, feels raw skin, nothing embedded, he guesses, if that's what bullets do. Maybe it grazed him. Not Evan . . .

Shot clean through. The work of a markswoman.

He pushes away the image of the bull's-eye in Evan's forehead, then is struck by a smell, so strange, sour brown sugar. He looks down at its source: on his shirt, red, sticky, Evan's blood. He tears at the button-down, animal-like, yanking it off, leaving himself with a T-shirt. He looks behind him, still clear, drops the shirt. Takes a deep, deep breath, wipes drizzle from his hair, nearly sopping, opens the café door, wincing at the jingle of bells. Looks down, shocked to see the iPad still in his hand.

Runs his hand along the back, feels the little metallic nodule, smaller than a pebble, than a baby mosquito. A bug.

Stuck with some adhesive. He flicks it off, watches it bounce onto the ground.

Looks up, shocked too to see no one look up. Smoking with self-consciousness, he feels like a gargoyle, a gigantic thumb sticking out, a glaring light, the sun. No one looks, not even the woman on the balcony, the one he realizes might help him yet. He puts his head down, beelines for the back stairs, fingering in his pocket, discovering the bill, pulls it out, a ten that feels like a miracle.

At the top of the stairs, she looks up, half smiles, then cocks her head, like: what possibly could've happened to you?

"They've finally figured it out," he says, trying to command calm, feeling that he's booming terror.

"Who's figured out what?"

"How to make it pour right when your meter is expiring."

"They got the shirt off your back."

Jeremy smiles, tries to, hopes he's smiling, tries not to look downstairs, toward the door. "I offer you a once-in-a-lifetime deal."

"You want to buy an umbrella?" She looks at his money.

"I buy you an organic donut and a coffee, or whatever you want. And a tea for me, and I go into the bathroom and dry off and try to restart this day."

She laughs. "I don't need your money."

"Please. No strings attached. I need some better karma."

She takes his money. "I'll buy my own."

She turns down the stairs. The second she's out of view, he begins to scramble through her pile of papers, underneath them.

It's a miracle, a real one. He finds just what he's looking for. He snags it.

He turns around, picks up the bag he left and sprints to the back of the loft, the other side of the balcony, the emergency exit.

Down slippery steel stairs, he finds himself in another alley, a veritable mirror of the one where he and Evan . . . he pushes away the image of felled Evan. Dead, right? Has to be dead. Jesus, Jeremy thinks, pictures it: He had a bullet hole in his head. Right in the middle. A black hole, seared.

And then another recognition: it was a woman, the shooter, in the alley, familiar. The same one from the log cabin? Short-haired, agile, she took shots at Nik and Jeremy, chased Jeremy.

He hears a siren. Cops coming. Is that good, or bad?

He looks across the alley, realizes the buildings on the other side are not businesses but residences. He starts jogging to his left, past the back of the movie theater. Away from the direction of the park, away from the café. On his right, a grinding noise. He jumps. It's a garage door opening. Jeremy instinctually presses himself against the wall, a move he instantly realizes makes no sense. He's trying to hide in plain sight. And why? Did someone hear the siren and decide to look? Probably not.

It's just someone pulling out of the garage. Someone, he can see now, in a heavy car, like a Mercedes, Lexus. Jeremy walks away from the wall, assumes a calm gait, passes across the other side of the garage, gives a hand wave, an instinctive gesture, a polite one, telling the driver: I'm here. The driver slides carefully into the alley, pulls out of the garage, turns on the car's wipers. It's a man, driving, sort of, also glancing at a phone, multitasking. Then reaching up to press a button over the visor. The garage starts to close.

The car lurches off.

Jeremy dives. Rolls.

He manages to get inside the garage just before it closes. Holds his breath. Listens. Senses. It's cool, dimly lit from a bulb enclosed in the garage door opener. No other sound. If someone is in the house, that someone makes no sound Jeremy can hear; he assumes that person wouldn't hear Jeremy either.

He looks around the garage—wooden shelving to his left neatly stacked with boxes, two mountain bikes hung from the ceiling, across the way, a several-step staircase, leading to a door, presumably leading to the house. He half sprints, half tiptoes across the garage to the stairs and sits against their side; from this spot, Jeremy would be hard to see at a cursory glance if there are people in the house and they decide to check the garage.

What difference does it make?

He's down to the final hours, maybe minutes or seconds, depending on how quickly he gets discovered by cops, or that sharpshooting woman who drilled a hole in Evan's head.

He scrambles in his pocket for his phone. He starts to dial Nik. Pauses, something nagging him. Not yet.

He reaches into the bag. Pulls out his external keyboard. He swipes the screen and pulls up the conflict map. All red.

2:22:19.

2:22:18.

2:22:17.

Why did the hours disappear this time? What has changed? He clicks on the update. There's a headline of an AP story: "Palestinian and Israeli Leaders Spotted in San Francisco." It's a half news story, half feature, wordplay, a question of whether there is a summit or a case of mistaken identity. Jeremy can't focus, it doesn't matter.

And another story: murals of lions spontaneously painted under the highway overpasses.

Dots connecting to dots.

Jeremy, clawing for sanity, ignoring the pulsing pain in his calf and a haunting image of another dead acquaintance, googles "Lion of Judah." He speed-reads the Wikipedia entry. To the Jews, the lion was handed down as a symbol from Jacob, the religion's patriarch, as a symbol of the tribe of Israel. To the Christians, the lion is Jesus, who came from the tribe of Judah.

Okay. And?

He looks up Lion of Judah and Custos. Guardian.

There are many, many entries. He can't possibly sift through them.

So much evidence, so many urgent priorities, so little clarity. A peace symbol on dead Harry's desk; a constellation of dishonest brokers surrounding Jeremy, all professing to want not to identify conflict but to bring peace; but not Jeremy, a devotee not of peace but of conflict, and somehow, now, the triggerman, who will set it all off. Or has he set it off already?

Why him? How him?

Because he's been taken advantage of? Because he's been manipulated? So easily?

He feels that pulsing around his clavicle, closes his eyes, pats the key fob. What makes Jeremy Jeremy? What makes him unique? This key, this thing that lets him inside this machine, this throbbing around his neck, the idea that he's not her, his mother, not her. He's holding the world at bay, with this key, afraid to share his secrets, to let go, not to be in control. Of everything, anything. The algorithm, a conversation, what gets ordered at the restaurant, how it's cooked. The key fob, right there, pressing on the edge of his neck, right there at the clavicle, the pulsing.

It's not cancer. Not like what ate away his parents from the inside. This is worse.

It's this thing.

He rips it from his neck.

I'm going to come for you, Emily. Kent. I'm not going out of this world alone. You're not going out of this world alone.

He looks at the random numbers generated on the key fob, connecting to some server somewhere, allowing him access, just him, to the computer. The conflict machine. Or is it the Peace Machine?

Flowing with his half-baked plan, he enters the numbers, followed by his (goofy) password. Tw1nkleKent1201.

Derivation: Twinkle, twinkle little fart, a joking rhyme told between him and Kent; then Kent's name; then four numbers corresponding to the day he met Emily.

Within seconds, he's in the guts of the program. He frantically makes a few keystrokes, tinkers with the program, a chance, a flier. Who knows? And what's the difference anyhow?

Can he rewrite the conflict? Can he rewrite himself?

He finishes his desperate act, drops his head, listens to the distant sirens. He picks up the phone. He starts to dial. He sees the hole in the middle of Evan's head. A bull's-eye. Satanic. And, more than that, a damning piece of evidence. The shooter was a professional, a crack shot, a markswoman. How come she missed at the log cabin?

With a deep sigh, he calls Nik.

Ten minutes later, the car pulls up in the alley and Jeremy gets inside. They drive in silence. Nik turns right out of the alley onto Masonic, heading toward an upward slope and, eventually, the water. A police car passes going in the other direction. Nik's knuckles clutch the steering wheel, white.

In Jeremy's head, dots connecting to dots. He's running algorithms, equations, in his head. He's allowing himself to see what they add up to, one of the stunning things they add up to.

"You are a patient man, Perry."

Nik crests the hill in silence. At the top, a miraculous view: the Golden Gate Bridge, the bay, and all of it suddenly highlighted by a break in the weather. A fogless midmorning stretch above one of mankind's greatest landmarks.

Jeremy, sensing something, turns around. He sees a blue van fall in behind. Its windows are tinted. He reaches into his pocket, feels his phone.

"There never was a cat burglar at your house. Remember, you told me you caught someone trying to break in, on the night my apartment was broken into," Jeremy says. "You lied about that. You were telling me that so that I'd think you were victimized too." He pauses. "And at the log cabin, that woman who shot at us. She was your ally too. She wasn't trying to actually shoot us, not to hit us. She was . . . . trying to scare me. Further the illusion that you and I are on the same side. If she really wanted to shoot us, to kill either of us, she is easily a good enough shot to have done so." He pictures the bullet hole in Evan's head. "Same woman who was dead-solid perfect with Peckerhead.

"It was not a bad head fake, Perry. I'd been wondering about you until she shot at us. Then I dismissed my reservations. Well played."

Nik glides to a four-way stop.

"I'm right, aren't I, Perry?"

They're on the edge now of the Presidio, the parklands that stretch from here to the ocean, the bridge. On the other side, a mile away at least, the log cabin. But between here and there, rolling hills, winding roads, massive eucalyptuses, mini-forests, the occasional brick building, a former armory or barracks turned rent-controlled residences.

"I'm calling you Perry because calling you PeaceNik now appears to be a grave misnomer.

"WarNik? Armageddon Nick." Jeremy looks at him, glaring at him, glowering. Looks again at the curvy road in front of them. "It was you the whole time."

He blinks, startled. "GuardianNik," he mutters, one of the last pieces coming together.

Chapter 47

I THINK WE'RE ON the same page." Nik's voice is soft, as always, hinting at deferential, certainly balanced, without irony or judgment. "Guardian Jeremy. You're the trigger-man, an honorary Guardian."

Jeremy reaches for Nik's hand and tears it from the wheel. Tries to, a random act of fury. Nik swats Jeremy away with an open hand, a powerful one. He not only dislodges Jeremy's grasp but plants a punctuating slam on Jeremy's chest. Jeremy momentarily loses his breath.

Nik swallows. "Please be patient," he says. "I've been, as you say, patient."

"Patient." Jeremy has to rasp it out. "Patient?!" He can barely catch his breath. If he attacks Nik, if he launches himself at this mutinous madman, then all could be lost. Any last-ditch hope.

Any chance to find Emily, and Kent.

Jeremy grits his teeth, swallows his instinct to physically attack. "Patient. I'll say. Four years, just sitting there, waiting. For . . ." He doesn't finish his question: for what?

The answer is obvious.

They are winding down a hill that twists to the right. But

Nik takes an abrupt left on a small frontage road. They're heading now to the west, down into a tree-shrouded part of the Presidio, the sky now blocked, the wet leaves having dripped onto the rutted road, creating a feeling they've descended into a rain forest. Ahead of them, by the side of the road, a sport utility vehicle. It suddenly pulls in front of them.

Jeremy looks over his shoulder. The van is still there. The one from the log cabin, from the morning they nearly were shot. And, now, in front, the SUV from the drive-by shooting of Evan. He looks back at Nik, wills his right hand to unfurl from a balled fist.

"You signed up with me from the very beginning to monitor the technology. You were waiting to see . . . you didn't want to see a prediction of war. You wanted to see a prediction of peace?" It's part question, part revelation.

"You have the best technology on Earth. You have an amazing mind, an Earthly treasure."

"You don't want peace?"

"More than anyone, Jeremy. Real peace."

Jeremy swallows. "The kind that comes with the Messiah."

Nik's silence carries affirmation. The cars wind to the right. They start to climb another hill. Ahead, Jeremy can see a break in the high trees, a little donut hole in the green density.

In his pocket, he fingers his phone. He holds it over the send button. On the text screen, a single word: "help." He's still not sure if it's time.

"So you just sat there, like an evil cherub, a knight guarding the holy grail."

"Neturei Karta."

Jeremy shakes his head. "What is it? Like a club? Like Dungeons and Dragons but for zealots?"

"The name is an oversimplification. It *was* a group of extreme Orthodox Jews who opposed the establishment of Israel, of a secular Israel. Much bigger than that now. It's all of us who believe that by secularizing that land, creating a worldly peace, we're foreclosing real peace, eternal peace. And, really, in concept, the Guardians long precede 1948, the creation of a secular Israel. We are ancient in our devotion to fulfilling God's covenant, securing a portal for his return. It is a rock-solid value that will save all of us, that so many people believe but so few are willing to defend. Now is the time."

Jeremy pauses for a moment, struck with a kind of obvious wonder, like someone staring at awe at the Grand Canyon despite having seen pictures of it a million times. What Nik is describing, as insane as it sounds, is not that far removed from a political rift that divides a nation, a world. Infuses hypercharged issues: Antiabortion; pro-choice. Gay marriage. Church and state. Will the Messiah return? Are we creating a world that will allow it?

And then there's the way Nik delivers it, with trademark nonchalance, humility, like explaining, when asked about the weather, that it's sunny but there could be rain.

"You're right," Nik says. "I was a bit like a knight guarding a grail. My job was to monitor you, the technology, to make sure we were the first to know about the likelihood of a secular peace, a false peace."

"A knight?"

"What?"

"Just a knight, or *the* knight?"

Nik doesn't respond.

Jeremy continues. "You were calling the shots. Orchestrating." An image comes to Jeremy. Nik using all the company's communications tools and, more than that, the opportunity to communicate globally with all kinds of actors, all without raising suspicion. After all, the company's job was to monitor international patterns, observe terrorist activity, even interact with the Pentagon.

"You were connecting with people on World of Warcraft. Your little gang exchanging messages, recruiting the like-minded, playing real war."

Nik looks deadly serious. "I don't crave power. I was called. Like you, I wound up in the middle of it, and I assumed the responsibility I was given." He clears his throat. "Anyway, we're more democratic than that."

"So you are in charge."

Nik almost smiles. "I couldn't believe they let those lions loose. They knew I wouldn't approve, so they didn't tell me. Guardians, they said, could not let the Lion of Judah die in his cell like a common mongrel. The troops took that one upon themselves."

It's a nonanswer but it seems to confirm Jeremy's terror; his loyal sidekick has been the point man on Operation Armageddon.

"It was an outrageous risk, letting those lions go," Nik continues. "Just the kind of thing that could get us attention from the press or police." Now he does smile, sadly. "Or your computer. It is so powerful, so sensitive. It sees things, almost as good as . . . He does. I guess you could say it was made in God's image."

Jeremy tilts his head, taking in Nik. "I always thought you were so modest."

"It is one of the highest callings."

"But that's not why you wear long-sleeve shirts and long pants, always. In fact, I can't say I've ever seen you wear shorts. Not once. Even when the fog parted in San Francisco and London."

Nik clears his throat.

"Let's see it," Jeremy says.

Nik swallows. Takes his right hand from the wheel and pulls up the shirt on his left arm to the elbow. Inside it, on the fleshiest part of his beefy inner forearm, beneath the bandage, the small tattoo of a lion on hind legs.

"Can't show you the leg while driving. Besides, we're here."

Jeremy eyes the bandage. "Did you really get hit, by a bullet, at the cabin?"

Nik shakes his head. A convenient scratch, he explains, from falling. Then he turns to Jeremy. "This will be a good vantage point."

Jeremy looks up. They're high atop the Presidio, pulling into a dingy gravel driveway, bumpy, lined with tall trees. In the distance, he can see a three-story brick structure. Seconds later, they're parked in front of it, a modest residence or administrative building. Brick, reddish, ruddy, white-trimmed window frames chipped and frayed from fog and neglect.

"Where are they?" Jeremy means Kent and Emily, which Nik obviously understands.

"We still need the code, Jeremy. All of it."

Jeremy hears a door slam. He looks up in the gravel semicircular driveway, grass growing through and around rocks. From the driver's side of the sport utility vehicle steps the short-haired woman who shot at him at the log cabin, and chased him, and then shot Evan. From the passenger side, a hefty bearded man. Both armed.

The driver of the van, maybe a tall male—hard to see through tinted glass—remains seated.

Jeremy opens his own door. As he does so, he hits send on his iPhone, then slips the device between the side of the seat and the door so that it falls into the cracks. Jeremy steps out of the car, feels his legs wobble, slams the door, the phone now inside. Nik comes around the front of the car. He nods to the woman and the bearded man while walking to Jeremy.

"The fob." He extends a hand.

Jeremy swallows, fingers the chain from around his neck. "You killed the lieutenant colonel, one of the Guardians did. You tortured him until he told you that I was the one who holds the detonation key. And then you killed him."

Nik looks down. "And then he died."

Jeremy considers the language, realizes Nik is trying to make the craziest distinction. The lieutenant colonel wasn't killed, Nik seems to be saying, not in a deliberate act; he died, just expired. Whatever. What's so obvious now to Jeremy, and so material, is that Nik's comments confirm what Jeremy had suspected, deduced. The Pentagon was using Jeremy as a piece of the Project Surrogate plan.

One mercenary group had half the dirty bomb.

Another had the other half of the bomb.

Jeremy had the detonation key. Princip.

"The Pentagon never cared about the computer. They wanted to send me to the Middle East. Carrying the fob," he says with quasi-revelation. "Then, what, they'd tell the mercenary groups, our terrorist allies, that I had the key, and I'd be abducted? Then the key used to detonate the bomb and take out Iran's nuclear arsenal. The lieutenant colonel must've been the one guy, or one of the few, who knew that I was the linchpin. Did Andrea know?"

"I didn't know. We didn't know. But, you are right, we knew

that the lieutenant colonel knew. He was the guy on Surrogate, the point man."

"They were using me all along. They didn't want my technology. They wanted a carrier pigeon. Someone who could move into and out of countries, someone with a safe passport, a civilian, someone unaware, uncorrupted."

Nik says: "You can't be corrupted. You're only out for yourself."

Jeremy thinks: When I was first seduced by Andrea, I couldn't find my key fob. They must've copied it.

"No," Jeremy blurts out. "They replaced it. They fitted me with their own access key. The detonation key. It looked just like my key fob and it was programmed to let me into my computer. But it also would work to set off the bomb." He shakes his head. "But how did your group get the bomb? Wasn't it supposed to go to separate, mercenary groups?"

Nik laughs, not condescendingly, like this is genuinely funny. He looks at the woman, as if asking permission to explain, and Jeremy sees she shrugs.

"We are, in a way, different groups. Some would call us militant Christians and Jews, some Rastafarians, like I said. Lucky for us that the Pentagon coordinated Surrogate independently with the Christian and Jewish factions. The U.S. government doesn't fully grasp what it's doing in the Middle East, and who it is doing it with. Partnerships there, it goes without saying, are notoriously risky."

"So they didn't realize the different groups were connected? They gave the two halves of the bomb to the *same* group?"

"Loosely. Guardians are everywhere. Not everywhere, but planted in enough places. We got lucky." He pauses. "Not lucky—"

"Lemme guess. Divine intervention," Jeremy interrupts, then says: "So would you have used the bomb on Iran?"

"If we'd have had the chance, of course. When it didn't happen, we had the bomb, but no access code. We plotted how we'd get it, and, when we got it, how we'd use it. And your computer helped us figure out when."

Jeremy lets it sink in, the cascade of betrayals. All these people around him, conspiring, coordinating, plotting.

"Where are they—Emily and the boy?"

Nik nods his head to the woman, who walks over to the van, her feet crunching on gravel. She opens the back of the van, revealing two people, tied together, back to back, white hoods on their heads.

Jeremy starts to run toward the van. "Emily!"

He's stopped in his tracks by Nik's beefy hand. And the site of the short-haired Sabra pointing a gun at Emily and Kent.

"Don't speak," the woman says to the pair. She has a pidgin accent, a bit of everything. "I am taking you inside a house where you may be reunited with your boyfriend."

"Mom?"

The woman slaps the white hood covering Kent's head. He whimpers. Jeremy starts to move again and feels Nik propel him backward with two forceful hands. "The code."

At gunpoint, Emily and Kent, hooded, stumble into the brick residence, through a front door with peeling paint and a torn door.

"The way you feel about them," Nik says. "It's the way I feel about all of it, the world."

Jeremy, without a millisecond of forethought, throws a wild punch at Nik. His arm whips through the air, a fist missile. Nik ducks to his right, evading the attack, finds his balance, springs forward with a counterattack. It's a vicious uppercut that sends Jeremy sprawling backward, then onto his ass on a patch of damp grass and gravel.

"I've taken so much shit from you. We all have." Nik doesn't sound angry, still his even-keeled self, almost like the punch was phlegm he needed to dislodge from his throat, now cleared. "Give it to me."

Jeremy fights for a breath. He reaches for the chain on his neck, pulls it over his head, the key fob attached. He tosses it to Nik.

"And your password. The detonation code, we're told, is both. However it is you get into your computer is how we detonate the bomb."

Jeremy pauses.

"Or they die," Nik says. He pauses, then says: "We'll know whether you're telling the truth because we'll test the code by logging into the computer. If it works, you're telling the truth and then you can be with them."

"For the next hour until the world ends. And then we're all dead."

Nik smiles patiently.

Jeremy swallows.

"TwinkleKent-one-two-zero-one."

Nik, without missing a beat, reaches into the car and pulls out a piece of paper and a thick, black pen. He hands it to Jeremy.

Jeremy looks at the building holding Emily and Kent. He looks around at the trees. At the woman with the short hair, the bearded man, the sky, the world.

He writes: Tw1nkleKent1201

He tosses the piece of paper to the ground. "Can I go inside?"

"Not until we see if it works."

"You're going to—"

"Not the bomb. Not now. Not for an hour or so. We needed to know where the meeting was taking place. It's been hell getting Evan to divulge the location. We worked sources, seduced executives, tried to get access to the network. It shouldn't have been that hard. After all, you and Evan were business associates. You'd think he'd have shared everything with us, the names of his partners, our potential partners. But it's funny how little he actually shared, or trusted you. Fortunately, Evan told you, and we had you bugged."

Jeremy shakes his head, not understanding.

"Stuck to the back of your iPad, just a tiny mike, very powerful, though. I knew you'd take it everywhere."

Now it makes sense.

"You put it there when we were driving around, when I went to find Emily and Kent at the Seal Rock. You needed me to elicit from Evan the precise location of the meeting." He pauses with another realization. "You tried to bring Andrea and Evan together to incite me, get me to confront them, confront Evan, do whatever was necessary to expose all their plans to you."

"And now we need to make sure the log-on code works for your computer, to make sure you're not bullshitting us. Wouldn't put it past you to want to . . . get the better of someone."

"Even you, my loyal battery mate."

Nik holds out his hand and Jeremy withdraws the iPad, runs his hand over the back, feels the spot where he'd found the bug. He passes the iPad over.

Then he watches his hefty assistant turned madman open the cover and then swipe and click until he arrives at the log-in screen. Nik enters a number from the key fob, then Jeremy's password.

"Good to go." The comment seems directed both at no one and at what Jeremy realizes is a growing posse. The big bearded man; a tall white man who had driven the van, now standing next to it; and a short woman with dark hair who had reappeared from the house. For a moment, Jeremy can't take his eyes from this dazzling creature, and her raw energy. Then he looks away. He doesn't see the guy with the jean jacket, the one who seduced Emily in the first place. He wants to kill that guy. First.

The bearded man walks over and takes the fob. He walks to the sport utility vehicle, and so does the woman.

"Stop!" Jeremy says. "Please." Pause. Again: "Please."

"A new vocabulary word for you." He nods to Jeremy, as if to say: speak your piece.

"Nik, Perry, whoever you are, look at the computer, the map. Just look at it."

Nik shrugs, looks down at the device, swipes. Jeremy can tell he's reached the conflict map when his eyes first blink rapidly, then stop and stare.

"You're not just going to destroy a plan to bring peace to the Middle East, the Fertile Crescent. You're going to destroy the world. Look how many people are going to die. I know you believe in the machine, or you wouldn't have shadowed me for four years. So just, please, look. How many innocent souls?"

Nik swallows. "What kind of world is this," he whispers. "What kind of world where the combative thrive, where the angry, the immodest and mean grow rich and fat? Where the humble servant winds up serving not God but his fellow man?

What kind of world where if you don't look the right way or go to the perfect school you're a second-class citizen, expected to carry everyone's water."

The most vulnerable Jeremy's ever heard Nik, maybe anybody's ever heard him. Nik clears his throat. He waves the woman and the bearded man into their car.

Jeremy drops to his knees. "Please. I'm begging you."

The tires of the sport utility vehicle spin on the gravel, get purchase, crunch away.

"It's a referendum," Nik says. The whisper is gone, and whatever deep personal well it drew from. "Technology won't save the world. Business and commerce won't save the world. Not science, not your machine. They are distractions, existential diversions. Everything we need, He already invented."

Jeremy feels momentarily struck by the eloquence of the lie, of its talking-point nature, of the misinformation. He says: "You know why the map is all red? Because you are choosing to hold forth about faith and the Messiah, to make your point, when the world is in the most precarious state. Conflict rhetoric rising, weapons of mass destruction rampant and in dangerous hands. You're throwing a spark into a bucket of flint and gasoline."

As he says the words, Jeremy realizes just how true that is; the reason the world is going to explode is not merely that Nik and his Guardians are setting off a dirty bomb; it's that, once the bomb goes off, the fragile world on the brink of conflict will come undone. The computer put all the pieces together.

"Nothing," Nik says.

"What?"

"Seventy-five million . . . people. Compared with eternal damnation, for all of us. It's nothing. If we allow secular peace to root in the Fertile Crescent, there can be no redemption. Ever." He looks at the house, then back at Jeremy. "Get up. Go inside. You can be with them. You've done much more of a service than you realize. You can take solace in that . . ."

"What"

"This thing is right. You were right." Nik looks down at the tablet. "Fifty-five minutes, seven seconds. Pretty much dead on." He smiles sadly. "Like I said, you're going to have quite a view."

CHAPTER 48

JEREMY ZOMBIE WALKS to the house. Realizes that Nik isn't following. No one follows, not the tall white dude, not two darker-skinned men Jeremy now realizes are lingering by the side of the house. One is smoking a cigarette. The air smells like pine and fog. Jeremy lets himself sense the world, appreciate it, for a millisecond, this imperiled Earthly existence.

He pulls on a worn brass handle and opens the front door, prompting a creak. He hears a man's voice say: "Up here."

Just inside the entrance, a wooden staircase that once would've been grand, bordering on majestic, born of a time of hand craftsmanship. But now its wear and tear and nicks and cuts are evident in light that is both dull and powerful, flooding in from the windows that checker the adjoining rooms.

At the top of the stairs, he sees a figure that fills him with fury. It's the man who broke into his house, the one from the café, the one who wheedled his way into Emily's life. Jeremy, in spite of himself, starts sprinting up the stairs. And he doesn't stop even when the man levels some sort of powerful weapon, a machine gun or something.

"If I bark," the man says seconds before Jeremy reaches him, "they die."

Jeremy freezes. He's two steps from the top, face-to-barrel. Behind the man, a hallway and three closed doors: left, right, straight ahead. "Where are they?"

The man gestures with a nod. "Middle. But first empty your pockets."

Jeremy pulls out his jean pockets, dislodging a dime.

"You looking for some more hair gel?"

"Cell phone." The guy doesn't take the bait. The opposite: "We are looking at a larger good and I'm deeply sorry for any trouble we've caused."

"Like killing Harry and Evan. How does it go: thou shalt not kill, unless it could lead to even more killing?"

"Go ahead."

Jeremy brushes past the man. He can't think of any productive way to attack, grab the gun, push the man down the stairs. All high-risk roads with no apparent reward. Jeremy reaches the door in the middle, turns back, sees the guy looking at him.

"The lions will die too."

The man grimaces. "Not in cages." He pauses. "Stay in the room." Pauses again. "It won't be long."

Jeremy turns back and opens the door. In the corner, beneath a picture window that stretches nearly the length of the wall, sit Emily and Kent; she's draped over him like a blanket. The pair practically entangled, a mother-and-child pretzel. She looks up. Dazed. Puts her head back down. "It's okay," she whispers to Kent.

Jeremy recognizes the invasion of a surprising, unwelcome thought: my mother would've been arguing with the guards, trying to escape, not enveloping me.

He sees a blur. Kent running toward him.

"You did this. You did this!"

Fury, tears, arms and fists whirring, half boy, half adolescent. "You hurt her! You hurt Mom . . ." He reaches Jeremy, arms flailing.

"Kent!" It's Emily.

Jeremy absorbs the modest blows, can't decide whether to protect himself or put his arms around the boy.

"Kent!" Emily repeats. She pulls her son from Jeremy, glowers at Jeremy, leers. "Don't say it. Don't say it."

"What, I . . ."

"It's our own fault, right? I should've known. I should've picked up this guy's bad intentions, erred on the side of defense, caution. I should put up boundaries and defend them at all costs. Like you."

Jeremy's eyes fill with hot tears. This is what she thinks of him. Even in this moment, she expects from him admonition, superiority.

"I'm sorry, I . . . Emily . . ."

"What? What? Did I hear that, right? Kent, did you hear that? Sorry. Sorry? What, is it new-vocabulary day for Jeremy?"

He shakes his head. Almost Nik's words when Jeremy had used the word "please."

He puts his head down. The word will end and these will be his final moments. Caged in the world he built.

"The cat's in the cradle," he mutters.

"Now some trick. You're going to make me guess your reference, chess, a setup? Show how superior you are, how inferior we are? I'm not them. I was never *them*, but to you everyone is a 'them.' It's not *us* and *them*. There never was an *us*. It's you and the rest of the world. And now you've drawn me into one of your wars with everybody else! They, they put a hood over Kent's head! I . . ."

Kent throws his arms around his mother's waist. She's run out of steam. The pair, though standing, seem to recoil in a hug. It dawns on Jeremy that Emily and Kent have no clue about what is happening. They think they've been kidnapped. Maybe they're collateral damage in some conflict that has embroiled Jeremy. That much is true, sort of, but a conflict the likes of which they can't possibly imagine.

Jeremy looks out the picture window, and he sees what Nik means by the remarkable view. He sees directly onto the Golden Gate Bridge, and beneath it. Especially beneath it. The top of the bridge is, predictably, enveloped by fog. But the bridge itself, and underneath it, clear. He can make out boats.

On one of them, a secret meeting is taking place to save the world. It will be ground zero.

"Please, please, Emily, let me explain."

She looks up from Kent. Calmly asks: "Can you get us out of here?"

He shakes his head. Allows himself to admit defeat. "No."

"Then go. Leave us. Get out!"

CHAPTER 49

H E STARTS TO say something. He can't think of what to
say. More than that, he can't make anything come out.
He turns around. Tears stream down his cheeks.

He walks to the door. He opens it. Discovers no one standing outside, or at the stair landing. Doesn't mean anything.
They're downstairs, out front, wherever. Whatever.

He pauses at the door.

"We could group the colors together. It is a good idea. It was
a good idea."

He shuts the door. He turns to mother and child.

"Kent," he continues. "We didn't have to do the corners
first, on the rocket ship puzzle."

It was the puzzle that Jeremy and Kent were doing when
they had their first big fight. The one where Kent challenged
Jeremy's authority and Jeremy snapped in his usual way.

"Jeremy, don't try your obtuse tricks with—"

Kent interjects: "Why can't I grow up!?"

Emily and Jeremy both look up, startled by the non sequitur. They catch eyes, like parents, then look back at the boy.

"What do you mean, sweetie?"

Kent answers his mother by sitting down.

"He doesn't like me when I'm not a baby."

She laughs, bitterly. "Me either." She looks at Jeremy. "Harry Chapin. 'The Cat's in the Cradle and the Silver Spoon.' The song. I get your reference. It's about neglecting your child. Not really the right reference, Jeremy."

He bites his tongue, his instinct to challenge her. He just meant that he knows he's created this world. He's reaping what he's sown.

She says: "That song is about a father and son. Your issue is around your mother, which is beside the point. Your *real* issue isn't that you learned how to neglect. Your issue is you never learned to let people have space. To be themselves. You can't love them for what they are, who they are. It's the opposite of what Harry Chapin is saying. You can't neglect anything. Not a flaw, a perceived flaw, a difference of opinion, not any threat to your way of thinking, your feeling of superiority, your need to feel superior. Just . . ." She stops. It's obvious. Just like his mother.

"Just like them," he says, letting his eyes gaze out the window. "Nik, the Guardians." He thinks: I'm like them, unforgiving, rigid, more willing to destroy the world than to let differences blossom. "Scorched Earth."

Finally, Emily gives him a softer look, not soft, but *softer*, a new look. She's said her piece. She's run dry of fury. It's not in her, and never was. Still, he doesn't feel any forgiveness, no latitude. Instead of walking forward, he sits. It's his own exhaustion coupled with a deliberate effort to be on their level, a rhetorical, strategic move that remains in him, an instinct he can't shed.

He notices Emily wears a watch. It's one he gave her. Rather, one he'd been given by some venture capitalist as a gift for her.

The fact she's wearing it gives him some hope; maybe it represents a subconscious act on her part—a sign that she has not abandoned him altogether.

"What time is it?"

She looks at the watch. "One thirty. Kent is hungry."

"Less than twenty minutes," Jeremy says. He's hit by a sudden urge to just sit like this, wait for the end, hope his desperate plan has worked and that the end might not yet come, not tell them what's happening.

But that's not fair. And, besides, telling them might allow him to bridge the gap, create a narrative, a different conversation to smooth their way into peace.

"Emily, we don't have much time."

Without further preface, he starts explaining.

Ten minutes later, they've all walked to the window, Jeremy finishing his story, all looking at the distant speck of a charter boat nearing the bridge.

"Ten minutes?" Emily exclaims.

He points to her watch and she holds it up. "Less."

"It's too impossible to believe."

"The boat is there, Emily. These people, downstairs, wherever, they have guns. We're not imagining this. This plot has been years in the making, decades, centuries. You're right, it's impossible to believe. The most powerful things are."

"Isaac," Kent whispers.

His hamster. "What will happen to him?"

"There is one, tiny possibility," Jeremy interjects. "One small chance."

He feels Emily's eyes on him.

"I swapped out the access code. A last-ditch thing, a Hail Mary, if you want to get biblical."

"What are you talking about?"

He explains. He tells Emily and Kent that he'd correctly guessed that the bomb needed an access code and that he himself, unknowingly for so long, was carrying the code: a combination of the random number generated by the key fob and Jeremy's personal password.

"You gave it to them?" Emily says.

"No. Not exactly."

He explains that, having guessed this is what they wanted, he created a substitute access code.

"But then how did it work to get into the computer?"

Jeremy says that, a few hours earlier, he was in a café where he saw a woman working with a key fob that looked very much like his own. A standard issue random-number generator. He took the fob when she wasn't looking. He tossed out his own actual fob. But not before he reprogrammed the algorithm with a new password.

"I'm not totally following, Jeremy. How long now?"

He looks at the watch. Six minutes.

"I knew that they'd test to see whether the access code was accurate, by making me log into the iPad," he says.

So, he explains, he programmed the iPad to accept *any* combination of numbers and letters. It, in effect, has no password at this point. "You could enter anything into it and get into the guts of the program. But they don't know that. They think that the number on the woman's key fob, combined with my password, is the key."

"Why not just change the access code and give them your key fob?"

"Because they'd have the actual number. Then, conceivably, they could make it work."

She blinks, calculating. He feels flush with love, attraction. She's his equal, intellectually, she just never needed to prove it. She's his great, great superior, emotionally.

"So will your plan work?"

He shrugs. "They bugged me, they could've found my fob, the real one. They've got a dirty bomb, a real one. So many possibilities. Chief among them: I could be wrong." He pauses. "There's a strong likelihood that I'm wrong and that my plan, this . . . last-ditch . . . this idea won't fool them. Besides," he says, then pauses again. "The computer still thinks the world is going to end.

"Last I checked."

"Hail Mary," Emily says absently.

He swallows.

"They took advantage of me, Em. I was set up from every direction. Used by the Pentagon, by Nik, by the venture capitalists, the peace and conflict community, people just preying on . . ." He pauses, continues: "On my tone-deaf talent."

Emily looks at him. He can see her deep nurturing instincts. He steps back to avoid her coming to his aid.

"I brought it on myself. I was deaf. I was the center of all of it, the world of peace and conflict, the plots and counterplots, but I was so busy attacking, preparing to attack, that I couldn't really listen . . . I couldn't . . ." He pauses, tries to catch his breath, puts his hand to his chest, where it used to ache all the time. It doesn't anymore.

"Listen."

"What?" she asks.

He wants to say: love. He can't get it out. A tear drips.

He feels Kent wrap a leg. Jeremy chokes back a tear, a sob, then doesn't—choke it back. He lets tears stream down his face. He feels Emily getting nearer. He wipes his cheeks with his palm and looks at the watch.

He looks at the watch. Two minutes.

"I wanted it to end a different way." He clears his throat. "But I did want it to end with you. Both of you."

He recognizes a terrible truth: even if the blast doesn't go off, the three of them will not possibly escape. "Just like the computer," he mumbles, "we know too much."

They look out the window, see the boat nearly beneath the bridge.

Ninety seconds.

He reaches for Emily and puts his arm around her. He wraps a hand around Kent, resting it on the boy's chest. Mother then kneels, putting her head next to the boy. "I love you more than anything. I'm sorry if I did anything wrong."

"You were perfect," the boy responds.

Jeremy listens, feels together with them, so apart. Emily's eyes are closed, her forehead touching Kent's, and Jeremy is sure she's praying.

Forty-five seconds.

He wants to tell them: please forgive me. But it's not about him.

Forty seconds.

"Look!" Kent points.

A small skiff, a dot, approaches the large boat. It must be the world killers, the Guardians, poised to set the world on fire. Poised, in their view, to save it.

It was right. The computer was right.

Twenty-five seconds.

The skiff nearly collides with the charter. It's hard to see what's happening.

Twenty seconds.

Jeremy feels himself kneeling. Joining the pair, huddling with them. He feels Emily lean in, touch her cheek to his cheek.

Fifteen seconds.

There's an explosion.

Outside the house, a flurry of gunfire. A cascade of rifles, shouts, drowned out by bang, bang, bang.

Emily turns to him. "Andrea," he mutters. She got his text message. Way too late.

Ten seconds.

They look out the window. They huddle.

More gunfire. Then something like a bomb going off, maybe a car exploding.

:05.

:04.

:03.

:02.

CHAPTER 50

:01.
   Jeremy closes his eyes.
   A deafening sound.

CHAPTER 51

:00.

CHAPTER 52

FREEZE!"

Jeremy turns around.

Men with guns. Police, federal agents, something. Flak jackets.

"Thank God." It's Emily.

Jeremy turns to the window. Squints to make clear what he's seeing: the world is still intact. The skiff, with the Guardians, jetting away.

"It didn't work. It didn't go off!" Emily.

He feels a hand on his back, another.

"Jeremy Stillwater?" A man's voice, the one attached to the heavy hand on his shoulder. "You're under arrest."

He turns. In the doorway, Andrea. Wearing a bulletproof jacket. And a grim visage. Black ash smudges on her cheeks. In her hand, some sort of heavy black handgun.

Jeremy: "Andrea. You got my text, you followed the signal."

Andrea: "I'd advise you not to say anything further."

Handcuffs clapped on him.

Emily: "What are you doing?"

The fed: "You're under arrest for the murders of Harry Ives and Evan Tigeson."

He looks at Emily, then at Andrea. "Tell them! About Surrogate!"

"I advise you to get an attorney, Mr. Stillwater," she says.

He searches her eyes, looking for a sign, a wink and a nod, an indication of whose side she's on. She says: "Dr. Ives was killed with one of your knives." It sounds almost apologetic. Like: there's nothing I can do.

The fed says to her: "Please don't say anything further."

"I . . ." Jeremy looks at the fed, then gets his footing, says: "They're getting away. You see we were held captive here." Turns to Andrea: "This is absurd. You obviously had to blast your way in here. It's not like I was standing outside with a gun. Whoever you killed, that's who did this . . . Harry, and Evan."

An arm yanks Jeremy through the door, and, several heavies at his side, he is escorted down the stairs. Outside. He sees carnage. The van in flames. A body. It's the guy in the denim jacket, bullet riddled, bloody.

Something next to him, on the ground, a glint of metal, a smolder of plastic. The iPad and its cover.

It was wrong. I was wrong.

Jeremy suddenly tears himself away from the beefy fed holding his left arm and sprints to the body prone beside the van. He dives at it, a human fury. "Freeze," he hears a chorus behind him say, then feels arms groping at him as he scrambles with his cuffed hand to tear at the shirt of the dead Guardian. Rips the garment, even as he's being ripped from the body. But before he's yanked away, he manages to do what he'd hoped: expose this Guardian's naked torso. On his chest, a tattoo. A lion.

From behind, Jeremy hears a seething whisper: "Next time, I shoot."

He turns, sees Andrea and others, scampering up. Among the group, a tall, thin woman in a flak jacket. It's Andrea's second, her assistant, hired gun, bloodhound. She catches Jeremy's eye and locks on to it until Jeremy turns back to Andrea. "Where's Nik?"

Andrea looks away.

The fed looks at the body on the ground, says to Jeremy: "Want to tell us the name of your accomplice?"

In the time it takes Jeremy not to respond, he gets yanked toward a black police car, no mercy now, and a hand pushes down on his head and shoves him into the backseat.

The car pulls away, Emily and Kent, standing at the front of the building, entangled, watching in disbelief.

Chapter 53

"Y OU HAVE THE right to remain silent."

"Shush, Kent." She looks at the boy, sitting cross-legged on the ground, looking at Jeremy, a mock serious look in his eyes. She looks at Jeremy, swallows.

Jeremy puts up his hands, surrender. He reaches into his pocket, withdraws it, empty-handed. He pulls his fingers across his lips, as if sealing them, then tosses away the key.

Emily exhales.

Kent smiles. "Let's do this one!" Jeremy twists his body, reaches behind him, picks up a puzzle box. On the cover, a large monster, Godzilla-like, stepping on a city.

"How about a different one, sweetie?" Emily says it to Kent, but looks at Jeremy.

He opens his palms, like, whatever, smiles.

Kent spills the pieces onto the floor. Jeremy feels something around his chest, a sensation that, for an instant, he can't interpret. Is it the pain, resurfacing? No, not that, it's smoother, duller, like the coursing of the morning's first cup of coffee, or tea. It feels like: thanks. He's struck by an urge to direct his appreciation, to express gratitude, to send it heavenward, thank somebody, or something. He realizes he's got tears welling, again, a lot of that lately. He drops his eyes and lets them focus on a puzzle piece, with green and a touch of slick gray, maybe Godzilla's toenail.

In his periphery, he allows himself to pick up the colors in Emily's modestly appointed living room, the red throw carpet, the brownish couch, the worn wood of the shelf over the fireplace. He feels the warmth again spread in his chest, such a far cry from the pulsing pain that plagued him until two weeks ago, when the world nearly ended.

When he removed the key fob from around his neck. When he pulled from his chest the symbol of his burden, his need to be right, his certainty of his righteousness. He didn't need an MRI. He needed to be relieved, to relieve himself, of his certitude, that singular belief in his own infallibility. Or, rather, he needed to admit to himself what he already knew: He was merely human. Not omniscient. The pain, the excruciating throbbing, was due not to cancer or disease but to a disconnect between the reality of an uncertain, chaotic existence and what he romanticized, idealized, needed.

"I had a fob, and Nik had a cross."

"What?"

He laughs. "Never mind. I'm waxing idiotic. How we doing this puzzle, Kent?"

"Let's put all the green pieces together."

He feels Emily's hand on his back, rubbing in a gentle circle. He takes a deep, appreciative breath. He picks up a puzzle piece with red jags, maybe fire jutting from a window of a building being stomped by Godzilla. He has another new sensation and tries to place it, and does: fear.

Yes, he's been temporarily exonerated of the murders of

Harry and Evan. There was sufficient doubt he could've pulled off such a crime, doubt cast by the conflicting physical evidence, his lack of any violent history, alibis that put him in too many places other than the murder scenes, particularly at the apparent times of death. Jeremy suspects he got some help from Andrea, or even those above her, suggesting to law enforcement that Jeremy was caught up in a larger terrorist-related plot, details missing, sotto voce, stuff that would fall under federal jurisdiction, the military.

Some suspicion for the murders has fallen on a woman who was consorting with high-tech execs, someone thought to be a prostitute, a woman described by Emily and Kent as radiant but heartless. She's thought too to have shot Evan. There are rumors that she goes by Janine, among other names, that her fingerprints have traveled the world. That she may have loosed a lion in the San Francisco Zoo. An assassin, a harlot, a zealot, but a practical one, the perfect terrorist. But rumors, ghost trails. The woman has not been further identified, or found.

Nor has there been any discovery of a bearded man, bomb parts that Jeremy alleges exists, or Nik. Perry. Whatever his name is. Gone, just as mysteriously and silently as he appeared one day those many years ago in the lab in Oxford.

Regardless, in a way, they've won. Not just because they've evaporated. But because they managed to head off the plans of the technology consortium to announce a development in the West Bank. Who knows why? Maybe Evan's death spooked them. Maybe they sensed danger. Maybe they just decided that their business is, plainly, business. No sense messing with efforts outside, as it is said, their core missions.

Jeremy glances at Emily and feels a surge of passion, not lust, just a craving to stay connected. He takes her in, pausing momentarily at her ankle, where he sees her blue-tinged Star of David tattoo. He's struck by her quiet observance of Judaism, how it bolsters her inner peace, how different from Nik's politicized version of religion. Who has the wisdom to know what's right?

Then he turns his attention to the cover of the puzzle box. One of Godzilla's feet pushes halfway through a building, a car pierced by the monster's toe. The other massive foot hangs in the air, poised to stomp, the edges of a setting sun peeking out from behind the furious green giant. At the edge of the image, a big white dog appears to sprint from danger.

"I know where he is."

Emily looks at him.

"You've done so well."

He takes her meaning: he's not touched a computer. He's even conceded that maybe Harry was right; computers, for all their power, might create major problems. Not just because they aren't human but because they make us less human. They make us less empathic. More computer communications, Harry has posited—or *had* posited—could mean more conflict. We don't see who we're talking to, we flame each other, we bully. We are inured to the responses we engender, just like, Jeremy thinks, I insulate myself from what everyone thought. Maybe, he's been thinking, he can do a little less of that insulating.

"It wasn't the computer that told me," Jeremy says to Emily.

It was an intuition, an impulse. And not one nearly so profound.

He stands up.

"Where are you going?"

"An errand. I promise." He feels too embarrassed to say now

what he's thinking but what he once would've said without reservation: I'm going to make the world a little bit safer.

"Kent, you're a big guy now, the man of the house. Please take care of your mother."

Kent looks up, blinks, something in his eyes, a question.

"Oh yeah, I'll be back. This puzzle better be finished when I get here."

CHAPTER 54

THE ANCIENT WALL seems to rise from the ground like a mirage, a chalky brown façade that can't help lending a terrible and awe-inspiring perspective. They've stood so long. They've withstood so much. They contain everything.

"You want here?" The Russian taxi driver's accent communicates decided impatience. Jeremy swallows a response.

He looks back over the walls that fortify the Old City. Jerusalem.

He nods. "Thank you." He hands the man money.

He stares at the Damascus Gate, the main entrance to Arab East Jerusalem, located on the city's northwest side. Arch-shaped, gray bricked, majestic and so fragile. How has it survived? He begins a purposeful march.

Inside, past security, he sees blue block letters on a white sign: VIA DOLOROSA.

The way of grief, the way of suffering. The winding walk; Jesus bearing his cross.

The name of Nik's dog. Rosa, short for Dolorosa.

Where else would a Guardian come? A Guardian? *The* Guardian.

Jeremy takes in the midday cacophony, the clanging of pots and pans, the merchant shouts and bickers from the hole-in-the-wall trinket sellers, apothecary, the butcher—this, the world's most ancient mall. A soldier walks by, a young woman, jet-black hair, jet-black rifle. Jews, Muslims, Protestants, Catholics.

Spitting distance from the Wailing Wall, the Jews' holy prayer site. Behind it, the Dome of the Rock, one of the holiest Muslim shrines. Here, the stations of the cross, the final steps of Jesus Christ.

Jeremy looks at a grimy-toothed boy, toes poking through sandals, dirt and grime pasted against his legs, smiling. Jeremy can't help wondering: Is this the portal—for the Messiah? For something? So much energy here. So much danger.

He sees Nik.

In a doorway, a face, that cherubic jowl, still visible but facing away, angled in the other direction. In a casual conversation with a man in a black robe. Nik, maybe sensing something, begins to turn toward Jeremy. Jeremy presses himself into a doorway, out of Nik's sight.

Jeremy takes a deep breath, pictures himself grabbing the gun from a soldier—trying to—and drilling a million holes into Nik. Instead, from his pocket, Jeremy extracts his phone. He dials. The line picks up.

"Shalom."

"Cute, Atlas."

"No."

"No, he's not there?"

"No, please don't call me Atlas." Unspoken: I can't handle that weight. Added again after a pause: "Please."

Andrea doesn't respond.

Jeremy says: "Yes, he's here."

There's a pause. "We've got it from here."

"You've got it from here." As in: yeah, right.

"Do you see the candlestick seller?"

Jeremy places a man along the dusty corridor, just a few feet ahead, sitting cross-legged on a blanket covered with silver candlesticks. The man's wrapped in a shawl, looking like something from an ancient bazaar. Jeremy grunts into the phone.

"Look behind him."

There's a doorway, closed on the bottom half, open at the top. Inside, a figure with a dark head covering. The figure pulls back the cover a tad, just enough. It's a woman, tall and thin, Andrea's aide-de-camp. A colleague Andrea has told Jeremy she trusts implicitly, brought on initially to help Andrea make sense of all the strange signs, and to help find the missing lieutenant colonel, Lavelle Thomson, their boss, the man behind Surrogate.

The woman covers her face again. Jeremy winces; posttraumatic stress disorder.

"What do you need me for?"

"No substitute for old-fashioned eyeball confirmation from a target's intimate."

Jeremy absorbs the jab; he was indeed intimate with Nik and yet, Nik was for so long invisible to Jeremy.

Andrea clears her throat. "Goodbye, Jeremy."

Jeremy slips out of the doorway, walking away from Nik. He allows himself a look over his shoulder, sees the Guardian looking in the other direction. He picks up his pace, hustles back toward Damascus Gate. He runs out of the city.

AUTHOR'S NOTE

ETUREI-KARTA IS A real movement and organization but I have taken substantial liberties in how I've presented it.

The name, Neturei-Karta, is the Aramaic term for "Guardians of the City." As described in the story, the name derives from an ancient story in which Rabbi Judah the Prince sent rabbi emissaries to inspect pastoral towns. In one, the emissaries asked to see the city guardian and they were shown a guard. The emissaries said this was not a guard, but a city destroyer. The townspeople asked who should be considered a guard, and the rabbis said: "The scribes and the scholars."

The name ultimately was given to a group of Orthodox Jews who banded together in 1938 to oppose the existence of the state of Israel.

That much is consistent with the explanation of the group on the web site of Neturei-Karta.

The web site explains that the group opposes a state of Israel because the concept of a sovereign Jewish state is contrary to Jewish law. Specifically, the group says, that law forbids Jews to return to the land of Palestine (from their exile) before the return of the Messiah.

And the web site says: "Jews are not allowed to dominate, kill, harm or demean another people and are not allowed to have anything to do with the Zionist enterprise, their political meddling and their wars."

But it also states: "The world must know that the Zionists have illegitimately seized the name Israel and have no right to speak in the name of the Jewish people!"

There have been reports that some members of the group praised then Iranian president Mahmoud Ahmadinejad and his anti-Zionist sentiments.

The idea that Christians and other groups have banded together with Neturei-Karta is pure fabrication. It is a partial fabrication that some fundamentalists in other religious groups—including Christianity—oppose a secular Israel. Some evangelicals fully support a return of Jews to Israel, a fully Jewish land, because they see it as a stepping-stone for the return of a Christian Messiah. It is not at all far-fetched that some of these people want to see Jews return to Israel, but not secular Jews, whose return could be seen not as a stepping-stone but as a misstep.

This book is not intended in any way as a condemnation of religion or religious heritage, which obviously brings peace and identity to millions. Rather, it is a playing out of views that linger not far beneath the surface for some fundamentalist sects.

Finally, the idea of a peace machine, a computer that could predict conflict, also is drawn loosely from real events. In my journalistic pursuits, I had the privilege of meeting a brilliant innovator named Sean Gourley. He's worked on research of "the mathematics of war." It entails predicting the timing and size of attacks. He cofounded a company called Quid, which uses Big Data—mountains of inputs—to try to predict outcomes in a variety of fields, including conflict and commerce. His technology aimed at predicting conflict is much more embryonic than the program in this story, but nevertheless is extraordinary. Sean, a great and gracious guy (who went to Oxford), is not anything at all like Jeremy Stillwater.

Acknowledgments

M Y HEARTFELT THANKS to a team led by Publisher Liate Stehlik at HarperCollins/William Morrow that is second to none and like family. Thank you for your support, partnership and friendship. A huge thank-you to Tessa Woodward, a terrific, patient editor of line and ideas. You went the extra mile on this one, and then some. And thanks to Jennifer Hart, Julia Meltzer, Andy Dodds, Alaina Waagner, Peter Hubbard, Nick Amphlett and Doug Jones.

Thanks to David Liss for, once again, sterling insights freely given. And to Susan Tunis, for crucial last-minute triage.

And to my parents for the kind of unconditional support I hope I am emulating with my children.

Thanks to Laurie Liss, a great friend and a great literary agent.

And, above all, thank you to my wife, Meredith, and our little angels, Milo and Mirabel. All my love.

About the Author

Matt Richtel reports for the *New York Times*, covering a range of issues, including the impact of technology on our lives. In 2010 he won the Pulitzer Prize for National Reporting for a series of articles that exposed the pervasive risks of distracted driving and its root causes, prompting widespread reform. He is the author of *A Deadly Wandering,* as well as three novels. A graduate of the University of California at Berkeley and the Columbia Journalism School, he is based in San Francisco, where he lives with his wife Meredith Barad, a neurologist, and their two children.

BOOKS BY MATT RICHTEL

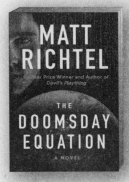

THE DOOMSDAY EQUATION
A Novel
Available in Paperback and eBook

From the Pulitzer Prize-winning *New York Times* journalist comes a pulse-pounding technological thriller.

A DEADLY WANDERING
A Tale of Tragedy and Redemption in the Age of Attention
Available in Hardcover and eBook

A landmark exploration of the vast and expanding impact of technology.

ALSO AVAILABLE

THE CLOUD
Available in Mass Market Paperback and eBook

When the next generation of technology seeps into the brains of the next generation of people, former medical student turned journalist Nat Idle must investigate and stop the invasion.

DEVIL'S PLAYTHING
Available in Mass Market Paperback and eBook

"A brilliant thriller that defies genre and scope; a twisted blend of Michael Crichton and Alfred Hitchcock." —James Rollins, *New York Times* bestselling author of *Altar of Eden*

AVAILABLE IN eBOOK

FLOODGATE
A Short Story

Available in eBook

On the eve of the presidential election, a conspiracy threatens to alter the outcome of the vote—and the future of American politics. At the heart of the plot is a powerful computer program, aimed at rooting out hypocrisy among politicians to expose their truths . . . and ours. Left to unravel the conspiracy is a bitter, hotheaded former journalist, but he's just not sure he cares enough to get to the bottom of it.